THE CHILDREN'S HOUR

Volume One
FIRST STORY BOOK

Volume Two
FAVORITE FAIRY TALES

Volume Three
OLD TIME FAVORITES

Volume Four
CARAVAN OF FUN

Volume Five
BEST-LOVED POEMS

Volume Six
STORIES OF TODAY

Volume Seven
FAVORITE MYSTERY STORIES

Volume Eight
MYTHS AND LEGENDS

Volume Nine
FROM MANY LANDS

Volume Ten
SCHOOL AND SPORT

Volume Eleven
ALONG BLAZED TRAILS

Volume Twelve
STORIES OF LONG AGO

Volume Thirteen
ROADS TO ADVENTURE

Volume Fourteen
FAVORITE ANIMAL STORIES

Volume Fifteen
LEADERS AND HEROES

Volume Sixteen
SCIENCE FICTION – GUIDE

Along Blazed Trails

A BOOK TO GROW ON

Consultant Editor for
Along Blazed Trails

CAROL RYRIE BRINK
Author
Newbery Prize Winner

CONSULTANT EDITORS FOR THE CHILDREN'S HOUR

CAROL RYRIE BRINK
Author
Newbery Prize Winner

JULIA CARSON
Author and Biographer

IRVING CRUMP
Editor and Author

HELEN DEAN FISH
Editor and Author

WILHELMINA HARPER
Anthologist, Librarian
Redwood City, California

WILLIAM HEYLIGER
Author,
Editor of Literature for Youth
The Westminster Press

SIDDIE JOE JOHNSON
Children's Librarian
Dallas Public Library
Author, Lecturer
Southern Methodist University

CORNELIA MEIGS
Author and Teacher
Newbery Prize Winner

NORMA RATHBUN
Chief of Children's Work
Milwaukee Public Library

MABEL L. ROBINSON
Author, Associate Professor
Columbia University

MARGARET JONES WILLIAMS
Director of Elementary Education
Cornell College, Iowa

MARJORIE BARROWS, *Editor*

Along Blazed Trails

MATHILDA SCHIRMER
Associate Editor

DOROTHY SHORT
Art Editor

THE CHILDREN'S HOUR

PRINTED IN THE UNITED STATES OF AMERICA

Acknowledgments

The editor and publishers wish to thank the following publishers, agents, authors, and artists for permission to reprint stories, poems, and illustrations included in this book:

APPLETON-CENTURY-CROFTS, INC., for "With the Forest Runners" from *The Forest Runners* by Joseph A. Altsheler, copyright, 1908, D. Appleton & Company.

BRANDT & BRANDT for "Western Wagons" from *A Book of Americans* by Rosemary and Stephen Vincent Benét, published by Rinehart & Company, Inc. Copyright, 1933, by Rosemary and Stephen Vincent Benét.

THE CATHOLIC BOY, for "The Boy Who Voted for Abe Lincoln" by Milton Richards.

CONSOLIDATED BOOK PUBLISHERS for illustrations by Eunice Young Smith for "Tomorrow Will Be Bright" by Mabel Leigh Hunt.

THOMAS Y. CROWELL COMPANY for "On the Mayflower" from *The First Year* by Enid LaMonte Meadowcroft, copyright, 1937, 1946, by Thomas Y. Crowell Company.

E. P. DUTTON & CO. INC., for "River and Beasts Betray" from *No Other White Man* by Julia Davis, published and copyright, 1937, E. P. Dutton & Co., Inc., New York; and "Daniel Boone" from *I Sing the Pioneer* by Arthur Guiterman, published and copyright, 1926, by E. P. Dutton & Co., Inc., New York.

HARPER & BROTHERS for "Christmas Horses" from *On the Banks of Plum Creek* by Laura Ingalls Wilder, copyright, 1937, Harper & Brothers.

HOUGHTON MIFFLIN COMPANY for "Disperse Ye Rebels" from *Johnny Tremain* by Esther Forbes.

ALFRED A. KNOPF, INC., for "Johnny Appleseed Visits Licking Creek" from *Little Brother of the Wilderness* by Meridel Le Sueur, copyright, 1947, by Meridel Le Sueur.

LITTLE, BROWN & COMPANY for "A Ride with Tom Thumb" from *The Little House on Wheels* by Marjorie Hayes, copyright, 1934, by Marjorie Hayes.

MCINTOSH AND OTIS, INC., for "The Feather of the Northman" from *Young Mac of Fort Vancouver* by Mary Jane Carr, copyright, 1940, by Mary Jane Carr.

THE MACMILLAN COMPANY for "Caddie's Silver Dollar" from *Caddie Woodlawn* by Carol Ryrie Brink; "The Willow Basket" from *Magical Melons* by Carol Ryrie Brink; "In a Covered Wagon" from *Drusilla* by Emma L. Brock; "A Pioneer Wedding" from *Five Bushel Farm* by Elizabeth Coatsworth; and "The Bears of Blue River" from *The Bears of Blue River* by Charles Major.

RINEHART & COMPANY, INC., for one illustration by Charles Child from *A Book of Americans* by Rosemary and Stephen Vincent Benét, copyright, 1933, by Rosemary and Stephen Vincent Benét

CHARLES SCRIBNER'S SONS for "The Master's Footstool" from *The School Bell Rings* by Evelyn Ray Sickels, copyright, 1942, by Charles Scribner's Sons.

STORY PARADE, INC., for "Old Sly Eye" by Russell Gordon Carter, copyright, 1945, by Story Parade, Inc.; and "The Three-Cornered Hat" by Russell Gordon Carter, copyright, 1941, by Story Parade, Inc.

THE VIKING PRESS, INC., for "The Saving of Boonesboro" from *Daniel Boone* by James Daugherty, copyright, 1939, by James Daugherty; and "A Message for Washington" from *In Calico and Crinoline* by Eleanor Sickels, copyright, 1935, by Eleanor Sickels.

THE JOHN C. WINSTON COMPANY for "Strangers in the Wilderness" from *With Daniel Boone on the Caroliny Trail* by Alexander Key.

LAURA BENÉT for "Horseshoe Nails," first published in *Story Parade.*

ELIZABETH COATSWORTH for "Mary Silver."

DEE DUNSING for "Tooth of the Great One," first published in *Boys' Life.*

MABEL LEIGH HUNT for "Tomorrow Will Be Bright," and "Johnny Appleseed's Coat," first published in *Story Parade.*

CORNELIA MEIGS for "Fox and Geese," "Hasty Pudding," and "Little Dog Star."

HARRY EDWARD NEAL and LESLIE GORDON PHILLIPS for "Frontier Blockade Buster" by Harry Edward Neal, first published in *The American Girl.*

EDGAR WYATT for "Apache Warpath," first published in *Story Parade.*

ALEXANDER KEY, JANET LAURA SCOTT, and KEITH WARD for illustrations.

Contents

ON THE MAYFLOWER   Enid LaMonte Meadowcroft   1
Illustrated by Matilda Breuer

FOX AND GEESE   Cornelia Meigs   10
Illustrated by Janet Laura Scott

THE MASTER'S FOOTSTOOL   Evelyn Sickels   20
Illustrated by John Dukes McKee

TOMORROW WILL BE BRIGHT   Mabel Leigh Hunt   26
Illustrated by Eunice Young Smith

HASTY PUDDING   Cornelia Meigs   36
Illustrated by Keith Ward

JOHNNY APPLESEED'S COAT   Mabel Leigh Hunt   47
Illustrated by Barbara Maynard

A RIDE WITH TOM THUMB   Marjorie Hayes   56
Illustrated by Janet Ross

THE FEATHER OF THE NORTHMAN   Mary Jane Carr   64
Illustrated by Frederick Chapman

IN A COVERED WAGON   Emma L. Brock   72
Illustrated by Carol Stoaks

WESTERN WAGONS
Rosemary and Stephen Vincent Benét   82
Illustrated by Charles Child

THE BOY WHO
VOTED FOR ABE LINCOLN   Milton Richards   83
Illustrated by I. Heilbron

THE WILLOW BASKET   Carol Ryrie Brink   93
Illustrated by Janet Smalley

THE LITTLE DOG STAR   Cornelia Meigs   102
Illustrated by Alexander Key

CHRISTMAS HORSES   Laura Ingalls Wilder   111
Illustrated by Matilda Breuer

CADDIE'S SILVER DOLLAR   Carol Ryrie Brink   127
Illustrated by Janet Smalley

JOHNNY APPLESEED
VISITS LICKING CREEK   Meridel Le Sueur   146
Illustrated by Barbara Maynard

STRANGERS IN THE WILDERNESS   ALEXANDER KEY   150
     Illustrated by the author

MARY SILVER   ELIZABETH COATSWORTH   159
     Illustrated by James Ponter

OLD SLY EYE   RUSSELL GORDON CARTER   173
     Illustrated by Lorence Bjorklund

THE SAVING OF BOONESBOROUGH   JAMES DAUGHERTY   181
     Illustrated by Henry C. Pitz

THE THREE-CORNERED HAT   RUSSELL GORDON CARTER   189
     Illustrated by Kay Lovelace

HORSESHOE NAILS   LAURA BENET   197
     Illustrated by Henry C. Pitz

FRONTIER BLOCKADE BUSTER   HARRY EDWARD NEAL   229
     Illustrated by James Ponter

DISPERSE, YE REBELS   ESTHER FORBES   238
     Illustrated by John Dukes McKee

A MESSAGE FOR WASHINGTON   EVELYN SICKELS   255
     Illustrated by Jack Roderick

TABBY'S TABLECLOTH   LOUISA MAY ALCOTT   264
     Illustrated by Salcia Bahnc

RIVER AND BEASTS BETRAY   JULIA DAVIS   277
     Illustrated by Lorence Bjorklund

THE PATHFINDERS:
LEWIS AND CLARK   EVA MARCH TAPPAN   289
     Illustrated by Jack Roderick
     Color illustration by Henry C. Pitz

WITH THE FOREST RUNNERS   JOSEPH A. ALTSHELER   295
     Illustrated by Walter R. Sabel

THE BEARS OF BLUE RIVER   CHARLES MAJOR   306
     Illustrated by John Dukes McKee

A PIONEER WEDDING   ELIZABETH COATSWORTH   314
     Illustrated by James Ponter

CUB PILOT ON THE RIVER   SAMUEL CLEMENS   321
     Illustrated by Robert Sinnott

APACHE WARPATH   EDGER WYATT   338
     Illustrated by Frederick Chapman

TOOTH OF THE GREAT ONE   DEE DUNSING   346
     Illustrated by Brinton Turkle

BUFFALO HUNTING   THEODORE ROOSEVELT   357
     Illustrated by Robert Sinnott

DANIEL BOONE   ARTHUR GUITERMAN   369
     Illustrated by John Dukes McKee

Introduction

A few years ago I had the privilege of talking with a very old lady whose memory went back to pioneer times. She could remember, as a child, living in a hastily-built stockade or fort during the Indian uprising of 1862 in Minnesota. She remembered picking the mud chinking from between the logs so that she could peep out and see the schoolhouse burning on the hill. A few days before she had gone to school there; now hostile Indians had set it afire. She remembered the sound that the schoolbell made as it fell through the burning roof.

"What terrible times those were!" I said. "How exciting it was to be alive then."

She put her small, withered hand on my arm, and said: "Yes, my dear, those were terrible times, but they were good times too. You are a writer, and I want you to write about the good times as well as the hard ones. We had to be brave, but also we had fun."

This volume of THE CHILDREN'S HOUR will give you a wide variety of pioneer stories to read and enjoy. You will find courage in these stories, and the will to meet adventure bravely, and I hope that you will find some fun too.

Almost everyone enjoys reading pioneer stories. There are a number of reasons why this is so. In the first place most of the pioneer stories that we read are true stories, or at least they are based on true experiences. If we have enjoyed a story, we are always doubly pleased to find that it is a true one. "Did this *really* happen?" we ask. If we find that it did, the story immediately becomes alive for us. "This really *did* happen!" we say in pleased surprise.

True pioneer stories have usually been told and retold by word of mouth before they were written down. Gradually the unimportant and uninteresting parts have been discarded, and the brave and fine parts have been remembered and emphasized. For this reason true stories are usually good and well-told stories.

Those of us who live in the West or the Middle Western part of the United States are not very far from the pioneers. Our grandparents or great-grandparents cut the logs to build their homes. They wove the wool from their sheep into cloth for their clothing. They studied by the light of home-dipped candles.

Now, only a few years later, we have prefabricated houses; chemically manufactured cloth for our clothing; and electricity, which not only lights our study tables, but performs all sorts of miracles of service for us. In a hundred years we have come from travel by ox-cart to travel by high-powered automobiles, Diesel trains, or machines that fly through the air like birds. I suppose that never before in the world has there been such a rapid change in the civilization of a region as we have experienced here in our last hundred years.

The adventurous blood of the men and women who went westward to seek new homes is still running in our veins, although the life we lead today is such a different one. So it is important for us to try to understand the life and character of our pioneer grandparents, in order that we may better understand ourselves and fit ourselves more comfortably into our brand-new modern civilization.

It is the pioneer spirit of going ahead into the unknown which has changed the United States in a few generations from a group of struggling colonies into one of the greatest nations on the earth. The first pioneers met the physical dangers of Indian warfare, wild animals, drouth, blizzards, grasshopper plagues. They learned to take care of themselves under all sorts of difficulties. They carried civilization through the wilderness until there were no more frontiers. No more frontiers? Ah, but there are always frontiers. Sometimes they are frontiers of the mind. We have our modern miracles of science only because pioneers of the mind were brave enough to push forward into unknown fields of thought. So, if it seems to us today that we do not have such opportunities for adventure as our great-grandparents had, let us stop and think for a moment. What are our opportunities for adventure? They are all around us.

When we read with what patience, skill, and responsibility great-grandfather drove his covered wagon across the desolate and dangerous plains, we see that we can use some of the same patience, skill, and responsibility in learning to drive a modern car through dangerous traffic.

If we admire great-grandmother's skill in weaving her own cloth, we may stop to think of the young chemists who are pushing forward into unknown thought and experimentation to bring us each year new materials made from such strange things as coal or glass.

Our modern doctors, who have already done so much to prolong life and make us healthy and strong, are still searching the unknown to find cures for many diseases. They are pioneers as truly as were our great-grandparents who searched the woods for healing herbs. The mathematician, the physicist, the social scientist, all the workers on the frontiers of knowledge are the pioneers of today. So, if we admire the faith and self-reliance that carried great-grandfather through his struggle with the wilderness, we shall be more ready to meet the perils of this atomic age with a faith and self-reliance of our own.

Yes, there are as many opportunities for adventure and achievement today as there were a hundred years ago. It may be harder for us to see and recognize them, but they are here for us—a modern challenge. If we can meet them with great-grandfather's courage, faith, and willingness to face the unexpected, then nothing should daunt us.

So, let's read and enjoy pioneer stories, remembering that, although our world is a different one, it is equally adventurous and exciting.

CAROL RYRIE BRINK
Consultant Editor,
Along Blazed Trails

Part I: FOR YOUNGER READERS

Enid LaMonte Meadowcroft

ON THE *MAYFLOWER*

ILLUSTRATED BY *Matilda Breuer*

MANY, many years ago two boats left England to come to this country. They were called the *Mayflower* and the *Speedwell*.

Before they were out of sight of land the *Speedwell* sprang a leak. Both boats put back to shore. Many of the people on the *Speedwell* were put aboard the *Mayflower*. Much of the *Speedwell's* cargo was put on the *Mayflower* too.

Once again the *Mayflower* set out to cross the ocean. She was alone this time and heavily loaded.

This is the story of the long journey of the little ship and of the brave people who sailed on her.

We call these people Pilgrims. But they had no such name for themselves. They were just plain people, setting out to build new homes. They wanted to live in a land where they could be free to think, and to live, as they believed God wanted them to.

You will ask, "Is this story true?"

It is just as true as I can make it. The children you read about were real children. The things I have told you about did happen, but perhaps not in just the way I have told you.

Remember that these people lived three hundred years ago. It is hard to know just how things happened then. They have left us records that tell us what they did, but they do not always tell how they did it.

1

THE *MAYFLOWER* rocked and tossed on the waves. In the sky a black cloud grew larger and larger. Lightning flashed. The wind whistled and cried.

"Get below, Giles Hopkins," called a man as he ran along the deck. He stopped to speak to a boy who held fast to the railing.

"I don't mind getting wet," the boy answered. "It's so crowded in the cabin, and half the people are seasick."

"Never mind that. It's not safe here. And you are in the way."

"Let me help then, Master Howland. I'm big enough," said Giles. But John Howland had already turned to go.

Suddenly the rain came. The boat tipped until she seemed to be lying on her side. The deck slanted so that the boy could hardly stand. He clung to the railing and shut his eyes to keep out the sight of the water. When he looked again the boat had righted herself. But John Howland had disappeared.

Giles ran to the side of the vessel. There was his friend in the water, splashing and yelling. A great wave rolled over his head and seemed to swallow him.

On the deck at the boy's feet lay a coil of rope. One end of it hung over the side of the ship.

"The rope! Grab the rope!" called Giles. He saw Howland grasp it and then disappear again under another wave.

Giles turned and ran down the deck. "Help!" he yelled. "Help! Help! Man overboard!"

· Several of the sailors came running in answer to his cry. They grabbed the rope and pulled on it. John Howland still clung to the other end. But it was a long rope, and he was far from the ship.

The men pulled him through the water as though he were a fish. Then slowly, slowly they pulled him up the side of the boat. He dangled at the end of the rope like a wet rag doll. The angry waves beat against him.

Then one of the sailors grabbed a large boat hook. He reached over the side of the ship and caught it in Howland's

clothes. So with the rope and the hook they tugged and pulled until they had him safe on board.

"Oh!" gasped John Howland when he could speak. "I have been nearer land than any of you. And I have swallowed most of the ocean. There can't be much left between us and America now."

Then he saw Giles standing near. The boy's hair lay flat on his head. Water streamed down his face and clothes. He was as wet as if he too had been overboard.

"You saved my life, boy," said Howland. "If you hadn't brought help it would have been the end of me. I couldn't have held on another minute. Now will you go below?"

"Yes, sir," said Giles. He watched for a minute while the men helped Howland to the steerage. Then he started down the ladder to the cabin.

It was almost dark in the cabin. The little ship still rolled and tossed. It was not yet safe to light the oil lamps or the candles.

All day the ship had been thrown about by the great waves. Everything in the cabin was upset. Boxes and cases would not stay in place. They slid back and forth across the cabin floor with each toss of the ship.

Some of the littlest children cried with fear. Many of them had been fastened in their bunks so that they would not be hurt by the sliding boxes or be thrown to the floor when the ship pitched.

The older boys and girls took care of the younger ones. Or they sat on benches at the long table in the center of the room and told each other stories.

Many of the women lay in their bunks too ill to move. Others who were well enough tried to care for them. They clung to the bunks and to the table as they walked about. They tried to keep away from sliding boxes and ran into each other.

Giles went to his mother, who sat on the edge of her bunk. A little girl was asleep in her lap.

"Where have you been, my son?" asked Mistress Hopkins. "I sent your sister to look for you some time ago. But Constance

4

said she could not find you. You are very wet. What have you been doing?"

"I was on the main deck," the boy answered. "Master Howland slipped and fell overboard. But he grabbed a rope that hung over the side, and we pulled him up. They have taken him to the steerage to dry him out. I was the one who called for help. He said I saved his life," Giles added proudly.

"Then I suppose it is a good thing you were there," said Mistress Hopkins. "Though I heard your father tell you to stay below today. Now change your clothes at once. There are some dry ones in our box if you can find it. I saw it slide under Mistress White's bunk a minute ago. If I move to help you little Mary will wake and she has just dropped off to sleep. Her poor mother is much too ill to care for her."

"It seems to me that almost everyone is sick," said Giles. "I'm glad the sea doesn't make me feel that way. I'm hungry."

"You'll get little to eat tonight, my boy. Just a bit of smoked beef, some bread, and some beer. No one has been able to light a fire all day. With the boat pitching so, it is not safe. Hurry now and get yourself dry or you will be sick too," said Mistress Hopkins.

"Yes, Mother," replied Giles. He pulled the box from under a bunk near by. Then he took out some dry clothes and went to the men's quarters to change.

After several days the rain stopped. The wind died down, and the sea was calm. It was cold but the sun shone. Sails were raised again, and the *Mayflower* sped on her way across the ocean.

Everyone felt better. The children had been shut up in the cabin for many days. Just to see and feel the sun made them race about the decks and shout for joy.

The women called back and forth to each other as they hung damp clothes out to dry. The sailors sang as they hammered down the hatches and coiled ropes.

Even the animals seemed glad that the storm was over. Ducks and chickens quacked and clucked. Goats and sheep and pigs bleated and grunted in their pens on the deck.

5

Some of the boys were playing soldier on the main deck. Wrestling Brewster was the leader. He had often watched the men as they drilled every day under Captain Standish.

"Hold your gun higher, Love," he commanded his brother. The little boy shifted his stick higher on his shoulder.

"You had better wake up, John Billington," Wrestling called to a tall boy at the end of the line. "The Indians will surely get you if you don't."

"I'm awake," growled John. "Awake enough to smell dinner. Say, what is the matter with Constance Hopkins? Look at her." He pointed to a girl who ran toward them. Several of the smaller children followed her.

"Guess what has happened! Oh, guess!" she cried. "I have a new baby brother. He was born last night. Mother just let me hold him for a minute."

"A baby brother," said Love Brewster. "What is his name?"

"It's a funny name," answered Constance. "Mother is going to call him Oceanus because he was born on the ocean. My big brother, Giles, is making a cradle for him out of an empty case."

"Oceanus Hopkins," said Wrestling. "That is quite a name. Perhaps I can help Giles with the cradle or make a box to hold his clothes."

"Now there are four of us; Giles, Damaris, Oceanus, and me," said Constance. "Oh, Wrestling," she added, "I forgot to tell you that your mother said your dinner was ready. She says you must hurry for the food is hot this noon."

"Hurray! Come on, Love," said Wrestling. The two boys started off to find their mother.

Hot food was a real treat on the *Mayflower*. There were only two ways in which it could be cooked, and both ways were hard. It could be put in a frying pan and held over a charcoal fire. Or it could be cooked in a kettle hung on an iron tripod, over a fire made in a box of sand.

Each day the food was taken from a common store. Even the smallest children knew that the food they carried on the boat must last them a long time. No one knew how long it might be before there would be any more.

6

Wrestling and Love dipped their spoons into the same trencher.

Wrestling found his mother standing over a steaming kettle in the shelter of the cookhouse. She was dishing food into a wooden trencher.

"It is a good stew, my son," she said when she saw Wrestling. "Dried beef, cabbage, turnips, and onions have gone into the making of it. After such terrible days of storm we all need something to make us strong. Take this for yourself and for Love." She held out a trencher filled with steaming stew.

"Thank you," said Wrestling. "It looks good, and I am so hungry." He reached for the wooden dish.

"Wait," said his mother, setting the dish beside her. "I have just remembered the Hopkins children. With a new baby to care for, Mistress Hopkins will not be cooking for a few days. Go and get them, Wrestling. Ask them to share our dinner with us."

"May we eat out here on deck, Mother?" asked Love as Wrestling ran to get Giles and his sisters.

"Of course you may," said his mother. "And so will everyone else. It is so good to see the sun again."

In a few minutes the children sat together on the deck. Wrestling and Love dipped their spoons into the same trencher. Giles shared his with Constance, and Mistress Brewster fed Damaris. There was little talking and a great deal of eating. Everyone was happy.

There were sunny days and stormy ones, but still the little *Mayflower* sailed the sea. Everyone was very tired of seeing nothing but water on all sides.

"We have been on this boat exactly sixty-three days," said Constance one afternoon. She and Giles were leaning against the railing watching the water.

"I know how long it is, because I counted this morning while I was waiting for everyone to wake up. I hate this boat. I hate living in that stuffy cabin with all those people. Sometimes I even hate Oceanus when he cries all night."

Wrestling, who stood near by, sighed deeply. "Sometimes I don't believe we'll ever reach land," he said. "My mother said last night that she wished we were back in Holland."

7

"Does she?" asked Giles. "I want to fight Indians and shoot tigers. The other day I heard two of the sailors talking about the Indians. They said that the Indians would eat us if they caught us. And they said—" Suddenly Giles stopped speaking. He looked carefully at the water. Then he pointed excitedly.

"Look!" he cried. "Do you see that?"

"What?" asked Constance. "Oh, that's only a dead tree branch. What do you care about that?"

"Silly!" said Giles. "Do trees grow in the ocean?"

"Look! Look! Come here," he called to some of the crew who were working near by. The sailors dropped their work and ran to his side.

"There—a tree branch!" exclaimed Giles. "It means land is near, doesn't it?"

In a minute the deck was crowded with excited passengers. All were eager to see the first sign of land. Long after the tree branch had floated past them, they talked about it.

"Watch for birds now," said one of the sailors. "If you see a wild duck or a goose you will know that we are really near the land."

So everyone who was able spent the rest of the day on deck. Each hoped to be the first one to sight land. But no one even saw a bird. At last it grew dark, and the children were sent below.

"Perhaps that branch came from a tree on an island, and we have sailed past it," thought Constance sadly that night. She crawled into the bunk beside her little sister and was soon asleep.

But all night long on the boat, men kept watch. Eyes peered eagerly into the darkness. There was much talk of what the next day would bring. Hearts were lighter, for surely now they were near their journey's end.

It was very early the next morning that the cry rang out, "Land ho! Land ho!" It woke all who were asleep in the cabin.

Men, women, and children rushed to the decks. The morning air was cold, and they drew their cloaks about them. They peered into the distance.

8

Yes—there it was. At first it was only a dim shadow on the horizon. Then as the *Mayflower* sailed closer, rocks and trees appeared.

Everyone was excited. Everyone was happy. The children talked together and planned what they would do when they got off the boat.

But the sailors shook their heads. It was land—but it was not the end of their journey. They knew that the land they saw was Cape Cod. They were far north of the Hudson River, where they had planned to go.

So they turned the ship south and sailed along the coast. About noon they came to dangerous waters. They were afraid the boat would be wrecked in the breakers.

Then the captain and the men held a meeting, and they decided to turn back to Cape Cod. All the afternoon they sailed north along the coast. When the children went to bed that night the ship was still moving through the water.

Early, early the next morning Giles woke and lay still for a moment wondering why he felt so queer. Suddenly he knew that the ship was not rushing through the water any longer.

He called Wrestling and the two boys hurried to the deck. The *Mayflower* was at anchor in Cape Cod Bay. Soon all the Pilgrims were gathered on the deck.

Before them lay a strange land. No friends were there to welcome them. There were no houses to shelter them and no stores where they could buy their food.

When they looked toward the shore they could see only rocks, sand, and a forest of trees. Indians and wild beasts might be hiding there. It was winter, cold and stormy.

Yet no one said he was afraid. No one said he wanted to go back to his home in Holland or in England.

Together they kneeled on the deck and thanked God because He had brought them safely to this land, where they could live as they thought He wanted them to. Then they began to plan at once for their new homes.

They were a brave people!

FOX AND GEESE

ILLUSTRATED BY *Janet Laura Scott*

IT WAS so early in the morning that Tibby was the only one astir, stepping carefully back and forth across the squares of sunshine on the floor of her room. The shadows of vine leaves danced in them and over her bare feet, for the fresh autumn breezes were blowing outside. Because it was Sunday, or First Day, as Tibby was taught to call it, everyone else in the house was sleeping late. They would get up at six o'clock today, when usually they all arose at half-past four. It was the first time, indeed, in all of Tibby's eight years of living that she had been the only one up and about in that busy Quaker household. She felt very old and important, as she slipped on her straight gray dress, pinned her white kerchief, and tiptoed down the stairs.

She had settled it all with her mother last night, just what she was going to do this morning, an undertaking that made her breath come a little quickly when she thought of it. Even now her heart was beating more briskly than usual as she moved about the kitchen, getting her own breakfast, a bowl of milk, brown eggs cooked the night before, late blackberries with cream, brown bread, and white cream cheese. Once she smiled, more than once she looked grave, and once even her face puckered to keep back the tears. She had a great deal to think about and to remember when she let her mind turn to all the things which had gone to the making of this plan. Outside she could hear the noise of the awakening ducks and hens in the poultry yard and the high, sharp hissing of the two big geese. The hot color flew to her cheeks as she listened, and her quick feet pattered even more quickly around the white-scrubbed table. The plan she had made had a great deal to do with the

10

henyard, and in particular, with the geese which were, or had been, her very own.

Yesterday—how long ago it seemed—her cousin, who was a year younger than she, had come to spend the day. Amanda Howe lived on the farm two miles to the westward. Past both Tibby's house and hers ran the road that led out from Philadelphia, through the green woods and fields of Pennsylvania. Both she and Tibby loved to help in the henyard, and each had her own possessions of which she was very proud. Amanda owned five clucking, speckled hens who laid the most generous number of eggs every day, while Tibby had her four little chicks and her two great gray geese. Both of them had longed, for months, for something else, for one, two or even three dear, small golden ducklings with broad flapping feet and flat light-yellow bills.

"How could we get some?" Amanda had asked with a sigh over and over. As she thought of it, Tibby hung her head, all alone in the kitchen, for if it had not been for her, she and Amanda would have been, that very morning, well on their way to owning those same much-desired ducks.

Amanda had come to visit the day before, and Tibby's grandmother had come the day before that. She lived in Philadelphia, the clean little city where the great Mr. William Penn had his townhouse, and where one could see his coach rolling down the cobbled streets, coming in from his farm at Pennsbury. Grandmother had stopped along the way, and had brought her youngest grandchild, Tabitha Watson, called Tibby for short, a very wonderful gift. "A clutch of eggs," Grandmother had called them, a whole dozen of duck's eggs in a round, brown basket. "Just put them under a good motherly hen," Grandmother directed, "and even though it is getting on to autumn, they should hatch out and do well. They ought to be the best and sturdiest ducks anywhere round about. Thou art to keep six for thyself, Tibby, and give six to Amanda the next time she comes over."

It happened, therefore, it just happened, that Amanda came next day. All morning the two little girls played in the hay-

11

ricks, in the barn, ran races down the paths of the vegetable garden, hung over the fence and watched the cocks and hens scratching in the henyard. "If we only had some ducks," Amanda sighed, for the twentieth time. And Tibby, it is hard to say it of her, but the truth must be told, Tibby said nothing at all.

They had dinner, they went out to gather chestnuts, the afternoon passed, and Amanda's father came for her. As he sat in the broad cart waiting for his little daughter to tie her bonnet on over her fair head, he spoke to Tibby's mother inside the door. "Art thou going to meeting tomorrow? I hear that Mr. William Penn himself is to ride out and be there, and the spirit should move him to speak to us. No one should miss it."

Tibby's mother told him that they were all coming, that certainly they must see and hear Mr. Penn. He it was who had founded Pennsylvania and had made it possible that people could live there in peace and comfort, with no question as to what they thought and to what Church they belonged. The Quakers, with their quiet speech and simple dress and plain, hard-working ways, were making a great success of living in Pennsylvania, with its soft winters and its long, beautiful golden autumns. On Sundays, when they all went to the meet-inghouse, they would sit in silent rows, no one moving or speaking until one or another felt the impulse to rise and say what he thought and felt about God and about how to live. It was known that Mr. Penn liked to ride out from town and join with the people in their meetings, but it happened that Tibby had never seen him. It would be a great Sunday, and the place would be full. Usually the thought of such a thing would have made Tibby happy and excited, and her gray eyes would have been wide at the news, and her round cheeks pink as she skipped back and forth in the house helping Amanda to get ready. But today her feet lagged, and she had no word to say. The whole day had passed, and she had not told Amanda about the duck eggs that Grandmother had left and how half of them were for her.

She had wanted ducks for such a long time, she could not,

she simply could not give them up. She kissed Amanda good-bye with a hard, cold little kiss, and watched her cousin climb into the cart. Amanda waved her hand as they rolled away, but Tibby did not see her, for her eyes were blind with tears. She was so wicked, but how, oh how, could she bear to part with those beautiful eggs that would some day become twelve sweet small quacking ducks.

"She wouldn't take as good care of them as I would," Tibby told herself fiercely. "We might lose some, there might be none left at all. But if we keep them—" But at that her selfishness and hardness gave way, for Tibby was not really so grasping a person as she seemed. Yes, the duck eggs were Amanda's; how wrong it was to try to keep her share from her. With a sudden change of heart Tibby rushed into the henhouse, upset the fat, gray hen who was sitting on the nest, bundled all the duck eggs into her white apron and ran through the gate calling, "Amanda, Uncle John. Stop! Wait!"

The cart was rattling so fast down the lane that they did not hear her. When they turned into the road, Tibby was sure, they must look back and see. She ran, she called, she was breathless. The horse was just turning the corner when, oh alas, she stumbled over a stone, she fell flat, and the duck eggs rolled and cracked and smashed all around her. The cart rattled out of sight; no one had looked back. There was not a whole duck egg left.

She got up, looked about her for a minute and wiped her eyes on the corner of her apron, which was stained with grass and the yellow of the eggs. She walked back to the house, threw herself into her mother's arms, and burst out crying. After a long storm of weeping she found breath enough to tell her mother the tale. "I am a wicked girl," she declared again and again. "I know I am. And now I am going to give Amanda my two gray geese, to make up for what I have done."

Her gentle mother was sure, with her, that such a plan was right. "It does not do to be selfish," she said. "There is never any happiness in that. And thou art fortunate in being able to undo, one day, the wrong thou didst on another." Together they planned that Tibby should get up early, drive the geese down the road to Amanda's house, and let her uncle take her with his family to the meetinghouse. "Thou canst find us there," Tibby's mother said. "We must not miss that, no matter what else there is to be done."

So here was Tibby, in her Sunday gown, with her white stockings and her square-toed shoes, all ready for meeting, but bound on a most important errand first. She finished her breakfast, set the dishes carefully together, swept up the crumbs, went to the door, and opened it.

Such a fresh, sweet morning as it was, with the trees dropping their brown and golden leaves, but with the air warm still as summer. The chickens were all busy in the poultry-yard, scratching and talking to one another. They came to the gate when they saw Tibby with her bowl of corn. The two geese, holding their heads very high, and stepping proudly, came out of the poultryhouse the last of all. Tibby's heart almost failed as she saw how big and stately they were. But no, there was nothing she would not give up if only she could feel comfortable inside again. While the other fowls were clucking and scrambling for the grain she drove the geese out of the gate and set off down the lane.

Geese walk very slowly. Their legs are so short that they can take only the smallest of steps, and they are giddy creatures, besides, easily distracted by anything they see along the road. Tibby had a little switch with which she turned them this way and that when they tried to stray. Sometimes she sauntered slowly behind, sometimes she ran frantically to turn them back from wandering, sometimes talked to them gently and sometimes shouted as they tried to plunge into the bushes and lose themselves. At last she managed to convince them that they were to walk, straight and steady, as good geese should, right down the middle of the road. They were tired of straying and seemed, finally, willing to walk in the proper way. They all moved along the wide road for a quarter of a mile, easily and straight. "Now," thought Tibby with a sigh, "we shall soon be there."

14

Tibby's task was not to be as simple as she hoped. A few people passed her on their way to meeting. They offered her a ride, but she said no, she must drive the geese and they, big fluttering things, could not well be taken up into a cart with the Sunday dresses. She walked on.

It was not only good Quaker farmers and their wives going to the meetinghouse who were out on that clear autumn morning. There were a few people in that neighborhood who were not Quakers and who did not spend Sunday in the same way. Far down the road Tibby heard an unexpected sound, the clear

15

blowing of a horn, then the baying of dogs. "The hunt," she thought. "The riders and the hounds are out after a fox again."

For a little while the sounds seemed to come no nearer; then there were shouts, loud, excited yelping from the dogs, and the thunder of hoofs down the road. Tibby saw the fox, running lightly, keeping to the open way until he saw a break in the bushes proper for making a dash into the woods. He passed close to her, he eyed the geese with a look that seemed to say, "Those creatures look interesting, but I have no time for them this morning." His red brush was held high; he was neither tired nor afraid; he gave the three of them a rapid, sidelong glance and was away into the woods. To Tibby it was so thrilling to watch the hunters come sweeping by that she forgot, in one fatal moment, what geese will do when they are excited. With one voice they screamed out, as geese can do, they fluttered their great wings, and dashed in among the trees and bushes. A few of the younger hounds stopped to make a dive at them, but then were ashamed and sped away behind the well-trained old leaders of the pack who would scorn to look at anything that was not a fox. The horses came pounding past. Tibby could hear the geese struggling among the bushes, still cackling and shrieking, getting farther and farther away. The last of the riders looked back at her as though he wanted to stop and help her, but there was a great shout from the woods, meaning that the fox had been seen, and he spurred onward, and she was left alone.

She stood still in the road, trying to choke back her tears. Should she give it all up and let the geese go? Certainly she had tried as hard as she could to make up to Amanda for keeping the duck eggs. How hard it was to set a wrong thing right. It could not be done! Yes—yes it could, and it would be done. Tibby dried her eyes so that she could see plainly. She was a little girl of spirit, and she was not going to be beaten. What she had set out to do, she was going to do to the end. She stepped from the road into the bushes, then into the wood, calling to her geese. A feeble, frightened little cackle answered her. The geese had not really run too far away.

16

It was a good half hour, however, before she managed to find them, fluttering and talking to each other in great excitement, and so wild that they tried to run through the thickets at the very sight of her. Very carefully and gently she drove them back to the road, spoke to them, quieted them, and at last got them to walk forward in their slow waddling gait toward Amanda's house. A quarter of a mile, half a mile, they were nearly there. Now they came at last in at the gate. Tibby had accomplished what she set out to do.

What hopes she had managed to keep up along the way sank as she came near the house. Of course she was later than she had meant to be, and now all the family had gone to meeting. The doors were closed, the sun shone on the steps, the bright autumn flowers swung in the breeze. But only the fat old shepherd dog was there lying on the stones in the sun and thumping with his tail to offer welcome for the absent household. Tibby walked steadily down to the henyard, opened the gate, drove in the tired geese and shut it with a determined click. She would see Amanda at meeting and would explain to her. But there was a long two miles to walk, and it was getting very late. Could she ever bear to walk in, after meeting had begun, and see all the glances turn in her direction, and hear her feet go thump, thump, thump, down the aisle of bare boards. And the great Mr. William Penn, would he turn about and look at her with reproof? Oh, she must hurry, she must get there in time, no matter how tired she was.

She started bravely, trudging along in the dust and the sunshine. Perhaps someone would come by whom she knew; she could be taken into one of the carts or chaises now, for she no longer had the geese with her. But nobody passed; they had all gone to meeting early, so that they should not miss Mr. William Penn. She could picture them all in their places, the rows of women's bonnets on one side, the men's broad hats on the other. On one of the benches in front, set facing the others, where the Heads of Meeting sat, would be Mr. Penn, very tall and stately and dignified, with a proud manner that would frighten little girls, most probably. She did not care much, now,

17

whether she heard him speak or not. But she must obey her mother, who had said that she must come to meeting, no matter what else there was to be done. She hurried all she could, but it was so hot and so dusty. The Sunday shoes were getting very heavy, and her hair was wet on her forehead. But still she plodded steadily onward.

Someone was coming on horseback, far down the road, someone in a hurry, for the horse was galloping. She looked back; it was a man riding alone. As he came nearer she saw that he was short and wide-shouldered, with rather a small face and large, dark eyes. He drew up beside her. He looked tired and dusty too, as though he, like herself, had come far and was in haste not to be late. How very kind his eyes were as he looked down at her.

"Art thou going to Merion Meeting, too?" he asked. "I think we both have need for hastening. Wilt thou get up behind me? Old Dobbin has carried double many a time, and my own daughter has always liked to ride behind me down the country lanes."

He held out his hand and she put her foot on the stirrup, as her father had taught her to do, and was up in one spring. Dobbin's gray back was wide and easy; she held to the strap at the back of the saddle, and they went on. The dust was not so bad now, and she could see the green fields behind the hedges and the song sparrows warbling as they went by. Now beyond a low hill they could see the roof of the meetinghouse. He asked her one or two questions, very kindly ones, although spoken as though he were a little out of breath with urging on his horse and galloping along the hot road. She found herself answering very freely and frankly, telling him of everything, from Grandmother's gift of the duck eggs, to the sweeping by of the hunt. He nodded wisely but did not make much comment, for they were just coming to the meetinghouse.

He helped her down and they went in, he by the men's door and she by the women's. She had thought she was going to be late, but no, meeting was only just beginning, almost as though they had been waiting for her and her companion. The doors

18

closed behind him as he came in. Someone spoke to him in a whisper and led him down to the front benches where he seated himself. Quiet, the complete, beautiful quiet of Quaker peace, spread through the big room.

Tibby never felt restless or fidgety at meeting, even though she sat on the bench by her mother, with her feet dangling, for a whole hour. She liked to look at the rows of pleasant, calm faces, under the bonnets, some wrinkled, some pink, all full of the still happiness that always seemed to fill that place. Across the way she could see the rows of men, their cheeks hard and ruddy from work on farms, their mouths stiff or firm or gentle, but they, too, all looking as though some secret of good and perfect living were being whispered to them as they sat there, silent and listening. The sun moved slowly across the floor, the windows were open to the warm autumn air, a bird fluttered on the sill and almost came in, a butterfly ventured inside for a little way, found it too shady and quiet for his liking and swung out into the sunshine again.

There was a little rustle, and someone got up to speak. It was the square-shouldered man who had brought her with him. He looked small as he stood there, but his voice, full and large and stately, went rolling through the whole place. And now she knew, suddenly, even before every head turned to listen, who this was. It was Mr. William Penn, not great and tall and terrifying, but with the kindest, gentlest, wisest face in the world, as he looked down at her.

"We are all bound to make mistakes," he was saying. "All of you have made yours and I have made mine. But there is always a way shown us for undoing them, and there is no peace like that which fills our hearts when we have toiled and struggled and succeeded in doing so."

She listened to every word, and yet she seemed scarcely to hear, for what he said was all a part of the perfect comfort and peace that stole through her tired body and into her beating heart. Beyond her mother, far down the row, Amanda was smiling at her. Everything was right, perfectly right, at last.

19

Evelyn Sickels

THE MASTER'S FOOTSTOOL

ILLUSTRATED BY *John Dukes McKee*

NAT was in danger of being late to school these mornings. For crossing Boston Common in 1775, where British troops were encamped, was a thrilling experience for a small boy. Each day promised adventure. Each step along the path might lead to danger. It was a perilous time. The feeling of fear was in the air. Quarrels between the American colonists and the mother country became alarming. As the weeks and months went by, more and more British soldiers arrived. What did their presence mean?

Nat could remember his first glimpse of the "Redcoats." He had thought the bright scarlet uniforms simply splendid. But soon he learned the truth. These men had been sent to force the people of Massachusetts to obey unjust laws made by a stubborn king. Then Nat, like many another Boston lad, had changed his mind. The brilliant uniforms were not fine at all. They were hateful! Now, whenever he passed a group of soldiers, Nat muttered the name by which the older folk called them.

"Lobsters!" he snorted, scowling ferociously. "Lobsters!"

Of course, he said it under his breath, always careful that the "Redcoats" did not hear him. But some day, he thought, he would be less cautious!

This morning he had almost reached the high fence which enclosed both the school and the gunhouse, when two British soldiers brushed briskly past him. A tall captain and his companion. Nat stared at their scarlet backs, and suddenly his resentment grew too strong for him.

"Lobsters for sale!" he cried shrilly and dodged into the schoolhouse. He peeped out from behind the door to see the effect of his daring.

The soldiers halted instantly. "The young rebel!" exclaimed the tall officer.

"You won't let him escape, sir?" cried his companion.

"Indeed I will not! I'll meet the rascal again. Then I'll settle with him!" The captain's voice was so threatening that Nat made up his mind the meeting must never take place. Not while he had two nimble legs! Not while he kept his Yankee wits about him!

But Nat soon forgot his enemy, for within the schoolroom Caleb Whipple was telling the other boys a piece of news that made Nat's young blood boil.

"Major Paddock is going to surrender our cannon to the British general!" cried Caleb. "My father overheard him say those very words!"

Surrender the cannon bought for the defense of Boston? It was incredible! At this very moment, two of those cannon stood in the gunhouse next door to the school.

"Major Paddock hasn't any right!" shouted one boy.

The schoolmaster drew near. When he overheard the conversation he cried, "Those guns have not been surrendered yet. Remember, two can play at the same game."

What did "Old Crusty" mean?

The master refused to say another word. Picking up a small cane, he brandished it threateningly above his head, demanding silence. But the boys were not frightened, for the master seldom whipped them. He had devised a far more ingenious method of punishment. He would pounce upon some rascal, seize him by the ear, and lead him squealing to the front of the room, where he would thrust him underneath the desk. The

21

master would then seat himself heavily in his chair, swing his large foot up and bring it down upon the squirming footstool.

Today the master opened the morning exercises by offering a prayer in which he called upon Divine Providence to bless the cause of the Patriots and aid them in defending their freedom. The deep, earnest voice made Nat's heart beat faster. If he were only a man and could carry a gun! He would make short work of the enemy! As the voice rose in earnest supplication, Nat pictured to himself the "Redcoats" falling thick and fast about him as he charged against them down the Common! How "Old Crusty" and the boys would cheer him when he returned after vanquishing the enemy!

A loud and solemn "Amen!" cut short his daydream. Nat knew then that the long prayer had ended. The "Redcoats" remained unchallenged upon the Common.

With measured tread, the Master began to pace back and forth across the room. Holding the lapels of his coat with both hands, he chanted in a solemn, rhyming sing-song, the names of the states, the largest towns of Massachusetts, and the rivers of Europe. He was just beginning on the prepositions when the schoolroom door was quietly opened and two men appeared. One was Deacon Whipple. The other was Nat's own father! What was he doing here in the schoolroom? Why was he so pale? Both men wore a look of grim determination. A hush fell over the scholars. The men spoke not a word. Quickly they crossed the room. Opening the door which led into the yard of the gunhouse, they stepped out leaving the door ajar.

For a moment no one moved. Each scholar felt that something of great importance was taking place. Then the master realized that the moments were flying. He began to lecture the boys upon keeping their own counsel.

"The Lord hath given man two eyes, but one tongue," he said in conclusion. "Therefore man should see much, but say little."

Scarcely had the master finished speaking, when Nat's father and Deacon Whipple returned, carrying the two guns which they had lifted off the cannon-carriage stored in the gunhouse.

Nat wanted to give three rousing cheers! His father would not let those guns be surrendered to the British! Never!

"Hide them in the woodbox!" cried the master. Instantly the guns were placed in the box. It was shoved under the master's desk. Then, as quietly as they had entered, the two men left the room. Not a moment too soon! Nat heard the sound of running feet. There was a commotion in the yard. A soldier shouted.

"They're gone! The guns are gone!"

"The rebels could steal the very teeth out of your head, with *you* keeping guard!" roared an officer.

"Not a man entered the gunhouse! I swear to it!" cried the sentry. "I stood guard in the doorway and never left my post."

"What about the back door?" snapped the officer.

The boys knew the answer. Nat could almost see his father and Deacon Whipple prying up the latch. Doubtless they had waited until the sentry's attention had been distracted by roll call. Then they must have stolen in and quietly lifted off the guns from the cannon-carriage.

"The guns can't be far away. The thieves must have left by this gate. But no! Here's a cobweb unbroken. Only one way is left! They must have come through the schoolhouse! Search the schoolhouse!" roared the captain.

No sooner were the words spoken than the master whispered to Nat, "Under the desk, lad!"

Quick as a wink, Nat saw the master's plan. He scrambled under the desk and flung himself flat upon the box which held the precious guns. The master dropped heavily into his chair and swung one foot up on Nat. The door burst open! Soldiers swarmed in. They were chagrined and thoroughly enraged to think that the guns had been stolen from under their very noses. They stormed about the room. They knocked over everything which might conceal the missing guns. When they came to the teacher's desk, they overturned it with a bang. What was their amazement to see a small boy, squirming uncomfortably under the master's heavy boot! They had heard of "the master's footstool." Never had they witnessed it!

23

mister
mckee

"Bless my bonnet, if it isn't the young rebel!" exploded the officer in charge of the search. He roared with laughter.

Nat broke out into a cold sweat. This was the officer whom he had taunted that morning. The one who had promised to settle with him the next time he met him!

"Crabs for sale!" mimicked the captain. "A squirming fresh crab!" He gave Nat a poke with the butt of his gun. Nat writhed, much to the amusement of the officer.

"Hold still, you rogue!" stormed the master, brandishing his cane. "Take care, that's my lame leg!"

Suddenly Nat's terror gave way to a fierce joy. The master was playing a part. Hadn't he said, "Two can play at the same

24

game"? Nat would help the master! They must manage somehow to keep the captain's attention centered on themselves. If they did that, he might not think of looking in the woodbox.

Nat sobbed and blubbered and whimpered. He begged to be allowed to get up, but the master only stormed louder. As for the captain, he laughed so hard the tears rolled down his cheeks.

Inwardly, Nat was chuckling. How well the deception was working! And all the time the captain thought himself so clever!

"You may settle my score with him, Schoolmaster," cried the officer, for he realized that he was wasting valuable time. Turning to his men, he snapped, "Search the yard!"

Out of the door the soldiers trooped. But long after they had gone, Nat continued to act as the master's footstool. Just in case the captain might return.

For two long weeks the guns lay hidden in the woodbox beneath "Old Crusty's" desk. Well did the scholars heed the master's counsel. During all that time, not a single boy, by so much as a word or glance, betrayed the secret hiding-place. Then, one day, Nat's father placed the guns in a large trunk, which he carried by wheelbarrow to a certain blacksmith's shop. Here the guns were hidden under a pile of coal. One dark night the blacksmith put them upon a boat and succeeded in smuggling them over to the American lines.

The morning after Nat's father had told him of the safe transfer of the guns, Nat crossed the Common with a light heart. His spirits soared! He was thinking how cleverly the Yankees had outwitted the British. "Redcoats!" Nat spat the words out of his mouth just as a tall British soldier loomed into view.

"Jumping Jehoshaphat!" gasped Nat. "It's the captain!"

With practiced eye he measured the distance to the nearest place of refuge. Assured that in case the captain gave chase, Nat himself could reach the spot first, he leaped into the air and cried shrilly, "Lobsters for sale!" Then he took to his heels and fled.

Mabel Leigh Hunt

TOMORROW
WILL BE BRIGHT

ILLUSTRATED BY *Eunice Young Smith*

ND in the middle of the night Trapper began to growl." Polly's voice held a breathless note. Her eyes were big.

"Then he barked, loud and sharp, and woke us all up," broke in Nancy, excitedly.

"But by that time Father was up, with his gun," added William.

"Goodness me!" exclaimed Docia. "What was it?"

"Just then Father fired," William went on. "He fired right through the tent at a—at a shape outside."

"It was more than a shape," cried Nancy. "It had a *foot!* Claws—that were reaching under the tent!"

"Yes, claws!" echoed Betsey. "If we'd been in a cabin instead of a tent, the—the beast couldn't have done that."

"Shucks, Betsey," scoffed William. "You're always harping about a cabin. If it was a panther—and it wasn't—a cabin wouldn't have made any difference. He'd a been on the roof, ready to drop down the chimney on us if he'd a mind to." William grinned in impish enjoyment of the girls' shudders.

"Hey!" called Peter, unimpressed by this rather common wilderness tale. "Be quiet, now. Let the varmints creep up real close. Then we'll scare the tails off 'em."

It was squirrels that Peter Moon called "varmints," and squirrels are very different from big beasts that prowl through the night. But Peter was interested in the business at hand.

26

He and his sister Docia had come from their father's cabin upstream to spend the day with their Harvey cousins and had at once joined them as they sat on the top rails of the fence surrounding the little cornfield. It was serious business—keeping the hordes of squirrels away from the precious corn. The crop must be saved to feed the little Harveys and their parents, Eli and Mary. It should feed, also, the horse that Eli had brought from North Carolina last fall. That was when he and his brothers and their families and Quaker kin and friends, numbering near one hundred strong, had come to settle in this new Ohio country.

At Peter's suggestion the children ceased their talk of last night's prowler. The hot and breathless morning matched their silence. Scarcely a leaf stirred. There was only the sound of the softly flowing water of Todd's Fork. And through the woods the children could hear the distant but steady blow of axes. One could always hear them—the axes of the Quaker pioneers.

In the stillness Betsey realized how much she missed the customary sound of Father's ax. Today, he had gone five miles to the gristmill on Dutch Creek. Betsey wished she could have gone, too. Perhaps, alone with Father, she might have mustered up courage to talk to him about staying in Ohio. Oh, why couldn't Father feel enthusiastic and settled here, as were his brothers Isaac and Joshua and Caleb, and the merry swarm of Betsey's cousins? Already this scattered colony was being spoken of as "Harvey's Settlement." How could it truly be called so, thought Betsey, if her father Eli and his five little Harveys were not here? Yes, *here*, in spite of perils and discomforts and fierce claws pricking at the walls of their tent. "I want to stay. I want to stay," fretted Betsey to herself.

Suddenly she almost tumbled off the fence. Such a din as broke the silence, and sent her thoughts helter-skelter.

"Shoo! Scat! Be off with thee—and thee—and thee!" yelled the other children, pounding with sticks on kettles and pails and fence-rails. A dozen squirrels scampered into the woods.

In the midst of the clamor Betsey slipped off the fence. She ran toward home. True enough, home was only a tent. It was

27

to serve through the summer, or until Father made up his
mind. Now an appetizing steam rose from a kettle slung over
an outdoor fire. Twelve-year-old Lydia was shoving bread
dough into an outdoor oven. She put her finger to her lips
in warning. "Thee, Betsey!" she whispered. "See what thee's
done—woke Mother up."

Mary Harvey opened her eyes and smiled at her daughters.
She was sitting in a rocker, in front of the tent. Betsey ran to
her. She picked up the turkey wing lying in her mother's lap.

"Thank thee, Betsey," sighed Mother, breathing in the cool-
ness made by the waving fan. "How very hot and still it is!
Even Trapper will not stir himself." She glanced at the dog
that lay with lolling tongue at her feet.

"Does thee feel very poorly, Mother? Oh, Mother," wailed
Betsey anxiously, "doesn't thee like Ohio, either?"

"Yes, child, it is a goodly country. But thee must cease thy fretting, and thee, Lydia. The decision to return to Carolina or to stay in Ohio must be left, and with patience, to your father. He knows not whether he acted wisely in coming north."

"I know one thing," declared Lydia, her mouth straight and stubborn. "Thee would get well in no time if Father would decide one way or the other."

"Hush," reproved Mother, sharply. "Thy father is thy father, wise, good, and loving. Who is thee?"

Lydia flushed. After a moment Mother took her hand. "Thee is my sensible little housewife," she said gently, "but made sharp beyond thy years because thy mother is so ailing." She sighed. "But there! Now come the other children, as hungry as bear cubs. Thee and Betsey will dish up."

"Um-mmm, I smell something good," sniffed Docia. "But we shall have to eat very fast, because brother Peter and cousin William said if we didn't hurry back and give them their turn at dinner they would begin chewing the bark off the fence."

"Stewed squirrel!" sighed Polly, gazing at her heaped plate. "We see squirrels. We chase squirrels. We eat squirrels."

"And very good eating it is, with Lydia's dumplings that are light as feathers," praised Mother. "Today, we also have a sauce made from the wild plums that Docia and Peter brought."

"I heard William and Peter whispering," confided Nancy. "They're planning on fishing, I think. So maybe—just maybe—we'll have fish for supper."

"I would be afraid to live in a tent," said Docia, suddenly changing the subject. "Indians and bears and bobcats! *Claws!*" Docia shuddered. "Why doesn't Eli build a cabin?"

"The gun is ever primed and at hand," said Mary Harvey quietly. "And Trapper is a good watchdog, as was proved anew last night."

"And the Indians hereabout are tame ones, thee knows, Docia," added Polly.

"And it is much cooler living in a tent in the summer," declared Betsey, lifting her head proudly against the thought of

29

the good square cabin where Docia lived. She could not resist adding, "But thee just wait, Docia Moon."

"What does thee mean by that?" demanded Docia.

"If thee wants to know," said Lydia, wise and sharp as a little old woman, "Bet is counting her chicks before the eggs are hatched. Our father will build us a cabin in good time, Docia, if he chooses so to do. If not, back we go to Carolina, so there!" Lydia's teeth fairly clicked together.

"I heard my father tell Mother," snapped Docia, "that the logs Eli Harvey had felled and trimmed may wait, but that winter will not wait on his dillydallying."

"Thee is a chatterbox, Docia Moon!" cried Betsey hotly.

"And thee is a saucebox, Betsey Harvey," quavered Docia, her lips trembling.

"Have done, now!" exclaimed Mother. "Where are thy manners, Betsey? Docia meant to speak no ill, I am sure, nor her father before her. Now thee and Docia run to the spring. A cloth wrung from cold water will cool my wrists and temples. Such a strange smothering weight on the air! See if any clouds begin to grow in the western sky, children."

When Betsey and Docia returned, laughingly sharing the burden of the brimming pail, they had forgotten their quarrel. "Thee needn't worry, Mother," reported Betsey. "The clouds piled up in the west are as fluffy and fair as beaten egg-whites."

"But dark along the edges," reminded Docia truthfully.

In the afternoon William and Peter fished where the water ran deep below the joining of Todd's Fork and Lytle's Creek. But as the heat and stillness grew, they returned. "The plaguy critters!" complained William, flinging down his pole. "Even the little shiners went off and stuck themselves under the rocks."

"Never saw such doin's," grumbled Peter.

"There's not a squirrel in sight, either," said Polly. "So we don't have to guard the cornfield."

"Something's brewing when even the creatures hide themselves away," declared Mary Harvey. "Peter, thee and Docia had best be safely at home."

30

Betsey walked with her cousins as far as the big oak. I'm 'shamed I called thee a chatterbox, Docia."

Docia squeezed her hand. "Thee could come and live with us if thy folks go back," she said. "We'd attend school together in the new schoolhouse."

"I wouldn't like Ohio much without my folks," answered Betsey. "I guess it isn't the place that makes home. It's the people one loves the best. But I hope—" Betsey turned and ran back to the tent.

She found her sisters busy with their knitting. William was raking up chips for the fire. They were all prattling about the journey north, almost a year ago.

"One day," said Mother, joining their talk, "we had climbed an endless weary way to the mountaintop. And from the valley below there came the chime of bells on some wagoner's teams. Somehow that far, lovely sound gave my spent spirit rest and courage. I shall always remember the brave, forward-going sound of the bells."

"Remember how—" William stopped. "Goodness, Mother," he exclaimed. "How queer everything looks! Kind of green—and kind of black. And there's Trapper sneaking into the tent with his tail between his legs. Mother! Listen!"

From afar, seeming to come over the treetops, came a strange steady droning. Swiftly it grew into a roar. "Maybe it's a big flock of pigeons," guessed Polly.

31

"It is the wind," said Mother. "Come into the tent, quickly."

"Has night come?" asked Nancy, catching at her mother's hand.

The Harveys could not see the fearsome shape of the cloud that darkened the August afternoon. But as the mother gathered her brood about her on the big bed that stood foursquare, the sides of the tent suddenly bellied out like an inflated balloon. The ropes creaked as they pulled at the pegs driven deep into the ground. "Will they hold?" screamed Lydia. She could not hear the answer, but in the white shimmer of lightning her mother's face shone pale and wide-eyed.

The children burrowed among the bedclothes, or held their hands over their ears, trying to shut out the noise of the storm —the heavy sweep of rain, the continuous boom of thunder, the wind, vast and violent, the splinter and crash of falling trees. Now and then they could hear Trapper whimpering under the bed. His fear increased their own terror.

Suddenly the earth shook as something struck it with a mighty crash. The dog leaped up to huddle and whine among the children. In his frenzy he knocked William off the bed.

"*Hark!*" thought the boy, scrambling to his feet. The wind had the voice of flight! It was sweeping on, wasn't it, beyond the encampment?

It was vanishing as swiftly as it had come. He called out above its dying roar. "Must've been the big oak that fell." He peeped through the tent-flap. "It's getting light, Mother. But I can't see much, 'cause so many boughs are piled at the door. Maybe we can't get out. Maybe Father can't see the tent."

"Pray God he stayed at the mill," murmured Mother.

Now the others ran to peer at the wreckage of the storm. Trapper sniffed at the edges of the canvas. But Betsey remained with her mother. "It's so nice and still," she sighed, "after—*that.* We never had a storm like that in Carolina. Now I know Father will take us back. I know it! Oh, Mother, we'd never have been so frightened if we'd been in a house—a real house." Betsey struggled against her tears.

Her mother gave her an affectionate little shake. "Better be

32

thee praying thy father is safe. And giving thanks that we are unharmed."

Suddenly Trapper began to worm himself frantically through the barricade of boughs. The children could hear him barking joyously through the woods.

Then came a hallooing. "Mary! Mary Harvey! Lyddy! William!"

"It's your father!" cried Mother. "Shout as loud as you can!"

"Here we are!" screamed the children. Now Father was tugging at the boughs. "Are you safe? Is Mother all right?" Now, while Trapper leaped and licked, Father gathered his family about him.

"Where's the horse?" asked William presently.

"I could not have brought him through the fallen brush," answered Father. "I left him at the Indians' camp. The storm did not touch them. It cut a narrow path, cleaner than the swath of a scythe. For instance, the north side of the cornfield is completely flattened, while the rest stands unharmed. With the Indians I watched the terrible cloud descend upon you. It whirled and twisted from heaven to earth like a great spinning snake. Never did I expect to find you alive. But come outside." Father's voice was strange. "Behold the miracle that saved you!"

He pointed upward. The trunks of two tall trees had been snapped by the storm. But, in falling, their branches had interlocked. One held and supported the other, high above the tent. They leaned above it in protection. "Now this is God's sign to me," said Eli Harvey huskily. "It is his word that I shall stay in Ohio. Here, in this spot where he has delivered my loved ones from destruction, shall I build my cabin."

Then Eli and Mary and their children knelt in thanks, not with bowed heads, but looking up in joy and wonder at the miracle of the leaning trees, at the clearing sky. And within the hour came Isaac and Caleb and Joshua to see what had happened to their brother's family. They brought food and news of other settlers.

"John Hadley's cow was killed. The chimney of the Moon cabin was blown down. In the midst of the storm a son was born to the Dakins. They have named him Preserved. A fit name unto the Lord."

The good Quakers nodded soberly. But they laughed and shook hands all around when Eli said he would stay in Ohio.

"When we have helped thee free the earth of wreckage," said Joshua, "thee will have a wider clearing than thee had counted on. All of us will help to raise thy cabin."

"Now, Mary," added Caleb briskly, "thee and the children must come home with me to dryer quarters."

"We have dry bedding in the oaken chest," answered Mother. "And we kept the big bed dry, for we were all on it. Even Trapper." Mother laughed gaily. "We shall stay here with Eli. He will need the helping hands of every one of us. And tomorrow will be bright."

Mother's voice rang. Somehow it reminded Betsey of the lovely thing she had said about the wagoner's bells—"the forward-going sound of the bells."

Before they left, the brothers helped Eli to bring dry wood from beyond the path of the storm. The fire they kindled leaped

34

and crackled. The children gathered around it gratefully, for the air was chill.

But Betsey was not cold. She felt warmed through and through by her father's promise, by her mother's new strength and happiness. It was as if Betsey already stood before the great, glowing hearth of the cabin that would soon be raised by helping hands—Betsey's home, snug and secure through all the bright tomorrows, in the new Harvey settlement of Ohio.

Cornelia Meigs

HASTY PUDDING

ILLUSTRATED BY *Keith Ward*

Iᴀ IT had not been for the thought of the hasty pudding, the little Stowe house would have been somewhat doleful that spring morning. As it was, there was hurry and bustle everywhere, with everyone telling everyone else what to do. The cold spring wind was banging the shutters, and every now and then a spurt of chilly rain would sweep across the gray hillside and throw itself against the windows. But no one—at least none of the children—noticed it at all. Ten-year-old Betty, who was to have charge of the house while her mother was away, was too full of questions about this and that to think about anything that might be going on outside. In fact, she was so busy asking questions that she did not always attend to the answers. Certainly she did not see that her mother's face looked troubled and that her father was whistling the tune that one only heard when he was a little anxious.

The small log house where the Stowe family lived was on the great far-spread hillside farm which their father had cut out of the Vermont woods for them. It had only one drawback, that of being very far from any town or other house. This was the time when the State of Vermont, with its tall mountains and narrow, green valleys, had but few people in it. Those who had been bold enough to clear the ground of forest and settle down to live there were very comfortable and happy, but they were not many. Twice a year it was necessary for Mr. and Mrs. Stowe to take the long journey to buy needed things at the nearest town, thirty miles away and on the other side of the mountain. They would be gone two days, but they would stop on the way and ask Great-Uncle Richard and Great-Aunt Clara, who lived fifteen miles down the valley, to come up and stay with the three children. But these two could not arrive so very soon, so that the three Stowes must spend the whole day alone. It was what every family, and every group of children, had to do in those early days of the settling of Vermont.

Therefore, it was Betty, with her straight shoulders, her quick feet, and her bright black eyes, who was to be in command while they were by themselves. Tom, who was nine, was perfectly able to carry the grain and water to the cows and feed the pigs. Martha was seven; she was to scatter corn for the chickens and help with the dishwashing. But it was Betty who must see that everything went properly, that the house was tidy, the meals cooked, and, if Uncle Richard and Aunt Clara should chance to be late, she must even see that everyone went to bed early, that the fire was covered, and the door barred.

On the evening before, Betty was sitting up in bed in her little room under the roof, wrapped up in a patchwork quilt, while she talked to her mother. "I must remember all those things," she said, "but I am not very good at remembering."

"No," her mother agreed, "you forget things easily, especially when you are in a hurry. But this kind of thing will help you to learn to remember. You *have* to remember when a whole family is depending on you. That is how I learned not to forget things."

Betty had a sudden feeling that was not quite terror, but something very much like it. Things were so safe and comfortable when her mother was there, and so different when she was gone. But she knew perfectly well that children had to stay alone when their parents went away to have the grain ground and to buy sugar and coffee and salt, and such things as they

37

could not get along without. Younger ones than she had managed, for they had to do it. Wildcats would call in the thickets on the mountainside; but everyone knew that wildcats never did harm to people, only to chickens and perhaps baby pigs. And there were other things—but she would not allow herself to think of them. She turned her mind stoutly to something else.

"Mother," she said, "I'm going to make them hasty pudding. They all like it so much, Tom particularly. You showed me once, and I know I can do it again. They will really understand that I can cook, when they see it come out of the pot all hot and smoking."

She let her mother tuck her in and listened to her footsteps as Mrs. Stowe went down to her own room below.

Betty went to sleep thinking of how fine it would be, that hot, spicy smell of the finished pudding, and what respect the other two children would have for her when she drew it out of the brick oven.

The log cottage was stout and warm, even though it was so small. There were two rooms below, the big kitchen where they all worked and ate and played, and the little bedroom behind it, where their father and mother, and Martha, the littlest girl, slept. Up under the roof were two tiny rooms for Tom and Betty, with the warm, stone chimney going up through both of them. There were no real stairs, only a broad, stout ladder, by which one climbed up from below. The children had known nothing else. They ran up and down like squirrels, thinking always that their house was the most beautiful and the most convenient one in the world. Betty, just before she went to sleep, could always see a picture of it behind her eyelids; how it looked to the stars, perhaps, or to the cold white moon coming up behind the mountains. It would be so small and square and tight, and its column of smoke would be going up so steadily and bravely in all that empty night of big white mountains and bright moon staring down.

In the morning, as has been said, her heart might have failed a little if she had not thought about the hasty pudding. Her mother showed her where everything was that she would need.

The ladder went crashing down into the room below.

Then, in a hail of good-byes and parting messages, Mr. and Mrs. Stowe climbed into the low wagon, clucked to the big gray horses, and were off.

"Be sure to keep the fire going. Be sure to bar the door well when it begins to get dark." Those were their mother's last words. It was so early that the clear, bright dawn was just lighting the stretch of sky above the hills. All the mountaintops were wrapped in a blanket of snow, but the long slopes were bare and dark, with here and there a glint of something sparkling, which was a little lake or an open stretch of some quickly running mountain stream. The wagon would be in sight for an hour, moving down the rough track which they called a road, and which wound away through the valley. Then presently, toward the end of the day, they would see a fat white horse coming slowly up and up the long way, a cart would stop at the door and Great-Aunt Clara would get down and say, "Well, children," just as she always did, and Uncle Richard would climb down after her, carrying the long rifle that always went with him, for who knew when one might meet a deer!

Betty turned away, finally, for nothing would be done in the house if they watched too long. She swept, she built up the fire, she skimmed the milk and kneaded down the bread. It takes a great many steps and a great deal of work to make even a little log house spotless and comfortable and warm. She had not known how often one had to put wood in the fireplace when one did it all alone. Tom was doing his full share in the barn, throwing down hay, putting fresh straw in stalls, bringing water and filling up mangers with corn. He and Betty exchanged shouts through the window and across the narrow yard, as they worked, each at his own task.

They lingered long over their dinner, because they had worked so hard all morning and because there was such an endless stream of jokes and stories to tell. Perhaps it was the fact that they must wash the dishes alone that made them slow about getting up and setting about another task. The rain had begun to come down steadily and streamed down the windows. It was only an April storm, they felt sure, but it might delay

Uncle Richard and Aunt Clara. Tom was tired from his busy morning and was willing indeed to sit on his stool beside the fire, even after Betty had asked him twice to go out and draw some water.

"There's no hurry about anything," he answered. "Why should I go out in the well in all this rain? I'll get some presently."

Betty, also, did not mind very much sitting in her mother's chair and looking, just looking, into the book which their mother had been reading to them last night. Little Martha, thoroughly tired out, curled up in the window seat; Tom dropped into his father's chair and was nodding, then finally went to sleep. Betty read on; she did not notice that the rain had stopped, that the sun shone briefly and then went under a cloud again. At last she jumped up and looked at the clock. The best part of the afternoon was gone. She must begin getting supper ready, build up the fire, put the kettle on to boil, and run out to milk the cow. Tom was only fairly good at milking, so their father said that Betty must do it.

She hurried to the barn with the empty pail in her hand; she was almost running when she came back with it full and foaming. The fire was bright on the hearth, Martha had been putting on extra logs. Now was the time for the hasty pudding. It was strange that their aunt and uncle had not come yet; but the heavy rain must have delayed them, and after all Betty could do very well at getting supper alone. Aunt Clara might scold a little when she found that Betty had let the work get behind. It was nearly suppertime, and she had not yet begun the pudding. They were going to have hasty pudding for supper, Betty vowed, if she had to toil until midnight.

Hasty pudding is not a real pudding at all, but porridge made of milk and flour, which if stirred smooth and combined with the proper flavors, can be made most delicious. Betty began to weigh and measure, but she was in such a hurry that she lost count of the cups of flour and had to measure and count again. At last she had the pudding mixed and set over the fire in the iron pot. It must cook slowly and be stirred again and again, and meanwhile she had a hundred things to do. Martha looked

40

tired and hungry. She sat down with a sigh and uttered the first lamentation of the day.

"I wish Mother were here."

Tom had come in from the barn. He had been working hard and was all ready to grumble. "Yes, if Mother was here we wouldn't have to wait like this for supper."

"I'm doing the best I can," returned Betty. She remembered just in time that she was in charge of the house and so managed to keep her voice from sounding snappish. "You'll see, supper will be ready before you know it."

She was feeling tired, too, and flurried at last, and not very sure of herself. She took off the cover of the pot and a delicious, comforting puff of fragrant steam came out. At least all was well with the pudding. The whiff of hot goodness made the others feel a little more cheerful. They could not help much, but they kept out of the way as Betty rushed from the fireplace to the table and back again. "In a few minutes now," she kept announcing, and at last gave the welcome news, "There, supper is ready." It was almost dark.

They pulled up their seats to the circle of firelight, for the evening was cold, as spring evenings are. The bacon was good, so were the potatoes, browned before the blaze. "But wait, just you wait," Betty kept telling them.

Now came the great moment. She went to the fireplace, took off the cover of the pot, and gave a final stir with the big spoon. The pudding was just the right thickness; here again was the marvelous smell pouring out. She had just lifted the pot, very carefully, off the fire, when she stopped suddenly. There was sound on the doorstep outside, an uncertain shuffling noise. Could it be Aunt Clara—could it be? It was in that second that she knew she had forgotten her mother's instruction, "Don't forget to bar the door as soon as it is dark."

She had forgotten. The door was shut, but the least touch on the wooden latch would open it. And the noise outside, what was it? Certainly not Uncle Richard or Aunt Clara.

She shot a glance of terror across the table. Tom had half risen from his stool; he, too, knew that this was an unusual sound. Martha alone was quite unconscious that anything was wrong. She took up her spoon and cried out in delight at the sight and the smell of the hasty pudding. But Betty stood, frozen, with the pot in her hand; for the wooden peg of the latch moved and the door swung open. The firelight showed two little glittering eyes, a smooth furry back; it showed, in short, that the thing which stood on the threshold was a round, plump, black bear.

Bears are not very terrible to see; they are not larger than big dogs, and their little pointed faces have always, somehow, a comic look. When one sees a bear one is not apt, at once, to feel frightened. But there is something about the idea of a wild animal from the woods coming into your house, a hungry animal which will take whatever it wants without asking, that is not soothing or comforting. Betty put down the pot with the pudding as carefully as she had taken it up, for even at this moment she could not drop anything that had seemed so precious. Then she cried out, "Run, Martha, run, Tom. Up the ladder. Let the bear have what he wants. Then he won't bother us."

Up they went, on feet that never stumbled, Betty helping Martha for fear she might fall. The ladder was steep, but they were so used to climbing it that they reached the top without a misstep, in spite of their breakneck haste. Once there, they sat down in a row, with their feet dangling over the beam which ran all across the house. Through Betty's mind there went over and over again the thought, "If I had remembered to fasten the door, if I had only remembered to fasten the door as Mother said. I was in such a hurry over the pudding that I forgot it." Even while she was so thinking, a draught of air, blowing through the house, caught the door and banged it to. The peg of the latch slipped as it often did when the door was slammed and it was fastened.

The bear stood staring at the fire for a minute, afraid of it, but enjoying its warmth. He came to the table, rose easily on his hind feet, and slipped the bacon off every plate. It was plain that he was pleased, he licked his jaws and looked about for more. He moved easily and quickly and neatly, like a dog which has been trained to stand on his hind legs. Suddenly he seemed to feel displeased over finding no more bacon, for he shouldered against the table and upset it. There was a great crash of broken china and of pewter spoons, while he snuffed and smelled among the wreckage, licking up what suited him. Still he did not seem satisfied and, as he turned about, a delicious fragrance seemed to come to his nostrils, the scent of the hasty pudding.

He swung round, came close to the hearth, and plunged his nose into the covered pot. The porridge was still hot, hot enough to burn his unaccustomed tongue and lips. He backed away, sat down on his haunches, and put both paws to his nose. He sat there, rolling from side to side, not in much pain probably, but in great anger and surprise.

The ridiculous sight was too much for Martha, and she laughed aloud. He lifted his head, listening, then turned about and, for the first time, saw the children. For a full minute they stared at each other. Then he got on all fours, came shambling across the room, and began to climb the ladder.

The three had not been greatly frightened, for they had seen bears at a distance before and had been told that they did no harm unless someone struck or hurt them. But to have a bear come climbing up to the perch upon which they sat, to the little loft where there was no room to move about, that was disturbing, very disturbing indeed. But up he came, rung by rung, for bears can climb as easily and neatly as they can do many other things. Betty, who sat nearest, knew that she must think of something quickly, now, before he came a step nearer.

The sides of the ladder, where they rested against the beam, were held between big spikes or nails, two on each side, so that the ladder was steady, but could be moved if necessary. "Tom, Tom," Betty ordered in a whisper, so that she would not excite the bear, "take hold of the other side of the ladder and pull, pull hard, so that we can push it out from the beam."

It took a strong jerk from both the children to wrench it free, and then a great push, with the weight of the bear on it, to shove it out so that it went crashing down into the room below. The bear tumbled lightly, like a cat, curling himself into a ball and rolling over and over, unhurt, as the ladder came down. He looked up at them, and there was still something so comic in his expression that they dared, finally, to laugh at him, loud and long.

He paid very little attention to them, once he found that he could not climb up to where they were. He poked about the room, examining everything with his little sharp eyes and his more dependable and most inquisitive nose. He looked into Martha's dollhouse and upset it; he pushed his nose into their mother's workbasket and spilled all the spools and balls of yarn; he tipped over a milk pan and left a puddle of milk and cream on the clean boards. The neat house began to look as though a tempest had blown through it, and still they could not seem to

44

have any hard feeling against a creature who was only looking about for his supper and was entertaining them so highly as he did it. No matter what he did, the three children could not get tired of watching him, or fail to burst out laughing at every new trick or mishap.

Betty looked up finally and saw that the stars were shining behind the little window in the roof. "Uncle Richard and Aunt Clara will certainly be here soon," she said.

Each of them in that minute was thinking the same thing, although it was Tom who spoke first. "Uncle Richard always has his rifle. When he sees the bear—" Martha set up a wail. "Oh, he couldn't, he mustn't. He shan't shoot our bear."

In spite of all the mischief he had made, the bear had begun to seem like a friend, a playmate who had amused them through an exciting hour. They forgot that he had robbed them of their supper and kept them prisoners up under the roof. Their only thought was how to save him when Uncle Richard came. "If there were only some way he could get out," Betty said. "But the windows are too little, and the door won't blow open."

Tom had an idea. He fumbled in his pocket and drew out a long piece of string. He tied a loop in the end of it, a very small loop. "Are you going to catch the bear with it?" Martha asked in wonder, but he shook his head.

Just opposite where they sat was another beam which ran along the top of the wall of the house. It was just above the door. Tom, by scrambling and swinging, once almost falling, got himself across to the beam, holding to the rafter above. He lowered the cord and tried to hook the loop over the latch of the door. Once he tried and failed, then he attempted it again. The bear began to be interested and came across to sniff at the cord. Tom gave a quick jerk (this time the loop had caught) and lifted the latch. The door swung open, and the bear went shambling out, to disappear in the shadows.

Uncle Richard and Aunt Clara appeared on the threshold only a few minutes later. They were, it may be said, considerably surprised. Tom had dropped down from his perch and had got the ladder into place again. Martha and Betty were just scrambling down into a room whose wild disorder looked like something in a bad dream. In answer to Aunt Clara's shocked exclamation, Betty only answered:

"Oh, that was just the bear! And, Aunt Clara, I know how to make hasty pudding. It was a wonderful one, only I hurried a little too much while I was getting it ready."

Mabel Leigh Hunt

JOHNNY APPLESEED'S COAT

ILLUSTRATED BY *Barbara Maynard*

M AYBE the boat's not coming, Ma." Seth's face was anxious. Resolutely he turned his back on the empty reaches of the Miami Canal. Perhaps if he could stop looking for the *Silver Bell*, she would come.

"Maybe the boat's sunk plumb to the bottom," fretted his twin, Sally. She moped drearily on one of the packing-boxes containing the worldly goods of the Rogers family.

"Ma!" Eight-year-old Susan's lips trembled alarmingly.

"Ma!" wailed Shadrach, casting himself upon his mother's knees. "You said we'd ride on the boat! You said—"

"Dry right up, all of you!" scolded Sarah Rogers. "You twins

47

starting such a hullabaloo! Five young 'uns—Seth, Sally, Susan, Shadrach, and Sharon Rogers—and not one of you with a mite of patience. Now hearken to me. Some time or other that packet will come. But when—that's a different matter." Ma suddenly cocked her head, listening. "There, now, what did I tell you?" she exclaimed.

From afar came a long-drawn bugling. The forest bordering the canal flung back the echo, clear and lovely. The children shot to the edge of the landing, tensely watching for the first glimpse of the *Silver Bell*. Ma stood up, bright-eyed, holding baby Sharon. And now, as if by magic, the sleepy Ohio settlement of Troy came to life. Eager and noisy, its inhabitants crowded to the landing.

Around the bend, along the opposite towpath, appeared a pair of gray mules. The morning sunlight flashed on their silver-mounted harness. Silver bells swung from their heavy collars. Their driver, but a moment ago plodding through the country quiet, now set his hat atilt, flourished his whip, and swaggered jauntily. "Giddap!" he shouted.

In tow of the mules, by means of a long rope attached to their collars, glided the *Silver Bell*. In the water her shadow

48

was reflected in bright, broken planes of color. Her underbody
was painted green and red, with accents of black. Dazzling
white was her cabin. Her twenty little windows boasted blue
shutters. Within hung crisp curtains of scarlet.

The Rogers children held their breath as the steersman, hand
on tiller, guided the boat toward the landing. The captain blew
one more blast on his horn. Across the canal the driver bel-
lowed at the mules to halt. The towline grew slack, trailing in the
water. Smoothly and silently the packet swam to her mooring.

Then what a hubbub of talk as captain and passengers clambered off! "And who might you be, stranger?" inquired the
villagers, with kindly curiosity. "What's the news down
Cincinnati-way? Nifty outfit you've got there, Captain Brown.
'Bout what speed you making?"

49

"Three and a half miles an hour," boomed the captain, proudly. "Sometimes as much as four."

"You don't say! Whew!"

The Rogers children could scarcely endure such leisurely talk, such dawdling. But at last they were aboard, bag and baggage. The boat resumed its way. In no time everyone on the *Silver Bell* knew that the passengers picked up at Troy were Sarah Rogers and her young 'uns from Clare County.

"Bound for Indiana," said Sarah, happily. "We change at Fort Wayne for another packet on the Wabash & Erie Canal. Travel as far as Lafayette, we do, where my man, Steve Rogers, will meet us. He's bought land there and an inn."

Once aboard, the slow, noiseless drifting of the packet seemed to cast a soothing enchantment over the spellbound Seth and Sally, Susan and Shadrach. The grown-up passengers murmured as drowsily as bees; all the nurslings slept; the tramp of the mules came muffled and measured. The children might have thought it a dream journey, had not the captain signaled so lustily at every flouring mill, every tiny settlement, every passing freight and passenger boat.

At noontide he blew the mightiest blast of all. The boat moored. They all piled merrily off and, at a nearby settler's house, stuffed themselves hugely with savory hot food.

It was mid-afternoon when the *Silver Bell*, gliding smoothly among her colored shadows, was hailed from the bank.

"Well, I'll be switched, if it isn't Johnny!" exclaimed a man close to Seth. "Look! And what's come over the old fellow, all fancied up like that?" The speaker turned to his deck companion. "It's dear old Johnny Appleseed. I didn't know he ever traveled by canalboat."

Seth slipped away to find his twin. "It's Johnny Appleseed, Sal," he whispered, and stared with round eyes as the packet sidled up to the shore. Ah, yes, Seth had heard of this odd character, who of his own free will had planted and tended apple orchards all through the new country of the Ohio. And when Johnny Appleseed leaped aboard, Seth managed to stand close —so close he could have touched the pilgrim's coat.

It was the coat that had caused the man on deck to exclaim. For above Johnny's worn moccasins and his tattered deerskin trousers, the coat seemed oddly magnificent. Sky-blue it was, very fine and soft, with elegant skirts, standing collar, and silver buttons. Neither did it match the pickax and spade that Johnny carried. Nor his hat—a cooking pan!

But no one laughed. Not after the word had spread that this was indeed the famous Johnny Appleseed. Now the *Silver Bell* seemed to move with a new pride, as if glorying in the knowledge that she carried one who was already half legend in the annals of the West—Johnny Appleseed, whose history was to outlast his orchards and all of those who journeyed with him this May day on the Miami Canal. The passengers crowded close to see and speak to him.

But as the afternoon shadows lengthened, there came a startling cry, "Man overboard!"

"No! It's a child! See, there he is! He's going under!"

How the passengers pushed and peered! How frantically every mother counted the noses of her flock! The mule driver halted his team. The boat stopped.

Above the wild cries Sarah Rogers heard Sally's scream. "Ma! It's Shadrach! Oh-h-h, Ma!"

Ma reached the stern in time to see Seth plunge to the rescue. Shadrach had disappeared. The channel was only four feet deep, but Shadrach was such a little boy.

"There he is!" yelled the crowd, as the child rose gasping to the surface. Their clamor rang in Seth's ears as with furious strokes he pushed toward his brother. But just as he was ready to grasp Shadrach's collar, he saw the boy lifted out of the water. Some strange giant claw seemed reaching from the sky.

Seth looked up, bewildered. On the deck stood Captain Brown, braced sturdily. He was holding a long pole. At its hook end there dangled, by the seat of his pantaloons, the dripping Shadrach. Amid cheers from the passengers, the youngster was hauled on deck.

Seth was dripping, too, when he climbed aboard. There had been no time, before his frantic plunge, to shed his coat. And

51

when little Shad had been revived, stripped, and wrapped in a blanket, Ma looked ruefully at Seth.

"Soaking wet you are, and that your only decent outfit! Probably won't be dry by morning. What you're going to wear I don't know, nor where I could find it among those boxes. But, there! I believe I do remember where I packed your long red woolens. Sally, lend your pinafore to Seth. He shall wear it over his underpants."

"Ma!" protested Seth, horrified. "A boy as big as me in a girl's pinafore! Everybody will laugh!"

Ma gave Seth a tender pat. "A hero can wear anything he's a mind to, 'thout folks laughing," she whispered.

To be called a hero! Seth was dumbfounded. "Shucks!" he muttered at last, " 'twas the captain saved Shad, not me."

"But you had the will," insisted Ma. "You made the effort. It's a'most the same. So you needn't mind the pinafore, Son."

Oh, but Seth did mind! And he was feeling not at all like a hero when Johnny Appleseed stepped up. He was pulling off his fine blue coat.

"Please, ma'am," he said, "I'd be proud could your boy wear this while his own clothes dry."

"But, Mister—" Ma cried, though her eyes were warm and deep, "what will you do for the lack of it?"

"A coat's a pesky burden," smiled Johnny. "Specially a fine one like this." He smoothed the sleeves of his shirt, stretching as if he were glad to be free.

Oh, how the sky-blue coat fairly swallowed Seth! And when he had donned his skin-tight underpants, he was a comical sight, if ever there was one. But every boy aboard gazed at him with envy.

As for him, he was completely dazzled. Even the experience of going through the locks at Junction, where the St. Mary's and St. Joseph's joined to form the Miami, even the knowledge that here the canal became the Wabash & Erie flowing into Indiana—that was certainly exciting, but not so deeply exciting to Seth as the feel of Johnny Appleseed's coat on his shoulders and the silver buttons under his proud touch. And oh, how everlastingly grateful he was to Johnny for saving him the shame of wearing a girl's pinafore!

At eight-thirty o'clock, there was the drawing of numbers for the sleeping berths. Ma, whose flock had barely escaped disaster that day, looked at Seth anxiously. "You'll have to bide in the men's cabin, Son. Now do take care of yourself, and mind you, don't sleep in Mister—in Johnny Appleseed's coat."

The berths were tiers of canvas shelves suspended by bars from the cabin walls. Each shelf was equipped with a thin straw pallet, a sheet, and blanket. Seth smothered his giggles as he peered down from his own top berth at the rows of shelves sagging so comically under the weight of the various passengers.

Many slept on the floor. They lay on benches, on and under tables. Their discarded collars and cravats, coats and waistcoats hung on ropes stretched from wall to wall.

But the precious sky-blue coat was not among these garments. Carefully Seth folded it across his body, one sleeve tucked underneath to keep it from slipping. And through all the clumsy settling-down, Seth kept an eye on Johnny. In the dim light he could make out the planter's spare figure. Above him sagged a huge mound of a fellow. There seemed scarcely room for Johnny to draw breath.

Soon there was a steady blast of snores. In Seth's dreams these ungodly sounds mingled strangely with the echoes of the packet horn, sweet and mournful and mysterious in the night.

Hours later he wakened. "Pa! Ma! Where am I?" he cried. Then he remembered, and was ashamed of his fear. He felt for the coat. It was safe. Peering through the shadow, he saw that the fat gentleman sleeping above Johnny had sagged yet lower. But Johnny—he was not there!

Tucking the coat under one arm, Seth swung himself down. There were grunts of protest as he picked his way among the sleepers on the floor. At the door he paused. In the half-light of early dawn he could see the shadowy figure of the steersman. On the towpath, mules and driver trod like inky ghosts.

Stealthily Seth tiptoed around the deck. And at the stern end, propped against the cabin's outer wall, lounged Johnny Appleseed. He looked up and held out his hand.

"It's you, lad," he whispered. "Couldn't you endure it, either? Put on the coat, and share my blanket. It's chilly. We must be quiet, for the captain, though snug in his cuddy, doesn't allow anyone on deck at night.

"I'll be leaving come morning, lad. I've had my fill of being packed away like a dead pig in a warehouse. Took me a foolish notion to travel by packet once in my life. It'll be the last time." He drew a deep breath.

Seth breathed deeply, too. After the close air of the cabin, how fresh and sweet was the scent of the forest! Little wavelets licked the sides of the packet as gently as kittens' tongues. And while the pale light grew, Seth fell asleep, nestling close to the loving-kindness of Johnny Appleseed.

As the passengers were going ashore for breakfast Johnny shook hands with Ma. "Now God go with you and yours," he said. "And you may have the coat for keeps, ma'am."

"You would give away such a fine coat as that?" asked Ma.

"I never felt it rightly mine," answered Johnny. "It was but given me in return for some apple seedlings. Besides, it's no coat for the wilderness. Nor for one like Johnny Appleseed, that runs free as a fox."

"I'm much obliged, then, I'm sure, Mister," said Ma, all ashine. "With close contrivin' I can tailor a handsome suit for Shadrach."

"But, Ma!" wailed Seth.

Quietly Johnny drew him aside. "I know, because it was mine, you'd like to keep the coat as it is, Seth, and thank 'ee for the compliment," he said. "But did you see the heartsome looks of your mother, when she saw in her mind's eye her little Shadrach tricked out in blue with silver buttons? Now let her be. *Giving*, lad—why it's one of the blessed things we mortals can do. So now if you'll part with the coat and smile in the doing of it, I'll give you something that's worth far more." Thrusting his hand into the front of his shirt, he drew forth a small buckskin bag. He loosened the string. Into Seth's cupped palm he poured a stream of brown seeds.

"Apple seeds, Seth, to plant in that new place of your pa's on the Wabash. Tend them well, and they'll grow into trees that will last nigh on a hundred years, and the miracle of their fruit will be repeated a hundred times. Think of that, lad!"

Seth lifted glad eyes. "Oh, Johnny, of course I'd rather have the seeds than the coat! 'Cause apple seeds—why, they're *you*, and all I've heard about you my whole life long! An' my pa will be *that* proud!"

"Some day, Seth," continued Johnny, "when there are apples in your pa's orchard, fair beholden I'll be should you give away seeds, too. I shall be gone; but to the folks living then, you must say: 'Remember, when these grow and bear fruit, it will be your turn to give away seeds. Because that was Johnny Appleseed's way, and Johnny Appleseed's faith in the future!'"

"That's not all I'll say," agreed Seth, with shy pride. "I'll say, ' 'Twas Johnny Appleseed told me, when I was a boy and wore his coat, that giving is good.'"

Marjorie Hayes

A RIDE
WITH TOM THUMB

ILLUSTRATED BY *Janet Ross*

"THREE miles to Baltimore," read the sign at the crossroads. Charles spelled it out laboriously, "B-a-l-t-i, Balti; m-o-r-e, more, Baltimore. What State is Baltimore in, Father?"

"Maryland. How many States have we been through now?"

"Vermont, Massachusetts, Connecticut, New York," chanted Charles. "Then New Jersey, Pennsylvania, Delaware, and Maryland. That's eight. Haven't we traveled a lot?"

"We keep going and going," said Lottie. "I should think the wagon would get tired."

Father laughed. "Only three miles more, did you say?" he asked Charles. "Then we'll be there by noon. How would you like to take dinner at an inn for a change?"

The children were delighted, for they had never eaten at a public place before, and Charles hoped that a lady with a parrot might come in, like the one in Pittsfield.

When they reached the city, Father chose an inn on the corner of a busy street. The dining room had two long tables at which several men and women were already seated, but Charles didn't see any parrot, although there was a canary bird singing away in a sunny window.

When they were finishing their beefsteak pie, the landlord stopped at their table. "I expect you came in to see the new steam railroad, sir," he said to Father.

"No," said Father.—"A steam railroad, you say? Pray tell us about it."

"Well," said Mr. Landlord, who was a very plump, rosy-faced man, with a big white apron tied about his middle, "a few months ago the new Baltimore and Ohio Railroad Company laid tracks from the city to Ellicott's Mills, some thirteen miles out, and have been running a horsecar there."

"I have heard about the horsecars in Quincy, Massachusetts," said Father.

"But some of the directors thought a steam engine, like they have in England, would be better," continued the landlord. "So Mr. Peter Cooper of New York, who owns the land through which the road runs, has built with his own hands a locomotive which he calls the 'Tom Thumb,' because it is so small. He had his trial run to Ellicott's Mills and back yesterday. Fifteen miles an hour he went and never turned over at a curve. A sight of people gathered to see him start, and today folks have been coming from a long way back in the country to have a ride."

"Marvelous!" cried Father. "It seems we have reached here just in time. Thank you for telling us.—How about a ride on the steam railroad, Vermont Roosters?"

"Yes! Yes!" cried Charles and Lottie, though they had no idea what a railroad was.

They had never seen Father so excited. He said they had eaten enough, and as soon as the landlord had given him directions for reaching the place where the railroad began, he bundled them into the wagon and set off at a gallop.

Very soon they met a great many people in buggies and wagons and on horseback, and even on foot, all going in the same direction. Then ahead of them they saw an enormous crowd, with the American flag waving on a tall pole over their heads, and they knew the train must be there.

Father tied the horses quite a distance away, because he thought they might be frightened of the engine, and he fastened Rollo in the wagon. Then, with the children clinging to his hands, he pushed his way through the crowd, eager for a glimpse of the wonderful locomotive.

57

There were two sets of tracks, side by side, running off into the woods, and on one of them stood the train,—an engine and one car for passengers. The engine didn't look the least bit like the locomotives of today. There was just a flat car, like a box cover on wheels, and on it stood a tiny little engine that the children hardly noticed, attached to what looked like a wash-boiler with a narrow smokestack at the top. The car for the passengers wasn't like a stagecoach, but was a flat car a little larger than the one that held the engine. It had a top over it and rows of seats across.

"But how can the train go without any horses?" asked Charles, after he had looked it over in silence for a moment.

"It goes by steam," explained Father. "Steam makes power to turn the wheels. It's a marvelous new invention which Mr. Fulton has used in his river boats, and which has even brought ships across the ocean. Listen and you will hear the steam beginning to come up."

Sure enough, Charles could hear a "Sh! Sh! Sh!—Sh! Sh! Sh!" from somewhere in the boiler. It grew louder, and pretty soon smoke began to pour from the stack. A man was shoveling some black stuff, which Father said was coal, into a door at the bottom, and the children could see a bright fire glowing there.

People were already taking their seats in the car, and Father said they had better buy their tickets at once. But when he went up to the man who had been selling them he said, "Sorry, all sold out, sir."

"You couldn't possibly squeeze us in?" asked Father.

The man shook his head. "She'll only hold thirty-six, and we've sold that many."

"Well," said Father to the children, trying not to look as disappointed as he felt, "I'm afraid we can't go, but we can watch the start, anyway."

Just then a man who had been standing behind him tapped him on the shoulder. "I've a ticket I'll sell you, stranger," he said. "I bought two, and now my wife, she's afraid to go, though we druv ten miles just to see the iron horse."

58

He was a very tall, thin young man, who looked as if he had grown too fast for his sleeves, Charles thought. But he looked down at them pleasantly and said it would be a shame for the "young uns" to miss the ride.

"How can we all three go in one seat?" asked Father dubiously. "The man says it's going to be crowded."

"You hold one young un in your lap, and I'll hold t'other," their new friend suggested.

Father said that would be very kind, and he bought the ticket at once. "You're sure your wife won't change her mind?" he asked.

Mr. Ward shook his head. "Nope, when she's got it made up, there ain't no changin'. She took a look at that ere Tom Thumb engine and she said, 'Mercy on us! That thing'll get so hot it'll blow up before the first mile.' She declared she was going back an' set in the wagon, and if I wanted to break my neck, I could do it alone."

Father smiled. "I think we'd better get our seats," he said.

As they stepped aboard the car, Charles noticed that Tom Thumb was puffing more loudly, "*Choo*-choo-choo! *Choo*-choo-choo! *Choo*-choo-choo!" as though he were eager to start. The seats in the car were nearly all filled, but they found two in the third row. Father took Lottie on his lap and Charles sat on Mr. Ward's knee. As Mr. Ward was on the end seat of the row, Charles could lean out and watch Tom Thumb.

Now every seat was taken, and five or six men were standing on the car with Tom Thumb. One of them was Mr. Cooper, and he was starting the engine. "All aboard! All aboard!" shouted the ticket man. "Keep off the tracks!" called someone else.

"*Choo*-choo-choo!" sang Tom Thumb more loudly. His wheels began to turn, and down the track he started, belching smoke from his chimney, with the passenger car following after.

How the crowd cheered! "Hurrah for Tom Thumb! Hurrah for Peter Cooper! Hurrah! Hurrah!" People were waving flags and handkerchiefs, and some of the passengers stood up and waved.

59

Charles sat clutching Mr. Ward's coat lapel tightly. They seemed to be going much faster than in the wooden wagon, and it seemed so queer to have the black smokestack of Tom Thumb in front of them, instead of Prince and Prancer. Soon they had left the crowd behind and were rolling along through the woods.

"It feels like we were on a sled," said Lottie.

"Ah, but Tom Thumb can go *uphill*," said Father, and sure enough, just then they began to go upgrade.

"Chug-chug-chug! Chug-chug-chug! Chug-chug-chug!" said Tom Thumb, breathing harder. But up the hill he went, pulling the car with its passengers behind him, and in a moment they were at the top and rushing down the other side.

"We'll be at Point of Rocks curve soon," said a man in front of Father. "I understand Mr. Cooper built Tom Thumb particularly to show that a steam locomotive can negotiate a short curve without any trouble."

Charles looked for the Point of Rocks curve, but he couldn't see it. Next thing he knew, they had whisked around it without tipping at all, and all the passengers were cheering.

When they arrived at Ellicott's Mills, they found another crowd, though not so large as the one in Baltimore, eager to welcome Tom Thumb. He came to a stop there, and Charles saw Mr. Cooper give him a big drink of water. Then, after a few minutes, he crossed to the other track and began the journey back to Baltimore.

And then the most exciting thing of all happened. When they had gone about halfway and were slowing down at the place called Relay House, for Tom Thumb to have another drink, they saw something ahead of them on the other track. As they came to a stop, they discovered it was the horsecar that had been carrying passengers before Tom Thumb was built, full of people and drawn by the finest horse owned by the stagecoach company, a spirited gray. It was headed in the same direction they were and had evidently been waiting for them.

As Tom Thumb drew alongside, the driver leaned out and shouted, "We'll beat you back to Baltimore, Mr. Cooper! Your old engine can't go any faster than we can."

"All right," said Mr. Cooper calmly. "I'm willing."

So, as soon as Tom Thumb had had his water, a man beside the track gave the signal, "Go!"

At the signal Mr. Cooper opened the throttle, the driver cracked his whip, the horse leaped forward,—but Tom Thumb stood still, because he had to get his steam up. The horsecar was quite a way ahead when he finally started. But then how he did go, and in a few minutes the train had caught up with the horsecar and there they were, racing neck to neck!

Then what a racket there was, with the two cars flying over the rails and the passengers cheering and shouting! More than half were standing up, and there was a man sitting on the roof of the horsecar, waving his arms. The driver yelled encouragement to his horse, and above it all Tom Thumb was singing away, "Choo-choo! Choo-choo! Choo-choo! Choo-choo!" He didn't seem excited at all. Charles wanted him to win, but he felt sorry for the horse, too.

Tom Thumb began to gain; then he passed the horse amid deafening cheers from his passengers. As he drew farther and

farther ahead, he seemed to say, "Ha! Ha! Ha!—Ha! Ha! Ha!—Ha! Ha! Ha!" Charles craned his neck to look back, and the horsecar was almost out of sight. Tom Thumb could afford to laugh.

But then an accident happened. A leather band somewhere on a wheel slipped out of place, poor Tom Thumb began to go more slowly, and finally stopped, while Mr. Cooper tried frantically to pull the band on again.

"Wal, I swan," said Mr. Ward. "That dratted horse'll beat us yet!"

"Mr. Cooper'll have us going again in a second," said Father.

But Mr. Cooper hurt his hand, and there was more delay, while Lottie, who had gotten a cinder in her eye, began to cry. Mr. Cooper worked over the wheel, and Father tried to get the cinder out, and meantime the horsecar, which had been just about to give up, came leaping by them, its passengers cheering in their turn.

By the time the engine was repaired, and the cinder out, it was too late. Although Tom Thumb went his fastest, the horse-car had too great a lead and reached Baltimore ahead of him.

"*Choo*-choo-o! *Choo*-choo-o!" he panted, as he drew up in the midst of the crowd, and Charles thought he was saying, "Too bad! Too bad!"

"I suppose he's too hot for me to pat," he said, as they got out and walked past the little engine.

"Yes, I'm afraid you'd have a burnt hand to remember him by if you touched that boiler," Father said.

"But be sure you do remember, young un," urged Mr. Ward, "that you rode behind the first locomotive built in America."

"Nasty old en-jine," said Lottie, "giving me a cinder! I'd rather ride in our nice wagon."

"I guess you'll have to, yet awhile, little Rooster," laughed Father. "But some day I believe there'll be a railroad all the way to Vermont, and you and Charles will think nothing of traveling on it."

"Y-y-y-y-e-s-s-s-s!" agreed little Tom Thumb, with his escaping steam.

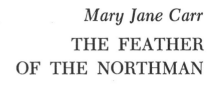

Mary Jane Carr

THE FEATHER
OF THE NORTHMAN

ILLUSTRATED BY *Fredrick Chapman*

ONALD MacDERMOTT was on his way
to Fort Vancouver. For days he and a group of trappers had
been traveling down the Columbia River in a fleet of canoes.
Through swift and smoothly flowing water, over rapids and
around whirlpools, they had glided along the great waterway.

It was Donald's first trip to the fort. His father, Big Mac, had
died only a little while ago. Now Young Mac, as his companions
called him, was traveling west to seek his fortune.

He was under the protection of his father's old friend, Henri
Le Grand. Henri had made up his mind that this thirteen-year-
old boy should grow up to be a man Big Mac could be proud
of. He had seen to it that Donald shared every hardship on this
trip, which, in the year 1832, had been full of hardship.

Many times they had had to leave the river and carry their
canoes and their supplies over rough trails. Every night a fire
was kept burning to frighten away wild animals. And the food
was bad.

Donald, though he was homesick and afraid, had refused
to let any of the men know how he felt. He had borne every
hardship without whimpering. Even the teasing of these rough,
good-natured woodsmen, he had taken in his stride, or at least
had tried to. But he had not returned their joking. And as the
miles increased between him and his home, he had grown
more sullen and quiet.

The men might lift their voices in loud song as they drove their canoes through the water, but not Donald. He sat in frowning silence. And when they joked, he set his mouth firmly and showed no trace of a smile. And so the men had made him the target of their fooling.

The teasing had increased each day, until Donald wondered how he could stand another hour of it. But still he held his tongue and his songs and smiles.

Now they were within one day's traveling of the fort. To-morrow the fleet of canoes would reach Fort Vancouver. Tomorrow he and the others would jump to land before the canoes had touched the shore. Tomorrow he was going to sing with the rest of them.

But deep in his heart there would be no singing, because Donald knew what the others didn't know. He knew that he was secretly afraid of this wilderness. That fear was the reason why he was sullen and homesick. It was the reason why he could not laugh and sing.

Now Donald lay wrapped in his warm beaverskin and watched the round, white moon climb high above the towering rocks that lined the opposite shore. Lying there, he fought his fear until, worn out with weariness, he dropped asleep.

He was awakened by a low snarl, which he recognized, even before he was fully awake, as the snarl of a timber wolf. His hand closed quickly on his gun, which lay on the ground beside him. He lifted his head cautiously and peered about.

He listened, hardly breathing. Had he only dreamed that threatening snarl?

It had seemed to come from near at hand. But now there was not a sound to be heard, other than the out-of-door sounds common along waterways at night—the hoot of an owl, the stir of wind in the branches, the soft lap of waves against the shore. The camp lay quiet and peaceful in the moonlight.

The bed of coals that had been the campfire drew his eyes. Those heaps on the ground beyond the fire must be Baptiste, the cook, and Jacques, huddled under their blankets, their feet to the warmth. In chill weather the men all slept close to the fires, but this night air was pleasant, and the trappers lay scattered around the camp. Some were in the open and some under the shelter of their upturned canoes.

The boy was surprised to see that no one was on guard duty. Did they believe this country so safe, then?

Donald looked for the sleeping place of Henri. He was relieved to see his friend lying only a few yards away, rolled in his Hudson Bay blanket. Henri never slept under a canoe unless it was storming. He didn't want walls of any kind around him when he was on the march.

It was a habit of self-protection he had formed in dangerous Indian country long ago. No matter how sharp a man's eyes might be, Henri said, they couldn't see through wood. An upturned canoe was too handy a hiding place for a red man bent on mischief. Too, Henri slept with his ears wide open. He would have been aroused the very first thing if any enemy, human or animal, had been prowling around the camp. That snarl must have been only part of a dream.

Donald's tight grip on the rifle loosened, and he was about to settle back into the warmth of the beaverskin robe, when a movement at the foot of his bed jerked him once more into sharp attention.

In the shadow of the upturned canoe, his eyes made out the form of a large animal. It was a timber wolf, ready to pounce.

The boy felt a chill, like a cold hand, run along his backbone. He paused for just a second while the chill shook him. Then he snatched his rifle and rose on his elbow. But before he could fire, the animal wobbled in a queer way, and then fell on its side at the foot of the bed.

Amazed, Donald lowered his rifle and stared. The fallen animal didn't move. It appeared to be dead, although no shot had been fired! Cautiously the surprised boy drew himself to a sitting position and gently poked the quiet figure with the barrel of his rifle. The figure did not move.

Then a smothered laugh from behind the canoe made Donald suddenly understand. The animal was dead! Its lifeless body had been propped up there as a joke on him!

Donald leaped over the body of the wolf and peered behind the canoe. Sure enough, there were Jacques and Baptiste, kneeling on the ground and shaking with smothered laughter.

"Shhh!" whispered Jacques, his finger on his lip. "Make no noise to wake that wolf, Young Mac! She is one big, bad, evil wolf, *non?*"

"Ho, little brother!" gasped Baptiste. "What are you doing out with your gun at midnight? Not hunting, surely?"

Suddenly the whole camp seemed to break into laughter. The boy turned to see figures rising from the ground all over the camp. Then he knew that the men had been only pretending sleep and waiting to see how the joke on him turned out.

At first a wave of anger swept over Donald, but it passed as quickly as it had come. He felt a little glow of pride. They had all seen that he was not a coward!

To be aroused from a sound sleep to find a snarling wolf at one's bedside—that was enough to frighten any man, surely! He had felt a touch of fear, to be sure, but he had thrown it off. Let them have their fun! They had seen that he was no coward. If he had covered his head and called for help— But no one could say that he had shown fear.

Resting one end of his rifle on the ground, the boy folded his arms across his chest, put one foot on the dead wolf, and faced the laughing camp with an air of triumph.

"Behold!" he cried in French. "Behold a real hunter!"

The men fell silent to listen.

"You call yourselves hunters!" Donald called out. "You boast of your fine shots! Many times I have heard you brag of how you killed a bear with only one shot. One shot, bah! *You* have to *shoot* to kill! But Young Mac has only to raise his gun, and the wild animals fall dead from fright! You have just seen it happen!"

Henri's powerful shoulders shook with laughter. Good enough! Young Mac was swaggering now in the true trapper style.

A roar of cheers went up from the men. The boy had turned the tables on them very neatly, and they were not only willing,

but delighted, to admit his victory. Young Mac was truly one of them—at last. He would have a tall tale of his own to tell now. They clapped one another on the back and shouted, "Ha! So you thought you were a hunter, eh? But *you* have to *shoot* to kill! Bah!"

Henri Le Grand finally quieted their cheers with an upheld hand. The guide went toward Donald, and the men drew near and formed a half circle around the two. The boy's eyes widened. His heart began to beat quickly, for he saw that Henri held in his hand a plaid ribbon with a red feather fastened to it. The men were perfectly quiet now, watching their guide and Young Mac.

"Tomorrow," said Henri, "Young Mac's first voyage comes to an end at Fort Vancouver. A long, hard journey it was, and he found fault not once. He took his place at the paddle with the best of you. Whenever it was necessary, he carried his heavy pack like a man. He ate what he was offered without a grumble. And when there was nothing in the pots for supper, he pulled his belt tighter and said not a word, though all his growing bones cried out for food. He sat tight when the canoes shot rapids. Not even at the Canyon of the Dead, where the tall white crosses tell of boatmen who died in the boiling water, did he show fear. Did any of you see him show fear?"

"*Non! Non!*"

"Now you have just seen him frighten a timber wolf to death. Is he not one of us? Is Young Mac not a Northman?"

"*Oui! Oui!*" the trappers shouted. "Yes! Yes! Behold Young Mac, the Northman!"

"You have learned the law of the trapper," Henri said to Donald, "the law that has made the sons of the fur trade able to look death in the face without blinking. You have learned well that law: to know fear, as all men must know fear, but not to be conquered by fear; to think clearly and quickly; to keep a high heart. It is decided that you have earned the right to wear the feather of a Northman."

Henri lifted his arms to place the band on Donald's head, a ribbon with the plaid of Big Mac's clan and a red feather.

"So tall the boy has grown!" the man thought. It seemed to him only yesterday that he had swung this lad up to ride on his shoulder along with his own son.

"Now then! It is done!" He pressed the headpiece in place. "Have you not something to say, Young Mac?"

"*Merci!*" said Donald almost in a whisper. He felt that he could not speak above the pounding of his heart.

"Oho!" laughed Henri. "Say more, Young Mac, and say it in English! That is the tongue they use at Fort Vancouver!"

Donald turned toward the watching men and saluted them gravely. He spoke in the language that he had not used for some time, not since Big Mac had spoken it with him.

"Thank you! I—I am very proud that you call me one of you. Thank you all. I shall keep forever the red feather to remind me that I am a Northman. And—some day we will go on another voyage—together."

The night air rang with the hurrahs of the trappers. While the cheering was still going on, Jacques and Baptiste climbed up a tree as quickly as squirrels.

"But, you two! Where are you going?" Henri shouted after them.

"We go to cut a lobstick!" Jacques shouted back. And Baptiste's voice called, as branches showered from the tree, "Yes! We mark forever the spot where Young Mac, a *real* hunter, saved his brothers from the fierce, evil wolf!" In trapper style the story was already growing tall!

"A lobstick for Young Mac, of course!" the men agreed, several of them leaping to join the two at work in the tree. And before long a tree was cleaned of its branches except for a little bunch at the very top. It would be a sign to all who came this way that something important in trapper history had happened on this spot.

Long after the silence of sleep had settled down on the camp, Young Mac lay awake. He had something precious to keep forever now—the Northman feather, a reward for his courage. Yes, and this night he had gained something more, something that would allow him to wear that feather with pride. It was an understanding that had come to him with Henri's words: "To know fear, as all men must know fear, but not to be conquered by fear."

He understood now that it was not unmanly to feel fear and to be lonely. It was unmanly only to let fear and loneliness conquer one.

The great men of the fur trade, even the strongest ones, had known fear. They, too, had been sick at heart sometimes, in the wild, lonesome countries where they had to spend months—years—of their lives. Maybe they, too, at times had felt that it would be easier to weep than to laugh.

His own father? Suddenly, with a clearness that startled him, there came to Donald a memory out of his childhood.

He had run in out of the snow, where he and a friend had been playing with Bairn. They had been trying to teach Bairn to draw a sled, when Bairn was still a puppy and didn't want to be taught such serious business. Donald had run into the house for a piece of harness and had been surprised to see his father sitting there with his face in his hands. He had asked, "Are you asleep?"

And his father had looked up with a strange smile and had said something strange.

"Not asleep! I was just remembering—"

The words had small meaning for Donald then, and he forgot them right away. Now when they came back across the years, he understood. His father, far from his home, had been lonely, remembering.

The boy put up his hand and touched the precious headpiece above him, which hung from the canoe. He marked the date well in his mind—October 18, 1832. He would not forget this day when the men had decided that he had earned the right to wear the Northman feather. He knew now that he could meet whatever hardships lay ahead with a brave heart. To-morrow—Fort Vancouver—let them come!

71

Over a hundred years ago when the Hodgetts family decided to go to Minnesota in a covered wagon they took with them Sarah's cornhusk doll, Drusilla. Here Drusilla tells about one of their adventures on the long journey.

Emma Brock

IN A COVERED WAGON

ILLUSTRATED BY *Carol Stoaks*

ALL that day and the next we crawled over the prairie. The road was very bad. It was almost no road at all, but just two wheel tracks across the prairie. The wagons shrieked and creaked as they tilted this way and that over the grassy tussocks. The log cabins with their plowed fields round them were far apart and looked like dark jewels in the bright prairie grass.

The prairie hens flew up with a clatter of wings before the oxen's hoofs. "Pigie, pigie!" they cried.

The sun was very bright and warm, and Mrs. Hodgetts and Aunt Polly were wearing their shaker bonnets to keep from getting sunburned. Aunt Polly was buttoned up in black gloves so that her hands would not freckle. Just to look at Will Smith was enough to make anyone afraid of freckles. His freckles ran together now. There was not a bit of skin between them.

"My, but it is warm," said Aunt Polly, unbuttoning her gloves.

"Minnesota can be very warm, they all say," said Mr. Hodgetts. He was mopping away the perspiration that was trickling down his long nose. "It feels like rain."

"Oh, what is that?" cried Aunt Polly, pointing toward a pile of things beside the road.

"It looks like a rubbish heap," said Mr. Hodgetts. "Things that people have thrown away. 'Help yourself,' the sign says."

There was an old bureau and a big old chair and a frying pan with a hole in it and a lot of other things.

72

"Oh, I mean the something that was moving. I don't see it now."

"Meouw!" said the something in a high thin voice.

"Oh, it's a kitten!" cried Aunt Polly.

"A little black kitten," said Sarah.

"And it is hungry," said Aunt Polly. "Give it to me, Will."

Will Smith picked up the kitten. It was very thin, and its eyes were half as big as its head.

"Oh, poor thing," said Aunt Polly. "I'll give it some milk."

"But we can't take the kitten along with us," said Mr. Hodgetts.

"But we can't leave it here to starve," said Aunt Polly.

"Well, no," said Mr. Hodgetts, rubbing his long nose. He really was a very kind man.

"And I'll give it some of my milk," said Sarah.

"And there is all that catnip I brought along in case we met a cat," said Aunt Polly.

"All right," said Mr. Hodgetts, "but we must hurry on to that clump of trees before the storm breaks. There is hard rain in those clouds."

The storm clouds climbed higher and higher over the blue sky. The bright lightning cracked them this way and that, and the thunder tumbled over the prairie toward us. The grass was even greener than it was in the sunlight. The wind of the storm laid it flat to the ground.

"Did you ever see anything so green?" asked Mrs. Hodgetts. She took off her bonnet and let the cool wind blow through her yellow hair.

The wind grew wilder and wilder and slapped the canvas loudly against the arched saplings. Then the big drops began to fall, bang, bang, on the canvas roof. The oxen wagged their ears and almost hurried a little. Daisy the cow said "Moo, moo," at every thunderclap. And just as the heavy rain began to fall, we rolled into the shelter of the thick oak trees.

Mr. Hodgetts shook the water from his clothes. He covered the oxen and Daisy with some old blankets and tied them close to the wagon.

It rained harder and harder. Mr. Hodgetts put pieces of canvas in the openings, and Mrs. Hodgetts lit the lantern that usually swung under the back axle of the wagon. There was no fire that night and no coffee nor bacon. They all crouched in the wagon and ate bread and jam and drank milk. The kitten had bread and milk without the jam.

The rain pattering on the canvas cover, and the warm oily smell of the lantern made everyone sleepy. But when they had crowded about and curled themselves up on the seats and round the barrels, no one could sleep. The rain came down in sheets. It poured right through the trees, and the sound of it on the canvas was so loud that we could hardly hear the thunder. No one slept a wink and no one was sorry when morning came.

But when they climbed out of the wagon, the sun was shining.

"Who would ever know it had been raining so hard last night?" said Aunt Polly.

"The roads will be bad," said Mr. Hodgetts, as he fastened the yoke over the necks of the two brown oxen.

The bumpy roads were sloppy, and the ruts were filled with

muddy water. The oxen's heavy feet splashed the water in brown fountains over themselves and over Mr. Hodgetts. He was wearing his high leather boots, but the mud went much higher than the boots. There were big spots of it like freckles on his face.

"You will be as bad as Will soon," said Aunt Polly.

Will made a face behind Aunt Polly's back, but she turned round just in time to see the end of it.

"Take care, Will," she said, twitching her earrings, "or you won't have any of those ginger cookies I'm going to make as soon as we get to Rich Prairie."

Mr. Hodgetts laughed between his freckles.

"We won't have the stove set up right away, Aunt Polly."

"O-oh," said Aunt Polly, "you wo-on't?"

"No. First of all I must plow and then plant some potatoes and some rutabaga seed. We must have food for next winter. And then before we unpack the wagon, we must build a house, one room to begin with. Will's uncle is going to help me, but even then it will be a while before we unpack the wagon. And the stove is at the bottom, you know."

"Do you calc'late it would be more than a week?" Aunt Polly asked, narrowing her forehead and lengthening her upper lip.

"Might be a month," said Mr. Hodgetts, just as a large splash of mud hit him in the face.

Aunt Polly smiled faintly and folded her gloved hands.

The sun was drying up the mud, but the water still lay in puddles in the ruts.

"Oop-hey, hey-ha-ha! Oh, oh, gee!" cried Mr. Hodgetts.

The oxen struggled through the mud with their bellies crouched to the ground. And then, bump, bang, rattle, the left back wheel of the covered wagon slipped into a pothole. Mrs. Hodgetts slid into Aunt Polly, and Aunt Polly slid into the canvas side of the wagon. The jam jar somersaulted off from the cherry chest of drawers, and the pans and kettles shot every which way, each with a louder bang than the others. The only reason that I did not fly somewhere was that Aunt Polly was sitting on me very hard indeed.

75

And no matter how much Mr. Hodgetts called, "Oop-hey-gee!" the oxen could not move the wagon.

"We're stuck," said Mr. Hodgetts, wiping the perspiration from his long nose and smearing the dirt over the freckles up and down his face.

"Laws-a-mercy," said Mrs. Hodgetts. "Do clean the mud off your face even if we are stuck."

She wet a washcloth in the water that had not slopped out of the pail and gave it to Mr. Hodgetts. He mopped and mopped.

"Right there by your left ear. No, there. Right in front of your ear. No, your left ear, not your right one. All right, it's gone."

"It's a deep hole, isn't it, John?" asked Aunt Polly.

"Well, it is deep, no doubt of that," said Mr. Hodgetts. "The wheel is in up to the hub."

Mrs. Hodgetts was climbing down from the wagon.

"We'll have to unload some," said Mr. Hodgetts.

"Oh, unload," said Aunt Polly. She was thinking. She looked in her bag for the boiled-icing recipe. Yes, there it was. And the smile on her wide mouth reached almost to her earrings.

Mr. Hodgetts unfastened the trailer and pushed it back a little. Then he took down Dickie's cage and opened the canvas

at the back of the wagon. He looked up and down the road. There was not another wagon in sight. He looked over the prairie. There was not a cabin anywhere. He was the only man for miles round.

It had taken all the cousins and the neighbors to pack the wagon, and now he would have to unload with only two women to help him. But Mr. Hodgetts always did whatever there was to be done. So he rolled up his sleeves and began. Mrs. Hodgetts and Aunt Polly looped up their full skirts to keep them out of the mud.

Of course, Mrs. Hodgetts really helped. She was a very strong woman and as good as half a man. They spread the canvas from the trailer on the prairie grass. Will and Sarah took the pots and pans and the packages of food that Mr. Hodgetts handed them and carried them over to Mrs. Hodgetts who piled them up on the canvas. And they carried the bundles of clothes and the bootjack and the other small things.

Aunt Polly ran round setting things straight.

"What a lark," she kept saying, "what a lark! Whoever expected this? We'll have to stay here all night, won't we, John?"

Mr. Hodgetts was looking at the chest of drawers and the trunks and the flour barrel.

"It may be a week," said Mr. Hodgetts. "I don't know how I am going to get them out."

Aunt Polly peered into the wagon. The stove was away up at the front. If the other things were taken out, the stove could be carried out too. She stood looking into the wagon and thinking. And when it came to thinking unuseful thoughts, Aunt Polly could think very well. She looked from the wagon to the ground and back again.

"I calc'late," said Aunt Polly, twisting her crooked mouth to one side, "I calc'late you could take that plow and rig it up with some ropes and some logs of wood and make a slope to slide the things down."

"The plow, slide things down the plow?" muttered Mr. Hodgetts, squinting his little eyes tight shut. "By gum, Aunt Polly, we could do that very thing!"

77

They fastened the plow to the back of the wagon and they laid down pieces of wood in the muddy road. And with Mr. Hodgetts on one side and Mrs. Hodgetts on the other and Aunt Polly in the middle to tell them whether things were coming down straight or not, they slid them from the wagon. The barrel of flour, the four-poster bed, the trunks and the boxes, the sacks of seed potatoes and the bags of seed corn.

"There are only a few things left," said Mr. Hodgetts. "We'll try it again."

"But shouldn't you take out the stove?" asked Aunt Polly.

"Oh, it is a hard thing to get out," said Mr. Hodgetts. "We have most of the weight out and we'll try it now. You two might push on the wagon."

"Oop-hey, ha-ha-gee!" cried Mr. Hodgetts, as he stood by the oxen and cracked his whip to urge them on.

The oxen pulled against the yoke until their eyes rolled big in their faces and the muscles stood out in large lumps on their legs. But the wagon wheel stayed fast in the pothole.

"Well, we *are* stuck," said Mr. Hodgetts. "You call to the oxen, Will, and I will try to lift the wheel."

But that did no good either.

"I suppose you will have to take the stove out," said Aunt Polly. The more excited she became, the more crooked was her smile. At that moment it was standing almost on end.

So they all slid the stove down over the plow, and Aunt Polly's Great-grandfather Timothy's sea chest and a few other things. The wagon was empty.

But would the big back wheel leave the pothole? It would not, no matter how hard they tried.

They all were hot and red in the face and hung their arms limply down beside them. There was only one of them smiling, and that one was Aunt Polly. She was grinning at the stove.

Mr. Hodgetts shrugged his tired shoulders. He looked up and down the road. No wagon was in sight. He looked over the prairie. No cabin had sprung up anywhere.

"There is just one thing to do," he said, "and that is to get a lever. We came through a grove of trees about a mile back. I'll

78

pry the wagon loose with a tree trunk. Where's my ax? Come on, Will."

"You would be gone a long time, John?" asked Aunt Polly.

"No, not very long. And as soon as the wheel is out, we'll pack up and go on again."

"O-oh, tonight?" said Aunt Polly.

"We must get to a stream, so we can clean up. Don't I need it?" asked Mr. Hodgetts.

Well, he did need it. His boots were mud inside and out. His trousers were muddy as far as they went. There was one large wagon wheel printed across his blouse, and the skin of his hands and arms you could not see at all.

"And you could do with a little cleaning yourself," he laughed, as he strode off with the ax over his shoulder.

"Oh, dear me!" cried Aunt Polly, all in a flutter. "Am I dirty?"

She looked in the piece of mirror that was fastened to the side of the wagon. There was a long streak of mud that climbed over her nose and slid down her right cheek.

She cleaned herself up and put Dickie's cage in the shade of the wagon. Then she settled herself in the low rocker beside the stove and wrote in her diary. She held up her little pink parasol to keep off the prairie sun.

Mrs. Hodgetts climbed up to the wagon seat and knit on a wool sock.

Sarah played house for a while among the boxes and furniture, with me and the black kitten for children. But the kitten had more important things to do, like chasing its tail and running after flies. So Sarah and I climbed up on the trailer to wait for Will and Mr. Hodgetts.

"I wish I could have gone with them," said Sarah to me.

We looked down the muddy road toward the grove of trees. At last we saw them coming. Will was carrying the ax, and Mr. Hodgetts was dragging a long tree trunk.

"Now, here we are!" called Mr. Hodgetts. "This tree should move that wagon."

He put the butt end of the tree trunk under the hub of the wheel.

"Call to the oxen, Will," he said. "Hit them up with the whip a little."

"Oop-hey, ha-ha-gee!" called Will to the oxen.

Mr. Hodgetts and Mrs. Hodgetts and Aunt Polly all hung their weight on the other end of the tree trunk, while Sarah and I pushed on the back of the wagon.

And, crack, squeak, rattle, the wagon started to move, and out of the pothole it rolled!

"There!" cried Mr. Hodgetts. "Now we are all right."

He stood looking at the pothole.

"It does not look so bad as it really is. How can we mark it so that the next people will see it and not get stuck too?"

Aunt Polly was thinking. "I calc'late I could make a sign," she said. "I have some things in my sea chest."

While Aunt Polly was hunting for the things in the sea chest, Mr. and Mrs. Hodgetts started to load the wagon.

"I'll have to tie ropes round things and drag them up," said Mr. Hodgetts. "Say, Aunt Polly, have you any rags there in your chest that I could wrap round things to keep the rope from rubbing?"

"Oh, yes, John," Aunt Polly answered. "Here is a soft rag. You can tear it open."

"Thanks. It's a good thing you brought a few extra things along, Aunt Polly," said he.

"Oh, yes, John," she said. She was so pleased that her jet earrings were bobbing madly against her round neck.

While Mr. and Mrs. Hodgetts were loading the things into the wagon, Aunt Polly took a piece of white cloth and some black oil paint. And she printed in very large letters:

BEWARE
POTHOLE
GO ROUND

Will and Sarah helped her put some sticks into the ground and fasten the cloth to them. Then they added a piece of red cloth to flutter in the prairie wind as a further warning.

"There," said Aunt Polly proudly, "I'm right glad I brought that paint along."

"It looks fine," said Mr. Hodgetts, as he hung Dickie's cage back in the opening of the covered wagon. "And it is so plain that anyone could read it."

"Oop-hey, ha-ha-haw!" called Mr. Hodgetts to the brown oxen, and creak, squeak, moo, the covered wagon and the trailer and Daisy the cow moved slowly on over the prairie grass beside the muddy road. They crept on until the sun was very low in the sky before they came to a stream.

"Here we'll camp," said Mr. Hodgetts.

"How you'll ever come clean, I don't know," said Mrs. Hodgetts, looking at Mr. Hodgetts who had almost disappeared under his mud covering.

"Oh, I'll wash off in the creek," he said.

"But your clothes," she said.

"The clothes," said Aunt Polly. "I calc'late that if we fastened all the muddy things in the running water, they would all be washed clean by morning."

And that is what they did. And they were all so tired that they went to sleep right after supper.

WESTERN WAGONS

Rosemary and Stephen Vincent Benét

They went with axe and rifle, when the trail was still to blaze,
They went with wife and children, in the prairie-schooner days,
With banjo and with frying pan—Susanna, don't you cry!
For I'm off to California to get rich out there or die!

We've broken land and cleared it, but we're tired of where
   we are.
They say that wild Nebraska is a better place by far.
There's gold in far Wyoming, there's black earth in Ioway,
So pack up the kids and blankets, for we're moving out today!

The cowards never started and the weak died on the road,
And all across the continent the endless campfires glowed.
We'd taken land and settled—but a traveler passed by—
And we're going West tomorrow—Lordy, never ast us why!

We're going West tomorrow, where the promises can't fail.
O'er the hills in legions, boys, and crowd the dusty trail!
We shall starve and freeze and suffer. We shall die, and tame
   the lands.
But we're going West tomorrow, with our fortune in our hands.

Milton Richards

THE BOY WHO VOTED
FOR ABE LINCOLN

ILLUSTRATED BY *I. Heilbron*

SAM ADAMS climbed to the wagon seat and spoke to the yoke of oxen. His father was out of sight now, over the hill, heading for the wheatfield. Jolting on the hard plank, Sam looked back and waved to his mother. She was standing in the middle of the farmyard, her yellow hair and gray calico skirt blowing in the brisk wind.

She waved anxiously. "Hurry now, Sam!" she called. "You know how much that wheat means to your pa. If those cattle get in before he gets the fence up—!" She left the sentence unfinished.

"I'll get there, Ma," he called back reassuringly. "Don't worry."

But he couldn't help worrying himself. A herd of cattle roving over the hills had already destroyed the Hillis's cornfield and the Moores' oats. It was Mr. Moore who had ridden over to warn Sam's father that the cattle were headed that way.

Sam gritted his teeth. That wheatfield meant everything to his father, to the whole family. If anything happened to it, next winter would be a barren one. Food scarce. Money scarcer. Sam could remember two years ago, when he had been only ten. All winter long there had been an empty ache where his stomach should have been. No. He didn't want another winter like that.

He tried to get the oxen to move faster. But the road was narrow and full of deep ruts. It was muddy, too, from yesterday's rain.

Bumping and sliding, the wagon, with its burden of fence rails, came finally within sight of the field.

83

Sam gave a glad shout. He was almost there, and the wheat was rippling in the wind, still untrampled. He could see his father riding along the far edge.

But Sam's shout had stopped the oxen. To them it had sounded like a call to halt. Too late, Sam tried to urge them forward. The right wheels were sunk deep, up to the hubs, in the sticky mud.

"Giddap," cried Sam desperately. It was no use. The wagon was stuck, glued to the slimy ruts. He lifted his head, opened his mouth to call for his father to come and help. The shout died in his throat. Thronging the hill beyond the wheatfield were moving cattle, a hundred head or more. They were coming steadily on toward the precious wheatfield.

No use now to call his father. They would never get the wagon out in time, nor the fence up. Could his father head the cattle off alone? If he did, it would be a miracle.

Sam choked. He had tried to be brave, but now tears came to his eyes. It was no use. The cattle would ruin the wheat. Eyes blinded, he slid from the wagon seat.

As he did so, he heard the familiar beat of a horse's hoofs behind. Someone was coming down the road!

Shouting hoarsely, Sam waved his arms and pointed to the wheatfield. Tears and excitement blurred his vision so that he could not tell if the man approaching were friend or stranger.

He backed against the wagon as the horse galloped forward, spurting mud toward him.

"Don't worry, son! Block up your wheels and put rails under them. I'll help head off the cattle."

He hadn't had time to see what the man looked like. Now, brushing the tears from his eyes, he stared after him in relief. Help for his father. The wheatfield had a chance now, maybe.

The man on the horse was long and lanky, Sam saw. But in heading off cattle, he was clever and successful. Soon he and Sam's father had managed to herd the steers away from the wheat. They thundered off, bellowing, in the direction they had come.

His heart hammering gratefully, Sam watched the stranger

dismount and talk with his father. Then he remembered the horseman's instructions for getting the wagon out of the mud.

Busily Sam started to work.

The cattle had been headed off for the time being, but no telling how soon they might come back again. The sooner he got the fence rails to the field, the better.

When he looked up again, the stranger had climbed on his horse and was riding off down the road at a canter, his lean form swaying awkwardly.

Mr. Adams crossed the field toward his son. He was mopping his brow with a large handkerchief.

"That was sure a close shave, son," he said, coming up to the wagon. "If it hadn't been for Abe, we'd have lost the wheat, sure. I never coulda headed them steers off alone."

"Abe who?" asked Sam. "A friend of yours, Pa?"

"Why, that was Abe Lincoln, son. He was on his way back to Springfield after making a speech some place. As for being a friend of mine, I guess Abe's just about everybody's friend."

"He sure was our friend, all right," said Sam gratefully. "What does this Abe Lincoln do, Pa? Is he a-farming, like us?"

"He's a lawyer, son; in politics, too. In fact, he's just been nominated for the presidency of the United States. On the new Republican party ticket. Don't know as he's got much of a chance, though."

"Why not?" asked Sam loyally. "I guess we'd be lucky, wouldn't we, Pa, to get a man as good as him?"

"You bet we would. But, you see, he's up against some pretty smart fellows. Men that makes a business of being smart. Educated folk. Stephen Douglas, for instance."

"But you're going to vote for Mr. Lincoln, aren't you, Pa? You'd like for him to be president, wouldn't you?"

"You bet I'll vote for him, Sam. Nothing can stop me from polling my vote for Abraham Lincoln, come November."

But something did stop Hank Adams from voting for Abraham Lincoln. In early July he was thrown from a horse and seriously injured. Judith, his young wife, and his son, Sam, were beside him when he died.

85

"Don't—forget—the—wheat, Sam. Take—it—into—Springfield."
He sighed, closed his eyes. "I—meant—to—take—it—in—election
day. When—I—voted—for Abe. Too bad."

Two weeks later Sam answered a knock at the door. Two
men stood outside.

"This the Adams farm?" asked one.

"Yes, sir. Will you come in?" Sam answered.

"Who is it, Sam?" called his mother. She came in, wiping her
red, roughened hands on her apron.

"I'm Joe Winship, mum," said the taller of the two strangers.
"And this is my pardner, Jerry Hogan. We've brought you a
letter from Mr. Abe Lincoln."

"From Abe Lincoln?" She took it wonderingly. "Why, it's
addressed to both of us, Sammy."

"To me, too?" asked Sam eagerly. "Open it, Ma. What does
it say?"

She looked up at the two men whom, in the excitement of

the letter, she had almost forgotten. "Oh, I'm sorry. I—I guess I've clean forgot my manners, gentlemen. Sammy, push up some chairs for Mr. Winship and Mr. Hogan."

"Oh, don't mind us, mum. We're just—just part of the letter, you might say," said Mr. Hogan, flushing.

But Sam ran for some chairs. When he came back, his mother had the letter open. She looked up from it, her face glowing.

"God bless Abe Lincoln," she said softly. "It's a beautiful letter."

"He's a kind man, mum," said Mr. Winship fervently. "There ain't many lawyers would let Jerry and me work out a debt like this, instead of paying straight cash."

"What does it say, Ma?" asked Sam eagerly.

"It says," replied his mother gently, "that Mr. Lincoln is deeply sorry to learn of your pa's going. And he hopes we'll be kind enough to let these two friends of his, Mr. Winship and Mr. Hogan, work out their debt to him for legal work by helping us with the farm work for a spell."

"Glory, Ma!" said Sam. "That means we'll have help threshing the wheat."

"You sure will," said Mr. Hogan, grinning widely. "All the help you need."

"I—I don't know what to say," said Mrs. Adams, choking. "It—it just seems like help from heaven. Of course, Sam's been doing fine, but he's a long way from being a man grown. How can I thank Mr. Lincoln?"

"We'll just tell him about the look on your face when you read the letter, Miz. Adams. That'll be thanks enough for Abe."

"Is that all the letter, Ma?" asked Sam. "Didn't he say anything about me? You said the letter was addressed to me, too."

"Why, yes, Sam. There is a note for you."

The boy took the page eagerly. It read: "Sam, I used to hear your father talk about what a fine, good boy you were. He was very proud of you. I know he's glad you're there to take care of your mother. Don't ever give up if you should get stuck in the mud again. There's always a way out. Something or someone will come along to help if you just keep trusting the Almighty."

Sam put the letter down. "Glory, Ma! Abe Lincoln's just got to be elected president. Why, I reckon he must be the best man in the whole world."

In November, Sam Adams took the wheat into Springfield to sell. It was fine wheat, he thought proudly, and he ought to get a fine price for it. Before they had left to go back to town, Joe Winship and Jerry Hogan had told him where to take it in order to get the best price.

It was good to know that his mother wouldn't have to worry about money all winter long. They'd have enough to eat now. He wished he could keep her from missing Pa too much. Maybe if he bought her something . . . something with the money she'd said he could have for his very own.

It was still early morning when he rolled into Springfield. There were a lot of people going to town—more than he'd ever seen before. The streets of the little town hummed with excitement. There was something in the air, something in the way women laughed and whispered, in the way men gathered in groups on street corners, that set young Sam Adams's pulses throbbing. Unusual happenings today, sure enough. He reckoned maybe it was a parade or a fair.

Then a group of men marched down the street bearing banners. A band played blaring music. The banners said: "Elect Stephen Douglas President."

Sam sat bolt upright, shocked. Elect Mr. Douglas? Why, it was Abe Lincoln they should be electing. His own pa had been going to vote for Lincoln.

He knew then why there were so many people here in Springfield today. It was election day—the day the people voted for President of the United States. He wondered why his mother hadn't told him. But they'd been working so hard lately that she must have clean forgot.

Well, he was here now, luckily. He'd go sell the wheat first, then come back. He got an even better price for it than he'd expected. The man who bought it, Mr. Salford, said he'd been expecting him. Joe Winship had told him about Sam.

"Too bad your mother couldn't come in to town, too," said Mr. Salford, helping Sam unload the bags of wheat.

"I reckon she'll be mighty sorry, too, when she hears it's election day," said Sam. "But someone had to stay and take care of the farm. There's only us two now."

"Well, you're a fine, strong lad," Mr. Salford said. "I'm sure your mother depends on you a good deal."

Sam asked the way to the nearest polling place. The town hall was closest, Mr. Salford said, waving good-bye.

The street outside the town hall was crowded. The sidewalks were clotted with gesticulating groups of men, all talking in loud voices or speaking in low confidential asides.

Sam nudged a man with a very red nose and fierce, black beard.

"Where do folks go to vote?" he asked timidly.

"Just follow the crowd," answered the man, waving a hand. "Just follow the crowd." Then, getting a good look at Sam.for the first time, he stared. "Are you figgering to vote, son?" He burst into loud laughter. "Well, if you do, don't vote for that scarecrow, Abe Lincoln!" A group of men near by also laughed uproariously.

Sam felt his ears get hot. He hurried past them. There were little booths in the room where people voted. As soon as one man left one of the booths, another man went in. Sam waited patiently for his chance. At the first opportunity he went into a booth.

"Hey!" said a voice. "A kid went in that booth! Yank him out."

They did yank him out. "But—but I want to vote," pleaded Sam. "I want to vote for Mr. Lincoln."

A man laughed. "But you're not old enough to vote, kid. You have to be twenty-one in order to vote." He gave him a shove. "On your way, son!"

"But please, mister—I'm voting for my pa. He aimed to cast his ballot for Lincoln."

"Well, he'll have to come himself," said the man impatiently. "Now go on—get out of here. You're just taking up floor space needed by legal voters."

89

"But my pa can't come himself," pleaded Sam. "Honest, mister, why ain't it all right for me to—"

The man beckoned two burly-looking men. "The youngster's stubborn, boys. I reckon you'd better show him the way out."

The two men took hold of Sam and lifted him squirming from the floor.

Two minutes later he picked himself up from the street outside. His best pants were torn. His hat had fallen into the gutter. His knees and one elbow were skinned. But worst of all was the way he felt inside. He'd failed. Failed both his pa and Mr. Lincoln.

He got up and picked his hat out of the gutter. It was crumpled and muddy. His eyes filled with tears. He tried to choke back sobs.

A heavy hand fell on his shoulder. Sam looked up, startled.

"Please, mister. I ain't doing anything. I'm going now."

"What's the trouble, son?"

Sam looked up into the face of a man so homely that, despite the kindness of his tone, the boy's fright returned. Maybe they'd sent this man to come and put Sam in jail. Maybe they put folks in jail for trying to vote when they hadn't ought to.

"Please, mister," he sobbed. "I didn't know it was wrong. I was just trying to help make Mr. Lincoln president."

"Were you now? And what makes you think he ought to be president?"

"Because he's so good," said Sam. "That's why I wanted to vote for him."

The long arm went around his shoulder, tightened. "You mean—you tried to cast a vote for him, son?"

Sam nodded. "I was going to vote for my pa, mister. He can't vote for Mr. Lincoln like he said he wanted to, because—because—he's dead, mister." He looked up proudly. "You see, my pa, he knew Mr. Lincoln."

The eyes that looked down at him were warm and pitying. All at once the man's face didn't look homely to Sam any more. Instead, it was the kindest face he had ever seen.

"What was your father's name, son?"

"Henry Adams, mister. We live out by Apple Creek. There's just my ma and me now, though. But Mr. Lincoln sent some men out to help us thresh our wheat, and so we won't have to worry all winter about having enough. My pa said Mr. Lincoln was always doing nice things like that. He was everybody's friend, he said."

"I knew your father, son. He was a fine man. I'm glad you got the wheat crop threshed all right."

"I'm glad, too," said Sam. But his face clouded again. "But my pa's going to feel awful bad, on account of not casting his vote for Mr. Lincoln."

"Is he?" said the man softly. "I reckon we ought to do something about that. You know, I haven't voted yet myself. I was kind of debating about the matter. You see, I'm not completely

91

convinced that Abe Lincoln is the man for president."

"But he is, mister. Honest he is. Pa said so."

"Well," the tall man drawled, rubbing his chin, "I don't know that I can sincerely cast my vote for Abe on my own account. But I'll tell you what I'll do. I'll go in and vote for Lincoln for your father's sake."

"Glory, mister!" Sam's face glowed. "That's sure fine of you. Me and my pa and ma'll be mighty grateful."

He watched the tall, thin figure mount the steps. He seemed to know a great many people, for he spoke to nearly everyone, nodding and smiling.

"I wonder who he is," thought Sam. "He's a mighty nice man, even if he wasn't quite sure about voting for Mr. Lincoln. I reckon that since he knew my pa, I should have found out his name to tell Ma."

It was getting late. He'd have to hurry if he wanted to get that present for Ma. He hastened along the street to the general store. The store was crowded. Sam had to wait a long time to get waited on. He came out, his arms full of packages, and went to find the team and wagon, still waiting patiently where he had left them.

He climbed to the seat and clucked to the horses. It was getting late. He'd have to hurry to get home before Ma began to worry about him.

As he started up, there was a commotion on the street. People were cheering and shouting. Towering above the crowd was the man Sam had persuaded to cast his father's vote.

Quickly he leaned down and called to a boy his own age, who was standing near the wagon.

"Say, can you tell me what that man's name is there? That tall one?"

The boy stared. "You must be from the country. Everybody in Springfield knows Abe Lincoln!"

Carol Ryrie Brink

THE WILLOW BASKET

ILLUSTRATED BY *Janet Smalley*

THEY'RE shiftless, that's what they are!"
said Mrs. Woodlawn decidedly. Shiftless was a terrible word
in pioneer Wisconsin. Caddie, Tom, and Warren exchanged
discouraged glances. They had been delighted to see the
McCantrys come back, even if the father, mother, and four
children *had* returned on foot, wheeling all of their possessions
in a wheelbarrow.

Mr. and Mrs. McCantry and the four children were standing
in the road now, casting wistful glances at the Woodlawns' cozy
white house while they waited for Tom and Caddie to inform
their parents of their old neighbors' return.

"But, Mother," said Caddie, "Emma is so nice, and all they've
got left is what they can carry in a wheelbarrow."

"They had just as good a chance here as the rest of us," said
Mrs. Woodlawn severely. "They had a farm, but they must
needs sell it for what they could get and go on to something
finer. And now, it seems, they are back with nothing but a
wheelbarrow."

"We must not judge people too hastily, Harriet," said Mr.
Woodlawn mildly, from the doorway.

"Oh, Father, we may ask them in for the night, mayn't we?"
begged Caddie.

"Well, now," said Mr. Woodlawn, with a pleasant wink at
Caddie over his wife's smooth, dark head, "we'll just let the

93

McCantrys go on to the next farm. The Bunns or the Silver-nagles will take them in for the night, and that will let us out of any obligation."

Mrs. Woodlawn whirled about with a suspicious look in her eyes and was just in time to catch her husband's smile and the tail-end of his wink.

"Go along with you!" she said, beginning to laugh herself. "I never intended to let them go without supper and a night's rest, and you know that. But I do feel better for having said what I think of them!"

Tom and Caddie and Warren raced away to invite the McCantrys into supper and comfortable beds. They were a dispirited-looking lot as they sat along the roadside, waiting for the hospitality of a former neighbor. The bottom of Mrs. McCantry's dress was draggled with mud and dust, and the two boys were barefoot, but Mrs. McCantry had a bonnet of the latest fashion trimmed with purple velvet pansies; and Pearly, the little girl who was next to the youngest, had a new gold ring.

Emma, the eldest of the four and Caddie's own age, slipped a warm brown arm through Caddie's and gave her a squeeze. Emma didn't have gold rings or bonnets with pansies, but she was brown and solid and comfortable, and Caddie liked her best of them all.

Mr. McCantry picked up the handles of the wheelbarrow, and Caddie thought that his shoulders looked rounder and more bent than they had when he went away. The wheelbarrow creaked as he trundled it up the path to the front door. Caddie could see that it contained some patchwork quilts and cooking utensils, a set of Mrs. McCantry's hoops, and a clock which was not running.

Mr. and Mrs. Woodlawn met the McCantrys at the front door.

"Well, well," said Mr. Woodlawn heartily, shaking his former neighbor's hand, "so you have come back to us again, McCantry? Dunnville is a pretty good place after all."

"It is that!" said Mr. McCantry. "I'm glad to be back. We've been a weary way."

94

"Now, Josiah, why do you say that?" cried Mrs. McCantry sharply. Caddie looked at her in surprise and saw that she had lost her discouraged look of a few moments ago and was quite the fine lady once again. "We have had a most edifying journey really," she said, "and spent some months with my brother who has a most elegant house which puts anything you have here in Dunnville quite to shame. Of course we were most elaborately entertained, and it is only by the merest chance that you see us in these circumstances. An unforeseen accident happened to our horse and carriage, and we just thought how healthful it would be to come along on foot."

"Yes, yes, of course," said Mrs. Woodlawn hastily. "Now do come in and wash yourselves for supper."

The two little boys went along with Tom and Warren, while Pearly was taken in charge by Caddie's little sisters, Hetty and Minnie. Caddie squeezed Emma's arm. "Come up to my room," she said.

"Wait," said Emma, smiling mysteriously. "I've got a present for you, Caddie."

"A present for me?" Caddie was incredulous.

"It's not very good," said Emma shyly, "but I made it myself. An old lady who took us in one night, when we hadn't any money, showed me how."

She fumbled through the untidy bundle of quilts and skillets in the wheelbarrow and brought out a little willow basket.

"Why, it's ever so pretty!" cried Caddie, sincerely pleased. "But you'd ought to keep it for yourself."

"Oh, I can make lots more of them," said Emma. "Big ones, too, but we don't have room to carry them, and I thought you'd like this little one."

"I'd love it," said Caddie. "Thank you, Emma."

Meals were always good at the Woodlawns', but any sort of company rallied Mrs. Woodlawn to extra effort. Tonight, besides the supper which she had already planned, she went to the smokehouse and took down one of the hams which had come from their own well-fed pigs and had been salted and smoked under Mrs. Woodlawn's own direction. With a sharp knife, she cut the tender pink slices and fried them delicately brown before heaping them on the big blue china platter. Each slice was half ringed around with a delicate layer of fat—just enough to give variety to the lean. Mr. Woodlawn filled the plates of the hungry-looking McCantrys with the generosity of a good host, and Emma and the littler boy fell to with a will. But Pearly set up a thin wail of protest.

"I can't eat this," she said, pointing an accusing finger at the fat.

"Me neither," said Ezra, her elder brother.

"Maybe Mama could cut the fat part off for you, Pearly," said Mrs. McCantry doubtfully.

"No," said Mrs. Woodlawn, with that gleam in her eye which

her own children had learned to obey. "If you can't eat that good ham just as it is, you're not very hungry. My children eat what is set before them with a relish. They know if they don't they can go to bed empty."

Over her tumbler of milk, Caddie saw with twinkling eyes that Pearly and Ezra were eating their fat with their lean. Personally she thought the fat was the best part, when it was all crisp on the outside and juicy on the inside, as Mother fried it.

The McCantrys stayed on for many days, but there were no more complaints about their meals.

Caddie and Emma enjoyed the time very much. Together they went down to the swamp where the young willows grew thickly, and the boys helped them cut slender, pliant shoots to weave more baskets. The Woodlawn land and Dr. Camden's land came together here at the edge of the swamp, and beyond their fences the swamp stretched away in a fairyland of tiny hummocks and islands on which grew miniature firs and tamaracks. There were wild rice in the swamp in the autumn and quantities of wild cranberries.

"What a pretty place this is!" said Emma. "If I were you, Caddie, I would build a little house on this hill overlooking the swamp. I like the nice, spicy swamp smell, don't you?"

Caddie remembered this later, when she heard her father and mother talking about a home for the McCantrys.

"Really, Harriet," said Mr. Woodlawn, "I've talked alone with McCantry, and they have reached rock bottom. He hasn't any money left."

"To hear *her* talk, you would think they were millionaires."

"I know, my dear, but she's a foolish woman. It's her foolishness that's brought them where they are, I think. But we can't let them starve for all that, and we can't have them living with us always either. Somehow we've got to set them on their feet once more."

"Well, Johnny, grumble as I may, I suppose that you are always right about such things. What had we better do?" sighed Mrs. Woodlawn.

"I thought we might give them a little land at the edge of our place somewhere. Perhaps one of our neighbors on the other side would contribute a little, too, and then all of the neighbors could get together and help build them a house. We could make a sort of raising bee out of it."

"A raising bee!" repeated Mrs. Woodlawn, her eyes beginning to shine. "Yes, we could do that."

"Oh, Father," cried Caddie, forgetting that she had not been included in the conversation so far, "that would be such good fun! And I'll tell you the very place for the house."

"You will?" laughed her father. "So you've already picked the site?"

"Yes, I have! It's that corner down by the swamp. Emma says she loves the smell, and they could get all the cranberries and wild rice they needed, and maybe they could sell what they didn't need, and they could make willow baskets out of the willow shoots and sell those, too."

"Willow baskets?" asked her father. "Sell willow baskets? You're going a little too fast for me, daughter. I'm lost in the swamp."

"Oh, wait!" cried Caddie. She was in one of her eager moods when ideas came too fast to be expressed. She flew out of the room and returned in a moment with Emma's basket in her hands. "Look! Wouldn't you pay money for a big basket, if it were as nicely made as that?"

Her mother took the basket in her own slender hands and looked at it carefully.

"Yes, I would," she said. "I believe a lot of people would. We've never had anyone around here who could make baskets."

"Well, we have now," said Caddie. "Can't we set the McCantrys up in business?"

"Where's my bonnet?" cried Mrs. Woodlawn. "I'm going to call on the neighbors!" Dancing with excitement, Caddie ran for her mother's tasteful gray bonnet.

"Thank Kind Providence, it doesn't have purple pansies on it," said Mrs. Woodlawn, as she went to the barn for a horse.

There was nothing like another's need to rally the pioneers

of that day. Dr. Camden joined Mr. Woodlawn in donating a good-sized strip of land at the edge of the swamp. Another man, who had plenty of timber on his farm, offered enough logs to build a cabin if others would cut and haul them. Men and boys, who had nothing to give but their time, gladly did the cutting and hauling. One neighbor offered a pig, another a cow, and a third the use of his horse and plow to break a garden spot.

On the day of the "raising," men and boys on horseback arrived early from all the country around and went to work on the cabin. The women and girls came along later in the morning with covered dishes and jars of pickles and preserves.

Mrs. Woodlawn and Mrs. McCantry with the help of the children had made tables by putting long planks on trestles near the site of the new house. Over an open fire were great pots of coffee and stone jars full of Mrs. Woodlawn's choice baked beans.

It was not often that the neighbors came together for a common purpose. They were a settled community now, and it had been a long time since one of them had had a raising for himself. There had been the time of the Indian "Massacree Scare," when they had all come together under the Woodlawns' roof for several days, but then they had been filled with fear and distrust. Now they came together in a spirit of friendship and helpfulness.

The children raced about playing tag and "Blindman's Buff" and "I Spy," while the men laid up stones for a fireplace and hewed and raised the logs one upon another to make the McCantrys' walls. The women unpacked baskets and laughed and chattered as they spread the feast. They were seeing friends and neighbors they had not seen for weeks, perhaps for months and years.

There was one thing which Mrs. Woodlawn and Mrs. McCantry had in common: they both loved a party. With happy, flushed faces, they moved about among the neighbors, shaking hands, filling coffee cups, and urging more beans or gingerbread on people who had already eaten their fill.

99

The swamp echoed with the ringing of axes and mallets and the cries of men as they heaved the upper logs into place. By sundown the McCantrys had a house of their own. All of the hard work was done and only the finishing was left for Mr. McCantry. As the neighbors prepared to depart, other gifts came out of their wagons: a sack of potatoes, a rocking chair, a bushel of turnips, a goosefeather pillow, strings of dried apples, a couple of live chickens.

At the last moment Mr. Woodlawn nailed up a shelf by the new fireplace. No one knew why until Caddie and Emma came breathlessly over the fields from the Woodlawns' house carrying the McCantrys' clock. Caddie and her father had sat up late in the attic shop the night before to take it all apart, clean it, and coax it to run. Now it ticked away on the shelf as gay as a cricket.

"There!" said Caddie triumphantly. "A house is ready to live in when a clock is ticking in it!"

"My land!" said Mrs. McCantry, "that clock hasn't ticked for years—just like us, I guess." Her bonnet was all crooked with excitement, and the purple pansies bobbed and trembled over one ear, but for once her eyes were perfectly frank and honest. "I know what you've been thinking of us, Mrs. Woodlawn," she said slowly. "Shiftless, you thought, and I guess you were right. But we've seen what neighbors can be like today. We're going to set right out to be good neighbors ourselves. You won't ever regret all that you have done for us!"

The two women smiled at each other in sudden understanding. Caddie and Emma smiled at each other, too, and hugged each other suddenly.

Mrs. McCantry meant what she said that day. For many years the family made a respectable living by selling cranberries and wild rice and the beautiful willow baskets which they all learned to make. And they were good neighbors.

Cornelia Meigs

THE LITTLE DOG STAR

ILLUSTRATED BY *Alexander Key*

DENNIS TURNER'S face was hot and the drops were rolling down his forehead; but he would not stop working before his father did.

"It is not every boy of eight who can help to build a house," Thomas Turner had said. Dennis kept repeating the words to himself as he toiled. "Not every boy of eight—"

It was also true that it was not every kind of a house that could be put up with the aid of a boy of that size and of his sister who was a whole year younger. This was a sod house, such a dwelling as we do not see anywhere today, such a house as the first settlers lived in on the western plains. Thomas Turner was a homesteader, a man who had moved out on the prairie lands of the American Middle West to make a home for himself and his family.

At that time the great plains held very few people. The Turners' nearest neighbors, the McKails, lived fifteen miles away. Sixteen-year-old Susy McKail sometimes rode across to see them and was their only playmate. Now and again they had a visit from a passing traveler; but often days and weeks passed with only antelope and jack rabbits for their daily company.

102

Since the only trees anywhere to be found grew along Sandy Creek ten miles distant, the Turners could not make their house of logs. Instead, Thomas Turner chose a place just below the crest of a low ridge which looked like a long wave in the sea of green land. He dug a hole the size the house was to be and about as deep as Dennis' head; then he cut squares of green sod and, with his children's help, built up the walls with the fresh-smelling blocks. The roof was framed of poles brought from the far-off creek valley. These he covered with sod and earth, and built a chimney out of sticks plastered with clay. When the low, green house was finished, with its narrow windows and heavily-framed door, it looked like a dwelling for gnomes and trolls out of a fairy story.

It was on the first frosty day of Autumn that they moved into the dwelling. Dennis and his sister Madge were as busy as ants running back and forth carrying bundles from the tent, where they had lived through the summer. It was at twilight that the first puff of smoke went up from the new chimney. Just above, a big blue and white star had come out to hang above the roof. Their father had taught them the names of all the stars, so that Madge knew it at once.

"Look, Dennis," she said, "there is Vega that used to come above the elm trees at home on the night before we went back to school."

"It doesn't seem so far from home when we can see all the same stars again," declared Dennis, "but there are a great many more here."

They had seemed very far from that town where they had once lived, where the steep roofs showed among the treetops and where the friendly voice of the schoolbell rang them up the hill every morning. Here there were no trees or hills, no school and no lessons except for those which they had from their mother beside the fire in the evening. But above them the sky showed its whole shining arch where they could see again all their old friends, the great orange-colored Arcturus, the Dipper, and the pale North Star. Very late that night Madge awoke and looked out of the tiny window above her bed. The stars had swung

across the sky so that she could not see Vega but could watch the big, ruddy-golden Dog Star, Sirius, coming up over the edge of the world.

"The Little Dog Star will come soon," she thought sleepily. "I must tell Dennis in the morning."

Of all the stars, they loved best that one which their father called Procion, the small Dog Star which follows the Great Dog Star and crosses the heavens in the late autumn and winter.

It was the very next day that the cabin had its first visitor. Strangers who came by were always on their way westward toward the Rocky Mountains and the sea. It was beginning to be said that there was gold in those mountains and that people could grow rich merely by washing it out of the river sands. The first guest, however, was not a stranger this time but an old friend. The Turner household was sitting at their supper, when horses' feet sounded outside, a tall man stooped to enter the low door, and a big voice said,—

"Have you any room here for Bill Simmons, and Bill Simmons's missus, on their way to California to get their share of gold?"

His wife looked thin and tired; but they both had much to tell of the great adventure of gold-seeking that was before them. Madge and Dennis went outside before they went to bed to look at the horses picketed in a restless stamping line on the frosty grass. Presently Bill Simmons and the children's father

104

came out also to see that all was safe for the night. Thomas Turner was having a chance at last to say what he thought of gold-seeking.

"I have seen many go hurrying west to get rich, but not yet have I seen one come back with his fortune made and his pockets bulging."

"You will see me," vowed Bill Simmons. "I'll be stopping at your door again when a year is out and I'll have gold enough in my pockets to make me rich all my days."

As he rapped out his pipe, their friend asked Dennis and Madge, "Do you like to live here?"

"Yes," they cried both together and began to tell him of the things that made them love the prairie, of the wild strawberries in the grass, warm and sweet in the sun, of the prairie hens clucking to their broods of shy brown chicks, and of the wide night skies with so many stars. But he shook his head as he listened.

"You will be powerful lonely," he declared. "Why, you haven't even a dog to play with, only a Dog Star!"

He and his wife rode away next morning. Dennis and Madge talked of them for weeks afterward, for they were the last travelers to pass before the winter came.

The two thought it was wonderfully exciting when the snow-drifts buried the little house to the roof. They loved to see the wide plain all glittering with sun-bright snow on a clear morning; they loved to sit by the roaring fire in the evening and think how safe and happy any place was where Father and Mother were. They loved also to peer out on bitter, sparkling nights and see the friendly light of the Little Dog Star.

Spring came, with flocks of long-necked cranes flapping overhead, their harsh loud voices dropping down out of the sky. Summer followed, hot and clear, with the winds blowing wavy patterns in the long prairie grass. Then came Autumn. The sod house was a year old, and they felt as though they had lived in it forever.

It was a cold morning in the late fall, with snow on the ground and the promise of more in the air. Mrs. Turner was just lifting the sizzling bacon from before the fire to set it on the breakfast table when the latch lifted and in came stumbling Susy McKail. She had ridden her pony many miles in the cold and the faint morning light to say, "Ma's been sick for a week, and last night Pa cut his foot and can't step. We—we need help."

Houses and farms were scattered far apart in that west country, but no one ever knocked at a neighbor's door to ask for help and asked in vain. Within ten minutes it had been decided that Thomas Turner and his wife must both go to the McKail's and that Susy should stay with Dennis and Madge.

"Perhaps we can come back tonight," Thomas Turner said, "but if it storms we shall have to wait for tomorrow."

"But tomorrow's Thanksgiving!" cried Madge. Then she was silent, for even she was old enough to know that when neighbors were in trouble, nobody spoke of feasts and holidays. They had talked a great deal of how they would celebrate the day and how thankful they must be that the harvest had been so good. Instead of a turkey, their father had brought in a gray sand-hill crane which, so he told them, would make a finer feast than any barnyard fowl. But of all this nothing was said now. A few sparse flakes of snow were already falling as the two rode away on the big farm horses and disappeared over the roll of the prairie.

By noon the snow was coming down thickly. It grew dark early, with the flakes flying in dense clouds and the cold wind booming across the prairie. Dennis fed the cows in the shed and Susy's pony, and carried in great armfuls of firewood just as he had seen Father do.

It was a strange bedtime without Mother there to tuck in the blankets and blow out the candle. Madge may have dropped a tear or two into her pillow, and Dennis shut his eyes tight, and stoutly made up his mind to sleep and make morning come sooner. When he awoke, however, it must have been midnight, and the sound of the driving snow had ceased. A drift had piled almost to the top of the window frame. He was anxious to see how deep the snow was and so huddled on some clothes and went pattering across the floor to open the outer door. He

106

peered through a crack, then flung the door wide open to listen. He had heard a far-off cry across the snow.

There were quick feet on the floor behind him and Madge and Susy came to stand at his elbow and hearken also.

"It's not Father," Madge said at once. Both of them would have known his voice in an instant.

"Somebody's lost," Susy said, reaching for her coat. Dennis was already buttoning his heavy rough jacket and was piling fresh logs on the fire.

"We can't leave Madge alone," began Susy, but Madge was winding her muffler about her neck and pulling on her mittens. How bitter cold it was as they all three came out of the door. The snow was frozen hard, and lay wide and white over all the still world. Dennis raised his voice in a mighty call. "We are coming," he shouted, and the voice answered again a great way off.

The stars were clear, but now and then a puff of light wind would carry into their faces whirls of flakes blown from the edge of a drift. The snow lay in ridges, one long drift after another. The three had not known how far a voice could carry across flat country in the stillness. They walked a long way with their feet beginning to grow heavy and their fingers numb.

"Look," cried Susy suddenly. Being taller than the others,

107

she could see farther across the ridges of snow. "I see someone."

"There are two," Madge said an instant later.

"Three," corrected Dennis. It was true that three stumbling, dark figures were struggling toward them and that the last lagging traveler was a woman.

"Is it you, Tom Turner?" asked the hoarse voice which had called them from afar, then added as they came nearer, "Great Heaven, it's Tom Turner's children!"

It was Bill Simmons.

"And can you show us the way?" quavered Mrs. Simmons, pressing forward to catch desperately at Susy's arm. "Or are you lost, too?"

"Why, yes—no—the house is—is right over there." Susy looked about her, beginning suddenly to be confused.

"No," declared Madge, "it's there. Don't you remember how we went around that long drift with the loose snow?"

It is easy to lose your direction on a flat, snow-covered plain. The low house, with its deep-buried windows was out of sight behind the high drifts. The blowing snow had covered the children's footsteps. For a long terrible minute, they all stood looking helplessly about them. Then Dennis touched his tall friend's arm.

"Do you see the Little Dog Star?" he said. "It stands straight above our chimney. That is the way home."

When at last they had got inside the safe shelter of the little sod house, when the fire had been heaped up to a roaring blaze, and the snow-covered travelers had been fed and warmed, there began to be told something of the story of how those three came to be lost. They had been making the eastward journey from California, and had been determined, in spite of storms and delays, to pass by the Turner cabin.

"We went wrong after we crossed Sandy Creek," Bill Simmons told them. "The horses could only flounder in the deep snow, so that we turned them loose to drift back among the trees where they would have some shelter from the storm. We thought that we could make the rest of the way on foot, but we missed the direction and would have been lost for good, Jerry

and the missus and I, if it hadn't been for you three and your Little Dog Star."

The big, loose-jointed man who was with them was called, it seemed, Jerry Owens. He was so shy that he could scarcely get out a word and turned red when anyone spoke to him.

Before day broke, Susy and Madge were beginning to make ready for the Thanksgiving dinner, cutting up pumpkins, stirring the batter for Indian meal pudding, and setting the sandhill crane to roast before the fire of coals. Susy was a good cook. "I have to be," she explained briefly.

When they had finished "as fine a dinner as man ever ate," as Bill Simmons said, Dennis asked a shy question.

"Did you find gold?" he begged to know.

"I did, indeed," Bill Simmons answered, "though I was tempted more than once to drop the heavy stuff on the snow. Gold isn't worth much to a man lost in the dark."

He pulled out one little buckskin bag after another and showed them the bright gold dust. Then he brought from an inner pocket a lump of white stone, with thick, crinkled, yellow gold covering half its surface. "That is a nugget," he said, "and it's for you. There are not many folks, even bigger ones than you, who will come out on such a night to show lost travelers the way home."

It was not until they were pushing back from the table that the big shy man cleared his throat and spoke suddenly.

"I have no gold nuggets to give ye, for I am one of those that has come back poor from adventuring in the West. There is but one thing I can do to make return for all ye have done for me. I'll sing ye a bit of a song."

And he sang. Ah, such a voice, big and rich and beautiful, singing all the songs that people love most to hear, Scotch songs, Irish songs, "Oh, Susanna," the song of the gold seekers. Last of all he drew a great breath and began that Thanksgiving hymn which the children had last heard in the white church on the town square in that far away country which their father and mother still called home.

> "Come you thankful people come,
> Raise the song of Harvest Home;
> All is safely gathered in,
> Ere the winter storms begin."

Bill Simmons had joined in a deep hum; his wife was singing, too, and so were Susy, Madge, and Dennis.

> "All the world is God's own field."

It was late afternoon and already dark, with the Little Dog Star bright above the roof, when the children's father and mother rode up through the snow to the door. They came in to see the three weary travelers sound asleep. Dennis was mending the fire while Susy and Madge were washing the dishes. They were stepping back and forth very lightly so that they should not waken their worn-out guests. Madge had taken the big gold nugget to prop open the door of the cupboard while she put away the cups and plates. All three were singing Jerry's Thanksgiving hymn very softly under their breath.

> "First the blade and then the ear,
> Then the full corn shall appear.
> Grant, Oh Harvest Lord, that we,
> Wholesome grain and pure may be."

110

Laura Ingalls Wilder

CHRISTMAS HORSES

ILLUSTRATED BY *Matilda Breuer*

SUMMER was gone, winter was coming, and now it was time for Pa to make a trip to town. Here in Minnesota, town was so near that Pa would be gone only one day, and Ma was going with him.

She took Carrie, because Carrie was too little to be left far from Ma. But Mary and Laura were big girls. Mary was going on nine and Laura was going on eight, and they could stay at home and take care of everything while Pa and Ma were gone.

For going-to-town, Ma made a new dress for Carrie, from the pink calico that Laura had worn when she was little. There was enough of it to make Carrie a little pink sunbonnet. Carrie's hair had been in curl-papers all night. It hung in long, golden, round curls, and when Ma tied the pink sunbonnet strings under Carrie's chin, Carrie looked like a rose.

Ma wore her hoopskirts and her best dress, the beautiful challis with little strawberries on it, that she had worn to the sugaring-dance at Grandma's, long ago in the Big Woods.

"Now be good girls, Laura and Mary," was the last thing she said. She was on the wagon seat, with Carrie beside her. Their lunch was in the wagon. Pa took up the ox goad.

"We'll be back before sundown," he promised. "Hi-oop!" he said to Pete and Bright. The big ox and the little one leaned into their yoke, and the wagon started.

111

"Good-bye, Pa! Good-bye, Ma! Good-bye, Carrie, good-bye!"
Laura and Mary called after it.

Slowly the wagon went away. Pa walked beside the oxen.
Ma and Carrie, the wagon, and Pa all grew smaller, till they
were gone into the prairie.

The prairie seemed big and empty then, but there was nothing
to be afraid of. There were no wolves and no Indians. Besides,
Jack stayed close to Laura. Jack was a responsible dog. He knew
that he must take care of everything when Pa was away.

That morning Mary and Laura played by the creek, among

the rushes. They did not go near the swimming-hole. They did not touch the strawstack. At noon they ate the corn dodgers and molasses and drank the milk that Ma had left for them. They washed their tin cups and put them away.

Then Laura wanted to play on the big rock, but Mary wanted to stay in the dugout. She said that Laura must stay there, too.

"Ma can make me," Laura said, "but you can't."

"I can so," said Mary. "When Ma's not here, you have to do what I say because I'm older."

"You have to let me have my way because I'm littler," said Laura.

"That's Carrie, it isn't you," Mary told her. "If you don't do what I say, I'll tell Ma."

"I guess I can play where I want to!" said Laura.

Mary grabbed at her, but Laura was too quick. She darted out, and she would have run up the path, but Jack was in the way. He stood stiff, looking across the creek. Laura looked too, and she screeched, "Mary!"

The cattle were all around Pa's haystacks. They were eating the hay. They were tearing into the stacks with their horns, gouging out hay, eating it, and trampling over it.

There would be nothing left to feed Pete and Bright and Spot in the wintertime.

Jack knew what to do. He ran growling down the steps to the footbridge. Pa was not there to save the haystacks; they must drive those cattle away.

"Oh, we can't! We can't!" Mary said, scared. But Laura ran behind Jack and Mary came after her. They went over the creek and past the spring. They came up on the prairie, and now they saw the fierce, big cattle quite near. The long horns were gouging, the thick legs trampling and jostling, the wide mouths bawling.

Mary was too scared to move. Laura was too scared to stand still. She jerked Mary along. She saw a stick, and grabbed it up, and ran yelling at the cattle. Jack ran at them, growling. A big red cow swiped at him with her horns, but he jumped behind her. She snorted and galloped. All the other cattle ran

113

humping and jostling after her, and Jack and Laura and Mary ran after them.

But they could not chase those cattle away from the hay-stacks. The cattle ran around and around and in between the stacks, jostling and bawling, tearing off hay and trampling it. More and more hay slid off the stacks. Laura ran panting and yelling, waving her stick. The faster she ran, the faster the cattle went, black and brown and red, brindle and spotted cattle, big and with awful horns, and they would not stop wasting the hay. Some tried to climb over the toppling stacks.

Laura was hot and dizzy. Her hair unbraided and blew in her eyes. Her throat was rough from yelling, but she kept on yelling, running, and waving her stick. She was too scared to hit one of those big, horned cows. More and more hay kept coming down, and faster and faster they trampled over it.

Suddenly Laura turned around and ran the other way. She faced the big red cow coming around a haystack.

The huge legs and shoulders and terrible horns were coming fast. Laura could not scream now. But she jumped at that cow and waved her stick. The cow tried to stop, but all the other cattle were coming behind her and she couldn't. She swerved and ran away across the ploughed ground, all the others galloping after her.

Jack and Laura and Mary chased them, farther and farther from the hay. Far into the high prairie grasses they chased those cattle.

Johnny, the cattle boy, rose out of the prairie, rubbing his eyes. He had been lying asleep in a warm hollow of grass.

"Johnny! Johnny!" Laura screeched. "Wake up and watch the cattle!"

"You'd better!" Mary told him.

Johnny Johnson looked at the cattle grazing in the deep grass, and he looked at Laura and Mary and Jack. He did not know what had happened, and they could not tell him because the only words he knew were Norwegian.

They went back through the high grass that dragged at their trembling legs. They were glad to drink at the spring. They

114

were glad to be in the quiet dugout and sit down to rest.

All that long, quiet afternoon they stayed in the dugout. The cattle did not come back to the haystacks. Slowly the sun went down the western sky. Soon it would be time to meet the cattle at the big gray rock, and Laura and Mary wished that Pa and Ma would come home.

Again and again they went up the path to look for the wagon. At last they sat waiting with Jack on the grassy top of their house. The lower the sun went, the more attentive Jack's ears were. Often he and Laura stood up to look at the edge of the sky where the wagon had gone, though they could see it just as well when they were sitting down.

Finally Jack turned one ear that way, then the other. Then he looked up at Laura, and a waggle went from his neck to his stubby tail. The wagon was coming!

They all stood and watched till it came out of the prairie. When Laura saw the oxen, and Ma and Carrie on the wagon seat, she jumped up and down, swinging her sunbonnet and shouting, "They're coming! They're coming!"

"They're coming awful fast," Mary said.

Laura was still. She heard the wagon rattling loudly. Pete and Bright were coming very fast. They were running. They were running away.

The wagon came bumpity-banging and bouncing. Laura saw Ma down in a corner of the wagon box, hanging onto it and hugging Carrie. Pa came bounding in long jumps beside Bright, shouting and hitting at Bright with the goad.

He was trying to turn Bright back from the creek bank.

He could not do it. The big oxen galloped nearer and nearer the steep edge. Bright was pushing Pa off it. They were all going over. The wagon, Ma and Carrie, were going to fall down the bank, all the way down to the creek.

Pa shouted a terrible shout. He struck Bright's head with all his might, and Bright swerved. Laura ran screaming. Jack jumped at Bright's nose. Then the wagon, Ma, and Carrie flashed by. Bright crashed against the stable, and suddenly everything was still.

115

Pa ran after the wagon and Laura ran behind him.

"Whoa, Bright! Whoa, Pete," Pa said. He held onto the wagon box and looked at Ma.

"We're all right, Charles," Ma said. Her face was gray, and she was shaking all over.

Pete was trying to go on through the doorway into the stable, but he was yoked to Bright, and Bright was headed against the stable wall. Pa lifted Ma and Carrie out of the wagon, and Ma said, "Don't cry, Carrie. See, we're all right."

Carrie's pink dress was torn down the front. She snuffled against Ma's neck and tried to stop crying as Ma told her.

"Oh, Caroline! I thought you were going over the bank," Pa said.

"I thought so, too, for a minute," Ma answered. "But I might have known you wouldn't let that happen."

"Pshaw!" said Pa. "It was good old Pete. He wasn't running away. Bright was, but Pete was only going along. He saw the stable and wanted his supper."

But Laura knew that Ma and Carrie would have fallen down into the creek with the wagon and oxen, if Pa had not run so fast and hit Bright so hard. She crowded against Ma's hoop-skirt and hugged her tight and said, "Oh, Ma! Oh, Ma!" So did Mary.

"There, there," said Ma. "All's well that ends well. Now, girls, help bring in the packages while Pa puts up the oxen."

They carried all the little packages into the dugout. They met the cattle at the gray rock and put Spot into the stable, and Laura helped milk her while Mary helped Ma get supper.

At supper, they told how the cattle had got into the haystacks and how they had driven them away. Pa said they had done exactly the right thing. He said, "We knew we could depend on you to take care of everything. Didn't we, Caroline?"

They had completely forgotten that Pa always brought them presents from town, until after supper he pushed back his bench and looked as if he expected something. Then Laura jumped on his knee, and Mary sat on the other, and Laura bounced and asked, "What did you bring us, Pa? What? What?"

"Guess," Pa said.

They could not guess. But Laura felt something crackle in his jumper pocket, and she pounced on it. She pulled out a paper bag, beautifully striped with tiny red and green stripes. And in the bag were two sticks of candy, one for Mary and one for Laura!

They were maple-sugar-colored, and they were flat on one side.

Mary licked hers. But Laura bit her stick, and the outside of it came off, crumbly. The inside was hard and clear and dark brown. And it had a rich, brown, tangy taste. Pa said it was hoarhound candy.

After the dishes were done, Laura and Mary each took her stick of candy, and they sat on Pa's knees, outside the door in the cool dusk. Ma sat just inside the dugout, humming to Carrie in her arms.

The creek was talking to itself under the yellow willows. One by one the great stars swung low and seemed to quiver and flicker in the little wind.

Laura was snug in Pa's arm. His beard softly tickled her cheek, and the delicious candy-taste melted on her tongue.

After a while she said, "Pa."

"What, little half-pint?" Pa's voice asked against her hair.

"I think I like wolves better than cattle," she said.

"Cattle are more useful, Laura," Pa said.

She thought about that awhile. Then she said, "Anyway, I like wolves better."

She was not contradicting; she was only saying what she thought.

"Well, Laura, we're going to have a good team of horses before long," Pa said. She knew when that would be. It would be when they had a wheat crop.

Grasshopper weather was strange weather. Even at Thanksgiving, there was no snow.

The door of the dugout was wide open while they ate Thanksgiving dinner. Laura could see across the bare willow-tops, far

117

over the prairie to the place where the sun would go down. There was not one speck of snow. The prairie was like soft yellow fur. The line where it met the sky was not sharp now; it was smudged and blurry.

"Grasshopper weather," Laura thought to herself. She thought of grasshoppers' long, folded wings and their high-jointed hind legs. Their feet were thin and scratchy. Their heads were hard, with large eyes on the corners, and their jaws were tiny and nibbling.

If you caught a grasshopper and held him, and gently poked a green blade of grass into his jaws, they nibbled it fast. They swiftly nibbled in the whole grass blade, till the tip of it went into them and was gone.

Thanksgiving dinner was good. Pa had shot a wild goose for it. Ma had to stew the goose because there was no fireplace, and no oven in the little stove. But she made dumplings in the gravy. There were corn dodgers and mashed potatoes. There were butter, and milk, and stewed dried plums. And three grains of parched corn lay beside each tin plate.

At the first Thanksgiving dinner the poor Pilgrims had had nothing to eat but three parched grains of corn. Then the Indians came and brought them turkeys, so the Pilgrims were thankful.

Now, after they had eaten their good, big Thanksgiving dinner, Laura and Mary could eat their grains of corn and re-member the Pilgrims. Parched corn was good. It crackled and crunched, and its taste was sweet and brown.

Then Thanksgiving was past, and it was time to think of Christmas. Still there was no snow and no rain. The sky was gray, the prairie was dull, and the winds were cold. But the cold winds blew over the top of the dugout.

"A dugout is snug and cozy," said Ma. "But I do feel like an animal penned up for the winter."

"Never mind, Caroline," Pa said. "We'll have a good house next year." His eyes shone and his voice was like singing. "And good horses, and a buggy to boot! I'll take you riding, dressed up in silks! Think, Caroline—this level, rich land, not a stone or stump to contend with, and only three miles from a railroad!

118

We can sell every grain of wheat we raise!" Then he ran his fingers through his hair and said, "I do wish I had a team of horses."

"Now, Charles," said Ma. "Here we are, all healthy and safe and snug, with food for the winter. Let's be thankful for what we have."

"I am," Pa said. "But Pete and Bright are too slow for harrowing and harvesting. I've broken up that big field with them, but I can't put it all in wheat, without horses."

Then Laura had a chance to speak without interrupting. She said, "There isn't any fireplace."

"Whatever are you talking about?" Ma asked her.

"Santa Claus," Laura answered.

"Eat your supper, Laura, and let's not cross bridges till we come to them," said Ma.

Laura and Mary knew that Santa Claus could not come down a chimney when there was no chimney. One day Mary asked Ma how Santa Claus could come. Ma did not answer. Instead, she asked, "What do you girls want for Christmas?"

She was ironing. One end of the ironing-board was on the table and the other on the bedstead. Pa had made the bedstead that high, on purpose. Carrie was playing on the bed and Laura and Mary sat at the table. Mary was sorting quilt blocks and Laura was making a little apron for the rag doll, Charlotte. The wind howled overhead and whined in the stovepipe, but there was no snow yet.

Laura said, "I want candy."

"So do I," said Mary, and Carrie cried, "Tandy?"

"And a new winter dress, and a coat, and a hood," said Mary.

"So do I," said Laura. "And a dress for Charlotte, and—"

Ma lifted the iron from the stove and held it out to them. They could test the iron. They licked their fingers and touched them, quicker than quick, to the smooth hot bottom. If it crackled, the iron was hot enough.

"Thank you, Mary and Laura," Ma said. She began carefully ironing around and over the patches on Pa's shirt. "Do you know what Pa wants for Christmas?"

119

They did not know.

"Horses," Ma said. "Would you girls like horses?"

Laura and Mary looked at each other.

"I only thought," Ma went on, "if we all wished for horses, and nothing but horses, then maybe—"

Laura felt queer. Horses were everyday; they were not Christmas. If Pa got horses, he would trade for them. Laura could not think of Santa Claus and horses at the same time.

"Ma!" she cried. "There IS a Santa Claus, isn't there?"

"Of course there's a Santa Claus," said Ma. She set the iron on the stove to heat again. . . .

Christmas Eve was the time when everybody was unselfish. On that one night, Santa Claus was everywhere, because everybody, all together, stopped being selfish and wanted other people to be happy. And in the morning you saw what that had done.

"If everybody wanted everybody else to be happy, all the time, then would it be Christmas all the time?" Laura asked, and Ma said, "Yes, Laura."

Laura thought about that. So did Mary. They thought, and they looked at each other, and they knew what Ma wanted them to do. She wanted them to wish for nothing but horses for Pa. They looked at each other again, and they looked away quickly, and they did not say anything. Even Mary, who was always so good, did not say a word.

That night after supper Pa drew Laura and Mary close to him in the crook of his arms. Laura looked up at his face, and then she snuggled against him and said, "Pa."

"What is it, little half-pint of sweet cider?" Pa asked, and Laura said,—

"Pa, I want Santa Claus—to bring—"

"What?" Pa asked.

"Horses," said Laura. "If you will let me ride them sometimes."

"So do I!" said Mary. But Laura had said it first.

Pa was surprised. His eyes shone soft and bright at them. "Would you girls really like horses?" he asked them.

"Oh yes, Pa!" they said.

"In that case," said Pa, smiling, "I have an idea that Santa Claus will bring us all a fine team of horses."

That settled it. They would not have any Christmas, only horses. Laura and Mary soberly undressed and soberly buttoned up their nightgowns and tied their nightcap strings. They knelt down together and said,—

> "Now I lay me down to sleep,
> I pray the Lord my soul to keep.
> If I should die before I wake
> I pray the Lord my soul to take,

and please bless Pa and Ma and Carrie and everybody and make me a good girl for ever'n'ever. Amen."

Quickly Laura added, in her own head, "And please make me only glad about the Christmas horses, for ever'n'ever amen again."

She climbed into bed and almost right away she was glad. She thought of horses sleek and shining, of how their manes and tails blew in the wind, how they picked up their swift feet and sniffed the air with velvety noses and looked at everything with bright, soft eyes. And Pa would let her ride them.

Pa had tuned his fiddle, and now he set it against his shoulder. Overhead the wind went wailing lonely in the cold dark. But in the dugout everything was snug and cosy.

Bits of firelight came through the seams of the stove and twinkled on Ma's steel knitting-needles and tried to catch Pa's elbow. In the shadows the bow was dancing, on the floor Pa's toe was tapping, and the merry music hid the lonely crying of the wind.

Next morning, snow was in the air. Hard bits of snow were leaping and whirling in the howling wind.

Laura could not go out to play. In the stable, Spot and Pete and Bright stood all day long, eating the hay and straw. In the dugout, Pa mended his boots while Ma read to him again the story called *Millbank*. Mary sewed and Laura played with Charlotte. She could let Carrie hold Charlotte, but Carrie was too little to play with paper dolls; she might tear one.

That afternoon, when Carrie was asleep, Ma beckoned Mary and Laura. Her face was shining with a secret. They put their heads close to hers, and she told them. They could make a button-string for Carrie's Christmas!

They climbed onto their bed and turned their backs to Carrie and spread their laps wide. Ma brought them her button-box.

The box was almost full. Ma had saved buttons since she was smaller than Laura, and she had buttons her mother had saved when her mother was a little girl. There were blue buttons and red buttons, silvery and goldy buttons, curved-in buttons with tiny raised castles and bridges and trees on them, and twinkling jet buttons, painted china buttons, striped buttons, buttons like juicy blackberries, and even one tiny dog-head button. Laura squealed when she saw it.

"Sh!" Ma shushed her. But Carrie did not wake up.

Ma gave them all those buttons to make a button-string for Carrie.

After that, Laura did not mind staying in the dugout. When she saw the outdoors, the wind was driving snowdrifts across the bare frozen land. The creek was ice, and the willow-tops rattled. In the dugout she and Mary had their secret.

They played gently with Carrie and gave her everything she wanted. They cuddled her and sang to her and got her to sleep whenever they could. Then they worked on the button-string.

Mary had one end of the string and Laura had the other. They picked out the buttons they wanted and strung them on the string. They held the string out and looked at it, and took off some buttons and put on others. Sometimes they took every button off, and started again. They were going to make the most beautiful button-string in the world.

One day Ma told them that this was the day before Christmas. They must finish the button-string that day.

They could not get Carrie to sleep. She ran and shouted, climbed on benches and jumped off, and skipped and sang. She did not get tired. Mary told her to sit still like a little lady, but she wouldn't. Laura let her hold Charlotte, and she jounced Charlotte up and down and flung her against the wall.

Finally Ma cuddled her and sang. Laura and Mary were perfectly still. Lower and lower Ma sang, and Carrie's eyes blinked till they shut. When softly Ma stopped singing, Carrie's eyes popped open and she shouted, "More, Ma! More!"

But at last she fell asleep. Then quickly, quickly, Laura and Mary finished the button-string. Ma tied the ends together for them. It was done; they could not change one button more. It was a beautiful button-string.

That evening after supper, when Carrie was sound asleep, Ma hung her clean little pair of stockings from the table edge. Laura and Mary, in their nightgowns, slid the button-string into one stocking.

Then that was all. Mary and Laura were going to bed when Pa asked them, "Aren't you girls going to hang your stockings?"

"But I thought," Laura said, "I thought Santa Claus was going to bring us horses."

"Maybe he will," said Pa. "But little girls always hang up their stockings on Christmas Eve, don't they?"

Laura did not know what to think. Neither did Mary. Ma

took two clean stockings out of the clothes-box, and Pa helped hang them beside Carrie's. Laura and Mary said their prayers and went to sleep, wondering.

In the morning Laura heard the fire crackling. She opened one eye the least bit, and saw lamplight, and a bulge in her Christmas stocking.

She jumped out of bed. Mary came running, too, and Carrie woke up. In Laura's stocking, and in Mary's stocking, there were little paper packages, just alike. In the packages was candy.

Laura had six pieces, and Mary had six. They had never seen such beautiful candy. It was too beautiful to eat. Some pieces were like ribbons, bent in waves. Some were short bits of round stick candy, and on their flat ends were colored flowers that went all the way through. Some were perfectly round and striped.

In one of Carrie's stockings were four pieces of that beautiful candy. In the other was the button-string. Carrie's eyes and her mouth were perfectly round when she saw it. Then she squealed, and grabbed it. She sat on Pa's knee, looking at her candy and her button-string and wriggling and laughing with joy.

Then it was time for Pa to do the chores. He said, "Do you suppose there is anything for us in the stable?" And Ma said, "Dress as fast as you can, girls, and you can go to the stable and see what Pa finds."

It was winter, so they had to put on stockings and shoes. But Ma helped them button up the shoes, and she pinned their shawls under their chins. They ran out into the cold.

Everything was gray, except a long red streak in the eastern sky. Its red light shone on the patches of gray-white snow. Snow was caught in the dead grass on the walls and roof of the stable and it was red. Pa stood waiting in the stable door. He laughed when he saw Laura and Mary, and he stepped outside to let them go in.

There, standing in Pete's and Bright's places, were two horses. They were a soft, red-brown color, shining like silk. Their manes and tails were black. Their eyes were bright and gentle. They put their velvety noses down to Laura and nibbled softly at her hand and breathed warm on it.

124

"Well, flutterbudget!" said Pa, "and Mary. How do you girls like your Christmas?"

"Very much, Pa," said Mary, but Laura could only say, "Oh, Pa!"

Pa's eyes shone deep and he asked, "Who wants to ride the Christmas horses to water?"

Laura could hardly wait while he lifted Mary up and showed her how to hold onto the mane and told her not to be afraid. Then Pa's strong hands swung Laura up. She sat on the horse's big, gentle back and felt its aliveness carrying her.

All outdoors was glittering now with sunshine on snow and frost. Pa went ahead, leading the horses and carrying his ax to break the ice in the creek so they could drink. The horses lifted their heads and took deep breaths and whooshed the cold out of their noses. Their velvety ears pricked forward, then back and forward again.

Laura held to her horse's mane and clapped her shoes together and laughed. Pa and the horses and Mary and Laura were all happy in the gay, cold Christmas morning.

CHRISTMAS SONG
Eleanor Underwood

Snowflakes shimmer in the air,
    Silver white, silver white,
Stars a-glimmer everywhere
    Christmas night, Christmas night.

All of us are watching them
    Through the snow, through the snow,
And remembering Bethlehem
    Long ago.

LIVING on the Wisconsin frontier in the 1860's was exciting for the six Wood-lawn children, Clara, Hetty, Warren, Tom, Minnie, and Caddie. There was much to keep them busy: hunting, picking berries, watching the neighboring Indians as they worked, and, of course, doing the household chores. The Saturday before our story begins the Woodlawns had invited the visiting Circuit Rider, Mr. Tanner, to dinner, and it was considered a great honor among the settlers to entertain the traveling minister.

Carol Ryrie Brink

CADDIE'S SILVER DOLLAR

ILLUSTRATED BY *Janet Smalley*

THE next day was Sunday, and, of course, the schoolhouse was opened and everyone went to church. Mrs. Woodlawn brought a bunch of her autumn flowers to decorate the desk. She had driven over early with her husband and Mr. Tanner to open and air the schoolhouse, which had been closed since summer. The children followed on foot. They had a mile to go, across a field and along a dusty road. They rubbed their feet through the tall grass by the schoolhouse gate to take the dust off their Sunday shoes. People from all the surrounding farms and home-steads had come to hear the Circuit Rider speak. Even Sam Hankinson was there, sitting in a back seat with his three little half-breed children about his knees. But his Indian wife stayed outside. Caddie peeped at them curiously through her fingers when Mr. Tanner's prayer grew very long. How would it be to have an Indian for a mother, she wondered? Then she looked at Mrs. Woodlawn, so fine in her full black silk with the cameo

127

brooch and earrings and the small black hat, and she was glad that this was Mother. And yet, she thought, she would not be ashamed of an Indian mother, as Sam Hankinson seemed to be ashamed of his Indian wife.

The next day the Circuit Rider rode away on his horse. Father set his clock upon the shelf to be mended later, and life went on again as usual. But now the children began to talk about when Uncle Edmund would come, for Uncle Edmund always came with the pigeons in the fall. He made his annual visit when the shooting was at its best, for he was an eager if not a very skillful sportsman.

Mrs. Woodlawn sighed. "No one can say that I am not a devoted sister," she said, "but the prospect of a visit from Edmund always fills me with alarm. My house is turned upside down, my children behave like wild things, there is nothing but noise and confusion."

"But Ma—" cried Tom.

"Don't Ma me, my child," said Mrs. Woodlawn calmly.

"But, Mother," persisted Tom, defending his hero. "Uncle Edmund knows the most tricks—"

"And jokes!" cried Caddie.

"Remember when he put the hairbrush in Caddie's bed?" shouted Warren.

"And the time he put a frog in a covered dish on the supper table, and when Mrs. Conroy lifted the cover—"

"That is enough, Tom," said his mother. "We remember Uncle Edmund's tricks very well, and I've no doubt we'll soon see more of them."

But she looked forward to her younger brother's coming just the same, and when the pigeons came and there was no Uncle Edmund, everyone felt surprised and concerned.

One night when they went to bed the sky was clear and the woods were still. But when they awoke in the crisp autumn morning the air was full of the noise of wings, and flocks of birds flew like clouds across the sun. The passenger pigeons were on their way south. They filled the trees in the woods. They came down in the fields and gardens, feeding on what-

128

ever seeds and grains they could find. The last birds kept flying over those which were feeding in front, in order to come at new ground, so that the flock seemed to roll along like a great moving cloud.

"The pigeons have come!" shouted the little Woodlawns. "The pigeons have come!" Even baby Joe waved his arms and shouted.

Tom and Warren armed themselves with sticks and went out with the hired men. But for once Caddie stayed indoors. She liked hunting as well as the boys. But this was too easy. This was not hunting—it was a kind of wholesale slaughter. She knew that the Indians and the white men, too, caught the birds in nets and sent them by thousands to the markets. She knew that wherever the beautiful gray birds went, they were harassed and driven away or killed. Something of sadness filled her young heart, as if she knew that they were a doomed race. The pigeons, like the Indians, were fighting a losing battle with the white man.

But John Woodlawn was not a glutton as some of his neighbors were. He said to Tom and the hired men, "There is not much grain left in the fields now. Drive the birds off and keep them from doing harm as well as you can, but don't kill more than we can eat. There is moderation in all things."

And so that night there was pigeon pie for supper. But on the Woodlawn farm no more birds were killed than could be eaten. After supper, Robert Ireton, strumming his banjo out by the barn, sang the song that everybody had on his lips at this time of the year:

> "When I can shoot my rifle clear
> At pigeons in the sky,
> I'll bid farewell to pork and beans
> And live on pigeon pie."

The three children, huddled around him on the chilly ground, hummed or sang with him, and all about them in the darkness was the rustle and stir of wings.

A few days later the passenger pigeons had disappeared as

suddenly as they had come. They had taken up their perilous journey toward the south. It was as if they had never passed by—except that the woods were stripped of seeds and acorns and dried berries, and some folks still had cold pigeon pie in their kitchens or dead birds on their truck heaps.

Then, after the pigeons were all gone, came a letter from Uncle Edmund announcing his arrival on the next steamer. The "Little Steamer," as everyone called it, came up the Menomonie River once a week as far as Dunnville. Its arrival was a great event, for all the letters from the East, all the news from the great world, most of the visitors and strangers and supplies came up the river on the Little Steamer.

The Woodlawn children begged to be allowed to go and meet Uncle Edmund.

"Certainly we can't take all of you!" said Mrs. Woodlawn. "I shall let Clara and Tom go, because they are the eldest."

Tom looked at Caddie and Warren with a superior smile. "Too bad you little children have to stay at home," he said, "but we can't take all of you."

"All right for you, Tom," said Caddie, "talking like that!"

She and Warren withdrew. They crossed the barnyard and climbed to the haymow. Nero went with them to the bottom of the ladder. He was quick to sense trouble of any sort and his tail wagged in mournful sympathy. Caddie and Warren buried themselves in the hay and talked things over. When Father or Mother made a decision, the Woodlawn children accepted it as final. There was very little teasing for favors in a large pioneer family. But not to meet Uncle Edmund was unthinkable.

"It's just because they haven't room for us in the wagon," said Caddie at last, "but if we walked—"

"Sure," said Warren, his face brightening, "and let's not tell them we're walking either. Let's save it for a—a surprise."

"Or maybe we could take one of the horses," suggested Caddie.

"Pete's the fastest," said Warren.

"Better take Betsy. Pete always runs for the low shed behind the barn and scrapes us off."

130

"Sure," said Warren, "we'll take Betsy!"

When the time came to meet the steamer, Clara and Tom, in their Sunday clothes, climbed into the wagon behind Mr. and Mrs. Woodlawn. Tom was a little sorry for Caddie and Warren, but he couldn't resist a smirk of satisfaction. Only, strangely enough, Caddie and Warren did not seem as depressed over being left behind as they should have been. They stood beside the wagon, grinning like two Cheshire cats. Hetty and little Minnie stood with them, looking properly wistful. The moment the wagon started Caddie and Warren made a beeline for the barn to get old Betsy and ride across the fields and through the woods.

Hetty saw them go, and instant realization of what they were going to do flashed across her mind. Here was something important to tell. "Father! Mother!" she shouted, running down the lane behind the wagon. "Stop! Stop! Father! Mother!" But her voice was lost in the rattle of wheels, and in a cloud of dust the wagon disappeared. Across the field in the other direction flew Betsy, the black mare, with only a rope and halter, and Caddie and Warren clinging like monkeys to her bare back.

Dunnville consisted of the schoolhouse which the children attended in winter and summer, a few log cabins, a store, and two taverns, one on either side of the river where the Little Steamer docked and turned around. As the Little Steamer came into sight, Mr. and Mrs. Woodlawn, Clara and Tom were standing on the dock ready with handkerchiefs to wave at sight of Uncle Edmund. Yes, Uncle Edmund was there. His round face was creased with smiles. His round eyes, behind his spectacles, twinkled with delight.

As soon as his voice could be heard over the sound of churning water, he shouted: "Hello there! Hello, Harriet and John! Hello, Tom and Clara! Hey, there, Caddie and Warren! Why don't you come on down?"

Caddie and Warren! The Woodlawns on the dock turned sharply around. There they were, Caddie and Warren, sitting on the bank above, their bare legs dangling, their hair shining. They grinned sheepishly.

"Well, of all things!" cried Mrs. Woodlawn, her clear brow darkening ominously. She was going to say a great deal more, but suddenly the Little Steamer docked with a bump and she was obliged to catch her husband's arm to keep her balance. Then they were all in Uncle Edmund's large, enthusiastic embrace—even Caddie and Warren. Uncle Edmund was so delighted that they had all come to meet him, that nobody could bear to tell him it had not been planned that way.

As they were walking up the path from the dock, Uncle Edmund began to fumble in his pocket. "Wait," he said, "I've got a present here for Caddie."

Caddie stopped in her tracks, speechless with joy. The others crowded around them. Out of his pocket Uncle Edmund took a fat little book. Caddie had never felt much need of books, but any sort of present was a rare delight. She took the little book from Uncle Edmund's hand and opened the cover. Whiz! Something long and green flew out at her and fell into the path. Uncle Edmund shouted with laughter, and Caddie laughed,

132

too, a little ruefully. She picked up the long green thing which lay in the path.

"That's no snake," she said. "It's got a clock spring inside it."

"Say, Uncle Edmund," cried Tom, "you'd ought to know you can't fool Caddie on snakes or clock springs. Try that on Hetty."

The next morning Uncle Edmund got out his gun and oiled and polished it. Then he polished his spectacles, for Uncle Edmund was near-sighted.

"Now," he said, "I've missed the pigeons, and that's a great pity, for a near-sighted man can always bring down a nice bag of pigeons. But I must do the best I can. Who will go with me to help me sight my game?"

Tom and Warren and Caddie stood beside him in breathless anticipation of this question. Uncle Edmund always asked it, and he always chose one of the three to go with him. More than one of them he would never take, for then, he said, they frightened the game away.

The three children spoke up with one voice: "I'll go, Uncle Edmund!"

Uncle Edmund looked them over critically. "Tom, you went last time I was here. You're pretty good, but you let a nice, fat squirrel get away. You remember?"

"Yah," said Tom, "but if I'd had the gun he wouldn't have got away."

"That's the trouble," said Uncle Edmund regretfully. "And Warren, here, talks too much. I might as well take a fife and drum corps."

"I wouldn't say a word," shouted Warren. "I wouldn't talk a bit. Just listen how quiet I could be."

"No," said Uncle Edmund, "I always have to fall back on Caddie in the end. I might as well start with her. She's as good as a pointer for showing me the game, and she never tells me how to shoot it nor reproaches me when I miss my aim. Come along, Caddie."

Caddie opened her mouth to speak. She was going to say: "It's too bad you little children have to stay at home. But, of course, we can't take all of you." But she closed it again with-

133

out saying anything. After all, she did hate to see Tom and Warren disappointed, and also she didn't want to find a frog in her bed or a pail of water arranged over her door in such a way as to give her a drenching when she came back.

As she trotted along beside Uncle Edmund, she was absolutely happy. It was perfect Indian-summer weather. The birch trees were all a-tremble with thinning gold. The oaks and sugar maples were putting on their vivid reds and orange hues, and river, lake, and sky were all sublimely blue.

Uncle Edmund and Caddie struck across fields and through the woods to the lake. Nero went with them, for, although he had not been trained as a hunter, he loved to go hunting, and he had a strong affection for Uncle Edmund. Half drawn up on the shore of the lake were the Woodlawn children's two prized possessions—a homemade raft, of small logs or poles fastened together with wooden pins, and the Indian canoe hollowed from a single log. The little Woodlawns could manage almost any craft in any kind of weather, but, although they spent half of their time on either lake or river, they had never learned to swim.

Caddie ran ahead, her golden-red curls flying in the breeze. She threw her weight against the canoe and pushed it into the water. Then, her eyes shining with mischief, she jumped in and caught up the paddle.

"Beat you to the end of the lake, Uncle Edmund," she called. Uncle Edmund could swim, but he was no hand with a boat. He managed to get the raft afloat, and he and Nero scrambled aboard. Then he began to pole it down the lake. It swung from side to side and seemed to defy all of his attempts at steering.

"Hey, you little whippersnapper, you!" he shouted at Caddie, shaking his fist good-naturedly.

Caddie came back laughing and circled around the raft in her canoe. "Oh, I'm sorry, Uncle Edmund. Honestly I am. But I can't help laughing. You look so funny. You can take the canoe coming back, and I'll take the raft, and I'll beat you that way, too. See if I don't!"

"Oh, you'll beat me that way, too, will you?" said Uncle

Whizz! Something long and green flew out.

Edmund, a fine edge sounding in his voice. "How much will you bet?"

"Oh, I haven't any money and Mother doesn't like us to bet, but I'll beat you just the same."

"All right," said Uncle Edmund. "You won't bet, but I'll tell you what I'll do. If you can beat me coming back, I'll give you a silver dollar, that's what I'll do. Mind—you take the raft and I take the canoe."

"Bully for you!" cried Caddie, echoing Tom's favorite expression. She was confident of winning. A silver dollar! The Woodlawn children never had much money to spend, and, in those days of wartime "greenbacks," a silver dollar was worth nearly three times the value of the paper dollar. Caddie was so delighted by Uncle Edmund's generosity that she offered to tow the raft to shore. But Uncle Edmund declined her offer and finally got himself awkwardly to the end of the lake. They beached their craft and started through the woods. But Uncle Edmund had forgotten something.

"Wait here a moment, Caddie. I left my gamebag back on the raft."

"I'll get it, Uncle Edmund."

"No, wait here. I'll go myself."

Uncle Edmund was gone quite a long time, but at last he returned with the bag.

Now they went slowly and quietly, Uncle Edmund peering through his thick glasses at the near-by trees, Caddie's bright eyes searching the more distant places. Nero walked beside them, deeply excited. His business was sheep and cows, not game, but, as Edmund often said, a little training would have made him an admirable hunter. Suddenly Caddie stopped, her body stiffened, she put a tense hand on Uncle Edmund's arm.

"There!" she whispered, pointing to the branch of a tree some yards ahead. A squirrel sat there motionless, trying to look like a part of the tree. Uncle Edmund followed the direction of her finger with his near-sighted eyes. He raised his gun to his shoulder. Bang! The report reverberated through the woods, shattering the silence into a hundred echoes.

"I got him!" shouted Uncle Edmund exultantly. "By golly, Caddie, I got him!" Caddie was as delighted as Uncle Edmund. She and Nero raced to retrieve the squirrel for Uncle Edmund's gamebag.

It was well along in the afternoon when they started back toward the lake. Uncle Edmund was treading on air, for he had three squirrels and a brace of partridges, and, for a near-sighted man, that was a good bag. Caddie's mind returned to the silver dollar she was going to win.

"Remember, I'm going to beat you across the lake, Uncle Edmund," she chirped.

"So you said. So you said," agreed Uncle Edmund jovially, chuckling to himself. He sprang into the canoe and pushed off. Caddie thrust the raft into the water and jumped on. Nero sprang on behind her, and Caddie began to pole the raft. She and Tom had handled the raft so often that she knew just how to manage it to the best advantage. A few deft strokes brought her alongside Uncle Edmund, who was hopelessly inefficient, even with such a delicate craft as a canoe. But something curious was beginning to happen to the raft. One by one the small logs of which it was built were beginning to float away. Caddie could not believe her eyes. She poled for dear life, but the faster she poled, the more quickly the logs fell away from the raft. The space on which she stood grew smaller and smaller. Someone had loosened all the pins which held the raft together! Bit by bit it was coming apart.

"Uncle Edmund!" shouted Caddie, red with surprise and rage. Uncle Edmund lay back in the canoe and laughed. In a flash Caddie knew why Uncle Edmund had taken so long to fetch his gamebag. The logs on which Nero stood came loose, and the old sheep dog plunged into the water and began to swim for shore. There were only three or four logs left together now, and it took only an instant for them to drift apart. Caddie went down with a great splash, and her shining head disappeared beneath the water like a quenched flame. Presently she came up again, sputtering and blowing, and caught desperately at the nearest log. When she felt its rough surface under her fingers, she stopped struggling and clasped her arms about it. She was used to the feel of water up to her neck, if only she had something to hold on to. But she was angry. It took a good deal to arouse Caddie from her good nature, but everyone's temper has its limitations, and Caddie's had been reached.

"Oh! Oh! Oh!" she sputtered, too angry to find any words.

Now that Uncle Edmund had had his little joke, he began to be worried. He brought the canoe around and helped Caddie into it. "Say, Caddie," he said, "I never thought that raft would come apart so quickly. Honestly, I just wanted to scare you a little. You don't mind getting a little wet, do you? Just for fun?"

Caddie sat in the bottom of the canoe straight and stiff. Streams of water ran down all over her and made a puddle around her. Her face was pale and her hazel eyes flashed cold fire, but still she couldn't find a word to say to relieve her bottled indignation.

"Oh, say, Caddie, don't take it so hard," coaxed Uncle Edmund. "It was just a joke. Listen now, I'll give you that silver dollar I promised; but say, don't tell your mother, Caddie."

At last Caddie exploded.

"Are you trying to bribe a Woodlawn, Uncle Edmund?" she shouted. After everything else, to attempt to bribe a Woodlawn was heaping infamy upon infamy.

"Oh, no! no!" protested Uncle Edmund anxiously. "It's just a gift, Caddie."

"I wouldn't take it," cried Caddie. "I wouldn't take it if it was the last silver dollar in the world! I wouldn't—"

"Now, now, Caddie," urged Uncle Edmund. "Here we are almost to shore. Now, listen, you just take off your dress and dry it in the sun, and I'll go back and collect the pieces of the raft. That's a good, sensible little girl."

Caddie stepped out of the canoe with the haughty air of a scornful but dripping princess.

"You do as I say, Caddie," urged Uncle Edmund anxiously, "and I'll be back in half an hour with the raft." Caddie shook herself like a wet dog. Angry as she was, she realized that it was better to dry herself in the sheltered, sunny curve of the beach than to walk home through fields and woods in her dripping clothes. She wrung out her dress and petticoat and hung them on the bushes. Then she lay down in the warm sand. Presently Nero, who had made his way along the shore, came and sat beside her, drying his own coat in the sun.

Uncle Edmund was gone a long, long time. When he returned at last, Caddie was sitting in the sun in a dress that was wrinkled but dry. She had had time to think over her adventure, and her usual good humor had got the better of her anger. She burst out laughing when she saw Uncle Edmund's red, perspiring face. Poor Uncle Edmund had paid for his misdeeds.

"By golly, Caddie, that was a hard job. I've had my come-up-ance-with, for once, my dear. But they're all here. I got every one." Behind the canoe he was towing the pieces of the raft, bound together with a rope which the children always kept in the bottom of the canoe. Caddie helped him pull the poles in to shore. He had managed to salvage most of the pins, too, and the two of them put the raft together once again.

"Well, I guess we're even, Uncle Edmund," said Caddie,

gravely smiling. She held out her small, brown hand.

Uncle Edmund shook it heartily, but he said, "No, Caddie, we're not even yet. I promised you a silver dollar."

"You said if I beat you to the end of the lake on the raft, or if I wouldn't tell Mother. But I didn't beat you, and I *am* going to tell Mother."

"Yes, yes, of course," said Uncle Edmund hastily, "but this dollar is just burning a hole in my pocket, my dear. Here, take it. It belongs to you."

Suddenly Caddie felt the weight of a silver dollar in the pocket of her dress. She put her hand in her pocket and the silver dollar felt warm and round to her fingers.

"Thank you, Uncle Edmund," she said.

They gathered up the gamebag and the gun, and started for home. Their three figures were silhouetted against the sunset, Caddie, Nero, and Uncle Edmund, and their three shadows trailed far out behind them. Uncle Edmund, with a lulled conscience, was whistling. But Caddie's mind was busy with the many, many ways in which one could spend a silver dollar.

[ALTHOUGH some months have passed Caddie still has not decided how to spend her silver dollar. Then, one day at school, something very unusual happened.]

In the middle of the morning, through the sound of droning voices chanting the reading lesson, a timid knock was heard on the schoolhouse door. Miss Parker, on her throne at the other end of the room, did not hear it. It came again and the children began turning their heads around to look at the door. First the outer door opened and closed. There was a moment of silence. Then the cloakroom door opened ever so softly, and an Indian woman entered the schoolroom in her silent moccasins. She stood a moment, troubled and ill at ease, searching the schoolroom with her bright black eyes. A large bundle which she carried she rested beside the door. Caddie knew who she was. She was Sam Hankinson's wife, the mother of the little half-breed boys who traded lunches with the Woodlawns. Her little boys turned now and saw her, and the youngest one held out his arms and gave a little stifled cry. With a swift movement, like a bird alighting from a low bough, the Indian woman ran to her children and knelt beside them, gathering first one and then another into her arms. She spoke to them in her own language, words guttural, broken, and soft as the chatter of a mother partridge to her brood. The boys answered in the same language, clinging to her and crying. By this time half of the white children were on their feet and Miss Parker had come down from her platform. The reading lesson was forgotten in a sudden sense of trouble and unrest.

"Ma! Ma!" cried the three little boys, clinging to the Indian woman and sobbing. Each of them in turn she pressed against her heart, then held each little brown head between her hands, pushing back the tangled hair, and looking earnestly into the face as if she would fix its image in her mind forever. When she had done this, she kissed each one upon the forehead and stood up. They still clung around her skirts, crying, "Ma! Ma! Don't go! Don't!"

The Indian woman put them away from her and stood straight and alone. The tears were running unheeded down her cheeks. To Miss Parker she said, "I go to my people." Then she turned and left the schoolroom. At the door she took up her bundle and swung it onto her shoulders. She did not look back. The cloakroom door closed, and then the outside door. They saw her pass by the window, going toward the woods. For a moment the only sound in the schoolroom was the sobbing of the three little boys.

Then Miss Parker said sharply, "Go on with your reading, please."

The drone of voices rose again. But it was as if a dark shadow or an icy wind had gone through the schoolhouse and changed everything. Caddie went on reading, but three bright tears fell on the page of her book and made odd little blisters over the type.

That evening she spoke about it to Mother.

"Why did she go away like that, Mother? She didn't want

to go and leave her children, and they didn't want her to go, either."

"It is hard to explain to you, Caddie," said Mother. "You see, Mr. Hankinson married her when there were very few white people in this country. He was not ashamed of her then. But now that there are more and more of his own people coming to live here, he is ashamed that his wife should be an Indian. I dare say the massacre scare had something to do with it, too. Folks seem to hate the red men more than ever they did before. Though why they should, I can't say. Goodness knows, the massacre was only in their own minds. But Sam Hankinson hasn't a very strong character. Now if your father had married an Indian—"

"Father marry an Indian?" cried Tom. "He never would!"

"Perhaps not," said Mrs. Woodlawn, smiling a little and tossing her head, remembering how pretty she had been as a girl in Boston. "But, if he *had*, you may be sure that *he* would never have sent her off because he was ashamed of her. No, not a good man like your father!"

That night, after Caddie went to bed, she lay thinking for a long time. Hetty and Minnie were sound asleep. Presently she got up and lit the candle. On the chest of drawers stood her little trinket box. She opened it and looked inside. There was the silver dollar, safe and round and shining. She took it out and held it to the candlelight. It was really beautiful—beautiful in itself, aside from what it would buy. Then she knotted it securely into her handkerchief, and put the handkerchief into the pocket of her school apron. After that she climbed into bed and went to sleep.

At school the next morning the little Hankinsons were late. Their hair was untidy and their round faces were stern and unsmiling. They were never good at lessons, and this morning they were worse than ever. Their eyes were swollen with crying. But Miss Parker was tactful and did not ask too much of them.

Caddie's eyes kept wandering to them over her books. It was hard to keep her mind on spelling and sums, when she knew

142

that they were sitting near by, so quiet and so full of hurt bewilderment. Then she felt her dollar, heavy in her pocket, and she was pleased that she had saved it for so long.

After school she laid her hand on Gussie's arm. He was not nearly so big as Warren and she had a motherly desire to pat his head, but she didn't.

"Gussie," she said, "you and Pete and Sammie come with me to Dunnville store. I'm going to give you a surprise."

The three little half-breeds looked at her in astonishment. For a moment they were surprised out of their sorrow.

"What for?" asked Gussie suspiciously.

"Just for fun," said Caddie with a smile. "I've got a whole silver dollar to spend," and she jingled it against a marble and a bit of slate pencil in her pocket.

"Candy?" suggested little Sammie, with a sudden glitter in his eye.

"Yes, sirree," said Caddie importantly. "Come along and see."

Mr. Adams of Dunnville store was accustomed to visitors after school. The children often came in with a penny or two, or sometimes only wishful looks, to examine the glass jars in which he kept brown hoarhound sticks or sticks of striped peppermint or wintergreen lozenges. But today he was quite amazed when Caddie Woodlawn, with the air of a queen, ushered in the three little half-breeds and laid a silver dollar on the counter.

"I want to spend it all, Mr. Adams," she said, "so you'll have to tell me when I've used it up. I want some hoarhound and peppermint and some pink wintergreens, and then I want three tops in different colors with good strong strings, and will you please tell me how much that is, because if there's anything left I want to get some more things?"

"Well, upon my word!" exclaimed Mr. Adams, "and bless my soul, too! But does your mother know you're spending a silver dollar, Caddie?"

"Not yet. But it's all right. It's my own dollar, and Father said I could spend it as I liked, and I'll tell Mother as soon as I get home."

The little Hankinsons looked on in amazement. The black mood of despair which had enveloped them all day had turned into wonder, and now wonder was rapidly giving way to incredulous delight. Candy! Tops! No one had ever bought such things for them before.

"Well, Miss Caddie, that comes to thirty cents," said Mr. Adams, when the bewildered boys with the help of Caddie had selected the candy and tops.

They were grinning now from ear to ear, and Caddie thought that, with so much money left to spend, she had better be a little wise. "I'd like to see some combs now, if you please. I'd like three small ones if they aren't too dear."

"Here you are, my girl," said the storekeeper, bringing down a dusty box from a shelf. He was smiling, too, by now, and almost as eager as the little Hankinsons to see what Caddie would buy next.

"I think," said Caddie, presenting the three combs, "that your mama would like you to keep your hair combed nice and tidy, and it'll be more fun if you've got combs of your own."

Unused to gifts of any sort, the small brown boys beamed as delightedly over combs as over tops and candy. Caddie looked inquiringly at Mr. Adams.

"It's not gone yet," he said encouragingly. "You've still got thirty cents."

Caddie examined her protégés with maternal eyes. Certainly their noses needed attention as well as their hair.

"I guess handkerchiefs had better come next," she said thoughtfully. "Thirty cents' worth of nice, cheerful, red handkerchiefs, if you please."

Mr. Adams had the very thing, large enough to meet any emergency, and of a fine turkey red. Caddie was satisfied, and the little Hankinsons were speechless with delight. The red was like music to their half-savage eyes. They waved the handkerchiefs in the air. They capered about and jostled each other and laughed aloud as Caddie had never heard them do before.

"Now you can go home," said Caddie, giving each of them a friendly pat, "and have a good time, and mind you remember to have clean noses and tidy hair on Monday when you come to school."

Dazed with their good fortune, they tumbled out of the store, whooping with joy and entirely forgetting (if they ever knew) that thanks were in order. Caddie and the storekeeper watched them race away, the red handkerchiefs flapping joyously in the breeze.

"Well, young lady," said Mr. Adams with an amused twinkle in his eye, "now your dollar's gone, and you didn't get a thing out of it for yourself."

"Oh, yes, I did, Mr. Adams!" she cried, and then she stopped. It was no use trying to tell a grownup. It was hard even to explain to herself. And yet she'd had her dollar's worth.

She found more words for it later when Tom, feeling himself for once the thrifty one, protested.

"But Caddie, you needn't have spent your whole dollar. You could have got them each a top or a hoarhound stick, and kept the rest for yourself."

"No, Tom, it had to be all of it. I wanted to drive that awful lonesome look out of their eyes, and it did, Tom. It did!"

Meridel LeSueur

JOHNNY APPLESEED
VISITS LICKING CREEK

ILLUSTRATED BY *Barbara Maynard*

THE people say they saw him everywhere.

My Grandmother said traders came through Licking Creek who said they had seen Johnny Appleseed in Missouri, Michigan, Indiana, and Kentucky.

Some would tell about seeing him walking with Indians in the Bad Lands. Others saw him paddling downstream in a hollow log chinked together with mud.

But everywhere he planted apple seeds. The first years he had to go back to Pennsylvania cider mills to pick the seeds out of the apple mash again, with the men making fun of him.

But the fourth year my Grandmother said, she heard the crows cawing one morning shriller than usual, and she ran out and saw Johnny Appleseed coming through the clearing, still with a gunny sack for a coat, the same old stewpot on his head, and a big prairie wolf loping beside him.

The child ran out and stopped when he saw the wolf.

"Hello, child," said Johnny. "This is my friend, the wolf. He was caught in a mantrap, and I set him free."

"Oh," said the child. "Your trees are very big now, Johnny Appleseed. I thinned them out for you, and everyone here has an apple tree at his door, the way you wanted it."

The child went dancing ahead shouting, "Johnny Appleseed is here. Here comes Johnny Appleseed!"

But when the mothers saw the wolf they screamed and ran into their houses, so Johnny had to tell him to wait at the edge of the forest.

It was soon spread around that Johnny Appleseed was in the village, and the people began to come in ahorseback and in wagons and afoot to see the man who had given them apple trees.

My Grandmother said that in the evening they all got together and gave a party for him in the biggest house in town. They all sat around the big fire, under the drying onions and corn that hung from the rafters, and Johnny told them about the country that lay west. He told about how he traveled the Old Indian trails from Fort Duquesne to Detroit by way of Fort Sandusky, one hundred and sixty miles through the forests, hills, and valleys, planting hundreds of apple seeds, going back to thin them out, repairing the fences.

He told how he had met a birdman named Mr. Audubon.

He told how he met a man in a coonskin cap named Daniel Boone, along the Indian trails.

After awhile he said, "Now do you want to hear some news from heaven?"

He took his Bible out of his blouse and he read to them, there, in Licking Creek, on the edge of the wilderness.

This is what he read: "In the morning, sow thy seed and in the evening withhold not thine hand, for thou knowest not whether shall prosper either this or that, or whether they shall be good alike. God giveth the increase."

They all liked the reading so much that Johnny said since there were not many books in Ohio he would share his with them. So he broke the book into three parts and gave the parts to the families and told them to pass the parts around.

He said there must be reading in America.

The people of Licking Creek, Ohio, made him a present of a leather bag for his seeds.

He would sleep in no bed, but lay down beside the dying fire, after he had taken his friend the wolf a bite to eat. He said he would be off at the crack of dawn.

And the child covered him over.

My Grandmother said she got up very early in the morning and was waiting for him at the forest's edge. She said it was a sight to see him walking through the sleeping town, a pig at his heels, the chickens and geese talking to him, and a billy goat who had taken a fondness for him nibbling at his coat tails.

My Grandmother said to him, "Johnny, winter is coming on, and from the coats of the animals it is going to be a hard one. You can't walk into the North without a coat."

She held up her husband's wedding coat. It was a coat

fine and warm, made Quaker style with bright silver buttons.

"Why," said Johnny, "I have a coat."

"Where?" my Grandmother asked. "That old sack!"

"As good clothing as any man needs," Johnny said.

"Put this coat on," my Grandmother said, and almost everyone obeyed my Grandmother.

"Take these shoes," my Grandmother said.

"I have a shoe," Johnny said.

"Going around in the snow one shoe on and one shoe off!"

"It saves a shoe," Johnny said.

"Take these stout shoes," my Grandmother said. "I don't want to be thinking of you when the winter winds blow, walking in your bare feet through the snow."

"My feet, ma'am, are the feet of my animal friends now. Do they ever want for a shoe?"

She said it was true, his feet were horny like an animal's.

"Good day to you," he said, and walked onto the ferry with the wolf. She heard him singing, the buttons of his new coat flashing in the rising sun.

> When the wintry winds blow
> Over the earth white with snow
> Where else can you find such delight?
> 'Tis a joy most complete,
> Mellow apples to eat,
> Round the fire on a cold winter's night.

My Grandmother said she looked back, and there were hundreds of little apple trees in the clearing all come from the seed he had planted that day many years before, and now there would be apple seeds at Licking Creek, and he would not have to go back to Pennsylvania, where men were laughing at him.

She said the next day an old trapper came into town and what do you suppose—he had on her husband's wedding coat, and she was going to have him locked up for stealing it, but the old man swore Johnny Appleseed had given it to him saying, "Take it. Your need is greater than mine."

"That man," my Grandmother would say, "didn't he beat all?"

149

Alexander Key

STRANGERS
IN THE WILDERNESS

ILLUSTRATED BY THE AUTHOR

DAN was nearly fourteen, long-legged and strong, but he was beginning to find it hard to keep up with his father's steady gait. The Squire moved swiftly through the woods ahead of him, a tall, lean figure in leggings and fringed hunting shirt. Strapped to his broad shoulders was a buckskin robe, neatly folded to hold two extra pairs of moccasins and a small bag of parched corn soaked in molasses. Dan's pack was identical, though in his hands he carried only a short staff instead of a rifle.

" 'Tis a long journey down into Caroliny," his father had said. "If'n ye go with me, thar must be no laggin'."

"I'll not lag," Dan had answered eagerly.

Why, this was the chance of a lifetime! Ever since he could remember he had been wanting to explore farther and farther beyond the narrow country where they lived. Each new day the Schuylkill region was losing more of its wildness. Settlers were appearing, building cabins, cutting trees, destroying game. . . . "It's gittin' built up so thick," the Squire had grumbled, "that a feller can't hardly breathe."

Dan felt the same way about it. But his mother had said, "That wilderness land is no place to take a wee lad!"

"Wee lad!" the Squire had scoffed. "Tush! Can't ye see he's nigh growed? 'Tis time he traveled a spell from home to git the feel of his man's legs. I own a smart piece o' land in Caroliny, an' it'll take two to scout it out an' tell whether 'tis fit for us to move there. But mind, Danny lad, if'n I take ye in place o' one o' the older boys, ye must play the man's part an' keep a sharp eye."

Well, a good many weeks lay behind them now, and some hundreds of weary miles over ridges and thick timber and deep streams that had to be crossed on a log. So far he had managed well enough and had given the Squire no cause for complaint. But his feet ached, he was hungry, and today his father had been walking faster than usual. Many times during the morning they had sighted deer within easy range, but the Squire had refused to risk a shot, even though they needed meat. Dan asked no questions, but he thought longingly of fresh venison roasted over a campfire.

Ahead, his father suddenly stopped beside a small stream that came tumbling down through the shadows. Dan turned, leaning his tired body on his staff. While he rested, his sharp blue eyes studied every detail in the gloom of the big trees.

Behind him a wood duck flew into a hole high up in a hollow trunk. A ruffed grouse resumed his drumming on a log, and a slim doe with a fawn tripped silently through a pool of sunlight. Dan's keen eyes missed nothing. If there was danger, at least it was not behind them.

"Danny," the Squire spoke abruptly. "Come here a minute."

His father was tugging thoughtfully at his short beard. "Son," he said, "thar's men about, an' I'm thinkin' they be Injins."

"Injins? How many? Where?"

"Danny boy, some day ye won't be havin' me around to answer all the questions. Supposin' as how ye use your own eyes an' tell me what ye see."

Dan's searching glance swept the ground. He stooped, intently studying the crushed blades of grass beside the narrow creek. Farther on was a broken twig and a few pebbles pressed into the hard ground, and in the clay by the water's edge was a small depression that could have been made only by the toe of a sharp-pointed moccasin. Dim, faint signs that only trained observers would notice.

"There was three of 'em," said Dan. "They crossed the creek here. Nigh two hours ago, jedging by the way the grass looks."

"Good," said the Squire. "Is that all?"

Dan took off his coonskin cap and scratched his head. "No, two went upstream. T'other went downstream."

"What kind of Injins was they?" asked the Squire.

"They—they warn't Cherokees."

"How d'ye know they warn't Cherokees? Ye never seen a Cherokee moccasin in your life!"

Dan rubbed his freckled cheek, thinking hard. "From the way they tromped around here, it seems like they was kinda lost. But I never hyeared of an Injin gittin' lost. Besides, a Cherokee is a mountain Injin—an' these footprints look like they come from the tidewater. Why—why, they must be white men!"

"Course they's white men!" laughed the Squire. "Now, what are white men a-doin' here on the edge o' the Cherokee country?"

"They warn't traders," said Dan, " 'cause they warn't a-walkin' heavy enough to be carryin' big packs."

The Squire stood a moment in thought. "Beyonst the high ground upstream, I'm thinkin', is the valley o' the Yadkin. Thar's where our land is, Danny, that we've come so far to see. Now, I'm a-goin' on over the ridge an' follow them two men. You slip downstream an' take a look at t'other man. They may be good people what's lost, or they may be bad men out a-stirrin' up trouble with the Injins. When ye finish scoutin', follow my trail to the other valley an' ye'll find me thar a-waitin'. But be careful—thar's Injins around."

"I know it," said Dan.

"How do ye know it?" murmured the Squire.

"Not by any real sign. I jest feel they's here."

The Squire peered at him sharply. "I always said, Danny, that ye was a born woodsman. That's why I brung ye in place o' the other boys."

Dan watched his father swing away into the shadows of the trees. He studied the creek several moments, his mouth tightened, and he started off down the bank.

He forgot his tiredness in the strange feeling of being suddenly alone in this great forest stretching dark and untouched around him for hundreds of miles. Virgin, unknown country that swept forever westward—no man knew how far. But he was not afraid. He had lived always in the woods and had learned to read and understand its secrets far better than those of the one or two books he had seen during his brief school days.

No, he was not afraid; but he would have felt better if he could have had a rifle like his father's. Rifles, though, were expensive and hard to get.

For an hour or more he followed the single trail. He went swiftly, silently, using an Indian's caution to keep himself hidden as much as possible. At the end of that time he saw where the man had leaped across the creek—something only a strong and agile person could have done. Probably a very young man, Dan thought, wading across after him.

There was a great deal of trouble up North, he knew—trouble with the French and their Indian allies. That was one of the main reasons why his father wanted to move South, before real warfare occurred. But suppose these three men were Frenchmen, sent down to talk the mountain Indians into mischief?

Dan stopped suddenly, considering what this would mean. If someone set the Cherokees on the warpath, it would not be safe to bring the family down here to settle. He had not as yet seen how the Yadkin valley looked beyond the ridge, but it must be like this—a wild, beautiful land of great trees, streams that ran clear and cold from the hills, and game everywhere. The very thought of living in such a region filled him with an excited longing. And over to the west were mountains, blue mountains filled with mystery.

The forest shut out the sunlight, but he knew from the deepening shadows that evening was near. If he did not find the man soon, it would be too dark to follow his father's trail. He would have to spend the night alone.

The man's footprints were easier to see now, for they were dragging as if he were tired. They led away from the creek, down a narrow ravine, and thence upward through a knee-deep layer of leaves to a ridge. Suddenly they curved back to a creek.

Dan approached the stream's edge carefully. It was not the same creek he had been on at first, though it looked very much like the other. He knew immediately that it must be a branch, and that the mouth of it was probably hidden by the dense azalea thickets he had noticed an hour ago.

It was twilight before he caught sight of the man he had been following—a tall, well-built young fellow in buckskins. But he was not a woodsman, for he wore a black tricorn on his head. Gentlemen from the tidewater wore hats like that—and Frenchmen from Quebec!

Dan crept silently forward, moving with the stealth of a fox from one tree trunk to another. The fellow had stopped, was staring about him with a puzzled look on his pleasant young face. Seeing no evil there, Dan stepped suddenly from his hiding place.

"Howdy, Mister Stranger!" he said. "Ye look kinda bewildered."

The fellow whirled around, raising his rifle. He dropped it when he saw Dan, blinked, and then smiled.

"Faith, you startled me!" he said. "I never dreamed I'd meet anyone like you in this place!"

Dan was usually timid with strangers, but there was some-

154

thing about this young fellow that made him feel friendly right away. He could not be much older than Dan himself. But he was taller than most full-grown men. In a few minutes they were talking like old acquaintances.

"My name's George," said the stranger. "Don't tell me you're all alone here!"

"No, the Squire's with me. I'm his son Dan. Him an' me come down to look at some land we own," Dan explained. "Course, Paw's not really a squire; but he was named that, you see, an' everybody calls him the Squire as if it was a real title. My, I'm glad you ain't no Frenchman!"

George laughed. "We're just hard-working surveyors from the coast. We came over to mark some boundaries on the Yadkin, but I'm beginning to believe that river doesn't exist! My friends went upstream to look around, and I'm afraid they went farther than they intended. Maybe if I give 'em a shot with the rifle—"

"No, no—don't shoot!" Dan interrupted quickly. "'Tain't healthy. Thar's Injins around!"

George looked incredulous. "I haven't seen an Indian for three weeks."

"They're here, somewhere," Dan insisted, "an' mebbe watchin' us right now. They been walkin' in the creeks, I think, so we wouldn't see their trails. They can't be on the warpath yet—cause an Injin always lets ye know first. But they know white men are here, an' they're waitin'."

"You seem to know a lot," George drawled. "Maybe you can tell me where my friends are, and how we can find the Yadkin."

"I'll take ye to the Yadkin in the mornin'," Dan promised. "It's too late now. We'll have to camp here tonight. Paw's likely found your friends already. Guess ye don't know ye got on the wrong creek, do ye?"

George's mouth dropped. "Don't you dare tell anybody I got lost," he said. "Faith, I'd never hear the last of it!"

They found a well-screened hollow behind a windfall, unrolled their packs, and made ready for the night.

"I'm so hungry," Dan said, "Why, I could chaw the bark off'n

155

a tree! I could catch some trout, only I hate to light a fire."

"I'm for taking the chance, friend Dan," said the other. "A man has to eat, and if the Cherokees come, why—we'll feed 'em!"

Dan stood irresolute, but hunger decided him. He opened the pouch at his belt and took out a finely braided horsehair line with a tiny hook looped in the end. He tied the other end to a short willow switch. George looked at him doubtfully while he caught half a dozen fat beetles under a log and attached one to the hook. "If you had a fish spear, young fellow," George said, "I'd be willing to bet on you, but—"

"You jest git a fire a-goin'."

Dan grinned and crept down to the creek. George plugged the pan of his rifle and snapped the flint upon a piece of flax dusted with powder. When the stuff was smoldering, he blew it into a flame and soon had a small fire going in the hollow.

In half an hour Dan returned. Strung on a stick were six large trout. George was even more amazed when Dan, lips tight, skewered all six fish and placed them over the coals.

"Gad, friend Dan, you act as if we were having visitors!"

"We are," Dan answered, in a voice that was not quite steady. "D—didn't ye hear 'em callin' a while back?"

"I heard a pair of wild turkeys gobbling."

"Well, they're the kind o' turkeys what like trout."

George stared at him. Suddenly he rose, peering into the dark beyond the fire. Dan whispered, "Put down your rifle! It's too late to run or fight."

Two tall straight forms appeared at the edge of the firelight. Almost instantly, two others appeared on the other side. Black, beady eyes squinted down at them from coppery faces.

"Cherokees!" George muttered.

Dan willed himself to stand, to smile into those dark unsmiling faces. He picked one that wore a tuft of red feathers in his hair and a necklace of bear claws. Only a leader would dress that way. Raising his hand, palm outward, he said, "How!" It was the way he had been taught to greet an Indian. George, smiling, did the same thing. Good for George!

The leader held out his palm, repeating the gesture of peace.

A rumbling "How!" came from his throat. Then he reached forward and briefly clasped each boy by the hand. Dan gaped at him—and suddenly remembered that Cherokees were not like other Indians. They greeted strangers as white men did.

Dan pointed to the fish. If they would sit down to rest and eat with them, all would be well. If they did not, he and the Squire might never hope to settle in the Yadkin country.

Suddenly, jabbering like four delighted schoolboys, the Cherokees squatted about the fire. Four pairs of hands reached out and plucked fish from the coals. Dan opened his bag of parched corn, and George produced a precious cake of maple sugar from his pack. "It looks," George whispered, grinning, "like 'tis going to be a regular feast."

It was, and all present enjoyed it thoroughly. When they were satisfied at last, the Cherokees gathered more wood for the fire and sprawled comfortably about it, heads nodding. George stretched beside Dan, his pack under his head.

"What do you think of 'em, friend Dan?" he asked quietly. "Seems as if they intend to camp with us the rest of the night."

"I ain't quite figgered 'em out yet," Dan whispered back. "But I reckon they be all right. They sure was hungry."

"And so was Mother Washington's son, George. I'll have to tell her all about this when I go home. How I met a young fellow named—but you haven't told me who you are yet."

"Boone. Dan'l Boone. But everybody calls me Dan."

"Well," George murmured, "I'm mighty thankful I met you —and that you know a thing or two about fishing. I just hope we can find Brent and Tucker in the morning. I—I feel sort of uneasy about them."

"Oh, we'll find 'em without no trouble," Dan assured him. "I reckon they're campin' with the Squire right now."

Dan, tired as he was, lay awake a long time, staring dreamily into the campfire. He was thinking of the high wall of blue mountains he had seen toward the west that morning and wondering what lay beyond. It was a mystery no white man knew anything about. Well—and some day soon now—he would cross that wall and find out for himself.

Elizabeth Coatsworth

MARY SILVER

ILLUSTRATED BY *James Ponter*

IT WAS late afternoon of an August day in 1725, and the Indian village of Saint Francis was filled with the stir of many returns: men returning from hunting and women from their work in the cornfields at the edge of the forest; even the children came running singly and in groups up from the Chaudière River, where they had been swimming and fishing or helping with the drying of the many eels that lay on the clean pebbles and the racks. The kettles in the long bark houses were boiling, and sinewy hands stretched toward the wooden bowls to fill them with succotash and venison.

Kanaskwa, the slave, was braiding her hair with an eelskin dyed scarlet. Except for its red and the bright blue of her eyes, she seemed in the dusky firelight of the long house like a girl made of doeskin: brown hair, brown face, and brown fringed dress and leggings were all much of one color. She was nearly fifteen, tall and well-made, but not pretty. It was for her voice that she was known in the village and valued by her master, Sawatis—that voice which sounded like a brook when she spoke and like a bird when she sang.

She was singing now to herself, a ritual song:

> "Deep the dew-water falls,
> No one comes close to me!
> Where are you, whippoorwill?
> Why am I waiting now,
> Calling you, calling you?"

"Come, the kettle is hot," said her mistress.

Kanaskwa swung her newly plaited braids in place with a

quick movement of her head and turned toward the fire where
Sawatis and his family were already seated on their blankets at
one end of the room which had three doors and sheltered three
families. But before the girl could move forward a child darted
in at another entrance.

"Kanaskwa," he said urgently, but in a low voice. "Quick!
The soldiers are coming for you again!"

Even as he spoke the girl turned and ran toward the nearest
door, but as she pushed aside the deerskin over the entrance a
tall young man in an English uniform entered, almost colliding
with her, and before she could twist past him, caught her firmly
by the wrist.

"Aha, my little fox!" he exclaimed in the Indian tongue. "Now
we have you, I think."

Blue eyes looked into gray for an instant, then the girl tore
her wrist free by a sudden fierce motion and whirled, only to
be caught at the shoulder by a hand swift as her own and pulled
back.

The Indians had not stirred from the blankets where they sat. They were eating as though nothing had happened.

Abruptly Kanaskwa gave up the struggle and stood quietly with expressionless face.

"That is better, wildcat," said the young man. "As far as I am concerned you could stay with the Indians forever, but the gentlemen in Boston have different ideas." He turned to her master. "I am sent by the commission again, Sawatis, and have brought the customary redemption money with me," he said, "though really you don't deserve it for the number of times you have hidden this girl, even though you knew the French governor himself had ordered her return to her family."

Sawatis looked at him quietly. "How are we to know of the affairs of Quebec? I go on hunting trips now and then in the forest, and the slave goes with me. But she is worth more than you have given: she is good with the corn and dresses a doeskin well. Besides that she sings. Kanaskwa, sing that we may hear you."

"I will not sing for these white thieves," answered the girl.

"You will do as I command," said her master.

Kanaskwa shrugged her shoulders wearily, and staring at the fire began to sing, making no effort to sing well, but her voice was beautiful in spite of her, and the house was filled with the low haunting music, so that the Indians at their fires stopped what they were doing to listen to her, and the soldiers in the doors forgot their grinning, and a softness came over the gray eyes of Colonel Caleb Greene.

> "Catching the darkness up,
> I hear the Eagle-bird
> Pulling the blanket back
> From the east, sleeping still.
> How swift he flies, bearing the sun
> to the morning!"

When she was silent, Colonel Caleb cleared his throat. He was a very young officer, just past his twentieth birthday.

"You are right, Sawatis," he said. "Here's another pound out

161

of my own pocket. But not another penny," he added, as the Indian opened his mouth to protest. "Don't forget I have the governor's warrant for fetching home Mary Silver, called Kanaskwa, the slave, and soldiers to carry it out. There's a new peace between France and England."

The Indian grinned and struck hands on the bargain.

"She's a good girl, but needs the stick," he remarked philosophically.

"Come along, Mary Silver," said Colonel Caleb. "If you have anything to bring with you, hurry and get it ready."

"I have nothing," she answered.

Her mistress came to her side with a blanket of wolfskins.

"Take this with you my daughter," she said with tears in her eyes. "Long shall I miss you in the field and in the lodge and in all the tasks of the day."

"Oh, do not let them take me, my mother," cried the girl suddenly with a sob.

"We can do nothing, my child," said the woman. "May thy road be straight. Farewell."

"Farewell," said Kanaskwa, holding up her head. "I shall never forget you. Some day I shall come back."

She looked about once at the Indians who looked at her, a long look from many pairs of black eyes that seemed to be saying:

"We shall be waiting. Come back to the corn and the forests. Come back, Kanaskwa."

Colonel Caleb made a gesture, and the girl walked to the door and out into the dusk of the village, while a soldier stepped to each side of her and laid a hand on her arm. The village was almost deserted, but from within the houses she heard the voices that she knew so well, and from beyond the willows sounded the great waterfall that had sung day and night in her ears.

Canoes with paddlers waited for them at the landing beach. Not until they were well out in the river did the hands leave her arms. The men talked together in French which she could not understand, as they paddled from the Chaudière into the wide

162

current of the Saint Lawrence, and slowly the sunset light faded out of the sky, and the evening star shone in the west, and then one by one the great constellations appeared. No one paid any attention to her, sitting in the center of the canoe, a prisoner among strangers, until at last Colonel Caleb turned about and spoke cheerfully. As she did not answer, he looked closely into her face in the starlight.

"Why, my child, you're shivering," he said in the Indian. "You would think we were enemies! It is to your own mother I am taking you, Mary Silver."

In the dim light she looked back at him, fearful and hostile. Did she not know what awaited her, never again to be allowed to step foot outdoors, to be tied into clothes that were a torture, and beaten because she did not know how to bake bread and pray as the Boston people prayed? Had not the Indians often told her?

If she was to be ill-treated, Colonel Caleb was slow to begin, waiting, she felt sure, until he had her away from Quebec and entirely at his mercy. Here there was still a chance that some-one might rescue her and send her back to the Indians, but in the French town no one paid any attention to a blue-eyed girl

163

in Indian clothes, for Indian prisoners were no rarity. Colonel Caleb took her to an inn where the innkeeper's wife bathed her and dressed her in European clothes and did up her hair under a French cap.

Then she took her down to Colonel Caleb in the inn parlor.

"Now, sir, where is your Indian girl?" she asked.

"Bless us," said the colonel, "I would never have known you, Mary Silver. Will you dine with me this evening?"

There was a twinkle in his eye as he looked at her. He was making fun of her, playing with her because she was in his power.

She met his look with her blazing blue eyes.

"A squaw does not eat with braves," she said.

"We are not squaws and braves, Mary Silver," he answered, his eyes twinkling more than ever.

Surely his apparent good nature was only to put her off her guard. She looked at him, defiant and forlorn.

"Kanaskwa!" he said sharply. "I am your master now. Sit down as I have bidden you." And the girl sat down. "Eat!" he said, and she ate, watching him carefully to see how he used his knife and fork and spoon and then making no mistakes.

He tried to talk, but she would not respond.

"I am to get your brother Nathaniel tomorrow," he said at last.

She could not keep the look of interest out of her eyes. Did she really have a brother, she wondered, or was he lying to her for some reason she did not understand?

"He has been as hard to get as you," Colonel Caleb went on. "This is the third time I have been here to Quebec after you two. Sawatis always got wind of my arrival and took to the woods; and the Tardieus, the French people who bought Nathaniel from the Indians soon after he was captured, claimed that the boy was dead. They had him hidden in Montreal, but I heard of it. And tomorrow the governor has commanded that he be brought here."

Dinner was finished, and he folded his arms and sat looking into the fire. Kanaskwa watched him. He was one of the Boston

164

men whom the Indians said were liars and thieves, all treacherous and cruel. He did not look to be these things, but young, courageous, and kind. Even so, she was prepared to believe the worst of him. For Indian stories told of being deceived by fine words and appearances, following some magician met in the forest and being lost forever. Perhaps the Boston men were like that.

She had almost forgotten that she, herself, was of their race.

The next morning she woke early in her high room, and glanced about, astonished to be alone, for she was accustomed to the Indian encampments where everyone—men, women, and children—slept crowded close together. She ran to the door, but it was, as she knew, locked on the outside. She ran to the little window, but she could only see a handful of sky and a bit of cobbled street below and the crowded houses opposite. The smells and the sounds were different. She was sick with homesickness for the things she knew and the ways to which she was accustomed. Here not a bird sang, not a breeze stirred in the trees; she was trapped, betrayed, and miserable.

She walked lightly about the room, testing the door to see if she might open it, examining the narrow window and the roof to see if there were a possible means of escape. In the darkness of the night before, when the landlady had brought her back to her room, she had taken off the French clothes and dressed herself again in her doeskin trimmed with beads and dyed porcupine quills. She had slept on the floor on the wolfskin blanket, disdaining the softness of the bed. How alone she felt, uprooted from the forest and river!

For several hours she stood by the little window looking out and watching, concentrating all her restlessness on the perceptions of her senses. In the middle of the morning, she saw approaching a boy about two years younger than herself, accompanied by soldiers. Her heart gave a great leap. She had seen her own reflection often enough in pools and kettles of water and was sure that this boy looked like her, but younger and less reserved. Surely this was Nathaniel, her brother, and at last she had someone who belonged to her.

165

In a short time Colonel Caleb sent the landlady to fetch Kanaskwa down. She exclaimed upon seeing the girl again in her Indian clothes. The colonel also gave a laugh at seeing her.

"Good morning, Kanaskwa," he exclaimed. "Here is your brother Nathaniel," and then speaking in French said to the boy, "and this is your sister Mary who has lived with the Indians."

The two looked at one another eagerly but there was an awkwardness between them, a brother and sister who could speak no word of each other's language.

"But soon," the boy said, smiling eagerly, "we shall be embracing our own mother, and already I have a dear sister!" As he spoke, he moved his hands rapidly like a Frenchman, trying to express his meaning, which Colonel Caleb was forced to translate. Kanaskwa smiled at him sadly.

"I shall go back!" she murmured.

"Eat your breakfast, children," the colonel said in two languages. "Now that you are both here, the sooner we get over the formalities and sail, the better."

From the deck of the sloop, *Perseverance*, Mary Silver, still in her Indian clothes, disconsolately watched Quebec fade from sight and the distant shores of the river slip by as they sailed down with the tide. It seemed as though she had always known those mountains and that great river and the dark forests along its banks. She thought of jumping overboard and trying to swim to shore, but Colonel Caleb's eyes were on her, and besides, she knew that she would never reach the bank. Nathaniel was soon helping the sailors, running errands, hauling rope, taking his turn at the tiller, but Mary Silver stood looking at no one, watching always the land they were leaving. She started and winced at a touch on her shoulder.

It was Colonel Caleb again, who sat down on the rail near her, one boot swinging.

"Tell me," he said, "why do you love the Indians? I have spent several years at the trading posts and have acted often as interpreter among them. I understand their customs. Now, it is usual when taking prisoners, especially children, to adopt

166

The door of the farmhouse opened, and a woman ran out.

them into the tribe. Why were you not adopted? Why do they still call you Kanaskwa, the slave, after ten years?"

The girl hid her face.

"Answer, Kanaskwa!" he said with authority.

"I would not!" she exclaimed. "They had killed my father. I can remember him lying on the ground, stripped and bleeding. I would not be adopted!"

"And yet," he exclaimed, "you fought like a wildcat to stay with them!"

"That is different," she flashed back. "I am afraid to go to the white people. My heart is sick for the things I know—"

She stopped, looking at him desperately.

"You are a fool, Mary Silver!" he said. "All your life with the Indians you have been beaten and made to do the heaviest work because you could not forget a dead father, and now when the chance comes to go back to your mother and your own kin, you sicken and grieve for these same men who killed him! You are too loyal, or not loyal enough! You walk with your eyes on the trail behind you! Look forward, Mary Silver, and take hope!"

"It is not in my head," she whispered, "it is in my heart where words cannot reach."

Every day Colonel Caleb talked to her of New England, trying to interest her and make her forget Saint Francis.

"You will like milking the cows," he said.

"Do they live in the house?" she asked.

"No," he answered, smiling, "they have their byres in the winter, and in the summer they stay in the fields."

"But I shall not be allowed to go to the fields."

"What foolish talk is this?" he exclaimed. "When your work is done you may go abroad as much as you like, I warrant."

She shook her head, her face turned toward the northwest whence she had come.

It was a fine bright day when they sailed into the quiet water of Pemaquid Harbor. The gulls were making a great commotion with the outgoing tide, and a kingfisher scolded at them from a dead oak tree. Nathaniel exclaimed with delight over everything, bidding a warm but hasty good-bye to the crew.

167

They spent the night at the tavern near the fort and in the morning hired three horses.

The farm where Mrs. Silver lived with Jacob Rising, her brother, was twenty miles away. Colonel Caleb would not be back at Pemaquid until the next night, but the *Perseverance* was to wait for him.

As far as she could remember, Mary Silver had never ridden a horse, but she was strong and supple and learned as soon as her brother the management of her mount.

With the motion of that strong body under her, and the joy of solid land beneath them and forest about them, an unthinking wildness seized the girl, and half in an access of gayety and half in earnest, she urged her horse to a canter. If she could only outrun the others and follow the hunting trails north and north until she got back to the Indian village.

But Colonel Caleb's horse overtook hers. His hand was on the bridle.

"You will tire your poor beast," he said with a grim smile. "I gave you the old horse, Kanaskwa."

But even if she could not escape, she could be happy for a little while, and she rode singing the Indian songs that she knew, while the other two listened amazed as always by the beauty of her voice.

By evening, when they came to the clearings of the Sheepscot, she was tired. Colonel Caleb inquired the way, and faces peered up at them as they sat in their saddles.

"Aye, they favor the Rising side of the family," said the woman of the house where they had inquired. "This will be a happy day for Alice Silver when her children come home."

"Aye, a happy day," said Colonel Caleb.

Now they had come to a farm running down to the river, and a man unfastened his oxen from a cart, waved to them, and hurried toward the house, leaving the patient animals standing where they were. The door of the farmhouse opened, and a woman ran out at the sound of the hoofs.

"Oh, my children! My children! Thank God you are come home!" she cried. "Mary! Nathaniel!" she began weeping and laughing, holding up her arms in the dusk as they slipped from their saddles to kiss her.

"Mother!" said Nathaniel—and the girl murmured something in Indian.

By this time their uncle had run up.

"A fine-looking pair of colts," he said to Colonel Caleb. "Now there'll be youth in the house, and my sister will have her own again!"

For a little while the bustle covered the awkwardness, but when they all sat down at the trestle table, it seemed strange that there were mother, daughter, and son, no one of whom could talk to any of the others. Colonel Caleb, who seemed preoccupied, acted as interpreter, but after a while conversation lagged. Everything—the blessing at the table, the food, the clothes, the furniture, the very feel of the air—was unknown to

169

Mary Silver. She felt her heart sinking and sinking. At dawn Colonel Caleb would go. Then she would be like a deaf and dumb person until she had learned this rumbling speech.

Something moved its sinuous length along the hearth, and Mary caught up the poker, but her uncle seized her arm, while everyone laughed.

"It is only an animal like a dog," explained the colonel. "It is called a cat and feeds on milk."

She dropped the poker, crimsoning with shame at having made herself ridiculous.

"They are very like the wildcats in the woods," added the colonel quickly, "and everyone knows, my sister, that *they* are dangerous."

Mary Silver shot him a grateful look from her blue eyes. Bedtime came early, for though the mother would gladly have looked at her redeemed children for hours, even she could see that they were almost exhausted.

When the girl said good night to Colonel Caleb, she added in a low voice: "My older brother, before we part, forgive me for all the trouble I have caused you."

"You have more than made up for any trouble, child," he exclaimed warmly. "But I shall see you before I go in the morning? And I'll visit you often—now that we are friends."

"You are good," she said very low, and before he could speak again, she had slipped silently out behind her mother who led the way with a lighted candle.

But Mary Silver was determined that by morning she would be far from the place on her way to freedom. This gentle, kind-faced woman was her mother, yet she could remember nothing of her: she was no more than a stranger. Mary had been stolen when she was six years old. Her mother had chanced to be at a neighbor's on an errand. Mary could remember seeing the sheep huddle together in a corner of the field and hearing her father say, "What ails the beasts, I wonder?" She remembered his dead body. That was all of her old life: there remained no memory of house and hearth, of spinning wheel and stable to make her return to her home easier for her and to deaden her

170

longing for the hard, casual, dangerous life she knew so well.

She could hear voices below as she knelt by the window in the room they had given her. When all were asleep she would steal out of the house and follow the north star toward the Penobscot. She would take food and in three or four days she would come on Indian villages where she could make herself known. She would go with the next party up the river toward the Saint Lawrence, and perhaps in a few weeks, at any rate by spring, she would be back at Saint Francis.

Outside the summer night was full of the sound of crickets. The stars wheeled slowly westward and a loon gave its melancholy cry from the river. She could hear the cattle moving a little in their stalls in the barn beyond the ell and the stamping of a horse.

A woman's voice was singing, softly and happily, a foolish old song:

"Alas! my love, you do me wrong
To cast me off discourteously,
And I have loved you so long,
Delighting in your company.
Green-sleeves was all my joy,
Green-sleeves was my delight. . . ."

Mary Silver did not understand the words, but the tune she understood. It brought back all the past. Suddenly she remembered a world of things, of lying in her mother's arms while her mother sang, of her doll Betsy who had fallen down the well, of Spot the old hound, and yellow Grizel the cow, all these came back, the singing, the spinning wheel, safety, and love. Now everything that had happened since seemed like a dream and lost its importance. The tears choked her—all her stoicism melted in a tender sorrow to the sound of her mother's singing; the last fear and distrust, the last memory of the lies that the Indians had told her flowed away with her tears.

There was much that her mind did not understand, but suddenly, unexpectedly, her heart was at home.

172

A frontier boy encounters
a savage panther.

Russell Gordon Carter

OLD SLY EYE

ILLUSTRATED BY *Lorence Bjorklund*

IT WAS a May evening in the year 1675. Alone in his father's log house on the northern edge of Dover township in the province of New Hampshire, Alben Hastings lit the lantern and opened his worn copy of *The Pilgrim's Progress.* Suddenly a loud commotion sounded in the direction of the barn—mad squeals, and frightened bellowings, and the hollow thudding of hoofs. Leaping erect, he seized his musket and, lantern in hand, went racing outside.

He was within a dozen yards of the barn, the wind singing in his ears, when the moon rolled from beneath a formation of ragged clouds, and he checked himself abruptly. There beside the shed lay the recently born calf, and over it crouched a big catlike creature, its solitary eye gleaming, its great round tufted tail weaving savagely to and fro—a panther.

Dropping the lantern, Alben raised the musket and fired, only to see the creature leap sidewise, apparently unhurt. The next instant it swept past him and vanished in the deep shadows between the house and the woods.

The boy clenched his teeth. "Old Sly Eye!" he muttered angrily, and his thoughts went swiftly back to the morning, two weeks earlier, when his father had set forth with Mr. Stephen Wainright on a trapping expedition beyond the Piscataqua.

"Yes, my lad," John Hastings had said then, "I know how much you would like to come along, but 'tis your duty to stay behind and look after your mother and sister. And mind ye keep a good watch over the livestock! I wouldn't want to come home and find Old Sly Eye had done to us what he's done to others."

Alben strode to where the calf was lying. It wasn't his fault that Old Sly Eye had managed somehow to break into the barn, for his father himself had said the barn was reasonably secure against varmints. The calf lay motionless—there was no question that it was dead. Within the barn the cow and the two oxen were still stamping about and letting out occasional bellows, but the boy was not so much concerned with them; they were safe and unhurt.

As Alben continued to stare at the calf, he thought of other plunderings within the township—cattle and swine slain by the big one-eyed panther that often killed for the mere sake of killing. Ever since the previous autumn Old Sly Eye had eluded the bullets and traps of the angry settlers—and tonight he, Alben Hastings, had had an easy shot at it and had failed to bring it down!

Well, regrets wouldn't help. Since the calf was dead, it would serve as food, and therefore the thing for him to do was to hang it on a tree or against the barn, high enough so that nothing could get at it. At the cabin—up in the loft, where he and his father were accustomed to sleep—there was a coil of rope he could use. Returning to the lantern, which had gone out, he picked it up and started for the house.

In the south, silver-edged clouds were racing past the moon. He wondered what the hour might be. Perhaps his mother and Rebecca would soon be coming home from the Wainright cabin, a mile or so to the west. They had gone over to help care for old Mrs. Wainright, who had fallen and broken a leg.

The door to the log house was swinging and creaking on its hinges, and as he shouldered his way inside, the wind caught it and thrust it shut behind him. Striding to the fireplace, he groped for the powder horn and bag of shot on the high mantel and reloaded the musket.

On the frontier a loaded musket sometimes meant the difference between life and death. After he had set it down, resting the muzzle against the wall, he crossed the hard-packed earthern floor to the ladder leading to the loft. It would be as black as midnight up there, but there was no need to bother with flint

174

and steel. He knew exactly where the rope was hanging.

With quick, sure steps he started up the ladder, but as his hands closed on the top rung he felt his heart tighten and his throat go suddenly dry. Something was in the loft—something heavy enough to cause the boards to creak! He was about to back downward when there was a snarl and a rush of padded feet, and the next instant a heavy body thudded against his shoulder and then hurtled past him, knocking the ladder violently sidewise. With a desperate lunge, Alben clutched at the edge of the loft, and for several seconds after the ladder had crashed to the floor, he clung there, his legs dangling. Then he succeeded in swinging himself upward.

Old Sly Eye! Crouching on the edge of the high platform, Alben felt the tumultuous pounding of his heart as he stared downward into blackness. The panther was over near the door; he could hear it crooning and snarling. He could hear the occasional thump and swish of its long heavy tail against the wall. Presently it moved, and he had a partial glimpse of it in a narrow band of moonlight slanting through an opening in the shutter across the south window. He saw its solitary gleaming eye, the other lost perhaps in an encounter with another panther. Then it vanished again in the blackness, and now he could hear it going round and round the room, hissing and muttering and making other catlike sounds deep within its throat.

Why had Old Sly Eye entered the house? Alben asked himself the question while he was groping about for something with which to defend himself. Was it in hope of finding another victim? Panthers as a rule kept away from humans, yet Old Sly Eye was no ordinary panther. Or was it, perhaps, curiosity that had prompted the creature to enter the partly open door? The boy could not be sure. He knew only that the panther was down there, unable to get out, and that he himself was in danger.

The loft held no weapon or heavy object that could be used as a weapon. In his two hands he held the rope. It was a stout, new, half-inch Portsmouth rope, more than a score of feet long —but what good was it? As he finally tossed it aside, he thought longingly of his loaded musket down near the fireplace.

The panther continued to move here and there, now and again passing through the band of moonlight. Every little while it would snarl in a way that made Alben shiver, and once he thought he heard it sharpening its claws on one of the logs. Or was it trying to reach the loft? The logs that formed the walls were unevenly placed—it might come slithering upward. And he was utterly defenseless, lacking even a knife.

Suddenly, with a feeling of icy water cascading down his spine, he remembered his mother and sister. Why had he not thought of them before? They, perhaps more than himself, were the ones who were in danger! Even at that moment they might be approaching the house. They would open the door and then—

Perspiration bathed his face and neck and armpits. With cold hands clutching one of the posts, he stared downward, lips drawn tight across his teeth. What could he do to warn them? Of course, if he should hear them coming he could shout; yet, even so, Rebecca might think he was joking. He remembered with regret some of the jokes he had played in the past. But it was possible that they might reach the door before he heard them. The thought of the two of them unsuspectingly entering the cabin sent a chill through him. "I must do something!" he said to himself.

Yes, but what? He was a virtual prisoner in the loft. There were no windows, and the only way to get down was either to jump or to slide down the rope secured to a post. In either case, the panther would be waiting for him. Again he thought of his musket. Was there any way he could reach it, perhaps with the aid of the rope? No, the weapon was too far away.

The more he pondered, the more he became convinced that the only thing to do would be to go down the rope and then make a rush for the door. It would take perhaps three seconds to go down the rope, and another three to reach the door—but during that time Old Sly Eye was not likely to be sitting quietly on his haunches! Alben drew his sleeve across his moist forehead. He was strong and active, but what chance would he have in a bare-handed struggle with a powerful panther? Nevertheless there seemed no other way.

Knotting an end of the rope securely round a post, he gathered up the rest of it, ready to toss it downward. His eyes had by now grown more accustomed to the darkness, and he thought he could make out the panther directly below him. He let the rope drop, and an instant later the house resounded to a frightful scream that set his teeth to chattering. He saw the creature bound through the band of moonlight and then heard it snarling over near the door.

While he waited, listening, he fancied he heard distant voices, as if his mother and sister coming through the forest might be talking to each other—or was it merely the sound of the wind? Raising his own voice, he shouted, "Mother! Rebecca! Keep away, there's a panther in the house!" There was no response. He waited a minute or two and then shouted again. Still there was no response. He had the sudden unhappy feeling that perhaps no one could hear him outside the stout log house—that no matter how much he might shout, it would do no good.

The night was silent now, save for occasional gusts of wind and the snarling of the panther and the thumping of its tail against the door. Supposing the door should suddenly open and Rebecca should call, "Alben, are you asleep?" Then the panther would leap and strike—and then—

It was more than he could endure! He must risk his life. He mustn't remain idle another moment. But if only he had a weapon of some sort—anything, even a short stick with which he could thrust! Maybe he could find a stick. He would make another search. It would take only a few seconds.

As he was feeling about in the darkness, his hands encountered the blankets that on cold nights he and his father used for sleeping. There they were, neatly folded against the wall. With a quick exclamation he seized one and shook it out. Here was something perhaps better than a stick! The blanket was thick and heavy—at least it would protect his face.

Holding it loosely over his left arm, he seated himself on the edge of the loft, ready to descend. The panther was still over by the door, and he imagined it waiting for him, teeth bared, claws prepared to strike and to rip. Again he thought of the musket. If only he could get his hands on it!

Still holding the blanket loosely over his left arm, he started downward. His feet had hardly touched the floor when a nerve-shattering scream filled the house and a glistening body flashed toward him through the band of moonlight. Crouching, he flung the blanket out protectingly almost at the instant the panther was upon him.

For perhaps half a minute it seemed that he and the panther and the blanket were all hopelessly entangled. He could feel the rough wool against his face. He could feel the weight of the creature upon him and smell the strong unpleasant odor of it. Then needle-like claws, caught in the folds of wool, were raking his back and shoulders. Lashing out with hands and feet, Alben tried desperately to free himself. A corner of the blanket covered his head. He reached upward, tore it loose, then rolled sidewise, all the while kicking and struggling.

Suddenly he was free! Rolling twice over, he sprang to his feet. The musket over there by the fireplace! Darting across the room, he snatched it up.

At that moment, above the snarls of the panther, still with claws entangled in the blanket, he heard voices outside. It was not the wind, it was not his fancy—the voices were real. With musket raised, he hesitated. Should he risk a shot in the darkness? If he were to miss, it might be fatal, not merely to

178

himself, but also to his mother and sister. No, he must not miss! Racing to the door, he flung it wide and leaped outside.

His mother and Rebecca were crossing the clearing from the western edge of the woods. Catching sight of him in the moonlight, the girl shouted, "Alben, what are you doing?"

He paid no heed to her. He was half a score of yards now from the open door of the cabin, musket raised, jaws set. The seconds passed while he waited, listening to the thumping of his heart.

"Alben!" This time it was his mother. "What is wrong?"

At that moment a great, tawny, glistening shape appeared in the doorway, its solitary eye gleaming. It swung its head first to the right and then to the left. It raised its voice in a prolonged scream. Then spying the boy, it came bounding forward.

A tongue of flame flashed from the musket, and the crash sent the echoes flying. They continued to tremble across the moonlit clearing while the panther lay twitching on the grass.

Alben strode to where it was lying. "Dead," he said to himself. "As dead as the calf!" But there were two bullet marks on the panther, one on the throat and the other on the side of the small narrow head, close to one of the rounded ears! Suddenly he understood. His first shot had not missed, after all! Probably it was that first bullet, momentarily bewildering the creature, which had caused it to seek shelter in the house.

"Alben, Alben! Oh, Alben!"

He turned to confront the others. Both were talking to him at once. "Your shirt, 'tis torn to shreds! And you are bleeding! Oh, Alben, are you badly hurt? Tell us what happened!"

He took a deep breath and then smiled. It was easy enough to smile now! "Not so very much happened," he replied slowly. "Yes, I know I'm a bit scratched an' torn, but after all, nobody could expect to fight Old Sly Eye bare-handed and not get himself hurt a little!" And then while they gazed at him, wide-eyed, he told them the whole story.

AFTER being captured by the Indians, Boone, the early explorer, was forced to live with them as the adopted son of the chief.

James Daugherty

THE SAVING
OF BOONESBOROUGH

ILLUSTRATED BY *Henry C. Pitz*

THE naked Indian children stared in wonder at Daniel Boone, and the lean wolf dogs snarled and snapped, not liking his strange white smell as he sat squinting at the fire in the smoky huts of Chillicothe. He was thinking his white man's thoughts as he watched the tall idle warriors and the bronze squaws grinding corn, scraping the skins, kneading the buffalo robes to make them soft. He had done very well pretending he was an Indian, pretending he was happy and satisfied, and pleasing the great chieftain Moluntha with his clever hunting. He looked wistfully at the fat Indian ponies, thinking of a dash for freedom when the right moment came. They had washed away his white blood in the river, pulled out half his hair, and painted him with strange symbols that meant he was the adopted son of the chief Black Fish. He knew by heart the strange rhythms of the mysterious ceremonial songs and dances. He was quick to share in the red laughter or laments.

One evening he came back tired from tedious labor at the salt licks to find the braves in war paint dancing to the pounding drums and shrill war chants. Sitting in his familiar place, he watched the wild frenzies rise and sway around the flicker-

181

ing campfires. There were five hundred warriors preparing for a surprise attack on Boonesborough. He knew how few were the defenders and that the fort was in bad repair. The whole settlement would be utterly unprepared. His hour had come, and he was ready. Before dawn he slipped out like a shadow and was gone. Now again he was the hunted fox of the wilderness with the red dogs in close pursuit.

"On the 16th I departed before sunrise in the most secret manner and arrived at Boonesborough on the 20th, after a journey of one hundred and sixty miles, during which I had but one meal." Brief autobiography. How did he know the way all the four days and nights with the Shawnee pack one jump behind?

He was not so young as he used to be, but tough and long-winded. When he came at last to the Ohio at full spring flood, he remembered he could not swim. It was a desperate tight spot he had known so often, but the angel of the wilderness showed him a leaky canoe stranded on a sand bar, and he made a swift downstream crossing on the yellow waters to the Kentucky shore that he knew like the back of his hand. Familiar landmarks cheered him. He shot a buffalo and cooked his first meal in four days. He was in sight of Boonesborough. He had kept his rendezvous with destiny.

It was a strange figure that came across the clearing into Boonesborough and said he was Daniel Boone. For weeks they had said Daniel Boone was a goner for sure this time. Even Rebecca's faith had failed, and she had returned with the family to the settlements. Boone was sorry, yet glad, too, for she was safe. His brother Israel and Jemima, his beloved daughter who had married Dick Calloway, were there to give him a warm welcome. But it was no wonder Rebecca had gone. Many a husband and father had never come back across the clearing.

The news of the coming Indian raid roused the settlers to action. The neglected log walls were repaired and everything made ready for an attack, the swift short Indian attack with which the borderers were familiar. But weeks passed and no

Indians were seen. Then another escaped white man brought in news that Boone's flight had delayed the Indians. Boone then took a raiding expedition across the Ohio and burned an Indian village, getting back just a few hours ahead of the great war party of over four hundred Indians with some forty French Canadians under the direction of their officer De Quindre.

There were about fifty men and boys, besides the women and children, behind the log stockade when the Indians surrounded the clearing of Boonesborough. Instead of the usual sudden attack, an Indian came out of the woods with a white flag and by calling back and forth arranged for a parley. Every hour of delay meant a nearer hope of reinforcement coming in from Harrodsburg. Three of the defenders met Black Fish, Moluntha, and Catahecassa near the fort for a powwow. There was talk of friendship and peaceful surrender. The chief promised that the whites would be taken safely on horses to Detroit if they surrendered peaceably. There need be no bloodshed if the Americans would agree to abandon the fort.

Boone said he would explain to his people and in two days give an answer. He was glad to find that the Indians had heard from a white captive that there were several hundred defenders in the fort. The Indians believed their offer of safety was sure to be accepted.

Inside the fort the chances were talked over and argued and weighed after the democratic way of the backwoods. The odds were ten to one and worse against defense, and not a man, woman, or child would be spared if— But the tough cantankerous spirit of the frontier urged: "Go ahead or bust." They would not have been where they were if they had not been stubborn survivors of a rough, tough, restless race who lived and died in their own independent way by the rifle, the ax, the Bible, and the plow. So they sent back the eagle's answer: "No surrender," the answer of the sassy two-year-old baby democracy, the answer of Man the Unconquerable to the hosts of darkness—"No surrender."

The iron-faced chiefs and the ornery Frenchman De Quindre took the answer grimly back to their council, while the settlers got in their cows, corn, and water from the spring without interference from the Indians. The next move was an Indian trick which was perfectly transparent to Boone, but he took the chances of playing it to win time.

The Indians proposed a grand council of nine on each side to sign a treaty of peace, after which they would depart, they said, like lambs. The council sat under the sycamore trees within rifle shot of the fort. At a wave of the hat from the delegates the riflemen in the fort were to open fire and cover the nine men's dash back when trouble started.

All day they sat in the shade and smoked, talked, and ate while a fancy treaty of peace, including a sworn allegiance to the British Crown, was agreed on, to be signed tomorrow at the same place. In the night an ambush of Indians was set around the treaty tree. The next day when the nine appeared from the fort, Black Fish met them with eighteen powerful young braves. After the signing came the two-to-one handshaking. Two Indians grabbed for each white man and a mob jumped from the laurel to finish the job. Then the nine Kentucky wildcats let loose with teeth and claws, and the fur flew. Shooting began and the nine raced for the fort. They had won the first round.

Next day there was a great hubbub in the forest, bugles

184

blowing and orders for retreat bawled out, and the pack horses were seen crossing the river at the ford. But the old border fox in the fort was not fooled. The gates of Boonesborough remained shut, and the Indian trick failed. The real danger was an Indian rush on the gates under a heavy fire from all sides. This was what kept the riflemen waiting and watching at the portholes day and night.

But to charge across the clearing under the fire of Kentucky rifles was so contrary to the Indian way of fighting that all of De Quindre's urging for a mass attack was useless. Instead, the savages remained under cover of the woods, firing continuously. Day and night under the heavy encircling fire of the enemy, the riflemen stuck to their posts, blazing away whenever an inch of Indian hide was exposed to view. The women passed out the scant rations and scarce water, loaded guns when the firing was fast, molded bullets, comforted the children, and prayed the prayers of the pioneer faith. Each slow day under the burning sun was an eternity; each night they thanked the God of their Fathers that some protecting angel had kept the gates.

From high up in a distant tree a sniper began sending bullets inside the fort and Jemima Boone was hit. Boone drew a bead at two hundred yards on the sniper as he was reloading and put a bullet through his head. The figure that pitched from the high tree was black Pompey. Colonel Calloway, of the old school, became irritated at Boone's cautious tactics and contrived an impressive wooden cannon. The roar and smoke of her first shot scared the Indians for about a mile out of range, but when the smoke cleared from her second blast she had burst wide open and was permanently disabled. But she was the wonder of the wilderness as long as she lasted.

More serious was the tunnel which the enemy was driving toward the fort. It carried to the defenders the sinister fear of exploding mines that would breach the wooden walls. Day by day they could hear the digging come nearer. It wore on their strained nerves like the gnawing of a rat in the night.

Hour by hour a week dragged on. In the inky blackness of the seventh night a bright flame suddenly shot across the clearing in a long arc and dropped on a cabin roof. It was the dreadful flaming arrow. Now they were dropping fast on the pine roofs of the cabins. Worse yet, the savages had crept across the clearing in the darkness and started fagot fires against the log palisade on all sides. The spreading glow lit up the clearing as the hungry little flames ran along the shingles. Against the glow the frantic silhouettes of the defenders trying to beat out the flames drew stinging gun fire from the enemy. Suddenly a figure leaped up on a burning roof and in a fury of flame and bullets beat out the fire. When he had finished he calmly jumped down to safety. But the fires along the stockade were taking hold, and the last remaining buckets full of precious water would be of no avail. The riflemen were standing at their

posts holding their fire, waiting for the final mass attack, and women stood clutching their children. To Boone it seemed the last card had been played and lost. As the red light flickered over his set face, suddenly he felt a drop of water strike the back of his hand, and as he looked up, heavy drops struck his face. In a few minutes the God-sent rain streamed down in drenching sheets. The burning stockade hissed, steamed, glowed, and went out. Something beyond human power had saved Boonesborough by the skin of its teeth.

Still the firing from the forest kept up incessantly. No one knew how near the tunnel was, but it seemed almost under their feet. The September pouring rain had soaked everyone to the bone. They would soon be passing around the last ration of food. Hope held desperately to ever slimmer chances. No Indian attack on a fort had ever been known to keep up so long.

Utter darkness of a night of lashing rain set in on the ninth day of the siege. In the fierce movement of the storm it seemed as though the savage demons of all the wild valley had come down for vengeance. It was a blind night when a man could not see the end of his rifle barrel. Nothing now could stop the mass rush of the savages across the clearing. The riflemen stood grimly at their posts in the pouring rain and waited. In the darkness time stopped. They shifted and growled, trying to keep their powder dry, and muttered to each other. At long last the night lifted. Out of the shapeless grayness the world was taking form. The morning came with no firing from the enemy, and the lookouts reported no signs of Indians in the forest. It looked like another false retreat. A scout came back with the news that the Indians were on the march this time for sure.

Then two white men crossed the clearing shouting and waving. One was Simon Kenton who had not been able to get through the lines. It was true that the Indians had gone. A surge of wild joy was in the hearts of Boonesborough when the log gates swung open and let out the starved cattle. There was whooping and firing to welcome eighty backwoodsmen from Harrodsburg, riding in too late for a rescue but in time for the celebration.

Russell Gordon Carter

THE THREE–CORNERED HAT

ILLUSTRATED BY *Kay Lovelace*

A MUSKET shot rang out sharply from the direction of Bemis Heights, the echoes rumbling across the upper Hudson. Seated in his small, flat-bottomed skiff, fishing line in hand, Joel Baldwin shaded his eyes against the almost level rays of the sun and squinted westward. In the stern a loose-jointed brown dog was also squinting toward the shore, its blunt muzzle sniffing the clear air.

"See anybody, Sandy?"

The dog stirred uneasily and continued to sniff.

Joel began slowly to wind up his fishing line. It was not the first time he had heard near-by firing, for it was the summer of 1777, and the armies of Gates and Burgoyne were across the river. But never before had he heard the sound of a musket so close.

Suddenly the dog jumped to its feet and gave a little yelp. The next instant Joel caught sight of a man on the winding road at the base of the Heights. He was running, and as he ran he kept looking back over his shoulder. Joel observed that he was clad entirely in black and wore a black three-cornered hat. A moment later the boy spied three British soldiers in scarlet coats emerge from the woods beyond the road, not more than a hundred and fifty yards behind the fugitive. He saw the leading Redcoat pause and raise his musket, but before he could take aim, the man in the black hat was out of sight round a bend.

Joel sat with hands clutching the gunwale, his heart pounding. The man in black, whoever he might be, was a fast runner, but it hardly seemed likely that he would escape, for a long stretch of straight road lay before him.

189

Perhaps the same thought occurred to the fugitive. At any rate, he suddenly did a strange thing. Still out of sight of his enemies, he snatched off his hat and hurled it into a thick clump of bushes, then ran a few yards and, turning abruptly, plunged into the woods. When the soldiers rounded the bend, he was nowhere in sight. Then one of them shouted and pointed up the slope, and a moment later the three of them disappeared in the woods.

Joel clenched his teeth, expecting presently to see the soldiers come out with their prisoner, but the minutes passed, and nothing happened. The minutes lengthened into a quarter of an hour, and still nothing happened. What did it mean?

Making his way to the bow of the boat, Joel began to haul up the heavy stone that served as anchor. The sky behind the western hills showed pink and gold where the sun had set. He supposed he ought to start down river for home—but over there somewhere on the western shore lay a black three-cornered hat! Seating himself at the oars, he headed the boat toward the shore.

Just where had the man tossed the hat? Joel and Sandy searched the bushes along the road for a considerable time before the dog at last crawled forth from a clump of alders, the hat hanging from his jaws.

"Good old Sandy!"

Joel examined the inside of the crown and was disappointed to find nothing unusual. He set the hat on his head. It fitted him perfectly. Well, that was something! He had always wanted a three-cornered hat.

"Sandy," he called. "Come, boy, let's go home!"

But Sandy, who had gone into the woods, paid no heed to the summons. Joel whistled to him, but still the dog failed to respond. Presently the boy heard him barking excitedly far up the hillside. "Found a woodchuck or somethin'. Reckon I'll have to go and fetch him."

Instead of setting off immediately, however, Joel removed the hat and once more began to examine the inside of the crown. This time he felt the crackle of paper under his fingers.

Paper? Was it customary to pad a hat with paper? Seating himself on a stone, he thrust two fingers under the lining at a place where the stitching was loose. A moment later, he drew forth a small square packet no thicker than a wafer!

He was about to open it when he jumped suddenly to his feet and, setting the hat on his head, thrust the packet hurriedly into his shirt front. Someone was approaching along the road!

As Joel stood waiting, he thought he understood why the man had thrown the hat away. The packet no doubt held something of great importance to the British, and if caught with it, he would be shot as a spy.

Three soldiers in scarlet uniforms came striding around the bend. At sight of the boy, they broke into a run.

"Who are you, and what business have you here?" the leader demanded as they halted in front of him.

Joel moistened his lips. Just what should he say? He was wearing the hat of a man who in all likelihood was a spy, and tucked into his shirt front was a packet that probably contained something of great military value.

191

"Come!" the leader said sharply. "Speak up!"

"My name is Joel Baldwin, and I live down river," the boy replied. "I've been fishing. That is my boat yonder. And," he added as an afterthought, "that is my dog barking in the woods. I reckon he's found a woodchuck."

The leader frowned heavily at him. "Aye, likely enough, but you've not yet told us your business here."

Joel had the uncomfortable feeling that the three Redcoats were looking at the hat and knew it belonged to the man they had been pursuing. With an impulsive movement he took it off and held it in his two hands.

"The truth is, Sir, I came here to search for this hat. You see," he added earnestly, "I was out yonder in my boat and could not help seeing the man you were trying to catch. His hat—er— went into these bushes as he fled toward the woods, and—and, Sir, after a long time had passed and no one appeared again on the road, I thought I would see if I could find it."

One of the soldiers muttered, "The young rebel has told the truth, methinks."

The leader took the hat and began to examine the inside of it. Joel saw his fingers tug at the lining, heard a sudden rip.

Far up the hillside Sandy was still barking. Listening to him, the boy felt a queer emptiness at the pit of his stomach. That was not a woodchuck the dog had found! The character of the barking had changed. It was louder, more furious, as if . . . Joel's throat went suddenly dry. What if the man in black were hiding there in the woods and Sandy had found him!

The leader of the Redcoats flung the hat abruptly to the ground and kicked it from him. Then with a grimy hand he began angrily to mop the perspiration from his face.

One of the other soldiers picked the hat up and tossed it to the boy. "Keep it, young rebel," he said. At the same time he lifted his head and gazed in a puzzled way toward the upper hillside.

The dog was barking more furiously than ever, each succession of barks ending in a high-pitched howl. No, Sandy never would bark like that over a mere woodchuck! As Joel set the hat on his head again, he pictured a man in black breeches and jacket lying in a hollow between two rocks while a brown dog danced about excitedly in front of him.

"That dog of yours makes a deal of noise," the leader remarked.

Joel said, "He's just a young dog, Sir."

One of the other soldiers observed, "Mebbe it's something bigger than a woodchuck he's found."

Joel's knees began to tremble.

The three soldiers looked as if they might be thinking of going into the woods again. Joel moistened his lips and said, "Reckon I'd best fetch the dog. He won't come if I just call."

He hesitated. Then, as none of the soldiers offered an objection, he entered the woods and set off up the slope. In less than a minute he was out of sight, making his way among great tree trunks and through thick masses of low growth. Once he thought he heard the leader calling, but the sound might have been merely the echo of Sandy's barking.

It was almost ten minutes before he came in sight of the dog. Sandy was leaping about at the base of an old rotting maple to the hollow upper part of which a man was clinging—a man wholly in black.

For several seconds he and Joel stared at each other while Sandy, silent now, squatted on his haunches, his sides heaving. It was the man who spoke first, his dark eyes wide with amazement. "Lad, that hat!"

At the same instant from somewhere down the slope came the sound of voices, then the swish of undergrowth. Joel caught his breath. He knew the meaning of those sounds. The soldiers, grown suspicious, were coming up the hill!

"Quick, Sir!" The boy's voice was hoarse with anxiety. "They're coming up through the woods, the Redcoats! Swing yourself to the ground!"

In a moment the man was beside him. "The hat—" he began again.

"Follow me!" Joel interrupted him. "I have a small boat—if we can reach it!" And with Sandy leaping ahead, he set off at

193

a run along the hillside, glancing backward now and again to be sure the man was following.

For perhaps two hundred yards they pushed southward while, farther down the slope, the sounds of the soldiers echoed through the woods. At last Joel turned sharply to the left where a deer trail led through a rocky ravine. Behind, the man was silent, evidently content to put his trust in the young lad who seemed so sure of himself.

The sky overhead was pink with afterglow when they finally reached the base of the hill. Off to the left Joel could see his boat drawn up along the shore. Between it and the edge of the woods lay a narrow stretch of green meadow. No one was in sight, and he ventured cautiously forth. Then beckoning with his hand, he turned and, with Sandy racing beside him, made at top speed for the skiff. As he ran he could hear the stranger's footbeats close behind.

They had almost reached the boat when Sandy, for the pure joy of it, began to bark! Joel struck at him with his hand, but the damage had been done. From up the slope came the sudden sound of angry voices.

"Quick, in you go!" the stranger ordered. Joel seized the dog by the collar and hauled him over the gunwale.

A musket cracked, and a bullet struck the water with a chug and a splash.

"Lie flat, lad, I'll take the oars!" The man in black spoke sharply in a voice of command. "Aye, that's right."

He gave a mighty heave against the bow and then threw himself forward as the craft swung out into the current. Another musket ball chugged into the water, then another. Seizing the oars, the stranger began to row with long, powerful strokes.

With an arm about Sandy's neck, Joel raised his head just as the fourth bullet tossed up a spurt of water within a few yards of the bow. Glancing backward, he saw the three Redcoats on the stretch of green meadow. Two of them were reloading.

In a few minutes the boat was well beyond midstream—a tiny object in the beginning twilight. The two or three shots that followed went wide of the mark.

The stranger murmured, "We be safe!"

Some twenty minutes later, in the gathering darkness, the man in black sent the skiff into a narrow creek mouth overhung with branches. "And now, lad, the hat—"

He had hardly spoken the words when a branch caught under the wide rim of the hat and swept it from the boy's head. Fortunately it landed in the boat, but as Joel picked it up, the stranger, catching sight of the torn lining, uttered a cry of dismay and dropped the oars. "The packet," he began in a shaking voice, "there was a small packet—"

"It is safe, Sir." And sliding a hand into his shirt front, Joel drew the packet forth.

"Eh?" exclaimed the stranger, seizing it. "You—you—"

"I had already taken it from inside the hat," Joel explained. Then while his companion listened, he gave an account of his encounter with the soldiers.

"Lad!" As the stranger spoke he grasped the boy's hand in both his own. "You have done a thing that puts me forever in your debt! This small packet—" He hesitated, then added, "Aye, there be no reason you should not know! It holds important military plans. Ere another hour they will be in the hands of General Gates. Now I must make haste—" And the stranger stepped ashore.

Joel wanted to ask a multitude of questions, but at the moment he could think of only one thing to say.

"Oh, Sir," he called, "the hat, you have forgotten it!"

From the darkness came a low laugh, then the words, "Keep it, lad, in memory of the service you have done your country!"

Joel sat for some time listening to the sounds of footsteps growing fainter and fainter. Who was the black-clad stranger? What was his name? No matter. The boy suddenly grinned and gazed downward at the hat—his hat!

Then, setting it firmly on his head, he pushed the skiff out into the current and began to row toward home.

Laura Benét

HORSESHOE NAILS

ILLUSTRATED BY *Henry C. Pitz*

THE broad Van Tassel farmhouse of West-
chester, New York, was witnessing a busy scene, this blustery
March morning of the year 1777. Day was barely breaking, but
a good horse stood saddled and neighing at the gate; a tall,
stocky young man in Continental uniform was turning to wring
his father's hand and give his mother a parting kiss. Two small
brothers, scarcely a year apart, had run out blubbering to his
horse's head, and a girl in her teens followed them slowly,
keeping close to her mother.

Another boy about thirteen, lean as a lath, watched the pro-
ceedings with dazed eyes. Cornelius Van Tassel, Junior, did not
comprehend as yet what Phineas's going to the war would mean
to all of them. Their Phineas, of whom Father was so proud,
was only nineteen, but he had been right-hand man on the farm.

Cornelius was the clumsy son. It was a source of great irrita-
tion to the father that his namesake was so unlike him. Even
now, his father spoke disapprovingly to him. "Cornelius, stir
those lazy beanpoles of legs and bring your brother's saddlebags! What are you gaping at? Haven't you ever seen anyone
ride before? Make things lighter for the one who's to do the
traveling and the fighting."

Cornelius went willingly enough to fetch the saddlebags and
lift them to the horse's back. He drew a soft sigh. How grand to
be like Phineas! Fearless, resourceful, able to do all the things
he himself could not do. The odd thing was that he felt no
jealousy but adored his brother quite as heartily as his father
did. Just now he took in every detail of the informal fighting

197

dress Phineas wore, the hunting shirt of deer leather, dyed green, and long leggings of the same.

The young soldier-to-be leaped easily to his saddle and took the bridle rein. "I'd best be off," he said gravely. "It's a long way to Peekskill, and eyes that I can't see will be watching, and guns lying in wait for me." Then looking at his brother, "Have a care of them all, Cornelius, while I'm away in the army," he said kindly, "we're patriots here, and their lot is a hard one. Father and Mother, Mary, the boys and little Leah—watch out for them. Remember there'll be one less to protect the farm and you'll have to grow up fast!"

Cornelius nodded, wordless. He wanted to be a patriot, too, but he was timid by nature and not gifted like Phineas. He waved bravely as Phineas swung his three-cornered felt hat. The horse trotted eagerly out of the enclosure and soon showed the road a good pair of heels.

His mother's eyes dimmed, and she went quickly into the house. Cornelius Van Tassel, Senior, as was his usual habit when disturbed, thought of half a dozen different things that might employ his second son's time when out of school.

This year of the American Revolution was black indeed for all the farmers living in Westchester County. It was called the "Neutral Ground" but really was not in any sense neutral. On the contrary, being fairly fertile, it was ravaged by two sets of foraging parties. These were called "Cow Boys" and "Skinners" because they drove off the cows and plundered the farmers of the neighborhood. Some of the robbers came from the British entrenched at Fort Washington; others were hangers-on of the American Army at North Castle and Peekskill, and some, alas, natives of the country itself, looking out for themselves. This guerrilla warfare caused untold evil to the neighborhood. Valuable cattle were driven off, barns set on fire, and innocent householders robbed of every slight treasure and bit of food they possessed.

Cornelius Van Tassel and others of his neighbors whose farms were on the old Sawmill River Road were all ardent patriots. No selfish desire to keep a whole skin in this struggle kept them

198

Cornelius lay on his stomach where he could spy on the highroad.

going. Because they were stanchly for the American cause, they had suffered most from raids and the loss of the crops upon which they were dependent for winter food. Therefore they had formed themselves into a company to defend families and possessions from the Cow Boys and straying parties of Hessian troopers. All who lived in this valley had determined on no compromise with the enemy. So they searched—and found—a rocky refuge on Beaver Mountain west of their settlement, and far enough off to harbor the women and children in case of attack. Here they kept a guard continually posted by a huge boulder called "Sentinel Rock" to give the alarm in case of need.

During the months that followed his brother's departure to join the Continental Army, Cornelius took his turn as watcher on Sentinel Rock. And sometimes he carried messages or provisions from one patriot to another, though these errands became increasingly difficult. Gloom had crept over Cornelius Van Tassel, Senior, when Phineas left him. Since that day he had grimly sent his second son on continual and even dangerous missions, to train him in self-reliance and to prevent his dreaming.

On a late September day in 1777, Cornelius was riding briskly, though very uneasily, home through his native country. He had been on an errand to his Uncle Dirck's to fetch a supply of flour and meal which the family badly needed. A wiry supple boy would not ordinarily have cast backward glances over his shoulder or urged his horse through gullies and darkening patches of woods. But today's trip had not been either safe or easy.

Young Cornelius was actually frightened. Once he was sure he saw a flash of bright red in the bushes and, instantly, he crouched close to the horse's head, digging determined heels into his flanks. It might be a red-coated grenadier! But the glint of color proved to be only a branch of maple leaves. Again, as the boy rode, he turned away his head that he might not see a shattered bridge or a wrecked and partially destroyed farmhouse. Even the once familiar road on which his horse was trotting had been almost obliterated by the continual marching of

199

soldiers' feet. Tramp, tramp, tramping for many months! He shivered to think of what had happened in a brief two years to everything that had been secure and sound in his life.

Suddenly, without any warning, he began to snuffle in a half-hearted fashion; then jerked the sleeve of his homespun hunter's shirt across his eyes, ashamed of such weakness.

"If I were only big and strong like Phineas, then I'd show Father that I want to help my country, too," thought Cornelius to himself. His nerves were worn down by the constant anxiety at home. He knew his mother trusted him, but his father's frequent scoldings and reproofs struck at his heart. And the trip today, so full of peril, had taken every bit of courage he could muster. He was riding the last horse left in his father's barn, the one ordinarily used for plowing. Should this animal be captured, there would be no means of getting about except on foot. But fortune had favored him, and it was with grateful relief that

200

he at last turned in at the familiar gate with full saddlebags.

His father spied him first through the barn door and came slowly out. His stern, harassed face relaxed somewhat. "Well, boy," he said in a gratified tone, "the luck was with you today. It cannot last. Make haste into the house with your provisions. Could Dirck and Ann spare flour and meal for porridge?"

"Yes, Father. They did not lose their crop as we did. But they have been beset many times!"

"I know it," said his father briefly. "It was good of them to spare us anything. Now the question is where to bestow it. I wonder had we better hide it here or near the Sentinel Rock."

Young Cornelius made no answer. He knew his father expected none. When he had stabled his horse, he threw down hay for him and then followed his father into the house, hurrying to warm himself at the log fire in the great spacious fireplace.

His mother, who had come forward joyfully to greet him, gave her son a reassuring smile. "At least we still have enough wood to burn," she said. She glanced ruefully at the gaps in the frame of the fireplace where the carved woodwork had been hacked by one party of raiders. Luckily the great andirons still stood, though many fireplaces in adjoining farms were without them.

Nevertheless, her heart was heavy as she went back to her place in the far corner of the room where the baby's cradle was rocking to and fro. She began singing gently an old proverb, "For want of a nail the shoe was lost, for want of a shoe the horse was lost, for want of the rider the battle was lost, for want of the battle the kingdom was lost. And all for want of a horseshoe nail." Her voice dropped sadly at the end.

Cornelius wondered why the kingdom (what kingdom was it?) could be lost for want of an old rusty nail? But he gave himself up to contented basking by the fire. Mary, the elder girl, was already stirring up their evening porridge, made possible by Uncle Dirck's contribution of meal.

For about an hour until supper was ready (and a good supper it was tonight), the Van Tassel family had peace. From the

201

father seated in his strong armchair pulling at his pipe to the pleasant-faced mother, and the younger children sprawled on the hearth, all was serene.

While they sat quietly by the fire, one of the younger boys said curiously, "Father, didn't one of the old Van Tassels once own a fortune? Wasn't our family rich after we first settled in America?"

His father puffed at his pipe. "No Van Tassel is prosperous in wartime; he is too busy fighting his neighbors' battles," he answered. "There was an old story, more legend than truth, that I heard as a child about my great-grandfather, old Jacob, who lived to be ninety-three. He struck good bargains in sheep and cattle. In his last years he lived alone except for a farm helper and became a miser. One day he died out here in the woods not far from this house. He had been seen, half an hour before, counting and muttering over gold pieces that he thought were leaves. At least so we were told. No truth in it, say I."

Small Peter, fascinated, listened breathless and hopeful for more of the legend, as did they all; but just then Mary called them to supper. Sitting around the oak table on which plates and mugs had been set, everyone ate, and ate heartily. In these highly uncertain days there was no telling when the next meal would be.

"You did your duty well," whispered his mother to Cornelius who always sat next her. She pressed his hand to show her approval and won a smile in return. However, Cornelius Junior noticed that his father's mouth wore a set expression and that he stopped often during the supper to listen to any sound the wind might bring.

Hark! He was not disappointed. Danger was on the way. Suddenly a long, clear, ringing blast on a bugle, blown by the guard stationed on the top of Sentinel Rock, warned them that a detachment of British soldiers had been sighted and was slowly but surely advancing. One boy dropped the scone he was buttering, another hastily scooped up the last of his porridge.

Cornelius said nothing but turned white as paper. "Father,"

he finally gulped, "can we get Mother and the children to the mountain in time and save what food I brought?" Cornelius had a way of asking at the wrong moment that irritated his father most.

"Hurry and help," was the only reply, in his father's gruffest tones.

The next few minutes turned the Van Tassel homestead into a scene of hasty and concentrated preparation. Food was gathered up and blankets. To Mother and the baby was given the one horse which should by rights have had a good evening's rest. The two cows and the few pigs were driven into the woods at the mountain's foot in the hope that they would not be discovered.

Cornelius Van Tassel, Senior, was joined by his neighbors, all excited and all carrying flintlock muskets. Soon a procession of women and children, escorted by their men, was wending its way up the Beaver Mountain trail to an inaccessible place. Here a natural rock platform with an overhanging precipice on the western side would protect them from bad weather. Earlier in the season they had brought up some rough tents and a few straw mattresses for the children. So they pitched camp. Most of the folk in their zeal to escape had forgotten to bring sufficient food with them. Should the soldiers be Delancey's Rangers and quarter themselves in one of the farmhouses for several days, the outlook was serious.

As she marshalled her family, Cornelius' capable mother said to him, laying her hand on the horse's flank, "I shall follow you quickly. Mary, come, take my place on the horse and hold the baby. I must hide a few things in a safe place. Cornelius, do you know of a hole somewhere for my best pewter teapot and silver spoons and pieces of plate?"

"Yes, I'll hide them for you, Mother. I know just the place! You join the others." Though shaking with fright, Cornelius received the package of precious things she gave him with great pride. Following at the tail end of the procession of fugitives, he dove into the woods that skirted the mountain's lower slopes. Running along a path he knew, he soon came to a tremendous

204

oak tree with wide-spreading roots. Here he dug frantically with a sharp stick to make an opening between the roots big enough for the fat teapot and the heavy pieces of plate.

As he scratched at the earth which came up in handfuls, his fingers plunged into a hole so deep that he nearly lost his balance and toppled into it. Then, to his terror, they touched something solid that was not a tree root nor a chunk of wood—something that felt like rough cloth. Oh, how heavy it was! He pulled and jerked with all his strength until he was soaked in perspiration. But he got more than he bargained for. Up came a heavy, dirty bag of some dark canvas, covered with mold and

tied tightly with a drawstring. Cutting this with his knife, Cornelius dared only snatch a hasty glance at what it contained.

Money? Yes, but what was it worth? Tarnished pieces that might be gold, medals and tokens! Some of the pieces had the head of a strange man on them. None of the coins were like those he had seen and handled. Probably they were very old. He dared wait no longer. Treasure or not, it was *his* now. He would not tell anyone; they might laugh. So Cornelius carefully buried his mother's pieces, thrust the bag back where he had found it, and scrabbled earth over them.

He was only just in time for he heard a long and peremptory whistle, that whistle his father used for calling members of his family together. His father must already be vexed at his absence. Half in a dream, vowing to return as soon as possible, Cornelius plunged on through the woods and up the mountain.

Now he remembered his mother's slower progress. What would she do if the rough soldiers came while she was still lingering about the house? The thought that she might have been delayed made his heart anxious. His fears for her increased when he reached the mountaintop and saw that she was not there with the others.

Afraid of angering his father, who was giving directions to some of the men, Cornelius ran to a sympathetic neighbor, Mistress Romer.

"Where is my mother? Have you seen her?" he gasped.

"Why, no, Cornelius! Where is she? I was just wondering if she had . . ."

Cornelius began to sob frantically. "She has stayed behind to hide things. Oh, why did she not start? I am fearful for her. I'm going back to help."

"Nay, nay, lad." Kind Mistress Romer grasped his arm. "You can do naught for your mother now. It's too late. Perhaps she had some good reason for staying behind. See, if you look down, you will see that the raiders are almost at the house! If you go after them, all of us here will fall captive to the enemy."

And then Cornelius Van Tassel, Senior, said in a bleak voice, "Oh, my wife, my wife! They must be holding her prisoner."

Indeed, to those who watched on the mountain in the autumn dusk, the situation looked perilous for Mistress Christina Van Tassel. Even with a spyglass, they could get but an inkling of what was taking place at the Van Tassel farmhouse. Soldiers with bright red facings on their coats had ridden clattering up and surrounded it.

Father Van Tassel looked the picture of woe but, when another half hour had passed, he said to Mary, "Your mother is a very wise woman. Look at the smoke rising! She must be cooking their supplies for them."

A column of friendly blue smoke began to rise upward through the dusky pall of evening. It was—it seemed—like his cheerful mother's signal to young Cornelius. "Yes," he thought to himself, "she must have lighted the big Dutch oven by the chimney, the one she uses on baking days."

He was interrupted by his father's gruff tones, "Stop mooning and help feed these children."

Indeed, here was a problem. There was a large troop of hungry children, and not every family had been forehanded enough to eat a good supper before word came to hurry to the mountain. Cornelius ran back and forth between the tiny cooking fire and the group huddled near it, making himself useful and praying that his mother was safe. The dark and chill of night settled down on them. Though many had empty stomachs, the fugitives finally fell soundly asleep for want of something better to do.

But Cornelius Junior's trouble weighted his heart and kept him dozing and waking. At dawn he sat up. His father, after sitting most of the night by the fire, was at last dozing. The spyglass had been left hard by. Cornelius picked it up and examined the house. Yes, his mother had put out a signal, one of which she had often spoken, that was to be a sign between them. An inconspicuous white rag was tied to a tree on the off side of the farm where the soldiers would not notice it.

Cornelius breathed a tremendous sigh of relief. Now he no longer feared for his mother's safety. What was more, he felt sure she would help them. All the food had been eaten but a little buttermilk and pork and a few half-spoiled apples. It might be possible to milk the cows if they had not strayed too far into the woods. He would make that his job and see his mother if possible.

Like an Indian treading cautiously on dry leaves, Cornelius stalked down the mountainside, threaded the woods, and reached the stone wall at the very foot of Beaver Mountain. Yes, he had guessed rightly, and that was such a comfort. On the other side of the wall was a queer, rough-looking bundle. He gathered it quickly in his arms and put his nose to it. Joy! Loaves of fresh-baked dark bread, rye and Indian, and a huge piece of cooked beef. Eggs, too.

He did not know that his devoted mother had been set by the enemy to bake for them as well as to roast the ribs of an ox in the big Dutch oven. Her hungry family and friends had weighed heavily on her mind. As soon as the soldiers were stuffing themselves and she could escape from the house an instant, she had slipped over to the stone wall and dropped her offering on the other side of it, hoping that Cornelius would come. Now he saw her! She stealthily waved her white apron from the door and instantly disappeared.

"Those cows next. I will find them," he said. First he had to climb up the winding path to the platform, deposit his store of bread and beef, and secure some article that would serve as a milking pail. A battered tin relic left behind on their last flight was all he could get. Hurrying with it to the woods, he at last found one of the cows caught by her horns in a bush. Soon milk was streaming into the pail.

At breakfast, several neighbors said, "Van Tassel, you have a capable son. No grass grows under his feet." But Van Tassel only grunted and replied briefly that he missed his pipe and hoped he would find it on his return home. He was not ready to give Cornelius any word of praise.

The British troopers found it to their interest to cool their heels in the comfortable Van Tassel homestead for several days. Meanwhile, a daily supply of food prepared by the mother of the family reached the party on the mountain, thanks to Cornelius, the messenger, who began to feel rather pleased with himself. Eventually the British became bored and took themselves off whence they had come.

Returning neighbors carried heavy and grieving hearts. Cornelius had listened to many tales of burned homes and pillaged barns that should have had hay enough for the coming winter.

"Even the Scarsdale tavern was burst open and sacked," one farmer related. "The troopers forced the doors because they heard that one poor, lone cow had been hidden in the parlor. The tavern keeper was trying to save his children's milk. The family saw her driven off for beef with much rude jesting."

"These are sorry and troublous times," said Father Cornelius gathering his wife and children around him by his own hearth again. "But—we shall yet win our freedom if the Lord gives us strength to hold out. Oh, if I could but send a good sum of money to the army. Gold and silver—that's what our men need instead of wretched script and paper shinplasters! But I have it not. We've been robbed twice. Our cattle are gone; we have not grain nor enough hay. Once we were comfortable, but now we are poor." And the good man, a truly sound-hearted patriot, shook his head and clenched his big hands until his face was flushed. Then, controlling himself, he turned sadly to his faithful partner and said, "Wife, all I can send to the Continental Army is a bushel of horseshoe nails!"

Mistress Christina smiled slyly and began to hum, " 'For want of a nail, the shoe was lost, for want of a battle, the kingdom was lost.' There is naught better than horseshoe nails," she answered. "Are they ready in a bag?"

"Yes," said the head of the family, turning to his son with a dour look in his blue-gray eyes. "You, Cornelius, must go on another expedition tomorrow if the horse is fit. You must carry the bag of nails."

"But Father, we may lose the horse. The men that are lurking around will certainly steal him from under me!"

"Nevertheless, I must get the horseshoe nails to the army. They are to go by way of neighbor Trump down the valley." His father's voice deepened. "You are to carry them for me."

209

"I promised Mother to cut and split wood for the fires tomorrow." Young Cornelius tried to find a good excuse to stay at home. "She used up all her supply while she was prisoner here."

"You have to act the part of an elder son and be my helper first of all." His father's tones were loud and commanding. "Do you understand that? Think of what your brother Phineas is doing for the cause. One day his horse may lose a shoe for want of a nail."

"Yes, sir," stammered Cornelius, more interested now that Phineas would profit by his efforts. He might have thought of this ride as a compliment to himself, had he not been so terribly tired.

"I have no one else I can send. We cannot trust neighbor boys who used to help us. I am counting on what sense you have and what speed you can make," added the older man. "I cannot ride forth myself, leaving your mother and the children undefended here in the house. Start tomorrow at daybreak. These falling days are short. Here . . ."

As he spoke, the big man rose and walked across the ample kitchen. Selecting one particular panel above the corner cupboard where pewter dishes were usually kept, he pointed it out carefully to his son. It bore marks of ill usage but was still intact. With a key Van Tassel set the whole panel ajar and took from the niche behind it two enormous bags of nails that shook and jingled.

"You are carrying aid to the army. Remember that," he said briefly—and handed Cornelius the bushel of horseshoe nails.

No one observed Cornelius when later in the day he crept out again to the woods carrying a blanket and picked up the bag of tarnished metal pieces that stirred in him thoughts of treasure. His mother had bidden him leave the silver and pewter in their hiding hole a while longer. But this was *his* discovery, *his* secret. He would keep the news of it to himself and tell no one, not even his loved mother. Perhaps the things were not worth anything. Then, again, they might be real treasure.

"Phineas ought to have everything we can do for him. Father's told me to take those nails to Trump for the army. I'd

210

like to do something by myself. Something to help. It might be good to put in this funny looking stuff I've found. It's a kind of treasure. The army needs gold and silver, but if horseshoe nails will help perhaps these old coins will help, too."

He wrapped the bag in the saddle blanket and lugged it out of the woods. Sneaking around by the back of the barn, he avoided the small boys who would be sure to ask him what it was. He dropped the blanket and its contents in the old part of the barn where there was nothing but a few rusted tools. Then he fetched the precious sacks of nails from his bedroom. The job of dumping out the nails and putting the coins underneath them took some time. His father would certainly miss him but that risk had to be taken.

As he sorted and packed in the old coins, he realized they would make the sacks top-heavy. Some of them would have to go in the saddle blanket. He searched in it for a slit and found one. By pouring some of his hoard into this slit, a few coins at a time, he succeeded in lightening the bags of nails. Should he

be overtaken on tomorrow's trip, the treasure would stand a better chance, unless thieves shook the blanket until it rattled.

Now that a secret was stirring his imagination, Cornelius started off next morning far less reluctantly, even eagerly. A most thrilling adventure lay before him. He carried treasure of which no one knew but himself. Suppose he and the horse never came back!

His mother had seen that he got a good luncheon to take with him. Indeed, she came out of the door with it in her hands, just as he and his father were carrying out the bags of nails.

"These bags seem a load heavier than they did yesterday," remarked the senior Cornelius, strapping them to the back of the saddle, "I must be getting old," and he wiped his forehead. Little did he know how grateful his son was for his help. Without it, Cornelius could never have lugged those sacks as far as the horse. "I see you have the blanket fastened on already," added his father. "Good luck now and off you go!"

His mother waved and blew him a kiss, one of the brothers struck the horse on the off flank, and soon Cornelius was out of sight, shortening his route down the valley by every brief cut he knew through the woods.

Every little while the fear that he might meet skulkers of the county or the British forces, be set upon and robbed of the hoard he had just found, sent cold and unpleasant shivers all up and down his spine. He comforted himself by remembering that this was a service he owed his country. And the thought of what he was carrying cheered him.

"It would be splendid if they could use these queer old coins and medals to buy food for the army, or coats or shoes. Our soldiers are all going ragged and barefoot, Uncle Peter said."

Nevertheless, the ride was gloomy. Woods and ravines were singularly quiet this morning, but the quiet was sinister, and the young rider felt it. After several hours he almost longed to see some living man besides the little woods' creatures that scurried about—squirrels, rabbits, young skunks.

Hunger at last was too much for him. Cornelius stopped the old horse and let him graze while he ate the bread and pork and apples and doughnuts he had brought with him. He had risen with the first light. Therefore it was only natural that a more adroit enemy than heavy-footed soldiers should overtake and capture him—sleep. He fell into a sound and heavy doze, lying hidden there in the bushes, one end of his horse's bridle in his warm hand.

Cornelius was roused into terrified reality by the sound of horses' feet. The sound came from a little distance at first, but the hoofs were pounding hard on the road and seemed to be going in the direction of Dunmow Farm, whither he was bound. Dragging his horse farther into cover under the trees, Cornelius lay on his stomach and crawled to a loophole between branches where he could spy on the highroad.

In another moment the riders clattered by. There were but three of them. That was better than he had feared. But it also marked them as raiding Cow Boys since they wore the informal threadbare uniform of the state militia.

"Oh, why did I ever fall asleep? It's true what Father says of me. I'm careless and irresponsible. I could have been at Dunmow Farm and delivered up the money by now. Then if it was stolen, at least he'd know I did the best I could. Well, the only thing I can do now is to follow them and see what they're up to."

Warily he trotted his horse along in their hoof prints, careful not to catch up with them. Being compelled to go slowly, it was a half hour before he came in sight of the small, quiet, out-of-the-way farm where he was to deliver up his trust. One glance at the place told him there was trouble ahead. Overturned objects in the yard showed signs of a struggle. Cautiously, he walked the horse up to the far side of the farmyard and peered around. Stamping told him that several horses were stabled in the barn. He knew that Farmer Trump kept but one horse.

Cornelius grew bolder. Unstrapping the bags from the saddle, he hid them in the underbrush and tied the horse where trees were thick and dark. Then he leaped the fence. On tiptoe he crept around to the partly opened door and took in a sad scene. There sat Farmer Trump in the large room that was both kitchen and living room, bound fast to one of his own wooden

213

chairs, a helpless prisoner! His shirt was torn, and there was blood on his cheek.

The boy's own blood boiled as he looked. He knew that Farmer Trump's sons were with the army but Deborah, his daughter, must be upstairs with the enemy. He could hear them searching the upper chambers and the girl's voice remonstrating with them. Where, oh, where, was the farm boy? If no one came to help him, how might these robbers be handled?

Then—everything happened at once! Down the stairs came one of the men, hustling pale Deborah before him. He was still demanding money.

"We have nothing of any value, if you would only hearken to me," she cried piteously. "So much of our gear has been stolen already. Leave us in peace, I beseech you."

"Give us that money, I tell you," he threatened. Taking the girl by her slender shoulders, he shook her violently until her cap flew off and her full print dress rustled. There was a faint tinkling sound and a tiny scrap of cloth containing a few pine-tree shillings dropped from its hiding place in her bosom.

"So," cried her tormentor. "You have lied! There it is!" Stooping forward greedily to pick up the tiny parcel of money, he knocked against the girl, who slipped on the steep little stairway and struck her head against a beam.

The sight of her, stunned and bruised, was enough to startle Cornelius into action. Darting forward he slammed the fellow over the head with his heavy pistol, and he tumbled to the floor. Cornelius picked up Deborah and carried her to the downstairs chamber. Next he swiftly cut Trump's bonds with a kitchen knife and used the rope to tie the arms of the robber. But where were his mates? There had been two others if this party consisted of the three Cow Boys who had passed him on the road.

"Where are the other two men who came with him?" asked the boy.

Trump nodded, motioned sadly toward the farmyard. Cornelius ran to the window and saw two men coming across the enclosure. One led the family cow and the other dragged by the heels a couple of freshly killed pigs. Helpless in their wake came

214

the farm boy whom they had bullied into showing them the
animal's hiding place.

Cornelius had only a few seconds to think. He had no wish to
kill in cold blood. They were coming across a wide space and
the barn, a high, strong and old-fashioned one, was behind
them. Stepping away from the open window, he took aim at
the barn and plugged its big wooden door with a bullet.

This unexpected shot, from a quarter that was supposedly
taken, startled the invaders. They lifted muskets which wobbled
in the air and missed fire. Cornelius fired a second shot. This
made them retreat in the direction of the barn and loose the cow,
which promptly galloped off.

William the farm boy, recognizing an ally at hand, suddenly

sprang forward from his position in the rear, covered the ground between the soldiers and the house before they could fire at him, stumbled in at the house door, and shut and bolted it with heavy bolts. Then he and Cornelius took each other's measure, for the farmer was still too weak and shaken to help them.

"Take this musket! See that it is loaded and guard the other window!" Cornelius commanded, loading and priming his pistols with what powder and ball he found to hand. The powder horn hung over the fireplace. So far he had been able to do nothing for poor Deborah, lying stunned in the inner room. But the two remaining thieves must not get away and spread an alarm.

Now both the Cow Boys in the yard fired. One bullet spattered against the fireplace, and the other dinted a panel of the cupboard. There must be no more of that. Pistol and musket cracked together, and when the smoke cleared, one man was holding his right shoulder, the other staggered with a bullet wound in his leg. Cornelius saw they were fast losing blood; so he and William dragged them into the house, secured their legs and arms. Their wounds were bound up and they were placed in the toolshed with their comrade to keep them company. The men threatened vengeance of the direst sort, but they were too weak to carry it out.

By this time, Deborah had recovered her wits and stood, amazed, in the doorway. "It's surely time I got supper for all of us," she said, heroically, smiling at Cornelius. She spoke as calmly as if the day had gone along naturally, and he smiled back as if brave deeds were nothing unusual for him. As the light waned, she set a pot of pease porridge on the fire with a skillet of johnny cake beside it. Slices of ham began to broil. William went out and caught the roaming cow, milked her and brought in milk for their tea, a homemade brew of herbs.

Up to this moment of a highly exciting day, Cornelius had had neither time nor opportunity to speak to Farmer Trump about the money he had brought. But something else must come first. His next duty was one of mercy. When supper was over,

216

he knew he must try to extract the bullets from his prisoners' wounds before they festered. But how, when he knew nothing of surgery?

Strangely enough, the farmer whom the marauders had so abused and injured was the one who came to their rescue. "I tended my own sick when my children were small and my wife ailing," he stated, and took from a press a small, much needed case of instruments. Deborah heated water and scraped up lint and tore old linen into bandages. The kitchen table was scrubbed, candles lighted, and one wounded man at a time hauled in and laid upon it. Even Cornelius winced at what had to be done. The bullet in the shoulder was near the surface and easily probed; the one in the leg had to be literally dug out.

When the wounded men were finally bedded in the shed, Cornelius and William sent Farmer Trump and his daughter to rest and took turns standing guard at the shed door. One of the Cow Boys had received no wound but only the stunning blow from Cornelius's pistol. He was the strongest; they scarcely dared take their eyes off him.

How slowly, oh, how slowly the hours dragged by till dawn began to filter in at the windows. Light coming now, thought Cornelius, numb and cold. His right foot had fallen asleep; he shook it violently. Things would be better, things—would—be —better—now. He yawned, weary with excitement and fatigue.

Then he felt a strong, heavy hand shaking him. "Master Cornelius. Master Cornelius! Wake up, wake!"

It was the stupid William, gaping with fright, whose eyes looked into his. "I must have slept, too," he blubbered, "and so he got away."

"Got away?"

"The big one," ejaculated William. His next remark was most disquieting. "He took *all* three horses."

"But the wounded ones? Are they gone, too? Go and look!"

"How could they be?" asserted William, peering farther into the corners of the shed. "They were too weak."

But a deadly fear nagged at Cornelius as he searched the shed and found their pallets empty. *He had fallen asleep again!* And

217

those rascals must have given him the slip just as day was breaking. Panic seized him. Had he carried the saddle blanket with the money in it into the house? Yes, he remembered that he had taken it upstairs when he brought his horse to the stable for the night. Yes, it was more by good luck than good judgment that the nails his father had sent had not gone with the Cow Boys.

Search revealed a red trail outside the door where the soldier with the injured leg had been hauled along between his two comrades. However, in their swift flight they had been compelled to leave behind them most of the slain porkers and the chickens. That was one good gained.

"Besides, those three prisoners would have eaten us out of house and home," pointed out Farmer Trump. "Who knows but their escape may be a blessing in disguise? Let's have breakfast and decide what to do next."

After breakfast, Cornelius and William went out to the bushes and hauled in the sacks of nails. Cornelius borrowed another small sack which he took upstairs. In this he put the coins taken from the blanket and dumped some nails on top of them. There were now three sacks instead of two.

"Neighbor Trump," he announced with dignity when William had gone outside to do the day's chores, "my father bade me deliver these horseshoe nails into your keeping to be sent to the army." And he set the smaller sack beside the large ones.

The farmer's face shone like a new moon on a crisp fall night. " 'Tis well come by, my boy, and going where it is needed. Have no fear. No eyes shall see the bags but Debby's and mine, and those of the messenger who will come by to get them today!"

"Father felt very sorrowful at not sending more," cried Cornelius. "He would fain have sent money."

"Of that we have none," said Trump sensibly. "I wonder— did any man see you on your way?"

"As far as I know none saw me," said Cornelius. He added impetuously, "Had not you and Miss Debby better come to us later for shelter and safety? We have our camp on the mountain, and there we could huddle in case of attack."

"What? Leave Dunmow Farm to the Cow Boys to burn,"

answered the farmer, spiritedly, "to burn and plunder now they've found their way here?"

Cornelius blushed. "True," he acknowledged, "but how will you manage to defend it?"

Trump laid his hand on his young friend's shoulder. "You came to us in the hour of need. Maybe the Lord will provide us with another helper should raiders return soon. Besides, after the messenger has come and gone with these sacks, under a disguise and on a hidden path, I can send word to my cousin and his lad who are at John Halterman's. They will step over and keep me company for a month. Their views are sound and William, though he is soft-witted, learned a thing or two last night or I'm much mistaken."

"Then, if I cannot help you further, I must away for home and quickly," cried the boy, anxiously. "How do I know what may not have happened there?"

Before the warm sun shone and the dry, ghostlike autumn wind rattled dead leaves along the road, Cornelius took his way homeward on Andy, the plow horse. It was a wonder that Andy had not been annexed by the devouring enemy, but he was thin and not young. Besides, Cornelius reflected, stroking the horse's mane, he might have whinnied at a strange touch and given the alarm. This mission, and an arduous one it had proved, was done.

Cornelius had only one regret. He would so have *loved* to see the disguised messenger who came for the sacks of nails and the *treasure*. In his ear rang the words of the song:

> "For want of a nail the shoe was lost,
> For want of a shoe the battle was lost. . . ."

At that moment he saw ahead of him a tall young man in a miller's smock, driving a cart with a sorry plug of a horse attached to it. When *he* in his turn saw Andy and his rider, the miller opened his mouth as if to ask a question, then thought better of it and passed on his way silently.

Cornelius wondered if this was the messenger of whom

219

Trump had spoken. Perhaps he wore the American hunting shirt under that very floury looking smock. Where was he bound for? No doubt the sacks of nails with the old coins lying snug underneath them would be taken for sacks of flour. That was an exciting thought and kept him company on his way.

His father's praise, valued like a shower of gold by his son because it was so rarely given, was his that night. So one boy climbed to his loft bed, happily. But now that he knew his father to be a link in the chain that was holding back the enemy, in this American fight whose outcome often looked so dubious, Cornelius realized that their homestead stood in great and immediate danger. His heart was troubled and his dreams, too. Would the miller get the bags and the money through the British lines or be taken prisoner and hanged?

For a full month after Cornelius's errand and subsequent adventure at Dunmow Farm, the Van Tassel family enjoyed a surprisingly peaceful interval. They all knew, and Cornelius Senior knew best of all, that this peace was only a lull. Raiding attacks might redouble in violence at any minute.

One morning early in November the whole household was greatly cheered by a messenger who came running over from Abraham Storm's tavern, bearing a sealed letter, evidently addressed to him for safe keeping. It was from their son and brother, Phineas, with the Continental forces. When the seal was broken it contained these few words:

"Dear Father and Mother. Do not be surprised to see me. At any time. This paper bears you my love. Phineas."

"What can the lad be doing?" asked Van Tassel. He turned pale, thinking of Nathan Hale's end and wondering if his son had been sent on some secret and dangerous mission.

The boy who had brought the note from the tavern turned and said, "Abraham Storm bade me tell you to be ready. The British are on the march this way again. Master Van Tassel, word has gone around that there is buried gold in this neighborhood somewhere. They want money and will get it. They are burning homesteads down"—and he was gone again like a rabbit before a hunter.

220

Van Tassel looked nonplussed. "Cornelius," he said harshly, "have you or Peter or Jake told schoolmates that foolish tale of old Jacob's gold pieces?"

Cornelius held his head high and looked his father straight in the eyes. "*No*, sir, no," he said with decision. "I haven't told anyone or even thought about it—much."

In spite of this alarming rumor, the note from Phineas made each and everyone in the house jubilant—the glad mother, Mary, the little brothers, and Cornelius. But Cornelius, while looking forward to the sight of Phineas, began to do some scheming and planning on his own account. Since the raid on the Dunmow Farm, he was sadder and wiser. What were they all to do in case of an attack so sudden that they could not make the steep, winding path up the mountain? Often he gazed at his father, wondering why he did not think of it. Several times he opened his mouth to ask his father's opinion on such an exciting idea. But his father, preoccupied to the extent of being quite gruff, was small comfort. As long as Cornelius plodded regularly to school, did his chores, fed the stock, split wood, and carried messages here and there, he did not confide further in him. "I could keep that boy busy all day here on the farm," he thought, "but he should be in the school. That is his due."

It was dull, this going to school in wartime. His father did not know that in the ever-shortening lonely and dank fall afternoons, Cornelius Junior was working as a beaver works on its dam. He had realized that the woods would be their safest and quickest retreat, those woods that skirted the lower slopes of Beaver Mountain. So one day he wandered into them with a sharp claspknife, valiantly cutting away branches and dead wood. Soon he came upon a curious opening where he had found the bag of treasure and hidden his mother's silver. Stooping down and examining it again, he judged it had originally been made by a bear or a fox and looked as if it might be of good size within.

Edging himself between the boulders at the mouth of the hole, Cornelius dropped on his knees and crawled in. The place was deep and smelt of leaf mold. It stretched a long way under

221

the tree, though it was shallow and not high. Human beings could harbor in such a burrow as well as animals. Why wouldn't it do as a refuge in time of need? However, he first searched the woods to see if he could do better. After a while he came back. He had found nothing so good.

In the next few days, Cornelius came back with an old spade and a pitchfork and thoroughly cleaned out the opening. Some still and hardly heeded voice seemed to whisper in his ear that it might be wanted. When he had cleaned everything up and made it look more like a dirt cellar than a wood cavern, Cornelius dragged in moss for beds. He even added to the moss by fetching a couple of the straw pallets they kept in readiness for the mountain. He controlled his longing to blurt out at home what he had arranged and thought of for them. Not even to his mother did he speak of this spot in the woods, but he marked the trail leading to it in ways of his own that could not be missed.

Mid-November days came and still no Phineas. His mother seemed to have a feeling he would walk in on them suddenly and, with Mary to help, she devoted herself to baking bread, making apple tarts and pies, and roasting a wild turkey that one of the boys had shot. Delicious odors floated around the farmhouse. Even the animals seemed to have a sense of expectation. To crown everything, there was a week of beautiful mild weather, the Indian summer following a spell of raw, autumnal rain.

One night when the golden hunter's moon rose late and swam high in the sky, Cornelius climbed to his bed in the attic which he shared with the boys. He climbed wearily. A sense of fear clutched at his heart, fear that he had not had for many a day.

"Something has gone ill with Phineas," he thought. "But why?" He thought the moonlight streaming in through those narrow panes under the eaves would keep him awake, but it did not. The day had been hard, and he fell asleep almost immediately.

He woke with a start. Something was the matter. He heard a threatening sound like the din of distant voices, angry voices, and the trampling of many horses' feet. Most of all a light shone into the attic, lighting it too brightly. It was not the moon but a strange scarlet glare that flashed and flickered.

Could it be fire? Were they to be attacked?

Leaping up from his pallet, Cornelius jerked on his heavy frieze jacket and boots. Next he shook and woke his sleeping brothers. All three of them rapidly slid down the ladder that led to the second floor, then clattered down the short and steep staircase, Cornelius carrying the blankets from their beds.

Their mother's strong voice was the only reassuring thing in the welter of confusion and fright downstairs. The boys snuffled and Mary, the baby in her arms, stood rigid with fear, while his father gave orders shortly and sharply.

"Our settlement has been surprised by Captain Emmerick's men, and they are many. Take your mother and the children up the mountain, Cornelius. The house is about to be surrounded, and probably they will try to burn it. They are burning Storm's tavern. Also they will take me prisoner for harboring Continental supplies. Your sister has some provisions. Quick! You must save yourselves."

Cornelius would like to have said, "There isn't time to get up the mountain, Father! It is useless to try." But he did not. What was the use? He closed his lips firmly. Was not the hole under the tree ready for them?

But—"Shall you stay here alone?" he ventured.

"Peter will join me. We will defend the place together. Cornelius, loose the cow and take her with you."

There was scarcely time to think of anything. Once outdoors, the bewildered family moved as in a nightmare. Mistress Van Tassel begged to stay with her husband. But there was the baby! All of them blindly and dolefully followed Cornelius to the stone wall, crossed it, and got into the woods, where the frightened cow had preceded them.

They were not one instant too soon. In fact, they had not gained their new hiding place before they knew the troopers were laying siege to the house. Cornelius helped his mother and sister through the narrow opening, the chubby baby was rolled in like a sack of meal, and he and the boys crawled in after them. When blankets and provisions had been arranged, all drew breath and stopped panting; but all shivered with fright and dampness.

Mother was saddest of all. "They will take your father prisoner beyond a doubt," she said. "He will never surrender. And then they will fire the house."

"Have they burned Uncle Peter's farm yet?" piped up one of the boys.

"Perhaps. But, Cornelius, how did you find this place?"

"I have had it ready for some time, Mother," he answered stoutly, though too agitated to smile.

"But—we had the mountain!"

"There was not time to toil up that path. We should have been set upon and captured."

Mother looked with admiration at her son and said, "Yes, it would have been hopeless."

So there, huddled together like foxes in a hole, the Van Tassels listened to all the dread sounds that made them fear for their father's safety. A wind had risen, and the commands of the soldiers and their yells sounded nearer and nearer. Cornelius longed to crawl out and dash to the edge of the woods where he could see the house. But he grew inches taller as he realized that all these people, even his stalwart mother, were dependent on him. A search party would not be likely to find their hole, for the opening showed very little from the outside. But they might capture Buttercup.

Slow and dismal half hours passed. Nobody could sleep, and they were all faint with hunger, yet they dared not eat while harkening to those alarming sounds. The wind brought a crackling in its wake, a smell of burning fodder, of charred rafters and singed hay.

"They have fired the barn," whispered their mother, in tears.

After what seemed like his whole thirteen years relived, Cornelius heard reverberations that made him think of a pitched battle. Cautiously he wriggled to the edge of their stifling little retreat. Should the British set these woods on fire, that would end everything! If he could only sneak down to the stone wall, on the other side of which their house lay, and see what had taken place!

What happened while Cornelius peeped was breath-taking. He found himself gazing on what was left of the Van Tassel barn. In fact nothing was left but the framework; and that meant a total loss of their hay as well. As to the dwelling house, one wing of it had been set on fire and then miraculously put out at the last minute, as charred rafters and a sickish smell of smoke and water testified.

225

He had expected to see his father, uncle, and their neighbors bound and marched off as prisoners. Instead, there stood Phineas, the long-absent Phineas, and a large party of Revolutionary soldiers and officers in their ragged coats, with smoking rifles, talking with his father under the trees. Every Redcoat was gone, save a few lying on the ground who would not rise again to go anywhere.

Reassured, the boy climbed over the stone wall and soon had his brother's hand in his, and was asking wondering questions.

"It was a sharp and bitter skirmish," said the young soldier. "General Putnam has moved his headquarters to White Plains. He sent us out as scouts to find the strength of the detachment of British left on the east side of the river. We *found* it, in very truth! My friends and I came up just as Emmerick's men had fired the house and were tying Father's hands behind his back. They had the house ablaze, and the struggle was to overpower the enemy and put out the fire. The wing is gone, and the household stuff with it. But now, boy, fetch Mother and the children from that mysterious place where you've hidden them—and quickly.

Soon the reunited group stood together. The mother kept gazing at her soldier son as if she did not believe him to be real. "O Phineas, son Phineas," she exclaimed, and no one could say words of praise as Mother said them. "You have saved your father and our home. But, see, here is your younger brother who has become a real man and a rescuer in your absence! He saved me and the children," and she looked fondly from one face to the other.

And to Cornelius's further surprise as they stood there, his father said to him quietly, "*Phineas* was the miller with the cart you told us about, our Phineas. He was the secret messenger." The corners of his stern mouth actually went down in a smile.

Next, and this whole scene was one long panorama of surprises, the elder of the two officers saluted Cornelius Van Tassel, Senior, and said courteously, "I serve as their paymaster, sir. The Continental Army appreciates your wonderful loyalty." There was real feeling in his voice. "Many horses will be shod

226

with the horseshoe nails you sent us, which were sorely needed. But many more of the enemy will feel the weight of your gift. With the money you sent, we have bought and had cast a fine piece of artillery, a field piece, and have purchased the powder and shot to go with it. We were grateful and thankful enough to get the gold in the bags—the money you must have worked hard to raise—over a thousand guineas it was. And we have a surplus which shall go to help the Army in some other way."

Van Tassel turned fiery red and looked stupefied. "I sent no money at all," he stated in bewildered tones, scratching his head. "I did try to raise funds and could not. I tried again and again. Having neither cattle nor grain I sent you some horse-shoe nails."

"I think, sir," put in Phineas stepping up, "my younger brother here may know something about this. 'Twas he who carried the bags."

The officer looked directly at Cornelius, who in his turn began to look very much embarrassed.

"I found it in the woods," he stammered. "A treasure—and I wanted to give it to the soldiers. But I did not know its worth."

"It was gold guineas of His Majesty's coinage right enough," spoke the officer.

"Then Uncle Jacob did bury it in the woods," muttered the boys' father.

Cornelius looked attentively at his toes. He heard the officer ask him his name, and he gave it hesitatingly.

"A good name for a good gun. We will call the artillery piece those guineas bought—CORNELIUS."

And the father added, grimly, "Our cause shall *not* be lost for want of a horseshoe nail. Horseshoes bring luck. You are a lucky boy, my lad!" He rested his hand on his second son's shoulder in pride and joy.

Harry Edward Neal

FRONTIER BLOCKADE BUSTER

ILLUSTRATED BY *James Ponter*

SHE hauled the bucket out of the well and poured the clear, cold water into the larger bucket on the ground, to take back to the new cabin. The cabin looked almost as strong as near-by Fort Henry itself—and it was, according to her brother Ebenezer, who had built both. She was proud of Ebenezer. She was proud of her other brothers, too—Silas and Jonathan and Isaac and Andrew. But Ebenezer was the one who always wanted to do things, always talked about the future, about building cities in the wilderness, making the frontier a place for homes and churches and factories. That was why he had built this fort on the banks of the Ohio River and had brought a handful of pioneers to make their homes here. Yes, Ebenezer had the true Zane spirit, and Elizabeth had it, too. She was here with her brothers instead of at her home in West Virginia—a fugitive hiding from the British—because of that Zane spirit.

This is how it happened.

Shortly after the start of the Revolutionary War, Betty Zane returned to her parents' home from finishing school in Philadelphia. Even then the British were marching through the countryside from Bunker Hill to the Carolinas, plundering as they went. Tales of British arrogance went before the soldiers and won them enemies in every town and hamlet.

William Zane, Betty's father, was a peaceful man of Quaker stock, opposed to violence. Betty, however, felt that it was wise

229

to fight for one's rights and to oppose injustice and cruelty and tyranny. One day the thud of hoofs was heard in the streets, and the Zanes looked out of their windows to see a troop of British cavalry approaching the house. An officer dismounted and pounded on the front door, which was opened by Mr. Zane.

"I want food and drink for my men," the officer said. "There are forty of us. Have it prepared immediately and don't make excuses. You American farmers have enough food hidden away to feed the whole British army."

Betty realized that her father and mother had no choice but to do as they were told. As her mother and father began to prepare the food, Betty looked out the window and saw the soldiers tethering their horses. The reins of the first horse were tied to the hitching post in front of the house. The reins of the second horse were fastened to the saddle of the first, the reins of the third were tied to the second, and so on. It was a strange way to tie horses, Betty thought.

The soldiers trooped into the house, and Betty went to the kitchen to help her parents, resenting the laughter of the red-coats in the other rooms, the thud of their boots on the clean floors. If only I were a man, Betty thought. But, she wasn't a man—she wasn't even a grown woman yet. She was just a seventeen-year-old girl, powerless to hurt the armed enemy.

Looking toward the street, she saw again how oddly the British horses were tied to each other, and suddenly a bold idea twinkled in her mind and sparked and leaped into a dazzling plan. Her whole body seemed to throb with excitement as she walked quietly out the back door and toward the street. She moved slowly—so slowly that anyone seeing her would never guess that she was about to strike a blow for liberty.

At the hitching post she patted the nose of the one horse whose reins were tied to the post and turned her head to glance at the house. The doors and windows were closed tight.

No one was in sight. Slowly, cautiously, Betty untied the reins with one hand as she kept patting the horse with the other. Suddenly she felt the loose leather in her fingers and knew the reins were free. She held them tightly, feeling the sweat in her

230

Betty wanted to laugh and cry, but she only kept looking back.

palm, as she forced herself to turn and look at the house again, half expecting to see a squad of redcoats aiming loaded muskets at her back. But no one was there. Quickly she passed the reins over the horse's head and climbed into the saddle.

"Come on!" she said softly, and jiggled the reins against the animal's neck. The horse wheeled away from the hitching post and the other thirty-nine mounts, all tied together, turned like a row of dancers and followed each other slowly down the road. Betty wanted to laugh and cry, but she only kept looking back at the quiet house, praying that none of the British would appear until she was out of sight.

She was close to the turn-off to the forest trail when, far back in the line, a horse neighed, and another. A moment later she saw a redcoat come out the front door. A second soldier appeared, and Betty heard their shouts. Were there also shots? She couldn't be sure. Desperately she slapped her horse's flank with her hand and kicked at his sides with her heels.

The horse leaped ahead into the friendly woods she knew by heart, woods in which the British would be lost.

Through the back trails she led her stolen enemy herd to the headquarters of General Washington and presented them to the Continental Army. Whether she gave the animals to Washington himself is not clear, nor is the location of his troops at that time. It was clear to Betty, however, that she would be hunted by every redcoat within miles, yet she wanted to return home to tell her parents she was safe.

Traveling by night, keeping under cover of the woods, she managed to get to the home of friends who carried a message to Mr. Zane that Betty was free and well.

But learning that some soldiers remained in the town with special orders to arrest her on sight, Betty decided she must get away before she got her helpful friends in serious trouble for concealing her. So, at a night meeting with her father, she obtained his permission to go to Fort Henry and join her brothers.

And here she was at the fort, dipping water out of a free well for a free life in a wilderness far from the nice school she had attended, far from her comfortable home.

As she carried her bucket to the cabin, Betty remembered the earlier Indian attacks when Ebenezer's first cabin had been burned to the ground. That had been in 1777 when the British and their savage allies swooped down on Fort Henry to kill the pioneers who would not surrender to the Crown. They had burned the few cabins outside the stockade, but the fort held, and finally the attackers were driven off. Now Ebenezer had finished a new cabin with a strong storehouse for gunpowder.

"Now let 'em come, if they want to," Ebenezer had said. "We'll show 'em next time."

If there were a next time, Betty wondered what she would do. As she looked at the log walls and the muskets over the mantel, and the rough bunk in which she slept, she could not help thinking how different life at Fort Henry was from the life she had known.

For one thing, the smells were different in the wilderness. There were no shops here with fragrant aromas of cinnamon and nutmeg and sugarplums and olives. There were only the smells of pine and of wood smoke, which Betty liked, and of fish and tallow candles, which she didn't like. She had no pretty taffetas and cambrics; instead she wore her blue or brown home-spun and calico dresses. Yes, life was strangely different here, Betty thought, and wondered once more how she, a girl from a Philadelphia finishing school, would act under fire in this wilderness.

Suddenly the cabin door opened, and Ebenezer came in. Betty saw he was excited.

"Get over to the fort," he told her. "Trouble comin'. Johnny Lynn, the scout, just came in from swimming the river. He saw a bunch of British and Indians on the other side heading this way. We'll be ready for 'em. Go on, now, get along with you."

Betty quivered with excitement. "But Eb—aren't you coming too?"

"I can do more right here. And don't you worry—they can't get us this time! Andy Scott and George Green are coming over with their muskets, and three of the womenfolk will help us load. I told Johnny Lynn and brother Jonathan to stay in the

232

sentry box and that you'd come and load for them. You remember how, don't you?"

"Of course."

"All right, then. Hurry up."

Betty left the cabin and sped across the clearing to the fort. Women and children and men from the twenty or twenty-five cabins outside the stockade hurried with her past the log gates. In a few minutes the gates were shut and barred, and people took posts around the fort.

Betty went directly to the white-oak log sentry box where her brother Jonathan and Johnny Lynn, the scout, peered through the musket openings toward the forest. They greeted her with smiles, calmly, as though an Indian attack were a daily occurrence.

Betty squinted through a crack between two of the logs toward the clearing near the river. Almost at the same instant she and Johnny Lynn cried out. "Look!"

The bright-red coat of a British soldier shone against the gold and brown of the autumn leaves. The British flag came into view, then there were more redcoats, intermingled with the buckskin worn by their Indian allies. Betty felt her throat grow dry and tight as she watched them approach. There were about fifty British soldiers, perhaps three hundred Indians. The garrison of the fort was outnumbered almost eight to one. And the Indians, Betty knew, all carried guns from the British arsenals on the Great Lakes.

A British officer called out: "In the name of His Majesty the King, I call upon you to surrender this fort."

Jonathan Zane squinted along the barrel of his musket, took careful aim. The shot exploded. The flagstaff carried by the British soldier splintered and fell, but the flag was immediately retrieved. Angrily the officer shouted a command. His men fired and took cover. The siege had begun.

Muskets boomed around the entire stockade. Shot after shot echoed from the cabin outpost where Ebenezer Zane and his friends helped to draw fire away from the fort. In the sentry box Betty doggedly molded bullets and loaded the muskets for Jonathan and Johnny. Bullets from enemy guns spattered against oak logs. Suddenly Betty squealed.

"You hit?" Jonathan asked anxiously.

Betty glanced at her arm. Wooden splinters from the logs were sticking into her flesh, driven in by the British bullets smashing against the wood. They hurt, but she was glad she wasn't shot. She pulled out the larger slivers and tried to laugh, but it wasn't easy.

"Good girl," Jonathan said.

When darkness fell the firing lessened, and there were only occasional flashes from the blackness of the woods, with answering shots from the stockade. Several of the cabins outside the stockade were set afire, but Betty saw that Ebenezer's still stood.

For three days and nights the siege kept up. Flaming torches were hurled at the fort, but were dislodged by the defenders before they could do any damage. On the morning of the fourth day Silas Zane, who was in command in the fort, came to the sentry box.

"I haven't said anything to the others yet," he told Jonathan, "but our gunpowder's practically gone. We never expected any

234

siege to last this long. Our extra powder is stored in Ebenezer's cabin, in the powder storehouse."

Betty understood the problem instantly. The cabin was nearly two hundred feet from the fort, across a clearing which could be raked by British and Indian gunfire. It would be almost sure death for anyone to cross that clearing. *Almost.* Perhaps she could do it. She could try. She could run fast. And she was a young girl—maybe they wouldn't shoot down a young girl. She grabbed Silas by the arm. "I'll go for the powder!"

Silas was so surprised he couldn't speak. He just looked at her rather queerly, then smiled and shook his head.

"It's out of the question," Jonathan said shortly. "Silas, you stay here. I'll go after the powder."

Betty wrung her hands in desperation. "No, no, Jonathan! I'm just a girl, don't you see? I'm not needed here as a man is. We can't let you go—we can't let any of the men go. There are few enough of them as it is. But I can go, and I won't be missed!"

The brothers glanced at each other, then Jonathan put one big arm around Betty's shoulders and hugged her. "I'd miss you."

"She's right, Jonathan," Silas put in. "We do need all the men. Betty's a Zane. She's one of us. We can't ask any of the other women to go. We'll let Betty go."

Over Jonathan's protests Betty climbed down from the sentry box with Silas and went to the gate where she took off her coat and dress and pinned up her petticoats to speed her dash to Ebenezer's cabin.

She felt weak in her stomach, and her legs seemed a little wobbly, but she tried to appear confident. "All right, Silas," she said. "Open the gate."

It seemed to her that she ran faster than an arrow could fly. She heard a few shots, but they served only to make her run faster. In a few minutes she reached the cabin door and sank, breathless, into Ebenezer's arms. He kissed her on the forehead and said, "You brave little fool! Where are your brains?"

She laughed as she fought for breath. "Get the—powder—out. I'm going to take some—back to the fort. Their supply is all gone. Whew!" She sat down, gasping.

235

"You'll do nothing of the kind," Ebenezer said. "If anybody takes powder back to the fort, I'll take it."

George Green and Molly Scott, who were in the cabin, agreed with Ebenezer. It was a man's job, not a task for an eighteen-year-old girl, and Ebenezer was adamant.

Betty stood up, squared her shoulders, and raised her head high. "Eb," she said solemnly, "I'm going back one way or another. Would you want folks to call your sister a coward? Do you want me to lose my faith in myself?"

Ebenezer looked at her for a long moment. Then without a word he strode to the powder storehouse and returned with a keg of gunpowder, which he held as he faced Betty. She knew he was going to let her go. Quickly she pulled the cloth from the rough table and tied it around her waist, like an apron. She held the free corners in her hands.

"Empty the powder into this."

Her brother lifted the keg and poured the powder into the cloth. Betty turned and walked to the door. The powder was heavy. At the door she peeked out, saw that the British and Indians were in the forest, perhaps preparing for a final onslaught.

"Quickly!" she cried. "Open the door!"

Betty darted out and began her dash across the field. Apparently the enemy realized what she was carrying. They began to shoot at her. She knew that one shot in the powder would probably blow her to kingdom come. The powder was even heavier than she thought, and the weight seemed to increase with each step. She prayed that she might not stumble and lose her precious burden. She heard a strange whistling noise and knew that a bullet had whizzed close to her head. Little spurts of dust around her told her that other bullets were nipping at her flying feet.

As she neared the fort she could hear the cries of encouragement from her friends, but it seemed years before she reached the stockade gate and almost fell into the arms of the men and women who held it open for her. Betty closed her eyes and breathed heavily, realizing only vaguely that someone was un-

236

tying the tablecloth and lifting the heavy weight from her arms and waist. Then she fainted.

When she recovered consciousness a few minutes later the guns were firing from the fort again. On that day, September 14, 1782, the enemy withdrew, and a British soldier fired the last enemy bullet in the Revolutionary War. It was answered by a shot from a musket in Fort Henry—the very last shot in the battle for American independence. And it was fired with powder carried through a hail of bullets by a brave American girl.

The Zanes founded Wheeling, West Virginia, Zanesville, Ohio, and other American towns. Betty Zane later married, had several children, and lived happily until 1823, when she died in Martins Ferry, Ohio. Her gravestone was marked, "Betty Zane—Heroine of Fort Henry," and the story of brave, beautiful Betty Zane was told up and down the Ohio River.

JOHNNY TREMAIN was apprenticed to a silversmith and came to know the famous silversmith, Paul Revere. When the British troops, under General Gage, occupied Boston, Paul Revere, with his friends Sam Adams, Dr. Warren, John Hancock, and Dr. Church, organized a system of spies against the British. Johnny, and his close friend Rab, a printer, became spies, and it was Johnny's job to linger around the stables of the British army. He was to pick up what news he could from the grooms, or from Dove, who was the Colonel's horseboy.

Esther Forbes

DISPERSE, YE REBELS

ILLUSTRATED BY *John Dukes McKee*

THE fourteenth of April, 1775.

General Gage had sent out spies, dressed as Yankee men looking for work. The spies came back on this day. All the colonels were at the Province House with General Gage listening to their reports. Joseph Warren knew this, and so did Paul Revere, even Johnny Tremain. It was easy enough to find out that spies had returned, were reporting to the commanding officer—but what had they reported? This was not known.

The fifteenth of April.

This fell upon Saturday. At every regimental headquarters the same general orders were posted, signed by Gage himself. All the grenadier and light infantry companies were to be taken off duty until further orders. They were to be taught some new evolutions.

Johnny himself read these orders posted in the lower hall at the Afric Queen. One man was grumbling, "New evolutions.

238

What was Grandma Gage thinking about?" But Lieutenant Stranger, as he read, whistled and laughed. "That," he said, "looks like something—at last."

Each regiment had two companies picked and trained for special duty. The light infantry were the most active and cleverest men in each regiment. Lieutenant Stranger was a light infantry officer. These men were lightly armed and did scout and flanking work. In the grenadier companies you found tall, brisk, powerful fellows, hard-fighting men, always ready to attack.

If you have eleven regiments and pick off from each its two best companies, it adds up to about seven hundred men.

All day one could feel something was afoot. Johnny read it on Colonel Smith's florid face. He was stepping across the Queen's stableyard very briskly and remembering to pull in his paunch. There was ardor in his eye. Was it martial ardor?

Lieutenant Stranger was so happy over something he gave Dove threepence.

Spring had come unseasonably early this year. In the yard of the Afric Queen, peach trees were already in blossom. Stranger was so happy something was bound to happen. Over on the Common Johnny found Earl Percy's regiment unlimbering, polishing two cannons. The soldiers were forming a queue about a grindstone sharpening their bayonets. What of it? They were always doing things like that. Did all this mean something?

He went to Mr. Revere's, whose wife told him to look for him at Doctor Warren's. The two friends sat in the surgery making their plans and listening to reports that were coming from all directions. Seemingly the excitement among the officers, the preparations among the soldiers, had been noticed by at least a dozen others. But where were they going? Who would command them? No one knew. Possibly only Gage himself, although before the start was actually made he would have to tell his officers.

All that day the British transports had been readying their landing boats. This might mean men would be taken aboard, move off down the coast (as Salem had been invaded two months before), or that they were standing by merely to ferry the men across the Charles River, land them in Charlestown or Cambridge. The work on the boats suggested that the men would not march out through the town gates. And yet . . . Gage might have ordered this work done merely to confuse the people of Boston. Blind them to his real direction. The talk at Doctor Warren's went on into the night.

Johnny relaxed on a sofa in the surgery as the men talked. He was ready to run wherever sent, find out any fact for them. It was past midnight. He would not have known he had been asleep except that he had been dreaming. He had been hard at work down on Hancock's Wharf boiling lobsters—he and John Hancock and Sam Adams. The lobsters had men's eyes with long lashes and squirmed and looked up piteously. Hancock would avert his sensitive face to their distress, "Go away, please" (but he kept pushing them under with his gold-headed cane). Sam Adams would rub his palms and chuckle.

Johnny woke up and realized that only Revere and Warren were still in the room, and they were talking about Hancock and Adams. These two gentlemen had left Boston in March. They were representatives at the Provincial Congress at Concord. The British had forbidden the General Court to meet, but the Massachusetts men had merely changed the name of their legislative body and gone on sitting. But did the British know that both these firebrands were staying at the Clarks' out in Lexington?

"It will do no harm to warn them," Revere was saying, getting to his feet. "I'll row over to Charlestown tonight, go to Lexington, and tell them a sizable force may soon move. They had best hide themselves for the next few days."

"And get word to Concord. The cannons and stores had best be hidden."

"Of course."

"Tell them we here in Boston have the situation well in hand. The second the troops move—either on foot or into those boats—we will send them warning in time to get the Minute Men into the field. I'd give a good deal to know which way they are going."

"Suppose none of us gets out? Gage knows we'd try to send word. He'll guard the town so well it will be impossible."

240

Johnny was still half awake. He yawned and settled back to think of those lobsters. With eyes like men . . . long lashes . . . tears on their lashes . . .

Revere was pulling on his gloves.

". . . Colonel Conant in Charlestown. I'll tell him to watch the spire of Christ's Church. You can see it well from Charlestown. If the British go out over the Neck, we will show one lantern. If in the boats—two. And come Hell or high water I'll do my best to get out and tell exactly what's acting. But I may get caught on my way over. Another man should also be ready to try to get out through the gates."

They talked of various men and finally pitched upon Billy Dawes. He could impersonate anybody—from a British general to a drunken farmer. This might help him get through the gates.

As Paul Revere with Johnny at his heels left Warren's a man emerged from the darkness, laid a hand on Revere's arm. In the little light Johnny recognized the rolling black eye, poetic negligence of dress. It was Doctor Church.

"Paul," he whispered, "what's afoot?"

"Nothing," said Revere shortly and went on walking.

"The British preparing to march?"

"Why don't you ask them?"

The queer man drifted away. Johnny was surprised that Revere would tell Church nothing, for he was in the very inner circle. Seemingly Revere was surprised by his sudden caution. "But I can't trust that fellow . . . never have, never will."

The sixteenth of April.

All over Boston bells were calling everyone to church. As though they had not a care in the world, the British officers crowded into the Episcopal churches, and army chaplains held services for the soldiers in the barracks. Paul Revere was over on the mainland carrying out his mission. Boston looked so usual and so unconcerned, Johnny began to wonder if they all had not made mountains of molehills, imagined an expedition when none was intended. But Rab was so certain the time was close at hand that he told Johnny that he himself was leaving Boston

241

mister
mckee

for good. There would be fighting before the week was out, and
he intended to be in it. Now he must report at Lexington.

Johnny took this news badly. He could not endure that Rab
should leave him: desert him.

"But as soon as the first shot is fired, no man of military age
can possibly get out of Boston. They'll see to it. It's now or
never."

He did not seem to feel any grief at abandoning Johnny, who
sat disconsolately on his bed watching Rab. The older boy was
cutting himself a final piece of bread and cheese. How many
hundreds of times Johnny had seen those strong white teeth
tearing at coarse bread. Rab had been eating bread and cheese
all through their first meeting—and that was long ago. It seemed

242

he'd be eating bread and cheese to the end. There was a sick qualm at the pit of Johnny's stomach. He couldn't eat bread and cheese, and it irritated him that Rab could.

The older boy was glowing with good health, good spirits. He was eighteen, six feet tall and a grown man. He looked it as he moved about the low attic, stuffing his pockets with extra stockings. Rolling up a shirt in a checkered handkerchief. He is leaving me—and he doesn't care—thought Johnny.

"Perhaps I'll go too," he offered, hoping Rab would say, "I'd give everything I've got—even my musket—if you could come," or merely, "Fine, come along."

"No, you can't," said Rab. "You've got your work to do right here in town. You stick around with your fat friend Dove. Gosh, I'm glad I'll never have to listen to Dove again. But you'll have a fine time with Dove, while I . . ."

"You know I cannot stomach Dove."

"No? I thought he and you were getting on fine together."

"And there's not one reason why I can't leave for Lexington too, except you don't want me."

He knew this was not true, but he could not help badgering Rab, trying to make him say, "I'll miss you as much as you'll miss me."

Rab laughed at him. He was going to leave and he wasn't going to be "slopped over." Johnny was gazing at him sullenly. Rab took the extra stockings from his pocket, untied his handkerchief, and added them to his shirt and other necessities.

"You *want* to go," Johnny accused him.

"Yes."

"Well, then—*go!*"

"I'm going fast's I'm able."

Oh, Rab, Rab! Have you ever seen those little eyes at the end of a musket? Rab, don't you go. Don't you go!

Rab was singing under his breath. It was the song of the Lincolnshire Poacher that Mr. Revere had taught Johnny and Johnny had taught Rab. There was something about Rab's singing, low, a little husky and not too accurate, that always moved Johnny. It was a part of that secret fire which came out in fighting, taking chances—and dancing with girls! The excitement glowed in Rab's eyes now. He was going to fight—and the thought made some dark part of him happy.

Johnny wanted to tell him about those eyes, but instead he said, "I guess you really want to get out to Lexington—and do some more dancing."

"Here's hoping."

From then on Johnny said nothing, sitting glumly on his bed, his head bowed. Then Rab came over to him and put a hand on his shoulder.

"Good-bye, Johnny. I'm off."

Johnny did not look up.

"You're a bold fellow, Johnny Tremain." He was laughing.

Johnny heard Rab's feet going down the ladder. The door of the shop closed after him. He ran to look out the window. Rab was standing outside the Lorne house shaking hands with his uncle, saying good-bye like a grown man. Now he was bending down to kiss Aunt Jenifer—not at all like a small boy kissing an aunt. He picked up Rabbit, who could toddle about, and kissed him, too. Then half-running, he passed lightly up Salt Lane and out of sight.

One moment too late, Johnny ran out into the alley. He couldn't let Rab go like that. He had not even said good luck, God be with you. Why . . . he might not ever see Rab again. He went back to his garret and flung himself on his bed. He half-wished he might cry and was half-glad he was too old for tears.

Today there was no sound from the shops and wharves. No cry of chimney sweep, oysterman, knife-grinder. The town was whist and still, for it was Sunday. As Johnny lay upon his bed, the church bells began to call for afternoon service. They babbled softly as one old friend to another. Christ's Church and Cockerel, Old South, Old Meeting, Hollis, King's Chapel. He knew everyone. He had heard them clanging furiously for fire, crying fiercely to call out the Sons of Liberty. He had heard them toll for the dead, rejoice when some unpopular act had been repealed, and shudder with bronze rage at tyranny. They had wakened him in the morning and sent him to bed at night, but he never loved them more than on Lord's Days when their golden clamor seemed to open the blue vaults of Heaven itself. You could almost see the angels bending down to earth—even to rowdy old Boston. "Peace, peace," the soft bells said. "We are at peace . . ."

Suddenly close by, over at the Afric Queen, the British drumsticks fell. The fifes struck up "too-too—tootlety-too." Even on Sunday they were out drilling. So were other men—even on Sunday. For instance, over in Lexington.

The sixteenth of April drew to a close.

Monday was a quiet day. Lieutenant Stranger looked very solemn. Maybe there was not to be an expedition after all.

The eighteenth of April.

By afternoon the sergeants were going about the town, rounding up the grenadier and light infantry companies, telling them (in whispers) to report at moonrise at the bottom of the Common "equipped for an expedition."

The sergeants would tap their red noses with their fingers and bid the men be "whist," but it was common knowledge in the barracks and on the streets that seven hundred men would march that night.

This very night—come darkness—the men would move, but in what direction? And who would be in charge of the expedition? Surely not more than one of the colonels would be sent.

Johnny, who had his own colonel to watch, Colonel Smith, hardly left the Afric Queen all day and helped the pot-boy serve drinks to the officers in the dining room. A young officer sitting with Stranger did say, as he stirred his brandy-and-water with his thumb, that he hoped before long thus to stir Yankee blood —and what of that? Colonel Smith did have an army chaplain to dine with him that day. Did that mean he was suddenly getting religious, as people are said to before they go into danger?

Of one thing Johnny was sure. Dove knew much less than he did. Dove was so thick-witted he had no idea anything unusual was afoot. He honestly believed that the grenadiers and light infantry were merely going to be taught "new evolutions." As

245

usual, Dove was too wrapped in his own woes to think much of what was happening about him.

By five Johnny thought he would leave the Queen and report to Paul Revere that he had discovered nothing new. First one more glance at Dove.

For once he found him hard at work, his lower lip stuck out, his whitish pig-lashes wet. He was polishing a saddle.

"That guy," he complained, "hit me for nothing. He said I was to get to work on his campaign saddle."

"Who's he?"

"Colonel Smith, of course."

"Did you do as he told you?"

"I tried. I didn't know he had two saddles. So I went to work on the usual one. I shined it until you can see your face in it. And he takes it out of my hands and hit me on the head with it. Says I'm a stupid lout not to know the difference between a parade saddle and a campaign saddle. How'd I know? Why, he's been over here about a year and that campaign saddle hasn't ever been unpacked. I had to get it from Lieutenant Stranger. How'd I know?"

Johnny said nothing. He realized he had heard something which conceivably might be important. Careful . . . careful . . . don't you say anything to scare him.

"Where's your polish? I'll help with the stirrups."

The instant Johnny went to work, Dove lay back on the hay.

"One of the stirrups wrapped 'round my head. Cut my ear. It bled something fierce."

Johnny was studying the saddle on his knees. It was of heavy black leather, brass (not silver) mountings. Three girths instead of two. All sorts of hooks and straps for attaching map cases, spyglasses, flasks, kits of all sorts.

Colonel Smith is going on a campaign. But perhaps not. He might merely be riding down to New York.

He leaned back on his heels. "Say, what if you and I took time out to eat supper? The Queen's cook has promised me a good dinner, because I helped them at table this afternoon. Roast goose. I'll fix it so you can get in on it, too."

246

"Oh, for goodness' sake—no."

"It's past five o'clock. Colonel can't be going anywhere tonight."

"Oh, for land's sake, Johnny, he says I'm to show him that saddle by six sharp, and if he don't like its looks he's going to cut me to mincemeat. He's always saying things like that. He's the . . ."

Johnny did not listen to what Colonel Smith was. He was thinking.

"Well, after that—when Colonel Smith has settled down to play whist. Can you get off?"

"Tonight isn't like any other night. He told me to bring Sandy around for him, fed and clean and saddled with this old campaign saddle by eight o'clock tonight . . ."

Colonel Smith is going on a long journey. Starting tonight at eight. It might be a campaign. He had an idea.

"I should think if the Colonel was making a long trip he'd take Nan, she's so light and easy to ride . . . if he has far to go."

"He does like her better—she don't jounce his fat so. He always rides her 'round Boston. But only yesterday he had Lieutenant Stranger take her over to the Common when the men were drilling. Stranger says she still is squirmy when she hears drums and shooting. I heard him say so."

247

"Oh." Drums and shooting. This was not to be a peaceful ride to, say, New York. His cloth whipped over the black saddle leather. He spat on it and rubbed even harder. The one thing he must not say was the wrong thing. Nothing was better than the wrong thing. So for a while he said nothing.

"Sandy's good as gold, but he's an old horse and a little stiff. His front left leg won't last forever."

"Colonel Smith didn't say he was going off on him forever."

This did not help much. But Dove went on:

"He and the horse doctor and Lieutenant Stranger were all looking at him just this morning. The horse doctor said old Sandy could do thirty miles easy. And Stranger said, no, he wouldn't swear you could get Nan on and off a boat without her fussing."

So . . . the campaign would start around eight that night. The Colonel's horse would be put on and off a boat. There would be a risk at least of drums and shooting. They were not going farther than thirty miles. Those men who thought the target of the expedition was going to be Lexington and Concord were right. And it would be Colonel Smith who would go in command.

All Johnny's hidden excitement went into his polishing. The brass mountings turned to gold. The black leather to satin.

"There! You take that in and show your Colonel!"

But he would wait one moment more, Dove might have something more to say when he came back from the Colonel.

Johnny went into Goblin's stall, but the horse pretended not to know him and put back his ears and nipped at him.

Sandy next. The big yellow horse carefully moved over to give him room in the stall, nickered a little. He fondled the broad white-striped face, pulled gently at the ears—little furry ears, lost in mane like a pony's.

"I guess," Johnny said, "it looks like you'll be seeing that Rab before I do. May be Lexington. You tell that Rab he'd best look sharp. Take good care of himself. Tell that Rab . . . oh, anything."

Dove came back in a jubilee.

"Colonel says I've done a fine job and so quick he's going to give me tomorrow as a holiday. He don't expect to get back

248

before night." Certainly this campaign was going to be a short one—if everything went as the British expected.

"It is tonight all right," Johnny said to Doctor Warren, "and Colonel Smith will command." He went on to tell what he had found out from Dove. That the expedition would start tonight and that Lexington and Concord were the likely objects, the men sitting about in Warren's surgery had already guessed. But they were interested to learn that the Colonel, and presumably his troops, expected to return to Boston the day after they set out and that he was to command them. Seemingly Gage, a punctilious man, had chosen Francis Smith because he had been in service longer than any of the other (and smarter) colonels.

"Hark."

Outside the closed window on Tremont Street a small group of soldiers were marching stealthily toward the Common. These were the first they heard. But soon another group marched past, then another. A man whose duty it was to watch the British boats at the foot of the Common came in to say he had actually seen the men getting into the boats, heading for Cambridge.

Doctor Warren turned to Johnny, "Run to Ann Street. Bid Billy Dawes come to me here, ready to ride. Then go to North Square. I've got to talk to Paul Revere before he starts. Both he and Dawes will be expecting a messenger."

Billy Dawes was in his kitchen. He was a homely, lanky, young fellow with close-set eyes, and a wide, expressive mouth. He and his wife had dressed him for the part he would play— a drunken farmer. His wife, who looked more like a schoolgirl than a serious matron, could not look at him without going from one giggling fit to another. She laughed even more, and Billy joined her, when Johnny came in and said the time had come. The young man stuck a dilapidated hat with a broken feather on his head, and his wife picked up a bottle of rum and poured it over the front of his torn jacket. Then she kissed him, and they both laughed. As he stood before them, his expression changed.

His eyes went out of focus. His grin became foolish. He hiccoughed and swayed. He both looked and smelled like a

249

mister
mckee

drunken farmer. But he did have money in his pocket which no country blade would have had after a big toot in town. He knew one of the soldiers guarding the Neck that night. He believed he'd get out all right.

The scene in the Dawes kitchen was so light-hearted and so comical—and Johnny as well as little Mrs. Dawes laughed so hard—he wondered if she had any idea of the risk her husband was running. For by any law of any land a man caught exciting to armed rebellion might be shot. The second the door closed after the young man, Johnny knew. Mrs. Dawes stood where her husband had left her, all laughter wiped from her face. Billy Dawes was not the only gifted actor in his family.

From Ann Street Johnny ran toward North Square. This he found crowded with light infantry and grenadier companies, all in full battle dress. They got in his way and he in theirs. One of the men swore and struck at him with his gun butt. The regulars were getting ugly. He could not get to the Reveres' front door, but by climbing a few fences he reached their kitchen door, and knocked softly. Paul Revere was instantly outside with him.

"Johnny," he whispered, "the *Somerset* has been moved into the mouth of the Charles. Will you run to Copp's Hill and tell me if they have moved in any of the other warships? I think I can row around one, but three or four might make me trouble."

"I'll go look."

"Wait. Then go to Robert Newman—you know, the Christ's Church sexton. He lives with his mother opposite the church."

"I know."

"They have British officers billeted on them. *Don't rap at that door.* Take this stick. Walk by the house slowly, limping, tapping with the stick until the light in an upper window goes out. Then go 'round behind the house. Tell Newman the lanterns are to be hung now. Two of them. He knows what to do."

As Johnny stood among the graves of lonely Copp's Hill looking across the broad mouth of the Charles, he could see lights in the houses of Charlestown. And over there he knew men were watching Boston, watching Christ's lofty spire—waiting for the signal. And as soon as they saw it, the best and fastest horse in Charlestown would be saddled and made ready for Paul Revere, who had himself promised to get over—if possible. Ride and spread the alarm. Summon the Minute Men. He watched the riding lights on the powerful sixty-four-gun *Somerset*. The British had evidently thought her sufficient to prevent boats crossing the river that night. She was alone.

The moon had risen. The tide was rising. The *Somerset* was winding at her anchor. The night smelled of land and of the sea, but most of all it smelled of spring.

Salem Street, where the Newmans lived, like North Square, was filled with soldiers. The redcoats were assembling here, getting ready to march down to the Common—and they would be a little late. Their orders were to be ready by moonrise. A sergeant yelled at Johnny as he started to limp past them, but when he explained in a piteous whine that his foot had been squashed by a blow from a soldier's musket and all he wanted

251

was to get home to his mama, an officer said the men were to let "the child" pass. Johnny was sixteen, but he could pull himself together and play at being a little boy still.

Downstairs in the Newman house he could look in and see a group of officers as usual, almost as always, playing at cards. Their jackets were unbuttoned, their faces flushed. They were laughing and drinking. There was on the second floor one light. Johnny couldn't believe anyone up there could hear him tapping in the street below. Instantly the light went out. He had been heard.

Newman, a sad-faced young man, got out at a second-story window in back, ran across a shed roof, and was in the alley waiting for Johnny.

"One or two?" he whispered.

"Two."

That was all. Robert Newman seemed to melt away in the dark. Johnny guessed what the little tinkle was he heard. Newman had the keys to Christ's Church in his hand.

The two friends, Paul Revere and Joseph Warren, were standing in the Doctor's surgery. They were alone. Revere was urging Warren to cross with him that very night to Charlestown. If there was fighting tomorrow, Gage would not hesitate to hang him—at last—for high treason. But Warren said no. He would stay and keep track of the British plans until the very last moment.

"The second a shot has been fired, I'll send a messenger to you," Revere promised.

"I'll wait until then. Why, Revere, I never saw you worry about anything before. I'll be a lot safer tonight than you'll be —catching crabs out on that river. Being shot at by the *Somerset*. And falling off horses—I'll not forget you and Parson Tomley's ambling jade."

He was always ragging Revere about falling off horses. It was some old joke between them which Johnny did not know, and both the men suddenly began to laugh. The mood between them had been heavy when Johnny came in, but now it lightened. They parted as casually as any friends who believe they

252

mister
mckee

will meet in a few days. But each knew the other was in deadly peril of his life. It was ten o'clock.

Doctor Warren told his colored man to make up a bed for Johnny in the surgery. The boy could not think of bed. He stole down to the Common to see the "secret" embarkation. It was almost over and was no secret. Hundreds of townsfolk stood about silently watching the boats returning from Cambridge shore and taking on yet another scarlet-coated cargo. But where these men were heading and who commanded them, scarce a man in the crowd knew except Johnny. Farther down the river he knew the *Somerset* was on guard. By now Paul Revere was in his boat, trying to steal around her. In Charlestown the horse waited for him.

He saw Sandy step into a boat with never a quiver. He recognized Lieutenant Stranger's own horse and for a moment saw the young man's dark face in the moonlight. Being a horse-minded boy, he noticed that there was a little trouble with a showy white horse built like Sandy, but much younger. This was Major Pitcairn's. Were the marines being sent as well as the grenadiers and light infantry companies? Or was the rough, genial, stout-hearted old major going along for the fun of it?

At least, he thought this observation important enough to report to Warren. Other spies had been bringing news of the embarkation. It had been noticed that Pitcairn was not in his usual tavern. He had been seen with a civilian cape wrapped about him heading for the Common. Doubtless he was going. Gage had sent him either because he knew he was a better officer than Colonel Smith or because he had a way with Yankees. Everyone liked the pious, hard-swearing, good-tempered Major Pitcairn.

A barmaid from Hull Street came in to say she had been watching the *Somerset* at just the time Bentley and Richardson were rowing Paul Revere to Charlestown. Not a shot had been fired. It was also known that Billy Dawes had woven and bribed his inebriated way past the guards on the Neck. And the horse he was leading and pretending to try to sell had not looked like much—a thin bony beast in a bridle patched with rope. It was one of the fastest horses in Boston.

Then Doctor Warren told Johnny to lie down and get some sleep. It was almost midnight.

Johnny took off his jacket and boots, rolled up in a blanket on the bed the Negro had made for him. The night before and the night before that he had been much upset over Rab's leaving. His thoughts had turned to the empty bed beside him. He had slept badly. Although people were still about the surgery, exchanging ideas, trying to guess what the future might be, he immediately fell asleep.

It was dawn. He was alone in the surgery and still sleeping. But out in Lexington on the Village Green the first shot was fired. One shot and then a volley. And Major Pitcairn was saying, "Disperse, ye rebels, ye villains, disperse! Why don't ye lay down your arms?"

The war had begun.

It was the dawn of the Nineteenth of April. But Johnny Tremain still slept.

Evelyn Sickels

A MESSAGE
FOR WASHINGTON

ILLUSTRATED BY *Jack Roderick*

LYDIA DARRAGH was raking the hot coals out of the chimney oven so that she could clap into it the weekly baking, when there came a mighty knocking at the front door.

"Thee will have to put these things in for me, Polly," she said to the girl who was helping her. Polly was a bound girl, who had been sent over from England and sold as a sort of household slave until she should have worked out her passage money. She was very young and flighty, and Lydia looked at her doubtfully.

"Now do thee be careful, Pol," she said kindly. "I'll not be gone but a moment. It is perhaps that British officer who likes to use our big room upstairs, so I had best be the one to go."

The knocking came again, louder than ever, and Lydia walked swiftly through the house to open the door. Sure enough, it was the British adjutant-general from the Golden Fleece Tavern across the street, where General Howe had set up his headquarters. He saluted her courteously.

"May I have a word with you within, Mistress Darragh?"

"Thee may," Lydia replied calmly, showing him into the long dim parlor.

"You know your large back room on the second floor," he began as soon as they were inside, "the one I have several times used to confer with my friends. You will kindly see that it is prepared for my use tonight. I have several friends coming. They will be here shortly after seven and will probably stay late. You will see that you and all your family are in bed early. When we

255

are ready to go, I will come and awaken you so that you can lock the doors after us. Do you understand?"

"I understand, and it shall be as thee says, friend," said Lydia. She spoke in the kindly, familiar way Quakers have, but there was not much enthusiasm in her voice. Though as a Quaker she did not believe in war and was not supposed to take sides in this one, Lydia Darragh very much disliked doing things for the British officers. For in her heart she believed passionately in the rebel cause. She had not protested as much as she felt she should have even when her oldest son insisted on enlisting in Washington's army.

"I know I can depend on your prudence and care," the adjutant was saying. "Until later, then." And he was gone.

Lydia closed the door and stood for several minutes with her hand on the knob, thinking. Why had the adjutant been so urgent and so solemn? Why must they all go to bed early tonight? He had never asked that before. *What were they going to decide in that room tonight?*

The gay voices of the children broke in on her reverie. They must have come in from their hour of play in the orchard. It was time Sarah and Deborah were at their knitting. And what might not Pol have done to the baking by this time? Well, well, she would lay the fire in the big room as soon as she got things straightened out in the kitchen. With so much to do, there would be no time to worry.

But as she went quietly about her work that day, Lydia Darragh could not get the adjutant's words and his important way of saying them out of her head. She kept seeing the little Patriot army shivering in the December cold at Whitemarsh, only a few miles outside the city. She knew that General Washington himself was in command there, and her own boy was one of the junior officers. Two months before, the Americans had been defeated at Germantown, and the British had marched into Philadelphia. Ever since then the two armies had lain inactive, watching each other. Lydia was sure this conference meant the British general was up to some mischief. *What was it?*

She thought the day would never end. Pol burned some of the

256

pies, and little Deborah did her knitting all crooked. Young John tore his knickerbockers, and William, Lydia's husband, came home late to dinner because he had been detained at the home of one of his pupils. But Lydia was used to days when everything went wrong and was never known to lose her temper or admit that she was tired. If only she could forget about that mysterious meeting!

At last seven o'clock came, and soon afterward the officers began to arrive. She showed them up to the big room, and when they were all there and the adjutant-general had closed the door on them, Lydia faithfully put the children to bed as she had promised. By eight o'clock William was in bed, too, and sleeping peacefully. He was not worried. A true Friend, he took no part at all in the war. Besides, he had not heard the solemn voice in which the adjutant had asked them all to retire.

When Lydia came up to their room and saw her husband already asleep, she lay down very quietly without undressing. She would have to get up later anyway, she told herself, to cover the fire and put out the light. But the longer she lay there the more impossible it was for her to sleep. What was going on in that rear room? She simply had to find out.

Scarcely realizing that she had made up her mind to do it, Lydia slipped off the high bed to the floor and glided noiselessly through the hallway to the door of the big room. Shamelessly she put her ear to the keyhole. She *must* know what they were saying.

At first she could not make out a word. They seemed to be all talking at once, and none loudly. Then the voices suddenly stopped, and after a moment of silence somebody cleared his throat and began to read an order. The words were very clear now. Lydia caught her lip with her teeth to keep from crying out.

"Tomorrow night," the voice was saying, "the troops will leave the city in secret to surprise and capture the American forces at Whitemarsh."

Lydia did not wait to hear any more. What more did she need to hear? She fled back to her room with her thoughts in a whirl,

JACK RODERICK

and quickly undressed and climbed into bed. She knew now what the meeting was about, but knowing had certainly not made her any happier! Was there nothing she could do to stop this terrible thing from happening?

About half an hour later she heard a knock at her door and knew that it was the adjutant come to say that the meeting was over. Of course she had not closed her eyes since getting into bed, but she pretended to be asleep and did not answer. It was not that she had any clear plan as yet, but whatever happened no one must know that she had been listening at the keyhole. She let the man knock again and again, each time more loudly and impatiently, before at last she pushed back the curtains of the bed, slipped into her nightgown (which we should now call a bathrobe) and sleepily opened the door.

"Did thee have to knock long?" she asked.

"Aye," said the officer a little curtly. "You are a good sleeper. We are through with your room now."

She locked the door after him, and went to the meeting-room to snuff out the candles and put out the fire. "No use covering the fire," she thought. "We have fire in the kitchen and doubtless they'll not want this room again for some time." For in 1777, of course, you thought twice before you put out a fire, since if there were no other fire in the house you would have to go to a neighbor's with a covered pan to get live coals, or take the trouble of kindling a fire with tinder, flint, and steel.

When Lydia was in bed again, she lay very quiet so as not to disturb William—who had scarcely stirred for all that knocking!—but she did not shut her eyes all night. She thought of telling William about what she had heard, but decided against it. He might get into trouble, and that would be especially hard when he had been so careful to remember he was a Friend and to keep clear of the war. No, if anything were to be done, she must do it herself. By dawn her plans were all laid.

It was still early when she woke William.

"Husband," she told him, "we used near the last of our flour yesterday for the baking. Today I must go to the gristmill at Franklin for more."

259

"Be it so," said William. He was not at all surprised, for Lydia often walked the five miles to Franklin and came back carrying a sack of flour. "Thee had better take Pol with thee."

"Nay," said Lydia positively, "I do not need Pol. She will be more useful at home." William protested a little at that, but in the end Lydia—as usual—had it her way.

No sooner was General Howe up than Lydia was at head-quarters asking for a pass to go through the British lines to Franklin. She had no trouble getting it, as she had been on the same errand so many times before. Then, with her pass safely tucked in her bosom and an empty bag over her shoulder, she set out, sturdily tramping through the new-fallen snow.

At Franklin she left her sack, saying that she would call for it a little later, and started on toward the American lines. Her heart was thumping violently under her prim Quaker dress, and under her big Quaker bonnet her eyes were burning with excitement. Perhaps she was going to save the life of her dear son, and the lives of thousands of others. Perhaps she was going to save the whole cause in which she believed, for the capture of Washington and his army would be almost too great a calamity for the Patriots to bear. She knew she was running a great risk in what she was doing; she hated that more for William and the children than for herself. She felt rather guilty, too, because she, a Friend, was mixing in a war. And she had eavesdropped and acted (though not spoken) a lie. But somehow Lydia was sure that after all she was doing right.

She hurried, because she did not want to be gone so long on her errand that anyone would suspect, either at Franklin or at Philadelphia. As she was nearing the American outposts, along came Lieutenant-Colonel Craig, whom she had often seen in the city, riding with a small band of cavalry. They were scouting about trying to pick up information. Little did they think what important information was hurrying along the snowy road to meet them!

Colonel Craig recognized Lydia and paused to greet her.

"And what are you doing out here all alone, Mistress Darragh?" he asked, drawing rein beside her.

"Do thee get down from thy horse, friend John Craig," said Lydia, "and walk a spell with me and I will tell thee." It had come to Lydia that she could save precious time by telling this trusty officer her secret, sure that he would take it swiftly to Washington.

"Gladly," said Colonel Craig, dismounting lightly. He looked at Lydia's serious face and ordered the soldiers to ride on ahead. "I see 'tis no light matter, Mistress Darragh."

"It is truth thee speaks," said Lydia, "for I bear heavy tidings. They are for thy General Washington's ears."

Craig glanced at her quickly. "Hum," he said. "Suppose you tell them to me. I will take them to him."

"Thee will not betray me?" asked Lydia urgently. "If the British officers knew I had a hand in this, it would go hard with me—and with my dear ones. Thee will promise not to betray me?"

"I promise," said Craig solemnly.

Then she told him. When she was through speaking, he wrung her hand in gratitude and, seeing that she was almost faint with weariness and excitement, he took her to a farmhouse near by and settled her comfortably at a table, bidding the woman bring her food. Then he left, to carry her message to Washington.

Lydia choked down a cup of milk and was on her way in almost no time. She stopped at the mill, shouldered her sack of flour, and tramped the five miles back to the city. Such good time had she made that no one thought of asking her why she had been so long away.

That night she sat alone in her room listening to the muffled sounds of the mustering of the British forces. When all was still again, she went to bed, but she got little more sleep tonight than the night before. And for the next two or three days she went about her duties as if in a dream. She dared not ask for news, though she thought she would die if she did not learn soon what had happened. Had her warning reached Washington in time? Had there been a battle? If so, who had won, and—most desperately important of all to her mother's heart—who had fallen?

The second day after the troops marched she was called to a neighbor's house to take care of a sick woman. For Lydia was an excellent nurse, and had been well known in Philadelphia for ten years as a sort of unofficial doctor. She helped support the family by her earnings at this work. This time she went eagerly, hoping that at the sick woman's house she might hear news of the armies. But everyone was so worried over the trouble at home that not a word was said of the war.

At last the troops marched back into the city. That afternoon there came a loud knock on Lydia's door, and there stood the adjutant-general again, looking much upset.

"Mistress Darragh," he said gravely, "you will be pleased to go with me to the conference room. I must speak with you alone."

Without a word Lydia followed him up the stairs. Her heart was pounding in her ears and she had to put out her hand now and then to touch the wall because a faintness had come over her. Had she been betrayed? What should she say? Would it be

262

wicked to lie about what she had done, to save herself and her family? And if she did lie, would he believe her? What would become of the children if—if anything happened to her?

The adjutant-general locked the door behind them and motioned Lydia to a chair. As soon as she turned to face him, her courage came back. "I am not afraid," she thought, "for surely what I did was right." She lifted her head defiantly and spoke in a clear, calm voice when she answered his questions.

"Mistress Darragh," he said, "were any of your family up late the night I entertained my friends in this room—on December 2?"

"Indeed they were not. Everyone was in bed by eight o'clock or before, just as thee bade."

"It is very strange," said he with a puzzled frown. "I cannot understand how the rebels could have got wind of our plan of attack, unless the walls of your house have ears. As for you yourself, I know you were asleep that night. I remember I had to knock several times before I could arouse you to let us out."

"So thee did," said Lydia. A great wave of relief had swept over her, and her voice was almost amused. So no one had betrayed her after all!—And what was this the officer was saying?

"Yet someone must have warned them, for when we got to Whitemarsh they had all their cannon in position and everything ready for a battle. It was not a pitched battle we went out for," he added ruefully, "and here we have marched back like a parcel of fools!"

So that was how Lydia Darragh heard how well she had served the Patriot cause. Nothing more was ever said to her about the matter—by the British. Long afterward, when the enemy had left Philadelphia and there was no longer any danger in its being known, Washington sent her a formal message of thanks. The story got around among the people of the city, and after many years it found its way into print.

But by that time Lydia Darragh had tended her last sick neighbor and raked the coals out of the oven for the last time. She died in 1789, the year in which George Washington, for whose cause she had risked so much, was inaugurated the first president of the United States.

Louisa May Alcott

TABBY'S TABLECLOTH

ILLUSTRATED BY *Salcia Bahnc*

N THE twentieth day of March, 1775, a little girl was trudging along a country road with a basket of eggs on her arm. She seemed in a great hurry and looked anxiously about her as she went; for those were stirring times, and Tabitha Tarbell lived in a town that took a famous part in the Revolution. She was a rosy-faced, bright-eyed lass of fourteen, full of vigor, courage, and patriotism, and just then much excited by the frequent rumors which reached Concord that the British were coming to destroy the stores sent there for safekeeping while the enemy occupied Boston. Tabby glowed with wrath at the idea, and (metaphorically speaking) shook her fist at august King George, being a stanch little Rebel, ready to fight and die for her country rather than submit to tyranny of any kind.

In nearly every house something valuable was hidden. Colonel Barrett had six barrels of powder; Ebenezer Hubbard, sixty-eight barrels of flour; axes, tents, and spades were at Daniel Cray's; and Captain David Brown had guns, cartridges, and musket balls. Cannon were hidden in the woods; firearms were being manufactured at Barrett's Mills; cartridge boxes, belts, and holsters, at Reuben Brown's; saltpeter at Josiah Melvin's; and much oatmeal was prepared at Captain Timothy Wheeler's. A morning gun was fired, a guard of ten men patrolled the town at night, and the brave farmers were making ready for what they felt must come.

There were Tories in the town who gave the enemy all the information they could gather; therefore much caution was necessary in making plans, lest these enemies should betray them. Passwords were adopted, secret signals used, and messages sent from house to house in all sorts of queer ways. Such a message lay hidden under the eggs in Tabby's basket, and the brave little girl was going on an important errand from her uncle, Captain David Brown, to Deacon Cyrus Hosmer, who lived at the other end of the town, by the South Bridge. She had been employed several times before in the same way and had proved herself quick-witted, stout-hearted, and light-footed. Now, as she trotted along in her scarlet cloak and hood, she was wishing she could still further distinguish herself by some great act of heroism; for good Parson Emerson had patted her on the head and said, "Well done, child!" when he heard how she ran all the way to Captain Barrett's, in the night, to warn him that Dr. Lee, the Tory, had been detected sending information of certain secret plans to the enemy.

"I would do more than that, though it was a fearsome run through the dark woods. Wouldn't those two like to know all I know about the stores? But I wouldn't tell 'em, not if they drove a bayonet through me. I'm not afeard of 'em," and Tabby tossed her head defiantly as she paused to shift her basket from one arm to the other.

But she evidently was "afeard" of something, for her ruddy cheeks turned pale and her heart gave a thump as two men came in sight and stopped suddenly on seeing her. They were strangers and, though nothing in their dress indicated it, the girl's quick eye saw that they were soldiers; step and carriage betrayed it, and the rapidity with which these martial gentlemen changed into quiet travelers roused her suspicions at once. They exchanged a few whispered words; then they came on, swinging their stout sticks, one whistling, the other keeping a keen lookout along the lonely road before and behind them.

"My pretty lass, can you tell me where Mr. Daniel Bliss lives?" asked the younger, with a smile and a salute.

Tabby was sure now that they were British; for the voice was deep and full, the face a ruddy English face, and the man they wanted was a well-known Tory. But she showed no sign of alarm, beyond the modest color in her cheeks, and answered civilly, "Yes, sir, over yonder a piece."

"Thanks and a kiss for that," said the young man, stooping to bestow his gift. But he got a smart box on the ear, and Tabby ran off in a fury of indignation.

With a laugh they went on, never dreaming that the little Rebel was going to turn spy herself and get the better of them. She hurried away to Deacon Hosmer's and did her errand, adding thereto the news that strangers were in town. "We must know more of them," said the deacon. "Clap a different suit on her, wife, and send her with the eggs to Mrs. Bliss. We have all we want of them, and Tabby can look well about her while she rests and gossips over there. Bliss must be looked after smartly, for he is a knave and will do us harm."

Away went Tabby in a blue cloak and hood, much pleased with her mission; and, coming to the Tory's house about noon, smelt afar off a savory odor of roasting meat and baking pies.

Stepping softly to the back door, she peeped through a small window and saw Mrs. Bliss and her handmaid cooking away in the big kitchen, too busy to heed the little spy, who slipped around to the front of the house to take a general survey before she went in. All she saw confirmed her suspicions; for in the keeping room a table was set forth in great style, with the silver tankards, best china, and the fine damask tablecloth which the housewife kept for holidays. Still another peep through the lilac bushes before the parlor windows showed her the two strangers closeted with Mr. Bliss, all talking earnestly but in too low a tone for a word to reach even her sharp ears.

"I *will* know what they are at. I'm sure it is mischief, and I won't go back with only my walk for my pains," thought Tabby, and, marching into the kitchen, she presented her eggs with a civil message from Madam Hosmer.

"They are mighty welcome, child. I've used a sight for my custards, and need more for the flip. We've company to dinner unexpected, and I'm much put about," said Mrs. Bliss, who seemed to be concerned about something besides the dinner, and in her flurry forgot to be surprised at the unusual gift; for the

266

neighbors shunned them, and the poor woman had many anxieties on her husband's account—the family being divided, one brother a Tory and one a Rebel.

"Can I help, ma'am? I'm a master hand at beating eggs, Aunt Hitty says. I'm tired, and wouldn't mind sitting a bit if I'm not in the way," said Tabby, bound to discover something more before she left.

"But you be in the way. We don't want any help; so you'd better be steppin' along home, else suthin' besides eggs may git whipped. Talebearers ain't welcome here," said old Puah, the maid, a sour spinster who sympathized with her master and openly declared she hoped the British would put down the Yankee Rebels soon and sharply.

Mrs. Bliss was in the pantry, and heard nothing of this little passage of arms; for Tabby hotly resented the epithet of "talebearer," though she knew that the men in the parlor were not the only spies on the premises.

"When you are all drummed out of town and this house burned to the ground, you may be glad of my help; and I wish you may get it. Good day, old crab apple," answered saucy Tabby, and, catching up her basket, she marched out of the kitchen with her nose in the air.

But as she passed the front of the house, she could not resist another look at the fine dinner table; for in those days few had time or heart for feasting, and the best napery and china seldom appeared. One window stood open; and as the girl leaned in, something moved under the long cloth that swept the floor. It was not the wind, for the March day was still and sunny; and in a minute out popped a gray cat's head, and puss came purring to meet the newcomer whose step had roused her from a nap.

"Where one tabby hides, another can. Can I dare to do it? What would become of me if found out? How wonderful it would be if I could hear what these men are plotting. I will!"

A sound in the next room decided her; and, thrusting the basket among the bushes, she leaped lightly in and vanished under the table, leaving puss calmly washing her face on the window sill.

As soon as it was done, Tabby's heart began to flutter; but it was too late to retreat, for at that moment in bustled Mrs. Bliss, and the poor girl could only make herself as small as possible, quite hidden under the long folds that fell on all sides from the wide, old-fashioned table. She discovered nothing from the women's chat, for it ran on sage cheese, eggnog, roast pork, and lamentations over a burned pie. By the time dinner was served and the guests called in to eat it, Tabby was calm enough to have all her wits about her; and pride gave her courage to be ready for the consequences, whatever they might be.

For a time the hungry gentlemen were too busy eating to talk much; but when Mrs. Bliss went out, and the flip came in, they were ready for business. The window was shut, whereat Tabby exulted that she was inside; the talkers drew closer together and spoke so low that she could only catch a sentence now and then, which caused her to pull her hair with vexation, and they swore a good deal, to the great horror of the pious little maiden curled up at their feet. But she heard enough to prove that she was right; for these men were Captain Brown and Ensign De Bernicre, of the British Army, come to learn where the supplies were stored and how well the town was defended. She heard Mr. Bliss tell them that some of the "Rebels," as he called his neighbors, had sent him word that he should not leave the town alive, and he was in much fear for his life and property. She heard the Englishmen tell him that if he came with them they would protect him; for they were armed, and three of them together could surely get safely off, as no one knew the strangers had arrived but the slip of a girl who showed them the way. Here "the slip of a girl" nodded her head savagely and hoped the speaker's ear still tingled with the buffet she gave it.

Mr. Bliss gladly consented to this plan and told them he would show them the road to Lexington, which was a shorter way to Boston than through Weston and Sudbury, the road they came.

"These people won't fight, will they?" asked Ensign De Bernicre.

268

"There goes a man who will fight you to death," answered Mr. Bliss, pointing to his brother Tom, busy in a distant field.

The ensign swore again and gave a stamp that brought his heavy heel down on poor Tabby's hand as she leaned forward to catch every word. The cruel blow nearly forced a cry from her; but she bit her lips and never stirred, though faint with pain. When she could listen again, Mr. Bliss was telling all he knew about the hiding places of the powder, grain, and cannon the enemy wished to capture and destroy. He could not tell much, for the secrets had been well kept; but if he had known that our young Rebel was taking note of his words under his own table, he might have been less ready to betray his neighbors. No one suspected a listener, however, and all Tabby could do was to scowl at three pairs of muddy boots, and wish she were a man that she might fight the wearers of them.

She very nearly had a chance to fight or fly; for just as they were preparing to leave the table, a sudden sneeze nearly undid her. She thought she was lost and hid her face, expecting to be dragged out—to instant death, perhaps—by the wrathful men.

"What's that?" exclaimed the ensign, as a sudden pause followed that fatal sound.

"It came from under the table," added Captain Brown, and a hand lifted a corner of the cloth.

A shiver went through Tabby and she held her breath, with her eye upon that big, brown hand; but the next moment she could have laughed with joy, for pussy saved her. The cat had come to doze on her warm skirts; and when the cloth was raised, fancying she was to be fed by her master, puss rose and walked out purring loudly, tail erect, with its white tip waving like a flag of truce.

" 'Tis but the old cat, gentlemen. A good beast and, fortunately for us, unable to report our conference," said Mr. Bliss with an air of relief, for he had started guiltily at the bare idea of an eavesdropper.

"She sneezed as if she were as great a snufftaker as an old woman of whom we asked our way above here," laughed the ensign as they all rose.

"And there she is now, coming along as if our grenadiers were after her!" exclaimed the captain as the sound of steps and a wailing voice came nearer and nearer.

Tabby took a long breath and vowed that she would beg or buy the dear old cat that had saved her from destruction. Then she forgot her own danger in listening to the poor woman, who came in crying that her neighbors said she must leave town at once or they would tar and feather her for showing spies the road to a Tory's house.

"Well for me I came and heard their plots, or I might be sent off in like case," thought the girl, feeling that the more perils she encountered the greater heroine she would be.

Mr. Bliss comforted the old soul, bidding her stay there till the neighbors forgot her, and the officers gave her some money to pay for the costly service she had done them. Then they left the room, and after some delay the three men set off; but Tabby was compelled to stay in her hiding place till the table was cleared and the women deep in gossip as they washed dishes in the kitchen. Then the little spy crept out softly and, raising the window with great care, ran away as fast as her stiff limbs would carry her.

By the time she reached the deacon's, however, and told her tale, the Tories were well on their way—Mr. Bliss having provided them with horses that his own flight might be the speedier.

So they escaped; but the warning was given, and Tabby received great praise for her hour under the table. The townspeople hastened their preparations and had time to remove the most valuable stores to neighboring towns, to mount their cannon and drill their minutemen; for these resolute farmers meant to resist oppression, and the world knows how well they did it when the hour came.

Such an early spring had not been known for years, and by the nineteenth of April fruit trees were in bloom, winter grain was up, and the stately elms that fringed the river and overarched the village streets were budding fast. It seemed a pity that such a lovely world should be disturbed by strife; but liberty was dearer than prosperity or peace, and the people leaped from their beds when young Dr. Prescott came, riding for his life, with the message Paul Revere brought from Boston in the night:

"Arm! Arm! The British are coming!"

Like an electric spark the news ran from house to house; and men made ready to fight, while the brave women bade them go and did their best to guard the treasure confided to their keeping. A little later, word came that the British were at Lexington and blood had been shed. Then the farmers shouldered their guns, with few words but stern faces, and by sunrise a hundred men stood ready, with good Parson Emerson at their head. More men were coming in from the neighboring towns, and all felt that the hour had arrived when patience ceased to be a virtue and rebellion was just.

Great was the excitement everywhere; but at Captain David Brown's one little heart beat high with hope and fear, as Tabby stood at the door looking across the river to the town—where drums were beating, bells ringing, and people hurrying to and fro.

"I can't fight, but I *must* see," she said; and, catching up her cloak, she ran over the North Bridge, promising her aunt to return and bring her word as soon as the enemy appeared.

"What news? Are they coming?" called the people from the

manse and the few houses that then stood along that road. But Tabby could only shake her head and run the faster, in her eagerness to see what was happening on that memorable day. When she reached the middle of the town, she found that the little company had gone along the Lexington road to meet the enemy. Nothing daunted, she hurried in that direction and, climbing a high bank, waited to catch a glimpse of the British grenadiers, of whom she had heard so much.

About seven o'clock they came, the sun glittering on the arms of eight hundred English soldiers marching toward the hundred stouthearted farmers, who waited till they were within a few rods of them.

"Let us stand our ground; and if we die, let us die here," said brave Parson Emerson, still among his people, ready for anything but surrender.

"Nay," said a cautious Lincoln man, "it will not do for us to *begin* the war."

So they reluctantly fell back to the town, the British following slowly, being weary with their seven-mile march over the hills from Lexington. Coming to a little brown house perched on the hillside, one of the thirsty officers spied a well, with the bucket swinging at the end of the long pole. Running up the bank, he was about to drink when a girl, who was crouching behind the well, sprang up and, with an energetic gesture, flung the water in his face, crying:

"That's the way we serve spies!"

Before Ensign De Bernicre—for it was he, acting as guide to the enemy—could clear his eyes and dry his drenched face, Tabby was gone over the hill with a laugh and a defiant gesture toward the redcoats below.

In high feather at this exploit, she darted about the town, watching the British at their work of destruction. They cut down and burned the liberty pole, broke open sixty barrels of flour, flung five hundred pounds of balls into the millpond and wells, and set the courthouse on fire. Other parties were ordered to different quarters of the town to ransack houses and destroy all the stores they found. Captain Parsons was sent to take pos-

273

session of the North Bridge, and De Bernicre led the way; for he had taken notes on his former visit and was a good guide. As they marched, a little scarlet figure went flying on before them and vanished at the turn of the road. It was Tabby, hastening home to warn her aunt.

"Quick child, whip on this gown and cap and hurry into bed. These prying fellows will surely have pity on a sick girl and respect this room if no other," said Mrs. Brown, briskly helping Tabby into a short nightgown and round cap and tucking her well up when she was laid down; for between the plump featherbeds were hidden many muskets, the most precious of their stores. This had been planned beforehand, and Tabby was glad to rest and tell her tale while Aunty Brown put physic bottles and glasses on the table, set some evil-smelling herbs to simmer on the hearth, and, compromising with her conscience, concocted a nice little story to tell the invaders.

Presently they came, and it was well for Tabby that the ensign remained below to guard the doors while the men ransacked the house from garret to cellar; for he might have recognized the saucy girl who had twice maltreated him.

"These are feathers; lift the covers carefully or you'll be half smothered, they fly about so," said Mrs. Brown as the men came to some casks of cartridges and flints, which she had artfully ripped up several pillows to conceal.

Quite deceived, the men gladly passed on, leaving the very things they most wanted to destroy. Coming to the bedroom, where more treasures of the same valuable sort were hidden in various nooks and corners, the dame held up her finger, saying, with an anxious glance toward Tabby:

"Step softly, please. You wouldn't harm a poor, sick girl. The doctor thinks it is smallpox, and a fright might kill her. I keep the chamber as fresh as I can with yarbs, so I guess there isn't much danger of catching it."

The men reluctantly looked in, saw a flushed face on the pillow (for Tabby was red with running, and her black eyes wild with excitement), took a sniff at the wormwood and motherwort, and with a hasty glance into a closet or two, where

sundry clothes concealed hidden doors, hastily retired to report the danger and get away as soon as possible.

They would have been much disgusted at the trick played upon them if they had seen the sick girl fly out of bed and dance a jig of joy as they tramped away to Barrett's Mills. But soon Tabby had no heart for merriment as she watched the minutemen gather by the bridge, saw the British march down on the other side; and when their first volley killed brave Isaac Davis and Abner Hosmer, of Acton, she heard Major Buttrick give the order, "Fire, fellow soldiers; for God's sake, fire!"

For a little while shots rang, smoke rose, shouts were heard, and red and blue coats mingled in the struggle on the bridge. Then the British fell back, leaving two dead soldiers behind them. These were buried where they fell; and the bodies of the Acton men were sent home to their poor wives, Concord's first martyrs for liberty.

No need to tell more of the story of that day; all children know it and many have made a pilgrimage to see the old monument set up where the English fell, and the bronze Minuteman standing on his granite pedestal to mark the spot where the brave Concord farmers fired the shot that made the old North Bridge immortal.

We must follow Tabby, and tell how she got her tablecloth. When the fight was over, the dead buried, the wounded cared for, and the prisoners exchanged, the Tories were punished. Dr. Lee was confined to his own farm, on penalty of being shot if he left it, and the property of Daniel Bliss was confiscated by the government. Some things were sold at auction, and Captain Brown bought the fine cloth and gave it to Tabby, saying heartily:

"There, my girl, that belongs to you, and you may well be proud of it; for, thanks to your quick wits and eyes and ears, we were not taken unawares, but sent the redcoats back faster than they came."

And Tabby *was* proud of it, keeping it carefully, displaying it with immense satisfaction whenever she told the story, and spinning busily to make a set of napkins to go with it. It covered the table when her wedding supper was spread, was used at the christening of her first boy, and for many a Thanksgiving and Christmas dinner through the happy years of her married life.

Then it was preserved by her daughters as a relic of their mother's youth; and long after the old woman was gone, the well-worn cloth still appeared on great occasions, till it grew too thin for anything but careful keeping, to illustrate the story so proudly told by the grandchildren, who found it hard to believe that the feeble old lady of ninety could be the lively lass who played her little part in the Revolution with such spirit.

UNTIL 1804 that part of the United States which lies west of the Mississippi and Missouri rivers had been unexplored. Thomas Jefferson, who was then president, wanted to know what this land was like, especially after the country bought Louisiana from Napoleon. He chose two able young men, Captain Meriwether Lewis and Captain William Clark, to lead an expedition, and so they became the first white men to enter this western territory. The following story tells of one of their adventures.

Julia Davis

RIVER AND BEASTS BETRAY

ILLUSTRATED BY *Lorence Bjorklund*

AND now farewell to the prairies, to the rich plains, the waving grass, the white drift of bloom on chokecherry and plum, the wild flowers and the grasshoppers, the abundant game and the turtle dove cooing in the willows. Farewell to the unbroken dome of the sky, which had covered the party for so long. They were entering a bleak and rocky country where the hills cut the sky in two and bore on their sides only pine and dwarf cedar and prickly pear. These were the Bad Lands, the "Deserts of America," the high and barren Black Hills of Montana.

Here they saw first the gray-green aromatic blanket of the sagebrush and smelt that pungency which haunts the Westerner and draws him forever back to the bare clean highlands. The pure air grew cold, ice froze on the canoes, and a light snow

Taken from *No Other White Men* by Julia Davis, published and copyright, 1937, by E. P. Dutton & Co., Inc., New York.

powdered the ground at dawn, though it vanished by noon-day. The buffalo disappeared, and the bighorn and mountain goat balanced precariously on the cliffs. The river ran in a swift and narrow channel between sheer rocks, and the men had to wade up to their armpits in the cold water, or stumble over yards of jagged shale which reddened with the blood from their bare feet.

When, on the third of June, they came at last out of these straits into a milder and more fertile country, where they could nurse their cuts and feast again on the buffalo, it was only to find that the river here betrayed them. All the way from St. Louis it had been the one sure thing in a land of the Unknown, the guide and compass, like a trusted relation sometimes difficult but always dependable. Now, before their astonished eyes, it divided into two streams of equal size, one flowing from the north, the other from the south.

Which was the true Missouri? The Indians had made mountains, falls, and grizzlies on their maps of sand, but they had drawn only one river rising in the Rockies with its headquarters near the Columbia.

The muddy water of the northern stream rolled slowly around its sandbars like the river they had known. It flowed through a sweet and open country, and on its banks, "one continued garden of roses, innumerable little birds sing inchantingly." The southern stream was so swift that the deer could not swim against it, so clear that the clean round stones could be seen nine feet below the surface. It sang like a mountain brook fresh poured from heaven, and it ran past high and barren land covered with prickly pear.

The Captains could not afford to make a mistake. If they took the wrong branch they would not find the pass through the mountains. If they wasted too much time they would lose the brief summer during which the mountains could be crossed. If they had to camp for another winter with supplies running low, "cold obedience" might take the place of "warm and zealous support" in the men. A year's delay might mean complete failure.

278

They called a halt, and for a few days Lewis explored the northern stream and Clark the southern. Back in camp they compared notes and agreed. The clear water was the true Missouri, for it rose in the mountains, while the other river must flow through the plains. When they called the men together and announced their decision there was silence. They all looked at each other with long faces. Some of them stared into the distance, others scuffed the ground with their toes.

"Speak out," said Clark, "what's on your minds?"

Each one waited for the next man to begin. Lewis grew impatient and turned to Patrick Gass.

"Come along, Pat. It's not like you to lose your tongue."

Pat was not happy to be chosen spokesman. His long lip trembled, he cleared his throat and rubbed his hand over his face.

"Well, sir—if you please—it's this way—"

He stopped and looked at the others for support.

"Yes, man. Out with it," said the Captain.

"What I would be after saying, sirs, is we'll go with yez wherever ye say. That right, men?"

The men looked relieved. Here was something they could assent to, and they gave a hearty chorus of "aye," "*mais certainement*," "you bet." Pat felt encouraged, and finished with a rush.

"Sure now yez can see for yourselves 'tis the north stream does look like the Missouri, so what else could it be?"

Once the ice was broken, everyone had a word to put in. Crusatte thought the south branch would soon leave them stranded in the mountains, and Crusatte was wise in river lore. Drewyer thought there would be no game on it. The Fields boys thought the current would be too swift for the canoes. They would all follow the Captains, but not a single one of them thought it was right.

The Captains heard them out, then retired to the white perogue to talk it over. They did not wish to be arbitrary. They had worked with these men month after month, had seen them suffer and not complain, had nursed them in sickness and tied up the inglorious wounds which come from labor, had commented time and again in the diaries on their cheerful cooperation. They knew and appreciated the qualities of each one—Crusatte with his skill and his fiddle, Pat, stout hearted and merry, Drewyer the invaluable, and Colter the second scout, Shannon with his boyish earnestness and enthusiasm, inseparable Reuben and Joe Fields, all the rest. They loved them as a father might his children. And for their part the men knew that the Captains asked nothing of their followers which they were not ready to do themselves, and shared every risk and hardship. Here in the wilderness this little lonely group of white men was held together by something stronger than the artificial tie of military discipline. They were not only officers and men, they were friends.

Late that afternoon the Captains called the men together again. They had not changed their minds, but they would have sure proof before they moved the party. The Indians had said that they would find great falls on the Missouri. Lewis and four men would go up the river until he found them, while Clark would supervise the making of a cache for superfluous stores, and then follow with the canoes.

The men gave three rousing cheers for the Captains, forgot their doubts, and happy to be again in agreement, called for the fiddle, and spent the evening dancing and singing, "in the most social manner."

Next day they started the cache. First they drew a circle on the grass large enough for a man to get his shoulders through, and took off the sod with care. Then they dug straight down for more than a foot. As they went deeper they widened it out until they had a hole shaped like a kettle, seven feet deep, and seven feet wide on the rounded bottom. Every bit of earth was handed up in a bucket, dumped onto a hide, and emptied into the river so that it would leave no trace. They lined the floor with small dead sticks and hay and covered it with well-dried skins. The goods which they meant to store had been sunning for two days to get dry and were packed in layers separated by sticks.

They put in bear skins, a few garments, all personal baggage which the men could spare, two of the best axes, some tools, powder and shot, and six kegs of provisions. It was a way of making sure that they would have what they needed for the journey home. With regret they decided that they could not carry the forge across the mountains. When the cache was tightly packed they covered the goods with dry hides, filled in the earth, replaced the sod, and only someone who knew where to look could have found it.

They took the red perogue and tied it fast to the willows on an island, knocked the corks out of the gauge holes, and covered it with brush to hide it and protect it from the sun. The seven men who had manned it were to divide up in the canoes. All who did not dig at the cache, dressed skins for clothing and moccasins.

Meanwhile Captain Lewis, with Drewyer, Shannon, Joe Fields, and Goodrich, marched off to find the falls. The Captain carried his gun and espontoon, or spear, and he had rolled his belongings in a blanket and strapped them across his back. "The first time in my life," he wrote, "that I ever prepared a burden of this kind, and I am fully convinced that it will not be the last." Because he had a slight fever, they made only twenty-seven miles the first day, but after he had cured himself with a draught of chokecherry tea they did better. They followed the cliffs along the river until Goodrich almost fell over one and was saved only by Lewis's presence of mind. After that they stayed on the high plains in spite of the prickly pear thorns which ran through their moccasins.

When the Captain was possessed by an idea he seemed unconscious of hills or cactus or heat. On the third day he made nine miles as usual before breakfast, and then sent Drewyer, Shannon, and Joe to hunt while he walked on with Goodrich. He did not waste breath in conversation, and it became a silent footrace for Goodrich, who was short and as fat as the hard life allowed. After an hour or so he had to give up and fall behind.

The Captain strode on, again alone, again ahead of all the

281

others, a long thin pole of a man with legs that worked as steadily as if they had been made of steel. He was one man, tireless, unyielding, in an immensity of barren broken earth, where his footprint was the only evidence of human life. The hot bright sun poured down on him, but he did not slacken pace as the hills grew steeper. His eyes were keenly observant, his ears tuned to the faintest bird call or beat of hooves on the ground. Suddenly he heard a sound like distant thunder.

There was not a cloud in the sky. The steady rolling reverberations did not die away as he walked in their direction, but grew louder. He was listening to the distant music of the falls.

He quickened his step and after a mile or so saw a drift of spray rising above the plains like a column of smoke. Another mile, and by noon he climbed a high rock and found himself looking down on a sight which filled him with exultation.

Below him a great body of water fell straight for nearly one hundred feet, black and smooth or breaking into white foam, while the sun made a brilliant rainbow in the mist above it. On a solitary rock in the middle of the falls was the eagle's nest which the Indians had described, which had been there for hundreds of years, and might be there for hundreds more.

Lewis sat down on his rock, and his spirit drank in the wild uncivilized beauty around him, from the black rushing water to the white unchanging cloudbank of the mountains on the far horizon. At last he remembered his duties, opened his blanket roll, took out his little red book, pen and ink horn, and began to write.

"Sublimely grand," he said, "and from the commencement of time concealed from the eye of civilized man." He filled several pages, then read what he had written and started to scratch out the pale flat words.

Since chaos, the river had poured over the cliffs waiting for one white man to come and tell the world that it was there. And he sat on his rock, not a poet, not an artist, trying to catch its majesty and put it down with a new quill pen which scratched abominably. He read again what he had written, and decided that bad as it was he would not be able to do any

282

better. He longed for that new fangled device, a "camera obscura." He was so absorbed that he was surprised when the men came up with a good supply of meat, and he realized that the sun was low, and the day was ending.

They feasted there, listening to the music of the falls, on buffalo humps and marrow bones, and fish which the Captain amused himself by catching, and their satisfied hearts gave good appetites, which they considered not the least of the luxuries. Next morning he sent Joe Fields back with a letter for Clark and set the rest of the men to dressing meat. For himself, he had acquired a strong taste for discovery, and he decided to walk on up the river for a mile or so, alone. Drewyer watched him go with narrowed eyes.

"The Captain he does not know this country," he said, "and he should not be so much alone in it."

"He told us he would go just a few miles," said George.

"That is not his way," Drewyer answered.

"Well," said Goodrich, running his knife expertly around a haunch of venison and tearing it off the carcass, "I guess he'll do as he pleases, and there ain't nobody going to stop him."

This seemed to sum up the subject so that there was nothing to add to it, and the other men fell to cutting up their sides of meat in silence.

Lewis strode along lightheartedly. He had so much to be satisfied about that morning that his responsibilities weighed on him less heavily than usual. Above the great falls he found another, and there heard the roaring of a third, and so he was led on and on until he had walked seventeen miles, and all the cascades were behind him and the river smooth again. Then a small tributary stream seemed to invite exploration, and Lewis could not resist it.

A herd of buffalo were grazing in a meadow by the side, and Lewis thought that it would be a good idea to kill one and leave it there, so that he should have something to eat in case he came back too late to reach camp that night. Shooting buffalo in that land of plenty was just about as exciting as shooting domestic cows would have been, but Lewis selected a small bull and put a ball through its lungs. It stood there in stupid amazement, head down, blood pouring from its mouth and nostrils, and as he waited for it to fall his heart contracted with pity in spite of all his hunting experience. He rested his rifle butt on the ground and forgot to reload it.

Suddenly he felt rather than saw something moving behind him and turned around. An enormous grizzly bear had crept up on him, and was only sixty feet away. Instinctively he swung his rifle to his shoulder, and then remembered that it was empty. He had no time then to waste getting out powder and ball and going through the complicated process of loading. He stood on a high open plain, no shelter anywhere, and the nearest tree three hundred yards away. In the split second which was all he dared use for thinking, he decided that he might make it if he turned and walked there quietly so as not to excite the bear.

284

As soon as he took a step, however, the bear rushed at him open mouthed as if it had been waiting for a signal. He ran then! He threw away his coat, which he was carrying on his shoulder, but hung on to his gun and spear as to a last hope. His legs worked like pistons, and his heart began to hammer. No matter how he drove himself the tree was still far away, and the bear steadily closer. It picked up his coat long enough to shake it, and he heard the sound of tearing leather. When he glanced over his shoulder again it was not more than twenty feet behind him, and he could see the wet shine of its black nose and the white hairs around its eyes. He gave up hope of the tree, and dashed into the river, thinking that if he made the bear attack him swimming he might be able to defend himself with his espontoon. He splashed out until the water lapped around the breast of his yellow hunting shirt, then turned and faced the bear with his espontoon raised shoulder high in his right hand ready to strike. He had dropped his gun and powder horn on the bank. He braced himself against the swift current and thanked heaven that there were stones under his feet instead of slippery mud.

The bear stopped on the bank, uncertainly. It did not understand a quarry which ran into the river and then turned in defiance instead of swimming away. Lewis decided to press his little advantage, so he shouted at it fiercely as if it had been a savage dog.

"Get out of here! Get out! Go home!"

The sound was like no sound the bear had ever heard, but it was loud and it was threatening. Lewis waved his espontoon. Suddenly the bear turned and ran off as fast as it had come. Lewis watched it for a second in astonishment, then waded ashore, picked up his gun and loaded it.

The bear did not turn back, and he saw it run for nearly three miles over the open plain, looking back occasionally as if it were afraid of being followed, and finally disappear into a distant grove of trees. He laid down his loaded gun and began to wring the water from his wet clothes.

The sunshine seemed to have a particular warmth and sweetness, and all his senses seemed sharpened. The enchanting bird songs were louder, the smell of the sage more pungently sweet. His sense of humor took hold of him, and he laughed aloud by himself to think how ridiculous he must have looked standing in the water and ordering the bear away. He could not imagine how he could have frightened it, but he found the result "not a little gratifying."

He wrung out his moccasins, put them back on, and walked up the bank, carrying his loaded gun. He went to get his coat and found that five razor-edged claws had slit it from shoulder to fringe in one sweep. It was not worth picking up.

In his heightened state of enjoyment the lure of discovery called to him more loudly than ever, and he continued his walk up the tributary river. About ten minutes later he saw in the distance a large skulking animal which he took to be a wolf.

Solitary wolves had grown to be a commonplace to the travelers and nothing to be afraid of, so the Captain did not change his stride. When he got to within fifty paces of it, however, he saw that it was not a wolf but a mountain lion. It crouched down in front of some rocks and waited for him, watching with round unblinking eyes as a cat might watch the approach of a mouse. He could see the tip of its tail waving slightly. The hair rose on its neck, its lips drew back, and its breath came out in a dry grating snarl.

Lewis stopped, rested his rifle on his espontoon to take steady aim, and fired. The lion roared and disappeared into its den. Lewis stood where he was until he had reloaded his rifle. He had had his lesson and was not to be caught a second time. Then he walked cautiously up to the rocks.

The dust around them was pitted by enormous padded feet. He examined the tracks and listened. The inside of the den was dark and completely silent. The lion did not move or come out, and as he could not be sure that he had hit it, for once caution ruled him, and he continued on his way.

But the beasts of the wilderness had not finished with him. Before he had walked more than a mile or two he saw a herd of buffalo grazing on the plain.

These animals were considered no more dangerous or alarming than domestic cattle, and it did not occur to the Captain to pay much attention to them. He had come to within a quarter of a mile of them, thinking of other things, noticing the colored rocks on the ground, the flowering herbs among the sage, looking for bear tracks, when suddenly he heard the pound of hooves. Three bulls had detached themselves from the herd and were charging him, their little tails high, their great horns lowered and shaking ponderously.

The Captain was amazed and then amused. He would run from a bear, he had respect for a lion, but he could not allow himself to be frightened by buffalo. He continued to walk quietly toward them, determined "at least to give them some amusement."

They thundered along together, snorting, thousands of pounds of muscle, blindly unintelligent. The dust rolled out in a train behind them. Lewis halted and stood perfectly still. Not more than fifteen feet away the buffalo stopped too. They stared at him, blinking their shaggy eyelids, puzzled by his immobility. Suddenly they wheeled, threw up their tails, and ran back to the rest.

The Captain had had enough. A land where even the buffalo were dangerous began to seem like a land bewitched. All the animals in nature had combined against him, and yet he bore a charmed life. Such luck could not last forever, not every ravening beast would be frightened when he came close to it. He decided not to go back for the buffalo he had killed in the morning but to strike across the plains to camp, although the red sun was already dropping below the horizon. He judged that it would be about twelve miles distant in a straight line.

The sun disappeared and the long twilight faded. The plains vanished into the darkness, and he walked alone in empty space. There were no landmarks visible, and he could not see to avoid the prickly pears. In the black silence the uncanny events of the day took on an air of unreality, and he would have thought that he had dreamed the whole fantastic story but for the cactus thorns which kept piercing his feet and reminding him unpleasantly that he was awake. The stars were out, and from them he took his direction.

After long hours he saw a pin prick of red light on the horizon. It was the campfire, and he made for it. As he drew nearer he could see his three men standing to one side with their guns in their hands, facing him and straining their eyes into the darkness. Drewyer had heard him long before he was visible. He shouted, and they rushed to meet him. They had been too anxious to sleep after the darkness fell. They had kept the fire going as a beacon, and were intending to start out on a search as soon as it was light.

Lewis sat down and finished off the remains of the supper. In the firelight he took seventeen thorns out of his aching feet. Then he lay down to sleep under a dwarf pine. He took a last sleepy look at the slow circling stars and saw a dark lump on the bough above him. He got up to look at it and found that it was a rattlesnake. This was the last straw. He killed it.

Eva March Tappan

THE PATHFINDERS: LEWIS AND CLARK

ILLUSTRATED BY *Jack Roderick*

AT THE close of the Revolution, the United States owned all the land from the Atlantic to the Mississippi and from Canada to Florida. France had lost Canada, but she still held the country between the Mississippi and the Rocky Mountains. Some twenty years after the war France needed money, and she sold this land to the United States at about two and a half cents an acre. The next thing was to find out what kind of country had been bought. The government asked Meriwether Lewis and William Clark, brother of George Rogers Clark, to explore it. It was thought that the best way would be to follow up the Missouri River, then to enter the Columbia River, and so get to the Pacific Ocean; but no one had any idea where the sources of the two rivers might be. The only way to learn was to go and find out.

No one knew what dangers there would be. There were stories of mountains so lofty that no man could ever climb them; of Indians more fierce and more cruel than any that had been known; but the stout-hearted company set out, not in the least frightened by all these tales. There were forty men or more in the party, the wife of the interpreter, and her baby, the youngest of American explorers.

This company was to do much more than simply to push through to the Pacific Ocean. They were to note the mountains and valleys and rivers; to draw maps showing where there were rapids or falls; to see what kinds of soil, trees, flowers, fruit, animals, and minerals there were in different parts of the country. In short, they were to keep their eyes open, and on their return to tell the government where they had been and what they had seen. One thing more they were to do, the most important of all, and that was to make friends with the Indians, to learn how they lived and what lands each tribe claimed, and especially to open the way for trading with them. It seems like going back to the days of Champlain to read the list of what the travelers carried to give or sell to the red men. There were beads, paints, knives, mirrors, red trousers, coats made gorgeous with gilt braid, and many other things that would please the savages.

Then they set out on a journey which proved to be two years and four months long. And such wonders as they saw! In one place the water had worn away the earth into such shapes that the explorers were sure they had come upon an ancient fort. In another was a wide river with bed and banks and falls and rapids, but not one drop of water. There were antelopes and prairie dogs and other animals which were new to them. There were buffaloes so tame that they had to be driven out of the way with sticks and stones. There were waterfalls so high that the water fell part way, then broke into mist, but gathered together again and made a second fall, which seemed to come from a cloud.

There were some things to meet that were not quite so interesting as double waterfalls. There were brown bears and black bears and grizzly bears, all anxious to greet them with a hug. There were long marches over ground covered with sharp pieces of flint, and there were other marches over plains where the thorns of the prickly pear pierced their shoes as if they were

290

J. RODERICK

only paper. Sometimes they were driven half wild with clouds of mosquitoes. "The Musquetoes were so numerous that I could not keep them off my gun long enough to take sight and by that means Missed," wrote Captain Clark in his journal. Captain Lewis once was separated from his men for a few hours, and in that time he met a grizzly bear, a mountain lion, and three buffalo bulls, all of which showed fight. Again he lay down under a tree, and when he looked up he found that he had a big rattle-snake for next-door neighbor. He nailed a letter upon a tree for some members of the party who were to come after him; but when they came they found that the beavers had gnawed the

291

tree down, carried it away to use in their dams, and so had stolen the whole post-office. One night the company camped on a sand bar in the river; but they were hardly sound asleep before the guards cried, "Get up! Get up! Sand bar's a-sinking!" They jumped into the boats and pulled for the farther shore, but before they reached it the sand bar was out of sight. There were other disturbances of their dreams. Another night they camped near an island which proved to be the home of ducks and geese and other wild fowl that quacked and hissed and made all the noises that they knew how to make, while the tired men rolled and tumbled and wished they had more quiet neighbors. Another night a buffalo dashed into their camp and ran between two rows of sleepers. And to cap the climax, the baby explorer had the mumps and was cutting teeth and cried all night.

Getting food was not always an easy matter. In one place they exchanged roast meat, pork, flour, and meal for watermelons; but they had not often so luxurious fare. Frequently they had nothing but a little flour or meal, and for a long while they lived on horseflesh and dogflesh. Often they were glad to buy eatable roots of the Indians. Sometimes the Indians refused to sell. On one such occasion, Captain Clark threw a port-fire match into the fire, and then took out his compass and with a bit of steel made the needle whirl round and round. The Indians were so terrified that the women hid behind the men, and the men hurried to bring him the roots that they had sullenly refused to sell. On the Fourth of July the explorers lived in luxury, for they feasted on bacon, beans, suet dumplings, and buffalo meat; but when Christmas came they had nothing but stale meat, fish, and a few roots. The Indians once cooked them some meat by laying it on pine branches under which were hot stones. More branches were put on top of the meat, then a layer of meat, then another layer of branches. Water was poured upon the mass, and three or four inches of earth spread over the whole heap. The white men did not like the flavor of pine, but they admitted that the meat was tender.

They tried to make friends with the Indians wherever they

went, by giving them medals and other trinkets that they had brought. They told them about the Great Father in Washington who wished them to be his children, and who would always be kind to them. Sometimes they shared their food with the red men. One Indian ate a piece of dried squash and said it was the best thing he had ever tasted, except a lump of sugar that some member of the party had given him. One tribe refused their whiskey. "I am surprised," said the chief, "that our father should give us a drink that would make us fools."

Talking with the Indians was not always easy. This is the way it was sometimes done. Captain Lewis or Captain Clark spoke in English; one of the men put what he had said into French; the interpreter put it into an Indian dialect that his Indian wife understood; she put it into another tongue which a young Indian in the party understood; and he translated it into the language of the tribe with whom they wished to talk. It was no wonder that whenever it was possible they avoided this roundabout method and used the language of signs. When a man wished to say, for instance, "I have been gone three nights," he had only to rest his head on his hand to suggest sleep and to hold up three fingers. He could say "I came on horseback" by pointing to himself and then placing two fingers of his right hand astride his left wrist. To hold a blanket by two corners, shake it over the head, and unfold it, meant "I am your friend; come and sit on my blanket." If the Indian accepted the invitation, the next scene was not very agreeable; for he would wish to embrace the white man and rub his cheek, thick with red paint, on that of his new friend.

One language was understood by all, the language of gifts. A string of beads went a long way in winning friends. The red men had their fashions in beads, however; blue or white beads were very welcome, but they cared little for other colors. They were fond of dancing. One evening several hundred Indians seated themselves around the white men's camp and waited till the violin struck up and a dance took place. After an hour or two, the white men said, "Now it is your turn. Show us how you dance." The red men and women and children sprang to their

293

feet and crowded together around an open space. A few young braves leaped into the space and carried on something that might be called a dance; but all that the rest of the company did was to sing and jump up and down in time with the music. They were as fond of games as of dancing. The most common game was one often played now by white children. A man passed a tiny piece of bone back and forth from one hand to the other, then held out both hands closed. The one who was playing against him pointed to the hand in which he thought the bone was. If he guessed right, he won the blue beads or another prize. If he lost, the other man won it.

So it was that, dancing, climbing mountains, shooting rapids, killing bears and mosquitoes, dragging canoes up rivers, making friends with the Indians, eating or fasting, the brave explorers made their way to the source of the Missouri, a streamlet so narrow that one of the men took his stand with one foot on either bank. Three quarters of a mile farther, they came to a creek running to the westward. This was one of the branches of the Columbia. Onward they went, and at last they stood on the shore of the Pacific. It was the rainy season. Their clothes and bedding were always wet, and they had nothing to eat but dried fish. It is no wonder that they did not feel delighted with the scenery. Captain Clark wrote in his journal that the ocean was "tempestuous and horrible."

At last they started on the long journey back to the east. There were the same dangers to go through again, but finally they came to the homes of white men; and when they caught sight of cows feeding on the banks of the river, they all shouted with joy, the herds looked so calm and restful and homelike. When they reached the village of St. Louis, they received a hearty welcome, for all supposed that they had perished in the wilderness. These courageous, patient men had done much more than to explore a wild country. Just as Columbus had made a path across the Atlantic, so they had made a path to the Pacific. They showed the way, and the thousands who have made the western country into farms and villages and cities have only followed in the footsteps of these fearless explorers.

The brave explorers made their way to the source of the Missouri.

HERE IS an exciting incident from a famous story of pioneer days.

Joseph A. Altsheler

WITH THE FOREST RUNNERS

ILLUSTRATED BY *Walter R. Sabel*

PAUL stopped in a little open space and looked around all the circle of the forest. Everywhere it was the same—just the curving wall of red and brown, and beyond, the blue sky, flecked with tiny clouds of white. The wilderness was full of beauty, charged with the glory of peace and silence, and there was naught to indicate that man had ever come. The leaves rippled a little in the gentle west wind, and the crisping grass bowed before it; but Paul saw no living being, save himself, in the vast, empty world.

The boy was troubled and, despite his life in the woods, he had full right to be. This was the great haunted forest of *Kaintuck-ee,* where the red man made his most desperate stand, and none ever knew when or whence danger would come. Moreover, he was lost, and the forest told him nothing; he was not like his friend, Henry Ware, born to the forest, the heir to all the primeval instincts, alive to every sight and sound, and able to read the slightest warning the wilderness might give. Paul Cotter was a student, a lover of books, and a coming statesman. Fate, it seemed, had chosen that he and Henry Ware should go hand in hand, but for different tasks.

Paul gazed once more around the circle of the glowing forest, and the shadow in his eyes deepened. Henry and the horses, loaded with powder for the needy settlement, must be somewhere near, but whether to right or left he could not tell. He had gone to look for water, and when he undertook to return he merely went deeper and deeper into the forest. Now the boughs, as they nodded before the gentle breeze, seemed to nod to him in derision. He felt shame as well as alarm. Henry would not laugh at him, but the born scholar would be worth, for the time, at least, far less than the born trailer.

Yet no observer, had there been any, would have condemned Paul as he condemned himself. He stood there, a tall, slender boy, with a broad, high brow, white like a girl's above the line of his cap, blue eyes, dark and full, with the width between that indicates the mind behind, and the firm, pointed chin that belongs so often to people of intellect.

Paul and Henry were on their way from Wareville, their home, with horses bearing powder for Marlowe, the nearest settlement, nearly a hundred miles away. The secret of making powder from the niter dust on the floors of the great caves of Kentucky had been discovered by the people of Wareville, and now they wished to share their unfailing supply with others, in order that the infant colony might be able to withstand Indian attacks. Henry Ware, once a captive in a far Northwestern tribe, and noted for his great strength and skill, had been chosen, with Paul Cotter, his comrade, to carry it. Both rejoiced in the great task, which to them meant the saving of Kentucky.

Paul's eyes were apt at times to have a dreamy look, as if he were thinking of things far away, whether of time or place; but now they were alive to the present, and to the forest about him. He listened intently. At last he lay down and put his ear to the earth, as he had seen Henry do; but he heard nothing save a soft, sighing sound, which he knew to be only the note of the wilderness. He might have fired his rifle. The sharp, lashing report would go far, carried farther by its own echoes; but it was more likely to bring foe than friend, and he refrained.

But he must try, if not one thing, then another. He looked up at the heavens and studied the great, red globe of the sun, now going slowly down the western arch in circles of crimson and orange light, and then he looked back at the earth. If he had not judged the position of the sun wrong, their little camp lay to the right, and he would choose that course. He turned away at once and then he walked swiftly among the trees.

Paul stopped now and then to listen. He would have uttered the long forest shout, as a signal to his comrade, but even that was forbidden. Henry had seen signs in the forest that indicated more than once to his infallible eye the presence of roving warriors from the north, and no risk must be taken. But, as usual, it was only the note of the wilderness that came to his ears. He stopped also once or twice, not to listen, but to look at the splendid country, and to think what a great land it would surely be.

He walked steadily on for miles, but the region about him remained unfamiliar. No smoke from the little campfire rose among the trees, and no welcome sight of Henry or the horses came to his eyes. For all he knew, he might be going farther from the camp at every step. Putting aside caution, he made a trumpet of his two hands, and uttered the long, quavering cry that serves as a signal in the forest. It came back in a somber echo from the darkening wilderness, and Paul saw, with a little shiver, that the sun was now going down behind the trees. The breeze rose, and the leaves rustled together with a soft hiss, like a warning. Chill came into the air. The sensitive mind of the boy, so much alive to abstract impressions, felt the omens of coming danger, and he stopped again, not knowing what to do. He called himself afraid, but he was not. It was the greater tribute to his courage that he remained resolute where another might well have been in despair.

The sun went down behind the black forest like a cannon shot into the sea, and darkness swept over the wilderness. Paul uttered the long cry again and again, but, as before, no answer came back; once he fired his rifle, and the sharp note seemed to run for miles, but still no answer.

Then he decided to take counsel of prudence, and sleep where he was. If he walked on, he might go farther and farther away from the camp, but if he stopped now, while he might not find Henry, Henry would certainly find him. Any wilderness trail was an open road to his comrade.

He hunted a soft place under one of the trees, and, despising the dew, stretched himself between two giant roots, his rifle by his side. He was tired and hungry, and he lay for a while staring at the blank undergrowth, but by and by all his troubles and doubts floated away. The note of the wind was soothing, and the huge roots sheltered him. His eyelids drooped, a singular feeling of peace and ease crept over him, and he was asleep.

It was yet the intense darkness of early night, and the outline of his figure was lost between the giant roots, but after a while a silver moon brought a gray tint to the skies, and the black bank over the forest began to thin and lighten. Then two figures, hideous in paint, crept from the undergrowth, and stared at the sleeping boy with pitiless eyes.

Paul slept on, and mercifully knew nothing of his danger; yet it would have been hard to find in the world two pairs of eyes that contained more savagery than those now gazing upon him. Their owners crept nearer, looking with fierce joy through the darkness at the sleeping boy who was so certainly their prey. Their code contained nothing that taught them to spare a foe, and this youth, in the van of the white invasion, was the worst of foes.

The boy still slept, and his slumber was deep, sweet, and dreamless. No warning came to him while the savage eyes, bright with cruel fire, crept closer and closer, and the merciful darkness, coming again, tried to close down and hide the approaching tragedy of the forest.

Paul returned with a jerk from his peaceful heaven. Hands and feet were seized suddenly and pinned to the earth so tightly that he could not move, and he gazed up at two hideous, painted faces, very near to his own, and full of menace. The boy's heart turned for a moment to water. He saw at once, through his vivid and powerful imagination, all the terrors of his position, and in the same instant he leaped forward also to the future, and to the agony it had in store for him. But in a moment his courage came back, the strong will once more took command of the body and the spirit, and he looked up with stoical eyes at his captors. He knew that resistance now would be in vain, and, relaxing his muscles, he saved his strength.

The warriors laughed a little, a soundless laugh that was full of menace, and bound him securely with strips of buckskin cut from his own garments. Then they stood up, and Paul, too, rose to a sitting position, gazing intently at his captors. They were powerful men, apparently warriors of middle age, and Paul knew enough of costume and paint to tell that they were of the Shawnee nation, bitterly hostile to him and his kind.

His terrors came back upon him in full sweep. He loved life, and, scholar though he was, he loved his life in the young wilderness of Kentucky, where he was at the beginnings of things. Every detail of what they would do to him, every incident of the torture was already photographed upon his sensitive mind, but again the brave lad called up all his courage, and again he triumphed, keeping his body still and his face without expression. He merely looked up at them, as if placidly waiting their will.

The two warriors talked together a little, and then, seeming to change their minds, they unbound the boy's feet. One touched him on the shoulder, and, pointing to the north, started in that direction. Paul understood, and, rising to his feet, followed. The second warrior came close behind, and Paul was as securely a prisoner as if he were in the midst of a band of a hundred. Once or twice he looked around at the silent woods and thought of running, but it would have been the wildest folly. His hands tied, he could have been quickly overtaken, or, if not that, a bullet. He sternly put down the temptation, and plodded steadily on between the warriors, the broad, brown back of the one in front of him always leading the way.

It seemed to him that they sought the densest part of the undergrowth, where the night shadows lay thickest, and he was wise enough to know that they did it to hide their trail from possible pursuit. Then he thought of Henry, his comrade, the prince of trailers! He might come! He would come! Paul's blood leaped at the thought, and his head lifted with hope.

Clouds swept up, the moon died, and in the darkness Paul had little idea of direction. He only knew that they were still traveling fast amid the thick bushes, and that when he made too much noise in passing, one or other of the brown savages would prod him with the muzzle of a gun as a hint to be more careful. His face became bruised and his feet weary, but at last they stopped in an opening among the trees, by the side of a little brook that trickled over shining pebbles.

The warriors wasted little time. They rebound Paul's feet in such tight fashion that he could scarcely move, and then, lying down near him, went to sleep so quickly that it seemed to Paul they accomplished the feat by some sort of a mechanical arrangement. Tired as he was, he could not close his own eyes yet, and he longed for his comrade. Would he come?

Paul's sensitive nerves were again keenly alive to every phase of his cruel situation. The warriors, lying almost at his feet, were monsters, not men, and this wilderness, which in its finer aspects he loved, was bristling in the darkness with terrors known and unknown. Yet his clogged and weary brain slept at last, and when he awoke again it was day—a beautiful day of white and gold light, with the autumnal tints of the forest all about him, and the leaves rustling in a gentle wind.

But his heart sank to the uttermost depths when he looked at the warriors. By day they seemed more brutal and pitiless than at night. From their long, narrow eyes shone no ray of mercy, and the ghastly paint on their high cheek bones deepened their look of ferocity. It was not the appearance of the warriors alone, it was more the deed for which they were preparing that appalled Paul. They were raking dead leaves and fallen brushwood of last year around a small but stout sapling, and they went on with their task in a methodical way.

Paul knew well, too well. Hideous tales of such doings had come now and then to his ears, but he had never dreamed that he, Paul Cotter, in his own person would be such a victim. Even now it seemed incredible in the face of this beautiful young world that stretched away from him, so quiet and so peaceful. He, who already in his boyhood was planning great things for this splendid land, to die such a death!

The warriors did not cease until their task was finished. It was but a brief one after all, for Paul had made no mistake in his guess. There was not time, perhaps, to take a prisoner beyond the Ohio, and they could not forego a savage pleasure. They dragged the boy to the sapling, stood him erect against the slim trunk, and bound him fast with green withes. Then they piled the dead leaves and brushwood high about him above his knees, and, this done, stood a little way off and looked at their work.

The warriors spoke together for the first time since Paul had awakened, and their black eyes lighted up with a hideous glow of anticipation. Paul saw it, and an icy chill ran through all his veins. Had not the green withes held him, he would have fallen to the ground. Once more his active mind, foreseeing all that would come, had dissolved his strength for the moment; but, as always, his will brought his courage back, and he shut his eyes to put away the hateful sight of the gloating savages.

He had never asked in any way for mercy, he had never

uttered a word of protest, and he resolved that he would not cry out if he could help it. They should not rejoice too much at his sufferings; he would die as they were taught to die, and he would show to them that the mind of a white boy could supply the place of a red man's physical fortitude. But Henry might come! Would he come? Oh, would he come? Resigned to death, Paul yet hoped for life.

He opened his eyes, and the warriors were still standing there, looking at him; but in a moment one approached, and, bending down, began to strike flint and steel amid the dry leaves at the boy's feet. Again, despite himself, the shivering chill ran through Paul's veins. Would Henry come? If he came at all, he must now come quickly, as only a few minutes were left.

The leaves were obstinate; sparks flew from the flint and steel, but there was no blaze. Paul looked down at the head of the warrior who worked patiently at his task. The second warrior stood on one side, watching, and when Paul glanced at him he saw the savage move ever so little, but as if driven by a sudden impulse, and then raise his head in the attitude of one who listened intently. Heat replaced the ice in Paul's veins. Had something moved in the forest? Was it Henry? Would he come?

The standing warrior uttered a low sound, and he who knelt with the flint and steel raised his head. Something had moved in the forest! It might be Henry. For Paul, the emotions of a life were concentrated in a single moment. Fear and hope tripped over each other, and the wilderness grew dim to his sight. A myriad of little black specks danced before his eyes, and the blood was beating a quick march in his ears.

The two savages were motionless, as if carved of brown marble, and over all the wilderness hung silence. Then out of the silence came a sharp report, and the warrior who stood erect, rifle in hand, fell to the earth, stricken by instant death. Henry had come! His faithful comrade had not failed him! Paul shouted aloud in his tremendous relief and joy, forgetful of the second warrior.

The kneeling savage sprang to his feet, but he had made a fatal mistake. To light the fire for the torture, he had left his

303

rifle leaning against the trunk of a tree twenty feet away, and before he could regain it a terrible figure bounded from the bushes, the figure of a great youth, clad in buckskin, his face transformed with anger and his eyes alight. Before the savage could reach his weapon he went down, slain by a single blow of a clubbed rifle, and the next moment Henry was cutting Paul loose with a few swift slashes of his keen hunting knife.

"I knew you would come! I knew it!" exclaimed Paul joyously and wildly, as he stood forth free. "Nobody in the world but you could have done it, Henry!"

"I don't know about that, Paul," said Henry, "but I'd have had you back sooner if it hadn't been for the dark. I followed you all night the best way I could, but I couldn't come up to you until day, and they began work then."

He glanced significantly at the leaves and brushwood, and then, handing Paul's rifle to him, looked at those belonging to the savages.

"We'll take 'em," he said. "It's likely we'll need 'em, and their powder and bullets will be more than welcome, too."

Paul was rubbing his wrists and ankles, where the blood flowed painfully as the circulation was restored, but to him the whole affair was ended. His life had been saved at the last moment, and the world was more brilliant and beautiful than ever. There was no more danger.

But Henry Ware did not lose his eager, wary look. It did not take him more than a minute to transfer the ammunition of the warriors to the pouches and powderhorns of Paul and himself. Then he searched the forest with keen, suspicious glances.

"Come, Paul," he said, "we must run. The woods are full of the savages. I've found out that there's a great war party between us and Marlowe, and I've hid the powder in a cave. I turned the horses loose, hoping that we'll get 'em some time later; but just now you and I have to save ourselves."

Paul came back to earth. Danger still threatened! But he was free for the time, and he was with his comrade!

"You lead the way, Henry," he said. "I'll follow and do whatever you say."

Henry Ware made no reply, but bent his ear again, in the attitude of one who listens. Paul watched his face attentively, seeking to read his knowledge there.

"The big war band is not far away," said Henry, "and it's likely that they've heard my shot. It would carry far on such a still, clear morning as this. I didn't want them to hear it."

"But I'm glad you did shoot," said Paul. "It was a mighty welcome sound to me."

"Yes," said Henry, with grim humor, "it was the right thing at the right time. Hark to that!"

A single note, very faint and very far, rose and was quickly gone, like the dying echo of music. Only the trained ranger of the wilderness would have noticed it at all, but Henry Ware knew.

"Yes, they've heard," he said, "and they're telling it to each other. They are also telling it to us. They're between us and Marlowe, and they are between us and Wareville, so we must run to the north, and run as fast as we can."

He led the way with swift, light footsteps through the forest, and Paul followed close behind, each boy carrying on his shoulder two rifles and at his waist a double stock of bullets and powder.

Paul scarcely felt any fear now for the future. The revulsion from the stake and torture was so great that it did not seem to him that he could be taken again. Moreover, they had seized him the first time when he was asleep. They had taken an unfair advantage.

The sun rose higher, gilding the brown forest with fine filmy gold, like a veil, and the boys ran silently on among the trees and the undergrowth. Behind them, and spread out like a fan, came many warriors, fierce for their lives. Amid such scenes was the Great West won.

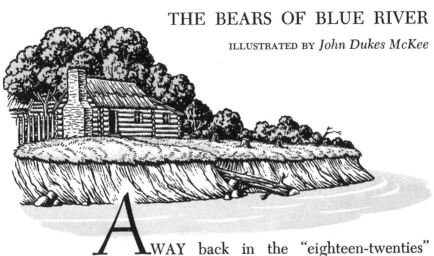

Charles Major

THE BEARS OF BLUE RIVER

ILLUSTRATED BY *John Dukes McKee*

AWAY back in the "eighteen-twenties" when Indiana was a baby state, and great forests of tall trees and tangled underbrush darkened what are now her bright plains and sunny hills, there stood upon the bank of Big Blue River, a cozy log cabin of two rooms—one front and one back.

Immediately at the water's edge was a steep slope of ten or twelve feet. Back of the house, mile upon mile, stretched the deep, dark forest, inhabited by deer and bears, wolves and wildcats, squirrels and birds, without number.

In the river the fish were so numerous that they seemed to beg the boys to catch them and to take them out of their crowded quarters.

South of the house stood a log barn, with room in it for three horses and two cows; and enclosing this barn, together with a piece of ground, was a palisade fence, eight or ten feet high, made by driving poles into the ground close together. In this enclosure the farmer kept his stock, consisting of a few sheep and cattle, and here also the chickens, geese, and ducks were driven at nightfall to save them from "varmints," as all prowling animals were called by the settlers.

The man who had built this log hut, and who lived in it and owned the adjoining land at the time of which I write, bore the

306

name of Brent, and his son Balser was the hero of the bear story which I am about to tell you.

Mr. Brent and his young wife had moved to the Blue River settlement from North Carolina, when young Balser was a little boy five or six years of age.

At the time when my story opens Little Balser, as he was called to distinguish him from his father, was about thirteen years of age and was the happy possessor of a younger brother, Jim, aged nine, and a little sister one year old, of whom he was very proud indeed.

On the south side of the front room of the log house was a large fireplace. The chimney was built of sticks, thickly covered with clay. The fireplace was almost as large as a small room in one of our modern houses and was broad and deep enough to take in backlogs which were so large and heavy that they could not be lifted, but were drawn in at the door and rolled over the floor to the fireplace.

The settlers had no stoves, but did their cooking in round pots called Dutch ovens. They roasted their meats on a spit or steel bar like the ramrod of a gun. The spit was kept turning before the fire, presenting first one side of the meat and then the other, until it was thoroughly cooked. Turning the spit was the children's work.

The daily food of the family all came from the farm, the forest, or the creek. Their sugar was obtained from the sap of the sugar trees; their meat was supplied in the greatest abundance by a few hogs, and by the inexhaustible game of which the forests were full. In the woods were found deer just for the shooting; and squirrels, rabbits, wild turkeys, pheasants, and quails, so numerous that a few hours' hunting would supply the table for days. The fish in the river, as I told you, fairly longed to be caught.

One day Mrs. Brent took down the dinner horn and blew upon it two strong blasts. This was a signal that Little Balser, who was helping his father down in the clearing, should come to the house. Balser was glad enough to drop his hoe and to run home. When he reached the house his mother said,—

307

mister
mckee

"Balser, go up to the drift in the river and catch a mess of fish for dinner. Your father is tired of deer meat three times a day, and I know he would like a nice dish of fried redeyes at noon."

"All right, mother," said Balser. And he immediately took down his fishing pole and line and got the spade to dig bait. When he had collected a small gourdful of angleworms, his mother called to him,—

"You had better take a gun. You may meet a bear; your father loaded the gun this morning, and you must be careful in handling it."

Balser took the gun, which was a heavy rifle considerably longer than himself, and started up the river toward the drift, about a quarter of a mile away.

There had been rain during the night, and the ground near the drift was soft.

Here, Little Balser noticed fresh bear tracks, and his breath

308

began to come quickly. You may be sure he peered closely into every dark thicket, and looked behind all the large trees and logs, and had his eyes wide open lest perchance "Mr. Bear" should step out and surprise him with an affectionate hug, and thereby put an end to Little Balser forever.

So he walked on cautiously, and, if the truth must be told, somewhat fearfully, until he reached the drift.

Balser was only a boy, yet the stern necessities of a settler's life had compelled his father to teach him the use of a gun; and although Balser had never killed a bear, he had shot several deer, and upon one occasion had killed a wildcat, "almost as big as a cow," he said.

I have no doubt the wildcat seemed "almost as big as a cow" to Balser when he killed it, for it must have frightened him, as wildcats were sometimes dangerous animals for children to encounter. Although Balser had never met a bear face to face and alone, yet he felt, and many a time had said, that there wasn't a bear in the world big enough to frighten him, if he but had his gun.

He had often imagined and minutely detailed to his parents and little brother just what he would do if he should meet a bear. He would wait calmly until his bearship should come within a few yards of him, and then he would slowly lift his gun. Bang! and Mr. Bear would be dead with a bullet in his heart.

But when he saw the fresh bear tracks and began to realize that he would probably have an opportunity to put his theories about bear killing into practice, he began to wonder if, after all, he would become frightened and miss his aim. Then he thought of how the bear, in that case, would be calm and deliberate and would put his theories into practice by walking very politely up to him, and making a very satisfactory dinner of a certain boy whom he could name. But as he walked on and no bear appeared, his courage grew stronger as the prospect of meeting the enemy grew less, and he again began saying to himself that no bear could frighten him, because he had his gun and he could and would kill it.

So Balser reached the drift; and having looked carefully about him, leaned his gun against a tree, unwound his fishing line from the pole, and walked out to the end of a log which extended into the river some twenty or thirty feet.

Here he threw in his line, and soon was so busily engaged drawing out sunfish and redeyes, and now and then a bass which was hungry enough to bite at a worm, that all thought of the bear went out of his mind.

After he had caught enough fish for a sumptuous dinner he thought of going home, and as he turned toward the shore, imagine, if you can, his consternation when he saw upon the bank, quietly watching him, a huge black bear.

If the wildcat had seemed as large as a cow to Balser, of what size do you suppose that bear appeared? A cow? An elephant, surely, was small compared with the huge black fellow standing upon the bank. It is true Balser had never seen an elephant, but his father had, and so had his friend Tom Fox, who lived down the river; and they all agreed that an elephant was "purty nigh as big as all outdoors."

The bear had a peculiar, determined expression about him that seemed to say,—

"That boy can't get away; he's out on the log where the water is deep, and if he jumps into the river I can easily jump in after him and catch him before he can swim a dozen strokes. He'll have to come off the log in a short time, and then I'll proceed to devour him."

About the same train of thought had also been rapidly passing through Balser's mind. His gun was on the bank where he had left it, and in order to reach it he would have to pass the bear. He dared not jump into the water, for any attempt to escape on his part would bring the bear upon him instantly. He was very much frightened, but, after all, he was a cool-headed fellow for his age. So he concluded not to press matters, as the bear did not seem inclined to do so; so long as the bear remained watching him on the bank, he would stay on the log where he was, and allow the enemy to eye him to his heart's content.

There they stood, the boy and the bear, each eyeing the other

mister
mckee

as though they were the best of friends and would like to eat each other, which, in fact, was literally true.

Time sped very slowly for one of them, you may be sure; and it seemed to Balser that he had been standing almost an age in the middle of Blue River on that wretched shaking log, when he heard his mother's dinner horn, reminding him that it was time to go home.

Balser quite agreed with his mother and gladly would have gone, as I need not tell you; but there stood the bear, patient, determined, and fierce; and Little Balser soon was convinced in his mind that his time had come to die.

He hoped that when his father should go home to dinner and find him still absent, he would come up the river in search of him, and frighten away the bear. Hardly had this hope sprung up in his mind, when it seemed that the same thought had also occurred to the bear, for he began to move down toward the shore end of the log upon which Balser was standing.

Slowly came the bear until he reached the end of the log, which for a moment he examined suspiciously, and then, to Balser's great alarm, cautiously stepped out upon it and began to walk toward him.

Balser thought of the folks at home and, above all, of his baby sister; and when he felt that he would never see them again and that they would in all probability never know of his fate, he began to grow heavy-hearted and was almost paralyzed with fear.

On came the bear, putting one great paw in front of the other, and watching Balser intently with his little black eyes. His tongue hung out, and his great red mouth was open to its widest, showing the sharp, long, glittering teeth that would soon be feasting on a first-class boy dinner.

When the bear got within a few feet of Balser—so close he could almost feel the animal's hot breath as it slowly approached—the boy grew desperate with fear and struck at the bear with the only weapon he had—his string of fish.

Now, bears love fish and blackberries above all other food, so when Balser's string of fish struck the bear in the mouth, he

312

grabbed at them, and in doing so lost his foothold on the slippery log and fell into the water with a great splash and plunge.

This was Balser's chance for life, so he flung the fish to the bear and ran for the bank with a speed worthy of the cause.

When he reached the bank his self-confidence returned, and he remembered all the things he had said he would do if he should meet a bear.

The bear had caught the fish, and again had climbed upon the log, where he was deliberately devouring them.

This was Little Balser's chance for death—to the bear. Quickly snatching up the gun, he rested it in the fork of a small tree nearby, took deliberate aim at the bear, which was not five yards away, and shot him through the heart. The bear dropped into the water dead and floated downstream a little way, where he lodged at a ripple a short distance below.

Balser, after he had killed the bear, became more frightened than he had been at any time during the adventure and ran home. That afternoon his father went to the scene of battle and took the bear out of the water. It was very fat and large, and weighed, so Mr. Brent said, over six hundred pounds.

Balser was firmly of the opinion that he himself was also very fat and large and weighed at least as much as the bear. He was certainly entitled to feel "big," for he had got himself out of an ugly scrape in a cool-headed manner and had achieved a victory of which a man might have been proud.

The news of Balser's adventure soon spread among the neighbors, and he became quite a hero; for the bear he had killed was one of the largest that had ever been seen in that neighborhood, and, besides the gallons of rich bear oil it yielded, there were three or four hundred pounds of bear meat; and no other food is more strengthening for winter diet.

There was also the soft, furry skin, which Balser's mother tanned, and with it made a coverlid for Balser's bed, under which he and his little brother lay many a cold night, cozy and "snug as a bug in a rug."

313

MANY years ago while Andrew Patterson was waiting for the return of his father's ship, he went to live in Happy Valley with Sally Smith and her three aunts, Deborah, Esther, and Nannie, her two uncles, Eben and Joseph, and the hired man, Jehoshaphat Mountain. When Aunt Esther announced that she was going to marry her cousin, Sam Hallet, there was much excitement in the family. . . .

Elizabeth Coatsworth

A PIONEER WEDDING

ILLUSTRATED BY *James Ponter*

ALL during the day before Aunt Esther's wedding and all that night it rained and rained and rained. The little house drummed with the sound, and sluices ran down the windows, and often as Aunt Esther ran to look out she could scarcely see ten feet away in that cataract that showed no signs of lessening.

But the wedding morning was as clear as crystal, and every grass blade and leaf glittered with a dozen prisms.

"Aunt Esther's going to be married! Aunt Esther's going to be married!" chanted Sally, hopping up so quickly that she dislodged Dinah from her place on the bed.

"Don't sing before breakfast, child," said Aunt Nannie, but she was smiling.

Even this morning of mornings, chores must be done, and the house left neat and in order. Sally fairly danced with impatience.

"The wedding won't be until eleven, child," said Aunt Nannie. "The minister has got to come up the river all the way from Bangor, and cross it as well. I'm thinking he'll have a muddy ride."

314

Outside Jehoshaphat Mountain was currying Dorcas and Peacock, while Andrew held their bridles.

"You'd better ride pillion with Uncle Joseph, Sally," said Aunt Nannie, "so as not to muss Aunt Esther's dress. And brother Eben and Andrew and Jehoshaphat Mountain can start a little early and walk."

"Let me walk with them, Aunt Nannie," said Sally with a little skip, but Aunt Nannie shook her head.

"You must learn to restrain your impatience," she said, jingling her eardrops disapprovingly. "There, child, in your excitement I believe you've forgotten to give your aunt the gift you have for her!"

So, indeed, Sally had. She swooped off to find her square of embroidery. Along the bottom, below the embroidered strawberry, the pink and the giraffe, she had written painstakingly with thread: "For dearest Aunt Esther from Sally, May, 1790."

Aunt Esther thought it very beautiful and so did Andrew when she darted out to show it to him, finished.

"Sally, this morning, is like a little swallow in the house," said Aunt Deborah and then she called gently, "Time to get ready now, Andrew, and I'll brush your coat for you and see about your hair."

Andrew felt very proud of his new family when they were all ready for the wedding. Of course, Miss Esther was loveliest of all in her white gown with the bands of colored embroidery on it, and her kid gloves. But his own Miss Deborah looked just as nice to him, and Sally in sprigged scarlet reminded him more of strawberries and cream than ever.

Miss Deborah said that Andrew looked nice, too, in his best suit that had lain unused in the pied calfskin trunk, and he stepped off very gaily with Uncle Eben and Jehoshaphat Mountain down the muddy road, wearing their boots, for the aunts would bring their shoes in the gig along with Miss Esther's riding dress and the hat with the feather which she was to wear when Sam Hallet took her up the river to their new-built house.

They were only halfway down the hill, for Uncle Eben never

315

hurried, and this morning the path was slippery, when the gig with the three ladies went by, Dorcas stepping gingerly; and then came Mr. Joseph with Sally perched behind him, her arms about his waist.

"All the pine trees have little white candles for Aunt Esther's wedding, Andrew," she called, as Peacock splashed past.

And Andrew, glancing at the pines, saw that their new tips were indeed like candles; but, of course, they had been that way half the spring.

All the way to the Hallets' house Uncle Eben was complaining because Hannibal had not been allowed to come to the wedding.

"I say nothing about Dinah," he declared. "No one wants a cat at a wedding. But a bear is a different thing, and Antic had a right to have a guest at such a frolic," and by the time they reached the Hallets' house Andrew was laughing so hard he had almost forgotten that he had ever been unhappy there. . . .

The house smelled sweet of lilacs that stood about in firkins and jugs, and the floor had been freshly sanded. Mr. Sam looked very fine in his pearl-colored breeches and best coat with the brass buttons, but he had no eye for anyone but Miss Esther. A dozen other people were there, and Tim Carey who had lingered to see the coat worn.

"And a finer-fitting coat at the shoulders, or a finer pair of shoulders to fit a coat to, you could ride a long day's journey and fail to find!" he kept declaring with as much pride as though he had made both coat and man.

"What a day it is!" everyone exclaimed. "I had been very fearful lest the wedding day should be rainy—I can't remember when I've seen such a downpour," and the talk buzzed busily.

But after a while people began to fall silent. It was long after eleven o'clock, and there was no sign yet of the minister. His would be a muddy ride, and they made allowances for slow going, but, after all, he should be here by now.

At last John and Andrew were sent down to the ferry to see if he were on his way. They found the ferryman, but no sign of the ferry-scow.

316

"Dang it," he said. "Look at the river! Never seed it so high myself. The dumb thing carried away my ferry last night in one of them thar freshets, and I'll be lucky if I find it inside a dozen miles."

"But why didn't you let us know?" asked John indignantly. "Everyone's been waiting."

"Let yer know soon's ye asked, didn't I?" returned the ferryman. "Shouldn't wonder if that warn't the reverent gent over thar now. He's been thar nigh onto half an hour, a-hollering."

Sure enough, the boys could hear words faintly coming to them across the river.

"Any crossing higher up?" came the voice of the man in black, still on his black mare.

"No, sir!" yelled back John. "Wait a little till we tell them."

"What say?" asked the voice.

"You yell," said John to the ferryman. "At least, you can do that much."

"'Tain't my fault that tarnation scow git away," said the ferryman, but he consented to yell.

Five minutes later the boys burst in among the wedding party, spreading consternation.

"River won't be down for a week, like as not," was the general opinion. "Suppose it'll just have to be put off."

But everyone knew that it was bad luck to put off a wedding. When a wedding was postponed, often as not someone died, and the young couple seldom throve.

Sam Hallet looked about the room, sweet with lilacs. He knew all the preparations his sister-in-law, Jennie, had made for the wedding breakfast, things that wouldn't keep for any week or so. He looked at Esther. Why, he had been looking forward to this day every minute, waking and sleeping, for months. A week?

Suddenly he had an idea.

"By the Eternal!" he exclaimed, slapping his thigh, and strode over to the bride and began whispering in her ear. Miss Esther blushed and then began to laugh.

"Why not, Sam?" she cried. "I think that would be a gay

318

wedding. And I don't wish to bring on bad luck, either."

"Friends and relatives," announced Sam, "Esther and I want to invite you to our wedding down by the river. The minister is here, and we're all here. I never heard tell that a little water flowing between altered anything."

Amid much laughter from the young and a few protests from the old, the party poured down the street. The air of late May was bright and warm about them, the sun shone, the birds sang, the little town stood among flowers. As the party went by, led by the bride and groom, others joined them, even to a few Indians from their settlement at the edge of the town. Almost every soul in the village crowded the bank above the ferry and listened among stifled titters and guffaws of laughter while the groom with his fine, carrying voice explained matters to the minister, still waiting on the farther bank.

There was an anxious pause while the solitary figure considered. Then everyone cheered when the reply came faintly:

"Can't see anything against it."

The minister got off his horse, and they could see him tying it to a tree and bringing his prayer book out of his saddlebag.

Uncle Joseph stepped forward and said quietly:

"Friends, we are about to witness a wedding—unusual, it is true, but solemn by its very nature. As brother of the bride, I ask you to behave as though we were in the church itself."

Sam and Esther stood facing the river, each with a brother near. Behind them stood the others, and at their feet flowed

the river, sparkling and swift. Sometimes the wind carried away the minister's voice, but then everyone knew the service so well that they could guess what had been said and go on from the next phrase that reached them. At the right moment Sam and Esther made their responses, Ephraim brought out the ring, and Joseph gave away the bride. When the prayer came, everyone, led by Aunt Nannie, knelt down in the wet grass (though more than one rose with stained knees), and Sally thought she had never heard a hymn sound so beautiful as when the birds twittered and sang it too.

But at last it was over and everyone was kissing the bride, and waving good-bye to the minister, who once more mounted his horse and turned its head downriver. Now Uncle Joseph led the gaiety. Back up the street the throng straggled, and all, invited guests and uninvited guests, crowded in to see the bride cut the wedding cake. Esther Hallet would never seem like a stranger to the people of Happy Valley after this! And how pretty she looked, laughing and rosy, her hair curling and a little out of place under the pushing of the river breeze, and how handsome and proud Sam Hallet looked today.

There was the sound of hoofs at the door, and Jehoshaphat Mountain led up Sam's two horses, Comet and Star with a side-saddle. Esther appeared from behind the quilt partitions in her riding dress and feathered hat, and Sam lifted her into her saddle and swung into his own. Now they were starting off for home—what a way to begin life together, riding side by side through the late spring! For a while all the children ran after them, but soon they dropped back and only Sally and Andrew still trotted along by the big horses. At the edge of the village Aunt Esther drew rein.

"That's far enough, children," she said. "You'll be out of breath," and she leaned down, and kissed them as they stood on tiptoe. "Remember to sleep on a piece of the cake and whatever you dream will come true. And I hope someday you may both have as happy a wedding as I have had."

And so, waving and blowing back kisses, pretty, gay Aunt Esther rode away with her husband.

320

Samuel Clemens

CUB PILOT ON THE RIVER

ILLUSTRATED BY *Robert Sinnott*

WHEN I was a boy, there was but one permanent ambition among my comrades in our village on the west bank of the Mississippi River. That was, to be a steamboatman. We had transient ambitions of other sorts, but they were only transient. When a circus came and went, it left us all burning to become clowns; the first Negro minstrel show that ever came to our section left us all suffering to try that kind of life; now and then we had a hope that if we lived and were good, God would permit us to be pirates. These ambitions faded out, each in its turn; but the ambition to be a steamboatman always remained. . . . Pilot was the grandest position of all. The pilot, even in those days of trivial wages, had a princely salary—from a hundred and fifty to two hundred and fifty dollars a month, and no board to pay. Two months of his wages would pay a preacher's salary for a year. Now some of us were left disconsolate. We could not get on the river—at least our parents would not let us. So, by and by, I ran away. I said I would never come home again till I was a pilot and could come in glory. . . .

I had been reading about the recent exploration of the river Amazon by an expedition sent out by our government. It was said that the expedition, owing to difficulties, had not thoroughly explored a part of the country lying about the headwaters, some

321

four thousand miles from the mouth of the river. It was only about fifteen hundred miles from Cincinnati to New Orleans, where I could doubtless get a ship. I had thirty dollars left; I would go and complete the exploration of the Amazon. This was all the thought I gave to the subject. I never was great in matters of detail. I packed my valise and took passage on an ancient tub called the *Paul Jones,* for New Orleans. For the sum of sixteen dollars I had the scarred and tarnished splendors of her main saloon principally to myself, for she was not a creature to attract the eye of wiser travelers. When we presently got under way and went poking down the broad Ohio, I became a new being and the subject of my own admiration. I was a traveler. . . .

The boat backed out from New Orleans at four in the afternoon, and it was our watch until eight. Mr. Bixby, my chief, straightened her up, plowed her along past the sterns of the other boats that lay at the Levee, and then said, "Here, take her; shave those steamships as close as you'd peel an apple." I took the wheel, and my heartbeat fluttered up into the hundreds; for it seemed to me that we were about to scrape the side off every ship in the line, we were so close. I held my breath and began to claw the boat away from the danger; and I had my own opinion of the pilot who had known no better than to get us into such peril, but I was too wise to express it. In half a minute I had a wide margin of safety intervening between the *Paul Jones* and the ships; and within ten seconds more I was set aside in disgrace, and Mr. Bixby was going into danger again and flaying me alive with abuse of my cowardice. I was stung, but I was obliged to admire the easy confidence with which my chief loafed from side to side of his wheel and trimmed the ships so closely that disaster seemed ceaselessly imminent. When he had cooled a little he told me that the easy water was close ashore and the current outside, and therefore we must hug the bank, upstream, to get the benefit of the former, and stay well out, downstream, to take advantage of the latter. In my own mind I resolved to be a downstream pilot and leave the upstreaming to people dead to prudence. . . .

I think a pilot's memory is about the most wonderful thing in the world. To know the Old and New Testaments by heart and be able to recite them glibly, forward or backward, or begin at random anywhere in the book and recite both ways and never trip or make a mistake, is no extravagant mass of knowledge, and no marvelous facility, compared to a pilot's massed knowledge of the Mississippi and his marvelous facility in the handling of it. I make this comparison deliberately, and believe I am not expanding the truth when I do it. Many will think my figure too strong, but pilots will not. . . .

At the time that wages soared so high on the Missouri River, my chief, Mr. Bixby, went up there and learned more than a thousand miles of that stream with an ease and rapidity that were astonishing. When he had seen each division *once* in the daytime and *once* at night, his education was so nearly complete that he took out a daylight license; a few trips later he took out a full license and went to piloting day and night—and he ranked A1, too.

Mr. Bixby placed me as steersman for a while under a pilot whose feats of memory were a constant marvel to me. However, his memory was born in him, I think, not built. For instance, somebody would mention a name. Instantly Mr. Brown would break in,—

"Oh, I knew *him*. Sallow-faced, red-headed fellow, with a little scar on the side of his throat, like a splinter under the flesh. He was only in the Southern trade six months. That was thirteen years ago. I made a trip with him. There was five feet in the upper river then; the *Henry Blake* grounded at the foot of Tower Island drawing four and a half; the *George Elliott* unshipped her rudder on the wreck of the *Sunflower*—"

"Why, the *Sunflower* didn't sink until—"

"*I* know when she sunk; it was three years before that, on the 2d of December; Asa Hardy was captain of her, and his brother John was first clerk; and it was his first trip in her, too; Tom Jones told me these things a week afterward in New Orleans; he was first mate of the *Sunflower*. Captain Hardy stuck a nail in his foot the 6th of July of the next year, and died of the lockjaw

323

on the 15th. His brother John died two years after—3d of March—erysipelas. I never saw either of the Hardys—they were Alleghany River men—but people who knew them told me all these things. And they said Captain Hardy wore yarn socks winter and summer just the same, and his first wife's name was Jane Shook—she was from New England—and his second one died in a lunatic asylum. It was in the blood. She was from Lexington, Kentucky. Name was Horton before she was married." . . .

He could *not* forget anything. Such a memory as that is a great misfortune. To it, all occurrences are of the same size. Its possessor cannot distinguish an interesting circumstance from an uninteresting one. As a talker, he is bound to clog his narrative with tiresome details and make himself an insufferable bore. Moreover, he cannot stick to his subject. He picks up every little grain of memory he discerns in his way, and so is led aside. . . .

A pilot must have a memory; but there are two higher qualities which he must also have. He must have good and quick judgment and decision, and a cool, calm courage that no peril can shake. Give a man the merest trifle of pluck to start with, and by the time he has become a pilot he cannot be unmanned by any danger a steamboat can get into; but one cannot quite say the same for judgment. Judgment is a matter of brains, and a man must *start* with a good stock of that article or he will never succeed as a pilot.

The growth of courage in the pilothouse is steady all the time, but it does not reach a high and satisfactory condition until some time after the young pilot has been "standing his own watch" alone and under the staggering weight of all the responsibilities connected with the position. When the apprentice has become pretty thoroughly acquainted with the river, he goes clattering along so fearlessly with his steamboat, night or day, that he presently begins to imagine that it is *his* courage that animates him; but the first time the pilot steps out and leaves him to his own devices he finds out it was the other man's. He discovers that the article has been left out of his own cargo

altogether. The whole river is bristling with exigencies in a moment; he is not prepared for them; he does not know how to meet them; all his knowledge forsakes him; and within fifteen minutes he is as white as a sheet and scared almost to death. Therefore pilots wisely train these cubs by various strategic tricks to look danger in the face a little more calmly. A favorite way of theirs is to play a friendly swindle upon the candidate.

Mr. Bixby served me in this fashion once, and for years afterward I used to blush, even in my sleep, when I thought of it. I had become a good steersman; so good, indeed, that I had all the work to do on our watch, night and day. Mr. Bixby seldom made a suggestion to me; all he ever did was to take the wheel on particularly bad nights or in particularly bad crossings, land the boat when she needed to be landed, play gentleman of leisure nine-tenths of the watch, and collect the wages. The lower river was about bank-full, and if anybody had questioned my ability to run any crossing between Cairo and New Orleans without help or instruction, I should have felt irreparably hurt. The idea of being afraid of any crossing in the lot, in the *daytime*, was a thing too preposterous for contemplation. Well, one matchless summer's day I was bowling down the bend above Island 66, brimful of self-conceit and carrying my nose as high as a giraffe's, when Mr. Bixby said,—

"I am going below awhile. I suppose you know the next crossing?"

This was almost an affront. It was about the plainest and simplest crossing in the whole river. One couldn't come to any harm, whether he ran it right or not; and as for depth, there never had been any bottom there. I knew all this, perfectly well.

"Know how to *run* it? Why, I can run it with my eyes shut."

"How much water is there in it?"

"Well, that is an odd question. I couldn't get bottom there with a church steeple."

"You think so, do you?"

The very tone of the question shook my confidence. That was what Mr. Bixby was expecting. He left, without saying anything more. I began to imagine all sorts of things. Mr. Bixby, unknown to me, of course, sent somebody down to the forecastle with some mysterious instructions to the leadsmen, another messenger was sent to whisper among the officers, and then Mr. Bixby went into hiding behind a smokestack where he could observe results. Presently the captain stepped out on the hurricane deck; next the chief mate appeared; then a clerk. Every moment or two a straggler was added to my audience; and before I got to the head of the island I had fifteen or twenty people assembled down there under my nose. I began to wonder what the trouble was. As I started across, the captain glanced aloft at me and said, with a sham uneasiness in his voice,—

"Where is Mr. Bixby?"

"Gone below, sir."

But that did the business for me. My imagination began to construct dangers out of nothing, and they multiplied faster than I could keep the run of them. All at once I imagined I saw shoal water ahead! The wave of coward agony that surged through me then came near dislocating every joint in me. All my confidence in that crossing vanished. I seized the bell-rope; dropped it, ashamed; seized it again; dropped it once more; clutched it tremblingly once again, and pulled it so feebly that I could hardly hear the stroke myself. Captain and mate sang out instantly, and both together:

The boat backed out from New Orleans.

"Starboard lead there! and quick about it!"

This was another shock. I began to climb the wheel like a squirrel; but I would hardly get the boat started to port before I would see new dangers on that side, and away I would spin to the other; only to find perils accumulating to starboard, and be crazy to get to port again. Then came the leadsman's sepulchral cry:

"D-e-e-p four!"

Deep four in a bottomless crossing! The terror of it took my breath away.

"M-a-r-k three! M-a-r-k three! Quarter-less-three! Half twain!"

This was frightful! I seized the bell-ropes and stopped the engines.

"Quarter twain! Quarter twain! *Mark* twain!"

I was helpless. I did not know what in the world to do. I was quaking from head to foot, and I could have hung my hat on my eyes, they stuck out so far.

"Quarter-*less*-twain! Nine-and-a-*half!*"

We were *drawing* nine! My hands were in a nerveless flutter. I could not ring a bell intelligibly with them. I flew to the speaking-tube and shouted to the engineer:

"Oh, Ben, if you love me, *back* her! Quick, Ben! Oh, back the immortal *soul* out of her!"

I heard the door close gently. I looked around, and there stood Mr. Bixby, smiling a bland, sweet smile. Then the audience on the hurricane deck sent up a thundergust of humiliating laughter. I saw it all, now, and I felt meaner than the meanest man in human history. I laid in the lead, set the boat in her marks, came ahead on the engines, and said,—

"It was a fine trick to play on an orphan, *wasn't* it? I suppose I'll never hear the last of how I was dumb enough to heave the lead at the head of 66."

"Well, no, you won't, maybe. In fact I hope you won't; for I want you to learn something by that experience. Didn't you *know* there was no bottom in that crossing?"

"Yes, sir, I did."

"Very well, then. You shouldn't have allowed me or anybody

327

else to shake your confidence in that knowledge. Try to remember that. And another thing: when you get into a dangerous place, don't turn coward. That isn't going to help matters any."

It was a good enough lesson, but pretty hardly learned. Yet about the hardest part of it was that for months I so often had to hear a phrase which I had conceived a particular distaste for. It was, "Oh, Ben, if you love me, back her!"

During the two or two and a half years of my apprenticeship I served under many pilots, and had experience of many kinds of steamboatmen and many varieties of steamboats; for it was not always convenient for Mr. Bixby to have me with him, and in such cases he sent me with somebody else. I am to this day profiting somewhat by that experience; for in that brief, sharp schooling, I got personally and familiarly acquainted with about all the different types of human nature that are to be found in fiction, biography, or history. The fact is daily borne in upon me that the average shore-employment requires as much as forty years to equip a man with this sort of an education. When I say I am still profiting by this thing, I do not mean that it has constituted me a judge of men—no, it has not done that, for judges of men are born, not made. My profit is various in kind and degree, but the feature of it which I value most is the zest which that early experience has given to my later reading. When I find a well-drawn character in fiction or biography I generally take a warm personal interest in him, for the reason that I have known him before—met him on the river.

The figure that comes before me oftenest, out of the shadows of that vanished time, is that of Brown, of the steamer *Pennsylvania*—the man referred to in a former chapter, whose memory was so good and tiresome. He was a middle-aged, long, slim, bony, smooth-shaven, horse-faced, ignorant, stingy, malicious, snarling, fault-hunting, mote-magnifying tyrant. I early got the habit of coming on watch with dread at my heart. No matter how good a time I might have been having with the off-watch below, and no matter how high my spirits might be when I started aloft, my soul became lead in my body the moment I approached the pilothouse.

I still remember the first time I ever entered the presence of that man. The boat had backed out from St. Louis and was "straightening down." I ascended to the pilothouse in high feather, and very proud to be semi-officially a member of the executive family of so fast and famous a boat. Brown was at the wheel. I paused in the middle of the room, all fixed to make my bow, but Brown did not look around. I thought he took a furtive glance at me out of the corner of his eye, but as not even this notice was repeated, I judged I had been mistaken. By this time he was picking his way among some dangerous "breaks" abreast the woodyards; therefore it would not be proper to interrupt him; so I stepped softly to the high bench and took a seat.

There was silence for ten minutes; then my new boss turned and inspected me deliberately and painstakingly from head to heel for about—as it seemed to me—a quarter of an hour. After which he removed his countenance and I saw it no more for some seconds; then it came around once more, and this question greeted me,—

"Are you Horace Bixby's cub?"

329

"Yes, sir."

After this there was a pause and another inspection. Then:
"What's your name?"

I told him. He repeated it after me. It was probably the only
thing he ever forgot; for although I was with him many months
he never addressed himself to me in any other way than "Here!"
and then his command followed.

"Where was you born?"

"In Florida, Missouri."

A pause. Then: "Dern sight better stayed there!"

By means of a dozen or so of pretty direct questions, he
pumped my family history out of me.

The leads were going now in the first crossing. This interrupted the inquest. When the leads had been laid in he resumed,—

"How long you been on the river?"

I told him. After a pause,—

"Where'd you get them shoes?"

I gave him the information.

"Hold up your foot!"

I did so. He stepped back, examined the shoe minutely and
contemptuously, scratching his head thoughtfully, tilting his
high sugar-loaf hat well forward to facilitate the operation, then
ejaculated, "Well, I'll be dod derned!" and returned to his
wheel.

What occasion there was to be dod derned about it is a thing
which is still as much of a mystery to me now as it was then.
It must have been all of fifteen minutes—fifteen minutes of dull,
homesick silence—before that long horse-face swung round
upon me again—and then what a change! It was as red as fire,
and every muscle in it was working. Now came this shriek:

"Here! You going to set there all day?"

I lit in the middle of the floor, shot there by the electric sud-
denness of the surprise. As soon as I could get my voice I said
apologetically, "I have had no orders, sir."

"You've had no *orders*! My, what a fine bird we are! We must
have *orders*! Our father was a *gentleman*—owned slaves—and

330

we've been to *school.* Yes, *we* are a gentleman, *too,* and got to have *orders!* ORDERS, is it? ORDERS is what you want! Dod dern my skin, *I'll* learn you to swell yourself up and blow around *here* about your dod-derned *orders!* G'way from the wheel!" (I had approached it without knowing it.)

I moved back a step or two and stood as in a dream, all my senses stupefied by this frantic assault.

"What you standing there for? Take that ice-pitcher down to the texas-tender! Come, move along, and don't you be all day about it!"

The moment I got back to the pilothouse Brown said,—

"Here! What was you doing down there all this time?"

"I couldn't find the texas-tender; I had to go all the way to the pantry."

"Derned likely story! Fill up the stove."

I proceeded to do so. He watched me like a cat. Presently he shouted,—

"Put down that shovel! Derndest numskull I ever saw—ain't even got sense enough to load up a stove."

All through the watch this sort of thing went on. Yes, and the subsequent watches were much like it during a stretch of months. As I have said, I soon got the habit of coming on duty with dread. The moment I was in the presence, even in the darkest night, I could feel those yellow eyes upon me, and knew their owner was watching for a pretext to spit out some venom on me. Preliminarily he would say,—

"Here! Take the wheel."

Two minutes later,—

"*Where* in the nation you going to? Pull her *down!*"

After another moment,—

"Say! You going to hold her all day? Let her go—meet her! meet her!"

Then he would jump from the bench, snatch the wheel from me, and meet her himself, pouring out wrath upon me all the time. . . .

Brown was *always* watching for a pretext to find fault; and if he could find no plausible pretext, he would invent one. He

331

would scold you for shaving a shore, and for not shaving it; for hugging a bar, and for not hugging it; for pulling down when not invited, and for *not* pulling down when not invited; for firing up without orders, and for waiting *for* orders. In a word, it was his invariable rule to find fault with *everything* you did; and another invariable rule of his was to throw all his remarks (to you) into the form of an insult.

One day we were approaching New Madrid, bound down and heavily laden. Brown was at one side of the wheel, steering; I was at the other, standing by to pull down or shove up. He cast a furtive glance at me every now and then. I had long ago learned what that meant; viz., he was trying to invent a trap for me. I wondered what shape it was going to take. By and by he stepped back from the wheel and said in his usual snarly way:

"Here! See if you've got gumption enough to round her to."

This was simply *bound* to be a success; nothing could prevent it; for he had never allowed me to round the boat to before; consequently, no matter how I might do the thing, he could find free fault with it. He stood back there with his greedy eye on me, and the result was what might have been foreseen: I lost my head in a quarter of a minute, and didn't know what I was about; I started too early to bring the boat around, but detected a green gleam of joy in Brown's eye, and corrected my mistake. I started around once more while too high up, but corrected myself again in time. I made other false moves, and still managed to save myself; but at last I grew so confused and anxious that I tumbled into the very worst blunder of all—I got too far *down* before beginning to fetch the boat around. Brown's chance was come.

His face turned red with passion; he made one bound, hurled me across the house with a sweep of his arm, spun the wheel down, and began to pour out a stream of vituperation upon me which lasted till he was out of breath. In the course of this speech he called me all the different kinds of hard names he could think of, and once or twice I thought he was even going to swear—but he had never done that, and he didn't this time. "Dod dern" was the nearest he ventured to the luxury of swear-

333

ing, for he had been brought up with a wholesome respect for future fire and brimstone.

That was an uncomfortable hour; for there was a big audience on the hurricane deck. When I went to bed that night, I killed Brown in seventeen different ways—all of them new.

Two trips later I got into serious trouble. Brown was steering; I was "pulling down." My younger brother appeared on the hurricane deck, and shouted to Brown to stop at some landing or other, a mile or so below. Brown gave no intimation that he had heard anything. But that was his way: he never condescended to take notice of an under-clerk. The wind was blowing; Brown was deaf (although he always pretended he wasn't), and I very much doubted if he had heard the order. If I had had two heads, I would have spoken; but as I had only one, it seemed judicious to take care of it; so I kept still.

Presently, sure enough, we went sailing by that plantation. Captain Klinefelter appeared on the deck, and said,—

"Let her come around, sir, let her come around. Didn't Henry tell you to land here?"

"*No*, sir!"

"I sent him up to do it."

"He *did* come up; and that's all the good it done, the dodderned fool. He never said anything."

"Didn't *you* hear him?" asked the captain of me.

Of course I didn't want to be mixed up in this business, but there was no way to avoid it; so I said,—

"Yes, sir."

I knew what Brown's next remark would be, before he uttered it. It was:

"Shut your mouth! You never heard anything of the kind."

I closed my mouth, according to instructions. An hour later Henry entered the pilothouse, unaware of what had been going on. He was a thoroughly inoffensive boy, and I was sorry to see him come, for I knew Brown would have no pity on him. Brown began, straightway,—

"Here! Why didn't you tell me we'd got to land at that plantation?"

"I did tell you, Mr. Brown."

"It's a lie!"

I said:

"You lie, yourself. He did tell you."

Brown glared at me in unaffected surprise; and for as much as a moment he was entirely speechless; then he shouted to me,—

"I'll attend to your case in a half a minute!" then to Henry, "And you leave the pilothouse; out with you!"

It was pilot law, and must be obeyed. The boy started out, and even had his foot on the upper step outside the door, when Brown, with a sudden access of fury, picked up a ten-pound lump of coal and sprang after him; but I was between, with a heavy stool, and I hit Brown a good honest blow which stretched him out.

I had committed the crime of crimes—I had lifted my hand against a pilot on duty! I supposed I was booked for the penitentiary sure, and couldn't be booked any surer if I went on and squared my long account with this person while I had the chance; consequently I stuck to him and pounded him with my fists a considerable time. I do not know how long, the pleasure of it probably made it seem longer than it really was; but in the end he struggled free and jumped up and sprang to the wheel: a very natural solicitude, for, all this time, here was this steamboat tearing down the river at the rate of fifteen miles an hour and nobody at the helm! However, Eagle Bend was two miles wide at this bank-full stage, and correspondingly long and deep: and the boat was steering herself straight down the middle and taking no chances. Still, that was only luck—a body *might* have found her charging into the woods.

Perceiving at a glance that the *Pennsylvania* was in no danger, Brown gathered up the big spyglass, war-club fashion, and ordered me out of the pilothouse with more than Comanche bluster. But I was not afraid of him now; so, instead of going, I tarried and criticized his grammar. I reformed his ferocious speeches for him, and put them into good English, calling his attention to the advantage of pure English over the dialect of the Pennsylvania collieries whence he was extracted. He could have done his part to admiration in a cross-fire of mere vituperation, of course; but he was not equipped for this species of controversy; so he presently laid aside his glass and took the wheel, muttering and shaking his head; and I retired to the bench. The racket had brought everybody to the hurricane-deck, and I trembled when I saw the old captain looking up from amid the crowd. I said to myself, "Now I *am* done for!" for although, as a rule, he was so fatherly and indulgent toward the boat's family, and so patient of minor shortcomings, he could be stern enough when the fault was worth it.

I tried to imagine what he *would* do to a cub pilot who had been guilty of such a crime as mine, committed on a boat guard-deep with costly freight and alive with passengers. Our watch was nearly ended. I thought I would go and hide somewhere till I got a chance to slide ashore. So I slipped out of the pilothouse, and down the steps, and around to the texas-door, and was in the act of gliding within, when the captain confronted me! I dropped my head, and he stood over me in silence a moment or two, then said impressively,—

"Follow me."

I dropped into his wake; he led the way to his parlor in the forward end of the texas. We were alone, now. He closed the after door; then moved slowly to the forward one and closed that. He sat down; I stood before him. He looked at me some little time, then said,—

"So you have been fighting Mr. Brown?"

I answered meekly,—

"Yes, sir."

"Do you know that that is a very serious matter?"

"Yes, sir."

"Are you aware that this boat was plowing down the river fully five minutes with no one at the wheel?"

"Yes, sir."

"Did you strike him first?"

"Yes, sir."

"What with?"

"A stool, sir."

"Hard?"

"Middling, sir."

"Did it knock him down?"

"He—he fell, sir."

"Did you follow it up? Did you do anything further?"

"Yes, sir."

"What did you do?"

"Pounded him, sir."

"Pounded him?"

"Yes, sir."

"Did you pound him much? that is, severely?"

"One might call it that, sir, maybe."

"I'm deucèd glad of it! Hark ye, never mention that I said that. You have been guilty of a great crime; and don't you ever be guilty of it again, on this boat. *But*—lay for him ashore! Give him a good sound thrashing, do you hear? I'll pay the expenses. Now go—and mind you, not a word of this to anybody. Clear out with you! You've been guilty of a great crime, you whelp!"

I slid out, happy with the sense of a close shave and a mighty deliverance; and I heard him laughing to himself and slapping his fat thighs after I had closed his door.

When Brown came off watch he went straight to the captain, who was talking with some passengers on the boiler-deck, and demanded that I be put ashore in New Orleans—and added,—

"I'll never turn a wheel on this boat again while that cub stays."

"The captain said,—

"But he needn't come round when you are on watch, Mr. Brown."

"I won't even stay on the same boat with him. *One* of us has got to go ashore."

"Very well," said the captain, "let it be yourself," and resumed his talk with the passengers.

During the brief remainder of the trip I knew how an emancipated slave feels, for I was an emancipated slave myself.

Edgar Wyatt

APACHE WARPATH

ILLUSTRATED BY *Fredrick Chapman*

THERE was peace in Apache Pass. The pass was a narrow trail that led through the canyons and gorges of the wild Chiricahua Mountains. Here, in their Wonderland of Rocks, lived the Chiricahua Apache Indians.

Five years before, Cochise, their great war chief, had promised the American commander at Fort Buchanan that his people would live in peace. Now, in 1861, white men rode safely through these mountains. There was no longer any danger of a sudden raid by yelling savages. Cochise had kept his word.

Almost everyone in the desert country had known that Cochise would keep his word.

The Indians said, "Cochise never speaks with two tongues."

White men said, "Cochise never lies. Truth and courage mean more to that Indian than his own life."

Now the United States Army post at Fort Buchanan in southern Arizona had an easier time. There were hostile Pinal Indians near by who lived west of the fort. But so long as Cochise's Apaches were peaceful, the Army could control the Pinals without much trouble.

But trouble was on its way to Apache Pass. It came when young Lieutenant George Bascom reported for duty at Fort Buchanan.

Lieutenant Bascom was new to the desert. He had never seen an Apache, but he was sure that he knew all about them. He

338

had read of Indian cruelty and torture. He had heard many tales of the Army's battles with fierce Indian tribes. He saw no difference between the Pinals and Cochise's Apaches. "Indians are Indians," he said. "The only good Indian has an army bullet in his heart."

One day a band of Pinals rode boldly past the fort. They swooped down on a near-by ranch that belonged to a white man named John Ward.

A Pinal Indian boy lived on the ranch with Ward. He was the son of a warrior who had been killed in battle. Ward had adopted him, but the Indians swore they would rescue the boy and take him home to live with his tribe.

One of the raiders snatched up the boy and galloped off. Other Pinals drove all Ward's cattle away. To confuse anyone who might chase them, the Indians rode far to the east—toward Cochise's country—before they turned toward the west and home.

John Ward tracked the Indians eastward to the San Pedro River. Then he hurried to Fort Buchanan. He poured out his story to Colonel Pitcairn Morrison.

"I want some soldiers," he shouted. "We've got to find Cochise and get back the boy and my cattle."

"Cochise is not on the warpath," said Colonel Morrison. "The guilty Indians must have been Pinals."

Ward pounded the colonel's desk. "I tracked them to the San Pedro. That's Cochise country. He's guilty, I tell you!"

"I'll send out some soldiers," said Colonel Morrison, "but I want no trouble with Cochise. We have his word to keep the peace—"

"The word of an Apache!"

"The word of Cochise," said the colonel, "is as good as the word of any man I ever knew, red or white."

He sent an orderly for Lieutenant Bascom and for Sergeant Bernard. The leather-cheeked sergeant had just ridden in from a long patrol. His bowlegs spoke of years in the saddle.

Lieutenant Bascom strode in. He saluted and stood stiffly at attention.

Colonel Morrison told them Ward's story. "Lieutenant Bascom, take Sergeant Bernard and twelve troopers. Take Antonio along. He's a Mexican who speaks Apache well. Ride to Apache Pass. See Cochise and ask him—"

"Ask him!" snorted Ward.

The colonel ignored Ward. "If the cattle were driven through Cochise's mountains, he'll know about it. If he knows, he'll tell you. He has helped us before. Good luck, Lieutenant."

The little column rode toward Apache Pass through forests of cactus and mesquite. The troopers, veterans of countless desert marches, relaxed in their saddles. Bascom rode stiff and erect. He spoke to Sergeant Bernard only to give his orders. He did not speak to his troopers at all.

John Ward rode at Bascom's stirrup. Every night at the campfire, Ward told stories of Indian battles and Apache cruelty. Bascom listened eagerly. Some of the tales were true. Ward made up many of them.

"All this talk about Cochise and peace is silly," Ward told the young lieutenant. "Every Apache is a killer. Cochise is as bad as the rest."

"I'll know how to handle Cochise," said Bascom.

After four days on the trail the troopers had left the desert. They climbed through steep canyons and camped that night high in the mountains. They were in the very heart of Cochise's country.

"Sergeant," called Bascom, "see that a white flag is raised over my tent."

They had been in camp just an hour when Sergeant Bernard shouted, "Here he comes! Here's Cochise!"

Bascom looked up startled. A few yards away were six Apaches.

"Which one is Cochise?"

"The big Indian in front."

So this was the great Cochise! Bascom's lips curled in contempt. He had expected him to look like a chief. This one wore no paint or feathers. Long muscles rippled under his copper skin as he advanced with the panther tread of the Apache.

340

Sergeant Bernard held the tent flap aside and motioned for the Indians to enter.

Cochise looked at the white flag. He nodded and went into the tent. The other Indians followed and sat in a circle on the ground.

John Ward and Antonio, the interpreter, went in next. Bascom waited a moment. Then he spoke softly to Sergeant Bernard. "Have the men surround the tent."

The sergeant protested. "Cochise is here under the guarantee of your white flag. We're in honor bound to respect it."

"What is honor to an Apache?" snapped Bascom. "Surround the tent!" He turned and went inside.

"Cochise," said Bascom sternly, "this man has lost his boy and his cattle. You or your people have stolen them. You will return them at once."

As Antonio translated these words, all friendliness left Cochise's face. He stared at Bascom.

"Tell the boy-soldier," he said, "that we have been at peace with Americans for many harvests. We have not killed. We have not stolen. When other Indians have done so, we have punished them. We will help you now to get back what you have lost."

Bascom hesitated. He looked at Ward. Ward was glaring at the Indian. Bascom turned back to Antonio.

"Tell Cochise that I say he lies!"

Cochise's face might have been carved from granite.

"Tell Cochise he is my prisoner!"

Cochise was on his feet in a single bound. His words exploded in the tent like bullets.

"Cochise does not lie!"

He towered over the startled Bascom. Now he whirled away and a long knife was in his hand.

"And Cochise is no prisoner!"

He leaped to the wall of the tent. One sweep of the knife split a long gash in the canvas.

He plunged through the torn tent and through the ring of soldiers that surrounded it.

341

The first shots of the troopers went wild. Cochise ran up the steep hillside. A bullet struck his thigh. He ran on. He reached the edge of the forest and disappeared.

The other Indians leaped out to follow him. One was quickly shot. One was pinned to the ground with a bayonet. Three were captured by Bascom's men.

That night, deep in the mountains, Cochise spoke to a few of his warriors. "We must have white prisoners to trade to the American soldiers who have captured our people. Attack stage-coaches and wagon trains. Remember, kill no Americans. Bring me white men—alive."

The braves galloped to Apache Pass. When morning came they had three prisoners. One of them was well-known to Cochise. He was Wallace, a stage driver whose route lay through the pass.

Lieutenant Bascom's troopers had worked all night to fortify their camp. Early in the morning there was a shout from the guards.

"Apaches!"

Led by Cochise, twenty Apache warriors rode out of the

forest. They halted at the rim of a little mesa that overlooked the white man's camp.

Today the tall Indian looked every inch a chieftain. His body was streaked with red, orange, and black. Eagle feathers sprouted from his headband. At his saddle was a rifle and in his hand a lance. Mounted on his favorite paint pony, he stared down at the camp.

There was a sudden movement among the Apaches. Wallace, the captured stage driver, was shoved forward.

"Bascom!" called Wallace. His voice trembled. "Cochise will trade our lives for the Indian prisoners."

"Let them go, sir," begged Sergeant Bernard, "or you'll start an Apache war that you can't finish."

Bascom was stubborn. "Tell Cochise to send back what he has stolen. If he doesn't, I'll hang the Indians!"

"Cochise is not guilty!" cried Wallace. "Let the Indians go! Let them go or we'll be killed!"

"He'll get his Indians," Bascom shouted, "when we get the boy and the cattle. Not before!"

In panic, Wallace tried to escape. He ran stumbling down toward the Americans. An Apache brave spurred his pony in pursuit. His lariat whistled through the air and its noose dropped over the fleeing Wallace.

The Apache whirled his pony. Wallace was jerked from his feet. His body bounced from rock to rock as the galloping pony dragged him back up the hill. At a signal from Cochise the Apaches dashed away through the woods. In a moment, all of them had vanished.

It was bright moonlight when the Indians reached the secret fortress that they called the East Stronghold. Smoke signals had been made. Runners had been sent to gather all the Chiricahua people.

Cochise stood erect on a great boulder. Massed about him were his warriors. He began to speak quietly.

"The soldiers at the pass have captured some of our people. Two have been killed. They will hang the others. We have killed three white prisoners. This is war.

"My children, this is a war that Apaches cannot win. Americans are as many as the grains of sand, as the blades of grass. No, we cannot win this war."

The warriors were silent. Cochise's voice rose on the night.

"We cannot win, but this I swear: I will live and die at war with the white men!"

A murmur began among the warriors. It became a shout. Soon Apache war cries, not heard in these mountains for five years, were ringing through the canyons. Cochise stood motionless on his boulder, his arms outstretched above the yelling, dancing braves.

In Apache Pass, Bascom's troopers hurried to break camp. They had to leave these mountains before Cochise could gather his fighting men.

As they rode down the trail, they saw the Apache smoke signals on the mountain peaks. At night each man slept with his gun. They did not dare to light campfires.

Antonio rode beside Sergeant Bernard as they came in sight of Fort Buchanan. "I wonder," said Antonio, "what the good Colonel Morrison will say when he learns that Bascom brings him not an Indian boy but an Indian war."

"I think the lieutenant is wondering about that, too," said Sergeant Bernard. "This war will last a long time. We'll fight it. And, of course, we'll win it. But a lot of people are going to get hurt because Lieutenant Bascom didn't know an honest Indian when he saw one."

That was the start of Cochise's long warpath.

It led him and the great chiefs who followed him—Victorio, Nana, Geronimo, and many others—into a hundred desert battles.

Seven years went by before a single white man spoke to Cochise and lived to tell of it. Twenty-five years of warfare passed before the Apaches were finally defeated. Most of the men who fought this war never heard of Lieutenant Bascom. They never knew that the fighting started because a stubborn man would not believe that "Cochise loves the truth more than his own life."

345

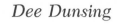

Dee Dunsing

TOOTH OF THE GREAT ONE

ILLUSTRATED BY *Brinton Turkle*

NEAR the edge of a broad, bubbling spring that stood among rank growths of custard apple, Matt Thompson found the fossil tooth. He picked it up and stood staring. Often he had found fossil teeth and bones near his home on Florida's frontier, but never anything so savage as the long tusklike thing that lay across his hand.

He took off his coonskin cap and ruffled his long tow hair excitedly. This was a tooth all right, a long front tooth. It wasn't chisel-shaped like the gnawing teeth of beaver or squirrel, but pointed like a cat's, with an inner cutting edge. Only, if it was a cat's tooth, it had belonged to the biggest cat that ever lived, and the most ferocious.

Again and again he turned the fossil over, chuckling with pleasure at the thought of what Little Knife would say. For the Mikasuki boy had long wanted one of these.

"Let us look for a tooth of the great one," he had urged many times in his queer jargon of Hitchiti and English. "With a tooth of the great one, we would be very strong and could do fine things. Only our chief has such a tooth, and it has made him powerful."

To the Mikasukis and Seminoles, this one rare tooth, owned by a chief, was strong medicine, although Matt did not know how they pictured "the great one." He had asked Little Knife, and the boy had spoken vaguely of a fearful creature that terrorized all others in the forest.

346

It was months since Matt had seen his friend, and then only for an hour when they had met by chance in the woods. They had seemed different to each other, and a new restraint had kept them from talking in their usual carefree manner.

Matt understood quite well what was wrong. It was the Treaty of Payne's Landing and the Treaty of Fort Gibson, signed by some of the chiefs and repudiated by others. It was the Indian agent's peremptory order that the redmen must leave Florida for a new reservation west of the Mississippi. And now that Christmas had passed, and 1835 would soon become 1836, schooners waited in Tampa Bay for Seminoles and Mikasukis to make the long trip west.

As he fingered the fossil, Matt felt a strong desire to keep it himself, for he was not without superstition. But the wish to please Little Knife was stronger, so he slipped the tooth into the front of his shirt, glanced at the afternoon sun, and started westward toward the Indian village.

As he walked through the warm forest flecked with sun and shadow, he thought of the hunting he had done with Little Knife in the woods below Fort Drane. Although the Indian had no rifle, he was skillful with bow and arrow, and Matt could not remember a time when their hunting bags were not weighted with partridge, squirrel, or rabbit. There was bigger game, too —deer for meat and hides, raccoon and otter for their valuable furs, and once a young bear. They had brought home the bear meat, although they had kept the robe for their own use, fleshing and tanning it themselves in the deep woods.

Little Knife had been a laughing, good-natured fellow in those days and a stout friend. He had not run when the bear charged, but waited beside Matt, hunting knife bared, until the white boy's bullet found a vulnerable spot. And when an eight-foot rattler coiled to strike Matt, the Indian had flung his tomahawk and broken its back, braving the revenge of Chitta-micco, king of the snakes.

Their most important secret had been a hiding place. Only a hollow oak not far from the Indian town, it was well concealed by a tangle of scrub and vine. They had carpeted the small "tree

347

room" with their bear robe. There was a carved niche in the wall for notes in picture writing.

Of late, Matt had visited the tree to leave messages and gifts—an odd-shaped coontiroot, a wooden carving of a deer, and last, a Spanish-looking button he had found buried deep in leaf mold. Although Little Knife had taken the letters, he never answered them. The gifts had remained untouched.

But surely this great tooth would be different, Matt thought. Freighted as it was with luck and power, it would tell Little Knife that Matt did not wish for "Indian removal," like other whites. Then the boys could be friends again.

Matt was within a hundred yards of the oak when a queer, measured thumping drifted to him on the wind. He paused to listen. Above the thumping rose a savage chant. It died with the wind, came again more strongly.

His breathing stopped for a minute. He knew that sound. It was an ominous one.

At first, he would not admit to himself what it was. But as it swelled and dropped away again and again, he could not deny its meaning. With slow horror, he faced it—the braves were making ready for war.

All his latent fear of Indian warfare blazed up and spread through his mind like a dry brush fire. He turned to run but halted when he had gone a few steps. What would his father say? Would he be ashamed of his son? Would he ask why Matt hadn't determined the strength of the Indians and reported to Fort Drane? Would he remind him that this news was vital to the safety of white families?

Knowing that he would, Matt turned reluctantly toward the sound. Rifle hanging in the crook of his arm, he moved carefully along the trail toward the village until he reached Broad Otter Creek.

It was necessary here to hide his trail, so he waded a distance downstream through the shallows, crept across on a fallen tree that spanned the dark current, and waded again, going more slowly now as the chant grew louder.

Where the song swelled to a roar that filled the woods, he

stepped onto the bank and worked his way slowly through a grove of close-grown elders interlaced with vines. From there, he could see into a clearing where the dance moved and coiled like a bright serpent.

The hundred or so warriors were dressed in gay calicos, trailing feathers, shells that rattled, and flashing breastplates. Their faces were smeared with red and black paint. As they chanted, they stamped or leaped into the air. Now and then, a brave slashed out with his tomahawk and gave a long war whoop as if he had struck a blow at the enemy. And beneath the yelling and singing, the drums moaned with persistent rhythm.

Matt crouched, torn with the violence of his feelings. These men—many of whom he knew—bore no resemblance to themselves. He thought of the time he had raised a panther kitten, loved it, and played with it, only to have it turn on him as an enemy. So it was now with these Mikasukis.

Then he saw Little Knife, wearing a yellow shirt and red turban topped with feathers. He, too, was painted red and black—red for blood, black for death. He, too, was dancing and yelling.

349

Matt had seen enough. Scared and sick with the portent of it, he began to creep back toward the creek. Slowly, so as not to snap a twig or cause a bough to wave, he moved through the elders. He had stepped into the river shallows and straightened up when suddenly the splash of running feet sounded behind him.

He whirled. A tall, half-naked brave loomed above him. A tomahawk flashed back, then forward. Matt dodged the blade, lost balance, and careened into the water.

With a thud the Indian was upon him. One long arm pinioned Matt's free hand. The other shoved his face down through the shallows into the sand. He struggled to jerk free, but there were more Indians now piling onto him. His gun was wrenched from his hands, his shot pouch torn off his shoulder.

They dragged him out of the creek, strangling but still fighting. He fought desperately all across the clearing. Only when they brought him before a shrewd looking old Chief, sitting cross-legged on the ground, did Matt stop, panting and glassy-eyed. This Chief he had seen before, in a long-ago, peaceful time, for around the old man's neck hung that rare tooth which Little Knife had envied.

The Chief held out a hand to quiet his braves. In Hitchiti he said, "Take the young warrior's knife, and see what he may carry with him."

Matt's captor yanked out the boy's hunting knife and dipped into his pockets. He did not find the tooth tucked away in Matt's shirt, and the boy faced the old Chief with no weapons but still possessed of the great medicine supposed to live in the fossil.

"Why are you here?"

Matt shook the water out of his hair and tried to answer boldly. "I came because of my friend, Little Knife."

The Chief eyed him. "I remember you," he said. "You have been among us before. You have hunted with Little Knife."

"Yes."

"You shall talk with him."

He asked that the boy be brought, and soon Little Knife was

pushed through the crowd of warriors. Slender and straight-limbed, he stood before the Chief. His tense mouth and gleaming black eyes held neither friendship nor hatred, and he made no attempt to smile or welcome Matt.

"Speak to the white boy," said the Chief. "Ask him why he spies on our village. Ask him if he is sent by the white general."

Little Knife began. His words were terse. Matt was hurt by his friend's attitude, but he answered in the same manner. He had come to see Little Knife, he repeated. No one had sent him. He had been surprised to see the braves in war paint.

Matt noticed that when Little Knife spoke of the white general and the Indian agent at Fort King, his face clouded with mistrust.

"Enough," said the Chief finally. "Let the drums beat again. I will talk with my top warriors. Eagle Plumes shall tie the boy until we finish our Council. Come."

Immediately, the drums began to sound; the Mikasukis returned to their stamping and chanting. A few older men stayed behind. They waited until Eagle Plumes had bound Matt's wrists with rawhide, then followed the Chief back into the village.

As Matt, trying to walk bravely, was led along behind them, the Indian women kept step with him, shouting names and threatening him with sticks. The Chief made no effort to stop them.

Near the center of the square, the old man turned off at a palm-thatched house. All followed except Matt and Eagle Plumes who entered the hut beyond. There Matt's ankles were bound, and he was left lying on a bear robe just within the open-fronted dwelling. Eagle Plumes kept guard outside.

At first the white boy felt only bitterness at Little Knife's betrayal and a numb hopelessness. In a few minutes the Chief Council would return with its verdict. They would not deal gently with him. Little Knife's cold, closed face had told him that the old days were gone and forgotten, that the Mikasukis were living a new day in which friendship would not be extended to the white race.

The sun dropped behind the hammock and flung deep shadows across the village. From the clearing came louder chanting and leaping fireglow.

Matt noticed that Eagle Plumes was interested in the ceremony. Each time he paced toward the lighted dancing ground, he went a little farther, craning his neck to see through the trees. Although he had preened himself when Matt was taken prisoner, he was bored now with sentry duty and wanted to rejoin the others.

Hope flared faintly in Matt. He looked around the square, saw that the women had drifted back to watch the war dance. The Chief still held his Council. If he could free himself and elude Eagle Plumes—

As he glanced around the hut hoping to see a knife somewhere, he saw only a long pipe laid across the rafter, clay vessels, animal hides, an assortment of bird wings, little bones, and animal tails that hung along one wall as if they might be part of someone's medicine bundle. To his disappointment, there were no knives, nor any instrument which might cut through his bonds.

As he rolled a little to one side, he felt a lump against his ribs. It startled him. He had forgotten the tooth. And suddenly, excitement flashed through him like a blinding bolt of lightning.

The tooth did have power—in its own way. It would help him now.

It was hard to get it out from under his shirt. But by raising his body off the floor, and pulling the tail from under his belt, he managed to shake the tooth out on the soft bear robe beneath him. He could not see the slicing edge, but he remembered how it had looked when he had examined it near the spring. Time and use had blunted it—yet it would do.

With stiff fingers, he found the edge and laid it upward. Then, carefully, watching the sentry, he pressed down on the rawhide thongs and sawed them against the blade.

It was slow, agonizing work. The tooth turned many times, and Matt had to right it. Every minute he expected to see the Chief's men emerge from the hut. But they did not come.

The rawhide seemed to loosen. Matt pressed down with a final, desperate effort that brought drops of sweat to his face. Suddenly, the thongs relaxed. His hands were free.

Eagle Plumes was coming toward the hut. Matt kept his arms behind him and lay still while the sentry peered at his prisoner, grunted, and turned away. Matt reached for the tooth instantly and sawed through the thong around his ankles.

Now was the time to go. The square was deserted. The sentry was gazing again at the war ritual.

Matt slipped the fossil tooth into his shirt again, crept out, got to his feet, and stepped into the hut's shadow. Although he trembled with excitement, he walked softly. Eagle Plumes did not turn his head.

Sliding gently as a pine bough in the wind, the boy moved toward the next hut, paused a moment in its shadow, then went on until he had reached the far end of the village. There he faded into the forest.

Comforting night sounds rose around him and drowned the faint noise of his footsteps: the soft hooting of a little owl, the rhythmic shout of a chuck-will's widow, and near by, the scurry of a woodmouse.

A trail led down to the river, and he followed it, ears alert for the sentry's cry if he should find his prisoner gone. But as Matt reached the stream, it was the sudden quiet that stabbed him. The war drums had died. The chant had ceased abruptly.

The boy halted, his feet in the lapping water, trying to fathom the meaning of this straining silence. As he stood there, a great yelling broke out and flowed like a river of sound into the village. It came straight the length of the rectangle and poured into the hammock behind him.

For a second he could not move. Then he took a huge leap across the shallows toward the dark center of the creek, dived, and swam with all his strength, not caring if he splashed or made a foaming wake, intent only on reaching the opposite shore.

Back of him the hunt fanned out through the hammock. Dogs were barking, torches flaring. A hound whined eagerly at the creek's edge where Matt had waded in. Three lights moved down to the water.

"There!" shouted a voice in Hitchiti.

Matt's feet struck bottom on the far side of the stream. Crouching, only his head above water, he moved in toward the bank. A rifle boomed, and a bullet spanked across the ripples. Then another. Its ball struck close.

Matt leaped to his feet. Two long jumps and he was on dry land, slipping into the dense undergrowth.

More rifles sounded. Their bullets tore into tree trunks and cut through foliage. One of them struck a pain-blade into Matt's shoulder.

The rifles paused. Men in canoes were crossing the river lower

354

down. Matt struck a trail and ran swiftly along it. His heart was pounding, and his feet seemed barely to touch ground. If not for that bullet in the shoulder, he could probably outrun them. With the wound, he dared not try.

Even as he made his decision, the strength began to ebb out of him. His legs turned trembly. He would have to hide.

Suddenly his legs would not carry him at all. He sought hastily for a shielding thicket. In the darkness he could see nothing but massed blotches of trees. Yet something about the trail was familiar. That shadow of vine ahead—the odd, looping arch of that branch. It came over him in a flood—this was the hollow oak, the hiding place!

He crawled into the small corridor which he and Little Knife had made in the brush and drew a vine across its entrance. Slowly, he made his way back into the oak and curled up in its shelter. Far back in the night, probably back at the creek, the dogs were yelping with frustration, unable to pick up the trail. Inside the hollow, the dead, still air in which he heard his own hoarse breathing was like another world.

Matt breathed a wordless prayer and put his hand on the great tooth. It would make a crude but effective weapon at close quarters. Even if it was Little Knife who entered the hiding place, Matt resolved that he would strike to kill. For it had become clear to him, as he lay bound in the hut, that he was white and they were red; that though other men had phrased the treaties which led to war, it was left to him to fight, no matter what his personal wish.

Again the hunt fanned out, although the dogs did not pick up the scent. Warriors with torches would be moving through the forest. They would be bold, for they knew he had no gun.

He shivered in his wet clothes. The wound had begun to pain, throbbing in the background of his thoughts. He saw again Little Knife's inscrutable face. Would his friend think of the hiding place and lead the warriors to it? Matt could only wait.

He became aware of a sound near the tree. Soft moccasins padded against the earth, and brushed the fans of the low palmettos. Outside the tree they stopped. A hand touched the grapevine that Matt had drawn across the entrance.

He clutched the tooth and waited, holding his breath. Again the leaves rustled. A flicker of torchlight sifted through the scrub and brightened the inside of the oak.

A voice called from farther off in the forest. "Have you found him, Little Knife?"

It was a moment before the answer came from before the tree. Then it rang out, strong and clear, in Little Knife's voice. And somehow, it reminded Matt of the day they had stood together before the charging bear, Matt with a single ball to stop the animal's rush, the Indian with only a keen blade.

"I cannot see him," the voice said. "Let us go farther into the woods."

Shortly before dawn, Matt crept out of the hollow oak and took the north trail. His shoulder had stopped bleeding, and he was stronger. The path was clear in the graying light.

The Indians had hunted for him half the night, but at last they had turned back and recrossed the creek. The war chant was not resumed, and Matt fancied the ritual would wait until the warriors moved farther south to another clearing which no white man could discover.

In other villages, he was thinking, there must be war dances, and probably somewhere in the Withlacoochee wilderness, there would be a meeting spot for all the braves where they could dance out their hatred together.

At a fork in the trail, he turned toward Fort Drane. In a few hours, he would be telling the army about the war ceremony. Then he could count his duty done and go home. His father would dress his wound, and perhaps he would look at him proudly as a father looks at a son who has behaved like a good frontiersman.

He no longer carried the fossil tooth. Back there in the hollow tree, it lay in the niche where so many letters and small gifts had been rejected by Little Knife. But this gift, Matt knew, would be found and cherished.

Theodore Roosevelt

BUFFALO HUNTING

ILLUSTRATED BY *Robert Sinnott*

HEN Independence was declared, in 1776, and the United States of America appeared among the powers of the earth, the continent beyond the Alleghanies was one unbroken wilderness; and the buffaloes, the first animals to vanish when the wilderness was settled, roved up to the crests of the mountains which mark the western boundaries of Pennsylvania, Virginia, and the Carolinas. They were plentiful in what are now the States of Ohio, Kentucky, and Tennessee. But by the beginning of the present century they had been driven beyond the Mississippi; and for the next eighty years they formed one of the most distinctive and characteristic features of existence on the great plains. Their numbers were countless—incredible. In vast herds of hundreds of thousands of individuals, they roamed from the Saskatchewan to the Rio Grande and westward to the Rocky Mountains. They furnished all the means of livelihood to the tribes of Horse Indians, and to the curious population of French Metis, or Half-breeds, on the Red River, as well as those dauntless and archtypical wanderers, the white hunters and trappers. Their numbers slowly diminished; but the decrease was very gradual until after the Civil War. They were not destroyed by the settlers, but by the railways and by the skin hunters.

After the ending of the Civil War, the work of constructing transcontinental railway lines was pushed forward with the utmost vigor. These supplied cheap and indispensable, but hitherto wholly lacking, means of transportation to the hunters; and at the same time the demand for buffalo robes and hides became very great, while the enormous numbers of the beasts, and the comparative ease with which they were slaughtered,

357

attracted throngs of adventurers. The result was such a slaughter of big game as the world had never before seen; never before were so many large animals of one species destroyed in so short a time. Several million buffaloes were slain. In fifteen years from the time the destruction fairly began, the great herds were exterminated. In all probability there are not now, all told, a thousand head of wild buffaloes on the American continent; and no herd of a hundred individuals has been in existence since 1884.

The first great break followed the building of the Union Pacific Railway. All the buffaloes of the middle region were then destroyed, and the others were then split into two vast sets of herds, the northern and the southern. The latter were destroyed first, about 1878; the former not until 1883. My own experience with buffaloes was obtained in the latter year, among small bands and scattered individuals, near my ranch on the Little Missouri; I have related it elsewhere. But two of my relatives were more fortunate and took part in the chase of these lordly beasts when the herds still darkened the prairie as far as the eye could see.

During the first two months of 1877, my brother Elliott, then a lad not seventeen years old, made a buffalo-hunt toward the edge of the Staked Plains in northern Texas. He was thus in at the death of the southern herds, for all, save a few scattering bands, were destroyed within two years of this time.

My brother was with my cousin, John Roosevelt, and they went out on the range with six other adventurers—a German-American, a Scotchman who had been in the Confederate cavalry and afterward in Maximilian's Mexican bodyguard, and four Irishmen. It was a party of just such young men as frequently drift to the frontier. All were short of cash, and all were hardy, vigorous fellows eager for excitement and adventure. My brother was much the youngest of the party, and the least experienced; but he was well-grown, strong and healthy, and very fond of boxing, wrestling, running, riding, and shooting; moreover, he had served an apprenticeship in hunting deer and turkeys. Their mess-kit, ammunition, bedding, and provisions were carried in two prairie wagons, each drawn by four horses.

The earth shook beneath their thunderous gallop.

In addition to the teams they had six saddle-animals—all of them shaggy, unkempt mustangs. Three or four dogs, setters and half-breed greyhounds, trotted along behind the wagons. Each man took his turn for two days as teamster and cook; and there were always two with the wagons, or camp, as the case might be, while the other six were off hunting, usually in couples. The expedition was undertaken partly for sport and partly with the hope of profit; for, after purchasing the horses and wagons, none of the party had any money left, and they were forced to rely upon selling skins and hides and, when near the forts, meat.

They started on January 2d, and shaped their course for the headwaters of the Salt Fork of the Brazos, the center of abundance for the great buffalo herds. During the first few days they were in the outskirts of the settled country, and shot only small game—quail and prairie fowl; then they began to kill turkey, deer, and antelope. These they "swapped" for flour and feed, at the ranches or squalid, straggling frontier towns. On several occasions the hunters were lost, spending the night out in the open, or sleeping at a ranch if one was found. Both towns and ranches were filled with rough customers; all of my brother's companions were muscular, hot-headed fellows; and as a consequence they were involved in several savage "free fights," in which, fortunately, nobody was seriously hurt. My brother kept a very brief diary, the entries being fairly startling from their conciseness. A number of times, the mention of their arrival, either at a halting-place, a little village, or a rival buffalo-camp is followed by the laconic remark, "big fight," or "big row"; but once they evidently concluded discretion to be the better part of valor, the entry for January 20th being, "On the road—passed through Belknap—too lively, so kept on to the Brazos—very late." The buffalo-camps in particular were very jealous of one another, each party regarding itself as having exclusive right to the range it was the first to find; and on several occasions this feeling came near involving my brother and his companions in serious trouble.

While slowly driving the heavy wagons to the hunting-grounds they suffered the usual hardships of plains travel. The weather, as in most Texas winters, alternated between the extremes of heat and cold. There had been little rain; in consequence water was scarce. Twice they were forced to cross wild, barren wastes, where the pools had dried up, and they suffered terribly from thirst. On the first occasion the horses were in good condition, and they traveled steadily, with only occasional short halts, for over thirty-six hours, by which time they were across the waterless country. The journal reads: "January 29th.—Big hunt—no water and we left Quinn's blockhouse this morning 3 A. M.—on the go all night—hot. January 28th.—No water—hot—at seven we struck water and by eight Stinking Creek—grand 'hurrah.'" On the second occasion, the horses were weak and traveled slowly, so the party went forty-eight hours without drinking. "February 19th.—Pulled on twenty-one miles—trail bad—freezing night, no water, and wolves after our fresh meat. 20th.—Made nineteen miles over prairie; again only mud, no water, freezing hard—frightful thirst. 21st.—Thirty miles to Clear Fork, fresh water." These entries were hurriedly jotted down at the time, by a boy who deemed it unmanly to make any especial note of hardship or suffering; but every plainsman will understand the real agony implied in working hard for two nights, one day, and portions of two others, without water, even in cool weather. During the last few miles the staggering horses were only just able to drag the lightly loaded wagon,—for they had but one with them at the time,—while the men plodded along in sullen silence, their mouths so parched that they could hardly utter a word. My own hunting and ranching were done in the North where there is more water; so I have never had a similar experience. Once I took a team in thirty-six hours across a country where there was no water; but by good luck it rained heavily in the night, so that the horses had plenty of wet grass, and I caught the rain in my slicker, and so had enough water for myself. Personally, I have but once been as long as twenty-six hours without water.

The party pitched their permanent camp in a cañon of the Brazos known as Cañon Blanco. The last few days of their journey they traveled beside the river through a veritable hunter's paradise. The drought had forced all the animals to come to the larger watercourses, and the country was literally swarming with game. Every day, and all day long, the wagons traveled through the herds of antelopes that grazed on every side, while, whenever they approached the cañon brink, bands of deer started from the timber that fringed the river's course; often, even the deer wandered out on the prairie with the antelopes. Nor was the game shy; for the hunters, both red and white, followed only the buffaloes until the huge, shaggy herds were destroyed, and the smaller beasts were in consequence but little molested.

Once my brother shot five antelopes from a single stand, when the party were short of fresh venison; he was out of sight and to leeward, and the antelopes seemed confused rather than alarmed at the rifle-reports and the fall of their companions. As was to be expected where game was so plentiful, wolves and coyotes also abounded. At night they surrounded the camp, wailing and howling in a kind of shrieking chorus throughout the hours of darkness; one night they came up so close that the frightened horses had to be hobbled and guarded. On another occasion a large wolf actually crept into camp, where he was seized by the dogs, and the yelling, writhing knot of combatants rolled over one of the sleepers; finally, the long-toothed prowler managed to shake himself loose, and vanished in the gloom. One evening they were almost as much startled by a visit of a different kind. They were just finishing supper when an Indian stalked suddenly and silently out of the surrounding darkness, squatted down in the circle of firelight, remarked gravely, "Me Tonk," and began helping himself from the stew. He belonged to the friendly tribe of Tonkaways, so his hosts speedily recovered their equanimity; as for him, he had never lost his, and he sat eating by the fire until there was literally nothing left to eat. The panic caused by his appearance was natural; for at that time the Comanches were a scourge to the buffalo-hunters, ambushing them and raiding their camps; and several bloody fights had taken place.

361

Their camp had been pitched near a deep pool or water-hole. On both sides the bluffs rose like walls, and where they had crumbled and lost their sheerness, the vast buffalo herds, passing and repassing for countless generations, had worn furrowed trails so deep that the backs of the beasts were but little above the surrounding soil. In the bottom, and in places along the crests of the cliffs that hemmed in the cañon-like valley, there were groves of tangled trees, tenanted by great flocks of wild turkeys. Once my brother made two really remarkable shots at a pair of these great birds. It was at dusk, and they were flying directly overhead from one cliff to the other. He had in his hand a thirty-eight-caliber Ballard rifle, and, as the gobblers winged their way heavily by, he brought them both down with two successive bullets. This was of course mainly a piece of mere luck; but it meant good shooting, too. The Ballard was a very accurate, handy little weapon; it belonged to me, and was the first rifle I ever owned or used. With it I had once killed a deer, the only specimen of large game I had then shot; and I presented the rifle to my brother when he went to Texas. In our happy ignorance we deemed it quite good enough for Buffalo or anything else; but out on the plains my brother soon found himself forced to procure a heavier and more deadly weapon.

When camp was pitched the horses were turned loose to graze and refresh themselves after their trying journey, during which they had lost flesh woefully. They were watched and tended by the two men who were always left in camp, and, save on rare ocassions, were only used to haul in the buffalo hides. The camp-guards for the time being acted as cooks; and, though coffee and flour both ran short and finally gave out, fresh meat of every kind was abundant. The camp was never without buffalo beef, deer and antelope venison, wild turkeys, prairie chickens, quails, ducks, and rabbits. The birds were simply "potted," as occassion required; when the quarry was deer or antelope, the hunters took the dogs with them to run down the wounded animals. But almost the entire attention of the hunters was given to the buffalo. After an evening spent in lounging round the campfire, and a sound night's sleep, wrapped in robes

and blankets, they would get up before daybreak, snatch a hurried breakfast, and start off in couples through the chilly dawn. The great beasts were very plentiful; in the first day's hunt, twenty were slain; but the herds were restless and ever on the move. Sometimes they would be seen right by the camp, and again it would need an all-day's tramp to find them. There was no difficulty in spying them—the chief trouble with forest game; for on the prairie a buffalo makes no effort to hide, and its black, shaggy bulk looms up as far as the eye can see. Sometimes they were found in small parties of three or four individuals, sometimes in bands of about two hundred, and again in great herds of many thousand; and solitary old bulls, expelled from the herds, were common. If on broken land, among hills and ravines, there was not much difficulty in approaching from the leeward; for, though the sense of smell in the buffalo is very acute, they do not see well at a distance through their overhanging frontlets of coarse and matted hair. If, as was generally the case, they were out on the open, rolling prairie, the stalking was far more difficult. Every hollow, every earth hummock and sagebush had to be used as cover. The hunter wriggled through the grass flat on his face, pushing himself along for perhaps a quarter of a mile by his toes and fingers, heedless of the spiny cactus. When near enough to the huge, unconscious quarry the hunter began firing, still keeping himself carefully concealed. If the smoke was blown away by the wind, and if the buffaloes caught no glimpse of the assailant, they would often stand motionless and stupid until many of their number had been slain; the hunter being careful not to fire too high, aiming just behind the shoulder, about a third of the way up the body, that his bullet might go through the lungs. Sometimes, even after they saw the man, they would act as if confused and panic-struck, huddling up together and staring at the smoke puffs—but generally they were off at a lumbering gallop as soon as they had an idea of the point of danger. When once started, they ran for many miles before halting, and their pursuit on foot was extremely laborious.

One morning my cousin and brother had been left in camp as guards. They were sitting, idly warming themselves in the first sunbeams, when their attention was sharply drawn to four buffaloes who were coming to the pool to drink. The beasts came down a game trail, a deep rut in the bluff, fronting where they were sitting, and they did not dare stir for fear of being discovered. The buffaloes walked into the pool, and, after drinking their fill, stood for some time with the water running out of their mouths, idly lashing their sides with their short tails, enjoying the bright warmth of the early sunshine; then, with much splashing and the gurgling of soft mud, they left the pool and clambered up the bluff with unwieldy agility. As soon as they turned, my brother and cousin ran for their rifles; but before they got back the buffaloes had crossed the bluff crest. Climbing after them, the two hunters found, when they reached the summit, that their game, instead of halting, had struck straight off across the prairie at a slow lope, doubtless intending to rejoin the herd they had left. After a moment's consultation, the men went in pursuit, excitement overcoming their knowledge that they ought not, by rights, to leave the camp. They struck a steady trot, following the animals by sight until they passed over a knoll, and then trailing them. Where the grass was long, as it was for the first four or five miles, this was a work of no difficulty, and they did not break their gait, only glancing now and then at the trail. As the sun rose and the day became warm, their breathing grew quicker; and the sweat rolled off their faces as they ran across the rough prairie sward, up and down the long inclines, now and then shifting their heavy rifles from one shoulder to the other. But they were in good training, and they did not have to halt. At last they reached stretches of bare ground, sun-baked and grassless, where the trail grew dim; and here they had to go very slowly, carefully examining the faint dents and marks made in the soil by the heavy hoofs, and unraveling the trail from the mass of old foot-marks. It was tedious work, but it enabled them to completely recover their breath by the time that they again struck the grassland; and but a few hundred yards from its edge, in a slight hollow, they saw the four buffaloes just entering a herd of fifty or sixty that were scattered out grazing. The herd paid no attention to the newcomers, and these immediately began to feed greedily. After a whispered consultation, the two hunters crept back and made a long circle that brought them well to leeward of the herd, in line with a slight rise in the ground. They then crawled up to this rise and, peering through the tufts of tall, rank grass, saw the unconscious beasts a hundred and twenty-five or fifty yards away. They fired together, each mortally wounding his animal, and then, rushing in as the herd halted in confusion, and following them as they ran, impeded by numbers, hurry, and panic, they eventually got three more.

On another occasion, the same two hunters nearly met with a frightful death, being overtaken by a vast herd of stampeded buffaloes. All animals that go in herds are subject to these instantaneous attacks of uncontrollable terror, under the influence of which they become perfectly mad and rush headlong in dense masses on any form of death. Horses, and more especially cattle, often suffer from stampedes; it is a danger against which the cowboys are compelled to be perpetually on guard. A band of stampeded horses, sweeping in mad terror up a valley, will dash against a rock or tree with such violence as to leave several dead animals at its base, while the survivors race on without halting; they will overturn and destroy tents and wagons, and a man on foot caught in the rush has but a small chance for his life. A buffalo stampede is much worse—or rather was much worse, in the old days—because of the great weight and immense numbers of the beasts, who, in a fury of heedless terror, plunged over cliffs and into rivers, and bore down whatever was in their path. On the occasion in question, my brother and cousin were on their way homeward. They were just mounting one of the long, low swells into which the prairie was broken when they heard a low, muttering, rumbling noise, like far-off thunder. It grew steadily louder, and, not knowing what it meant, they hurried forward to the top of the rise. As they reached it, they stopped short in terror and amazement, for before them the whole prairie was black with madly rushing buffaloes.

Afterward they learned that another couple of hunters, four or five miles off, had fired into and stampeded a large herd. This herd, in its rush, gathered others, all thundering along together in uncontrollable and increasing panic.

The surprised hunters were far away from any broken ground or other place of refuge; while the vast herd of huge, plunging, maddened beasts was charging straight down on them not a quarter of a mile distant. Down they came!—thousands upon thousands, their front extending a mile in breadth, while the earth shook beneath their thunderous gallop, and as they came closer, their shaggy frontlets loomed dimly through the columns of dust thrown up from the dry soil. The two hunters knew that their only hope for life was to split the herd, which, though it had so broad a front, was not very deep. If they failed they would inevitably be trampled to death.

Waiting until the beasts were in close range, they opened a rapid fire from their heavy breech-loading rifles, yelling at the top of their voices. For a moment the result seemed doubtful. The line thundered steadily down on them; then it swayed violently, as two or three of the brutes immediately in their front fell beneath the bullets, while the neighbors made violent efforts to press off sideways. Then a narrow wedge-shaped rift appeared in the line, and widened as it came up closer, and the buffaloes, shrinking from their foes in front, strove desperately to edge away from the dangerous neighborhood; the shouts and shots were redoubled; the hunters were almost choked by the cloud of dust through which they could see the stream of dark huge bodies passing within rifle-length on either side; and in a moment the peril was over, and the two men were left alone on the plain, unharmed, though with their nerves terribly shaken. The herd careered on toward the horizon, save five individuals who had been killed or disabled by the shots.

On another occasion, when my brother was out with one of his Irish friends, they fired at a small herd containing an old bull; the bull charged the smoke, and the whole herd followed him. Probably they were simply stampeded, and had no hostile intention; at any rate, after the death of their leader, they rushed by without doing any damage.

But buffaloes sometimes charged with the utmost determination, and were then dangerous antagonists. My cousin, a very hardy and resolute hunter, had a narrow escape from a wounded cow which he followed up a steep bluff or sand cliff. Just as he reached the summit, he was charged, and was only saved by the sudden appearance of his dog, which distracted the cow's attention. He thus escaped with only a tumble and a few bruises.

My brother also came in for a charge, while killing the biggest bull that was slain by any of the party. He was out alone, and saw a small herd of cows and calves at some distance, with a huge bull among them, towering above them like a giant. There was no break in the ground, nor any tree nor bush near them, but by making a half-circle, my brother managed to creep up against the wind behind a slight roll in the prairie surface, until he was within seventy-five yards of the grazing and unconscious beasts. There were some cows and calves between him and the bull, and he had to wait some moments before they shifted position as the herd grazed onward and gave him a fair shot; in the interval they had moved so far forward that he was in plain view. His first bullet struck just behind the shoulder; the herd started and looked around, but the bull merely lifted his head and took a step forward, his tail curled up over his back. The next bullet likewise struck fair, nearly in the same place, telling with a loud "pack!" against the thick hide, and making the dust fly up from the matted hair. Instantly the great bull wheeled and charged in headlong anger, while the herd fled in the opposite direction. On the bare prairie, with no spot of refuge, it was useless to try to escape, and the hunter, with reloaded rifle, waited until the bull was not far off, then drew up his weapon and fired. Either he was nervous, or the bull at the moment bounded over some obstacle, for the ball went a little wild, nevertheless, by good luck, it broke a foreleg, and the great beast came crashing to the earth, and was slain before it could struggle to its feet.

Two days after this event, a war party of Comanches swept down along the river. They "jumped" a neighboring camp, killing one man and wounding two more, and at the same time ran off all but three of the horses belonging to our eight adventurers. With the remaining three horses and one wagon they set out homeward. The march was hard and tedious; they lost their way and were in jeopardy from quicksands and cloudbursts; they suffered from thirst and cold, their shoes gave out and their feet were lamed by cactus spines. At last they reached Fort Sniffin in safety, and great was their ravenous rejoicing when they procured some bread—for during the final fortnight of the hunt they had been without flour or vegetables of any kind, or even coffee, and had subsisted on fresh meat "straight." Nevertheless, it was a very healthy, as well as a very pleasant and exciting experience; and I doubt if any of those who took part in it will ever forget their great buffalo-hunt on the Brazos.

DANIEL BOONE

Arthur Guiterman

Daniel Boone at twenty-one
Came with his tomahawk, knife, and gun
Home from the French and Indian War
To North Carolina and the Yadkin shore.
He married his maid with a golden band,
Builded his house, and cleared his land;
But the deep woods claimed their son again,
And he turned his face from the homes of men.
Over the Blue Ridge, dark and lone,
The Mountains of Iron, the Hills of Stone,
Braving the Shawnee's jealous wrath,
He made his way on the Warrior's Path.
Alone he trod the shadowed trails;
But he was lord of a thousand vales
As he roved Kentucky, far and near,
Hunting the buffalo, elk, and deer.
What joy to see, what joy to win
So fair a land for his kith and kin,
Of streams unstained and woods unhewn!
"Elbow room!" laughed Daniel Boone.

On the Wilderness Road that his axmen made
The settlers flocked to the first stockade;
The deerskin shirts and the coonskin caps
Filed through the glens and the mountain gaps;

Taken from *I Sing the Pioneer* by Arthur Guiterman, published and copyright, 1926, by E. P. Dutton & Co., Inc., New York.

And hearts were high in the fateful spring
When the land said "Nay!" to the stubborn King.
While the men of the East of farm and town
Strove with the troops of the British Crown,
Daniel Boone from a surge of hate
Guarded a nation's westward gate.
Down on the fort in a wave of flame
The Shawnee horde and the Mingo came,
And the stout logs shook in a storm of lead;
But Boone stood firm and the savage fled.
Peace! And the settlers flocked anew,
The farm lands spread, the town lands grew;
But Daniel Boone was ill at ease
When he saw the smoke in his forest trees.
"There'll be no game in the country soon;
Elbow room!" cried Daniel Boone.

Straight as a pine at sixty-five—
Time enough for a man to thrive—
He launched his bateau on Ohio's breast,
And his heart was glad as he oared it west;
There were kindly folk and his own true blood
Where great Missouri rolls his flood;
New woods, new streams, and room to spare,
And Daniel Boone found comfort there.
Yet far he ranged toward the sunset still,
Where the Kansas runs and the Smoky Hill,
And the prairies toss, by the south wind blown;
And he killed his bear on the Yellowstone.
But ever he dreamed of new domains
With vaster woods and wider plains;
Ever he dreamed of a world-to-be
Where there are no bounds and the soul is free.

mister
mckee

At fourscore-five, still stout and hale,
He heard a call to a farther trail;
So he turned his face where the stars are strewn;
"Elbow room!" sighed Daniel Boone.

Down the Milky Way in its banks of blue
Far he has paddled his white canoe
To the splendid quest of the tameless soul—
He has reached the goal where there is no goal.
Now he rides and rides an endless trail
On the hippogriff of the flaming tail
Or the horse of the stars with the golden mane,
As he rode the first of the blue-grass strain.
The joy that lies in the search he seeks
On breathless hills with crystal peaks;
He makes his camp on heights untrod,
The steps of the shrine, alone with God.
Through the woods of the vast, on the plains of space,
He hunts the pride of the mammoth race
And the dinosaur of the triple horn,
The manticore and the unicorn,
As once by the broad Missouri's flow
He followed the elk and the buffalo.
East of the sun and west of the moon,
"Elbow room!" laughs Daniel Boone.

Index

ALCOTT, LOUISA MAY, Tabby's Tablecloth, 264
ALTSHELER, JOSEPH A., With the Forest Runners, 295
Apache Warpath, Edgar Wyatt, 338
Bears of Blue River, The, Charles Major, 306
BENÉT, LAURA, Horseshoe Nails, 197
BENÉT, ROSEMARY and STEPHEN VINCENT, Western Wagons, 82
Boy Who Voted for Abe Lincoln, The, Milton Richards, 83
BRINK, CAROL RYRIE, The Willow Basket, 93, Caddie's Silver Dollar, 127
BROCK, EMMA L., In a Covered Wagon, 72
Buffalo Hunting, Theodore Roosevelt, 357
Caddie's Silver Dollar, Carol Ryrie Brink, 127
CARR, MARY JANE, The Feather of the Northman, 64
CARTER, RUSSELL GORDON, Old Sly Eye, 173, The Three-Cornered Hat, 189
Christmas Horses, Laura Ingalls Wilder, 111
CLEMENS, SAMUEL, Cub Pilot on the River, 321
COATSWORTH, ELIZABETH, Mary Silver, 159, A Pioneer Wedding, 314
Cub Pilot on the River, Samuel Clemens, 321
Daniel Boone, Arthur Guiterman, 369
DAUGHERTY, JAMES, The Saving of Boonesborough, 181
DAVIS, JULIA, River and Beasts Betray, 277
Disperse, Ye Rebels, Esther Forbes, 238
DUNSING, DEE, Tooth of the Great One, 346
Feather of the Northman, The, Mary Jane Carr, 64
FORBES, ESTHER, Disperse, Ye Rebels, 238
Fox and Geese, Cornelia Meigs, 10
Frontier Blockade Buster, Harry Edward Neal, 229
GUITERMAN, ARTHUR, Daniel Boone, 369
Hasty Pudding, Cornelia Meigs, 36
HAYES, MARJORIE, A Ride with Tom Thumb, 56
Horseshoe Nails, Laura Benét, 197
HUNT, MABEL LEIGH, Tomorrow Will Be Bright, 26,
     Johnny Appleseed's Coat, 47
In a Covered Wagon, Emma L. Brock, 72
Johnny Appleseed's Coat, Mabel Leigh Hunt, 47
Johnny Appleseed Visits Licking Creek, Meridel Le Sueur, 146
KEY, ALEXANDER, Strangers in the Wilderness, 150
LE SUEUR, MERIDEL, Johnny Appleseed Visits Licking Creek, 146
Little Dog Star, The, Cornelia Meigs, 102
MAJOR, CHARLES, The Bears of Blue River, 306
Mary Silver, Elizabeth Coatsworth, 159
Master's Footstool, The, Evelyn Sickels, 20
MEADOWCROFT, ENID LaMONTE, On the Mayflower, 1
MEIGS, CORNELIA, Fox And Geese, 10, Hasty Pudding, 36,
     The Little Dog Star, 102

Message For Washington, A, Evelyn Sickels, 255
NEAL, HARRY EDWARD, Frontier Blockade Buster, 229
Old Sly Eye, Russell Gordon Carter, 173
On the Mayflower, Enid LaMonte Meadowcroft, 1
Pathfinders: Lewis and Clark, The, Eva March Tappan, 289
Pioneer Wedding, A, Elizabeth Coatsworth, 314
RICHARDS, MILTON, The Boy Who Voted for Abe Lincoln, 83
Ride With Tom Thumb, A, Marjorie Hayes, 56
River and Beasts Betray, Julia Davis, 277
ROOSEVELT, THEODORE, Buffalo Hunting, 357
Saving of Boonesborough, The, James Daugherty, 181
SICKELS, EVELYN, The Master's Footstool, 20, A Message for Washington, 255
Strangers in the Wilderness, Alexander Key, 150
Tabby's Tablecloth, Louisa May Alcott, 264
TAPPAN, EVA MARCH, The Pathfinders: Lewis and Clark, 289
Three-Cornered Hat, The, Russell Gordon Carter, 189
Tomorrow Will Be Bright, Mabel Leigh Hunt, 26
Tooth of the Great One, Dee Dunsing, 346
Western Wagons, Rosemary and Stephen Vincent Benét, 82
WILDER, LAURA INGALLS, Christmas Horses, 111
Willow Basket, The, Carol Ryrie Brink, 93
With the Forest Runners, Joseph A. Altsheler, 295
WYATT, EDGAR, Apache Warpath, 338